BLACK LEATHER SERIAL MURDER

Also by the author

Improbable: Male Love Stories

Fairy Swatter: Short Stories

Accidental Parents

Queer Queries

BLACK LEATHER SERIAL MURDER

Book Two of the Queer Queries Mystery Trilogy

PETER MELILLO

Published by Querelle Independent, a division of Querelle Press LLC
www.querellepress.com

Cover design by DesignCrowd
Typeset by Raymond Luczak

ISBN: 979-8-9925443-0-5 print edition
ISBN: 979-8-9925443-1-2 e-book edition

Distributed by Ingram Content Group: ingramcontent.com

Printed in the United States

First edition 2025

Dedicated to:

Felino Jojo Manansala
May 6, 1948 – January 29, 2024
Dear friend ready with a smile and missed by all you knew.

REST IN PEACE

Chapter 1.

The intercom beeped and lit up blinking its little green light. That meant my three o'clock appointment had arrived and was now waiting. Damn! Once again, despite trying to do better, I'd let time writing clinical notes between clients run over. But, hey, I was getting better at time management or that's what I told myself.

I stuck my head through the open office door to see one person sitting in the waiting area. The new patient looked on guard, maybe even a little pissed off. Couldn't be at me, we haven't met yet. He did not look like my usual new patients, overanxious, jumping out of their own skin expecting to be disappointed by yet another professional. Disappointing expectations was my specialty … well, not this time.

Taking a minute to observe a little longer, the waiting new patient became fully engrossed manipulating a cellphone held tightly in two hands. His eyes were transfixed on the phone's little screen. Not able to catch his attention from my office doorway I walked over, leaned down, and softly said, "Hi. I'm Oliver Kulgul, might you be Tyrell Joyner?"

Without looking up, he muttered, "That's me." After his requisite time-interval, Tyrell Joyner finished texting, stood, made eye contact, and said, "Hey. I like to be called TJ. Would you prefer a fist bump or elbow greeting?"

I was trying to decide if he was rude on purpose, just thoughtlessly inconsiderate, or didn't care how he was perceived. As my curiosity rose, without forethought I said, "Whatever floats your boat TJ."

Acting full of himself, puffing out his chest, Mr. Joyner stood at my height, six foot one, moved with confidence like he was comfortable in his own skin and knew his way around a gym. I outweigh him by fifty or sixty middle-age pounds. The contrast between us didn't stop with weight, my people came from Scandinavia long ago. When I worked for Parole, my parolees called me white bread for being so blond and blue eyed. Joyner looked to be fidgeting for an opening to elbow or fist bump me in greeting as offered.

At that point, not sure I wanted a friendly greeting, and anxious to get on with what should be a short conversation, I abruptly turned my back and walked to my office. Moving, I chastised myself with the thought, *Now who was being rude?*

Another thought intruded and I wondered *Who is in charge here?* I stopped and said, "Thinking about it, around here I prefer a good old-fashioned unhygienic pressing of the flesh for greeting," turned, and put my hand out for a shake. *My office my greeting.* But I was ready for a bone crushing gym-built protest grip for being an old stuffed shirt out of current fashion.

His gray-blue eyes showed disappointment at having to shake this old fuddy duddy's hand. I still go to the gym regularly and was prepared for opposition. Instead, he yelped, "Good God, man, don't break my hand, I'm a successful artist and need it to work."

"Oh, sorry, I sometimes forget how strong my grip is, my husband and I work out together. He's closer to your age than mine. The hand sanitizer dispenser is right over there." Scolding myself for bad behavior, I said, "TJ, it's nice to meet you."

Following where I pointed, he crossly squirted clear hand antiseptic into his palm. He angrily looked to be taking a moment to consider leaving rather than staying. Meanwhile I gestured for him to follow me into my office. After another moment's extra contemplation, head down, wearing an angry face, he followed me.

My mind's balance restored; I did my usual new client assessment. TJ's complexion was a rich caramel-candy-color. Short black dreadlocks with multi-colored beads hung above intelligent piercing eyes shining out of a hairless, attractive young man's angry face. He gave off more than an in-charge-big-boss vibe. His appearance could easily pass for eighteen until he opened his mouth to show a graduate level education's vocabulary, thinking, and self-assuredness.

Mr. Joyner was dressed in an expensive-looking, custom-fitted, soft black leather cowboy jacket with long leather fringe hanging under each sleeve and across the back yoke. He wore it over a fitted black T-shirt that showed where the leather jacket gapped open in front. His stonewashed black denim designer skinny leg jeans showed off a big package. His cowboy boot was highly polished shiny black, sterling-silver inlayed and toe tipped completed his outfit.

Once inside my office, wearing a custom-made dark business suit accented by an Italian silk neutral colored tie I said, "Pick a chair, any chair that suits you."

"Then I'll sit behind your desk."

Surprised I said, "The top is all cluttered from work in progress. You'd be more comfortable in one of these two matching brocade armchairs or the sofa. I guarantee they are comfortable."

"I'm sure that's true. But you said I could pick any chair. If I sit *behind* your desk, there won't be as much power imbalance."

Thinking he meant by having my big desk between us, but to be sure I said, "What imbalance are you feeling?"

"Only one of us in this room has a PhD, and you have two. Then there is the all-American matter of you being white and I'm not."

Resigned I said, "You present a strong case, I yield. For privacy's sake, let me shuffle the paperwork on the desk first. We don't want to upset U.S. Congresses'

HIPPA rules." He had deftly regained control after the elbow bump did not happen. This was going to be a short interview, so why compete with him? I got busy scooping up open case files to place out of sight on top of my office conference table in the back of the room.

With aplomb Mr. Joyner seated himself behind my big, hand-carved antique, dark-red mahogany desk with me in one of the armchairs facing him, he said, "Ah, nice and roomy. I could get used to this."

"Don't get too comfortable. I'm sorry to say a mistake was made. This practice is referrals only from psychotherapists or psychiatrists. In other words, we don't see anyone without a referral letter preceded by a lengthy phone call between professionals. I can assure you when I uncover the source of the mistake there will be consequences. That's a promise. You have my sincere apology for this inconvenience. As a courtesy I wanted to tell you personally face to face."

"When I called for this appointment, I told the receptionist my granduncle was a friend of yours. I guess that wasn't written down."

Quickly rescanning the intake form, I said, "Hmm, no, that's not noted here. We've been using temps lately."

"My uncle never was a therapist. But if you only take patients from other shrinks, you must be some kind of super consultant. That does explain why I just paid your front desk $5000 for this initial consult."

Back in familiar territory I said, "That fee covers more than a forty-five-minute therapy session. My regular ongoing fee amounts to much more, and we seldom take insurance."

"Wow, and I thought I made out like a bandit, profit-wise."

"What we do here is not much like traditional psychotherapy."

"Then today is a big disappointment for us both. I didn't come here for psychotherapy and want my money back." With that said Mr. Joyner stood.

I also rose-up and prepared to lead Mr. Joyner to the front desk for his refund, when he said, "My granduncle is going to be extremely disappointed about being wrong. He spoke highly of you like you were old friends."

My surprise probably showing on my face I said, "What's your uncle's name?"

"Willis Washington." He said the name with a mixture of awe and something stern in his voice. "We were close friends when he lived up here. He's my maternal grandmother's youngest brother."

"Jasmine. How is she doing?"

"She died two years ago. It was Covid-19 pneumonia. Grandma and my granduncle haven't gotten along of late, so he didn't come to the funeral. Not that it would matter to her or the rest of us. He's a stubborn old coot who brought northern honor to our southern family."

"Let's start again." And we both sat down. "What did my old friend Willis say I could do for you?"

Perking up after a slight deflation, TJ said, "He said, Okay, Oliver is the only person, that he knew, who could help me. If anyone could."

"You didn't answer my question."

"Google says you do hypnosis."

He still had not answered my question but appeared to go on guard. "Depends, the reason why? Willis sent you to me for hypnosis, really?"

Then he ejaculated loudly, "No. My husband is in jail accused of murder. My overpaid lawyer wants him to plead guilty. I know he didn't kill anyone; that's not in his nature. If he takes the plea deal, he'll be in prison for about twenty years of a life sentence. If he pleads innocent and is found guilty it's life without the possibility of parole. That means I'd never see the man I love free again. I love Asa with all my heart and know he'd never kill anyone least of all a stranger for no reason." TJ sat back in my desk chair and glared at me defiantly.

Used to having clients' outbursts in my office, as calmly as humanly possible I said, "What evidence does the prosecution have against your man?"

Locking eye with me, still defiant, he said, "They have the murder gun found near Asa with his fingerprints on it." He broke the stare, looked down defeated and said, "My lawyer says its open and shut."

Without intending to, out of old habits I shifted into private detective mode. I had not realized I missed being a gumshoe and said, "What does your husband say?"

"He says he doesn't remember any of it. I know he is innocent. Asa claims he blacked out while out with friends. He has no recollection other than having a beer in a bar and then waking up naked in an empty parking garage near a gun with his fingerprints and a dead guy."

I found myself taking notes like in the old PI days. "Does he blackout often? Where were you when this happened?"

"No, never. I was in Europe for an installation of my artwork. Asa wasn't feeling well, or he would have come."

I paused note taking, looked up, and asked, "What were you and your uncle expecting from hypnosis?"

His face showed he was back on solid ground with the question. "Granduncle Willis said you know things are seldom what they appear. He thinks the case against Asa is too pat to be for real." Then TJ scanned my face to see if I agreed.

"Whose idea was hypnoses? That doesn't sound like old school Willis."

Looking like he was back on the hot seat he said, "I read in an airline magazine sometimes blackouts are opened to illumination during hypnosis. Can you recommend someone to find out what happened between Asa going to a bar with friends, waking up near the murder weapon, and a dead body in front of him?" This was said in a defeated tone of voice and face to match it.

"If you glance at my achievement wall, over there on the left, the laminated parchment plaques says I attained the highest degree hypnotherapist certification.

That plaque and four bucks will get you a ride on the New York City subways." As soon as I said the words I wished I could take the attitude back.

Defiance back on his face. "Yes or no, can you open a blackout?"

"Depends."

Back to where we started, he said, "Are you always this hard to get along with? You remind me of my granduncle."

Put in my place I explained hypnosis seldom gets much recall from a black hole caused by overindulgence in substances. On the other hand, a blackout from terror, over exertion, or any other form of physical or mental exhaustion, then there is a better than even chance of some memory recovery. But hypnosis is not an exact science. Then there was the matter of his husband being in jail, detention rules seldom allow for exceptions for trance induction.

TJ became adamant Asa wanted out of jail any way possible. So, TJ required extraordinary ways around the rules to get him out, no expense spared. Then I explained we did not know if his husband was even susceptible to deep trance hypnosis. Going to extremes to hypnotize him, where it may not be allowed, sounded like a big, probably wasted effort for nothing.

First looking slightly deflated then brightening to take command, TJ smirked and said, "You said probably, so, hypothetically, there is a statistical probability you could make hypnosis work."

I explained the probability is, twenty percent of the population goes into deep trance right away, and twenty percent can't be hypnotized no matter what. That leaves sixty percent that can be induced into some kind of a trance but not easily, or without a lot of time and effort. With repeated determination some of the sixty can dig deeper into their subconscious for some results. But it is a statistically bad crap shoot.

Paying attention to my words and then to show who was the boss, TJ said, "If you are worried about my paying for your ongoing long-term services, don't be, like you, I'm a multimillionaire. I'll pay whatever it cost for as long as it takes."

His words caught me off guard, without forethought my mouth said, "How do you know what I'm worth."

In charge of the conversation, he lectured me saying, "Dr. Kulgul, you should know my being Black doesn't mean I'm poor. My artwork sells for millions."

My hackles bristled as I said, "We've just met, and it's presumptuous of you to think that I assume all Black people are poor. Just what has my worth to do with why you are sitting here in this office?"

He met my challenge with his own fight face on. "It's important to me, *you know*, money is no object to get my husband out of jail, I miss him, and I never back down from a fight, ever. I'll pay whatever it takes to get him home."

"I haven't been a private detective for several years. But just so you know I find your attitude abrasive, and that's not helping."

He heard me and back pedaled. "I had my staff check you out. You're like my granduncle Willis, not a quitter. Now that we have that out of the way, how *do you* get in jail to hypnotize Asa?"

While I was thinking, *He cannot have any friends, and I don't need this crap*. My mouth said, "If your husband is willing to change to a less dogmatic lawyer, Willis and I know one who may give him a shot."

A look of relief washed over his face. "Now you're talking. Damn, I finally got you moving."

"No disrespect or offense intended but your attitude isn't helping ."

"Yeah, yeah, I've heard all that before, like I give a shit. Try to stay on topic will you. That's what I'm paying you for."

Wondering why I bothered I said, "A word to the wise, TJ. I doubt my lawyer will be interested in working with your attitude, it sucks. Just so you know, even if everything goes according to your plan, anything uncovered under hypnosis is not admissible in court."

TJ physically showed he was hearing me, not always a given. "Anything I can do to get my man free, I will. Even if I must temporarily change my attitude, if that's even possible."

I got up and retrieved a clipboard with a fresh form on it and sat back down. "Since you're already here, let's do a new intake form that reflects the real reason for your visit. Then *you* find out if your husband will accept a new lawyer and get back to me."

"If he does?" His facial muscles relaxed into hopeful for the first time since he arrived.

"If he does and my lawyer is available, and willing to put up with your abrasive personality, we'll let her handle it ..." Once again, I chastised myself for letting my irritation show.

Back a couple of paces from hopeful TJ said, "Okay, okay. I'm just wondering if you and my granduncle are so close, how come he didn't tell you I was coming?" That said he dropped the expensive pen he'd been playing with onto my desktop for emphasis.

"Since Willis took early retirement from the police department to raise horses in Mississippi, he and I have not had much to talk about. He and his kids love horses, me not so much."

"Does he know you are no longer a private detective?"

"I doubt it. I changed careers after he retired. I knew he'd have a problem with me changing jobs again. He'd complain I change jobs so often I'm not reliable."

"He talks just like that. It's his old school ways. I try to copy his style, but he's better at it in a nicer way."

With something definite to agree about I said, "He's one in a million."

"Uncle Willis doesn't value my art much either, but it brings me big bucks and fame."

"I see here on this previous intake form you have a local address. I thought you lived in and were from Florida."

"My husband and I moved up here six months ago. I told you my maternal grandmother died, we were caring for her, then things went from bad to worse culturally in Florida."

"Curious, how did culture get you packing?"

TJ told me the Florida state legislature and fascist governor passed a 'You Can't Say Gay' bill and then started burning LGBTQ books in libraries and schools. Between institutionalized bigotry and global warming dissolving the coastal boundaries, he and his husband felt it was too unhealthy to stay in Florida. Especially since Disney and other large corporations are moving their operations to Sanctuary States to protect their workers' rights.

"I have a gallery up here that's been showing and successfully selling my work for years. Now Asa manages granduncle Washington's properties up here too."

"Manages?"

"You know collects the rent, handle repairs, and deal with asshole problem tenants."

"According to this old initial interview you list your occupation as artist. Most artists I know aren't multimillionaires, or at least without a lot of hoopla and pyrotechnics to get there. What's the secret to your success?"

TJ explained he made mobiles that produce acoustic sounds as they move, usually by wind, some have electric motors. Also, he made musical instruments from found objects that can play the chromatic scale for successful hip-hop groups. He told me I would not believe how much one of his big mobiles sells for as part of a newly constructed building's lobby. Architects love to include his work in theirs these days. It sets them apart from their peers.

Keeping us on track I said, "I'd like to see your work sometime. *But for right now,* I'd like to know about you and your husband."

"We met during college freshmen orientation, he was seventeen, I was eighteen. Now I'm twenty-seven and he's twenty-six. I know I look much younger; I still get carded and it's not from virtuous living, I can tell you that. Asa looks young for his age too it's by association."

"You look at least a decade younger than your years."

"It makes no difference to me."

"People come to this office with serious problems. It used to be they expected me to risk my life to help them feel safe. Nowadays clients are willing to spend months on a waiting list to pay me a lot of mullahs, *so they can take risks to feel better.*"

Looking around where I work like an auction appraiser, TJ said, "I can see there is nothing cheap about your office."

"I never took frivolous cases, and don't ever intend to. In the past Willis and I went to the mat for each other for years. First when I was a parole officer then me as a private dick. Neither owes the other anything, we've paid forward. He and I were there for each other, guns smoking or otherwise more time than I care to count."

Putting on a plastic smile, TJ said, "All right, I guess the most significant thing to tell about me is I am biracial. That is mixed race in other words if it isn't obvious. Asa Mulroy is white, never knew a Black person before me, and he got quite a disturbing education about race in America for loving me. I do not know if you can understand this Dr. Kulgul, but I am a better me because of Asa's love and our fighting in our face racism and BDSM discrimination."

Having been born in the US, I think I understood racism from a queer white privileged ex parole officer's perspective. But what was meant by BDSM exactly? After a long pause looking me up and down, TJ stated for Asa and him BDSM was like religion with rules and rituals. Except they were not required to believe in supernatural powers, other superstitions, or bullshit. It occurred to me we'd gotten off track into an area uncomfortable for me at that moment.

Reading my reaction TJ made an abrupt transition, and simply said Asa was born in Maine. Then after a reflective interval said there were not any darkies in his part of rural Maine, and so at first TJ became an oddity. He told me what I already knew from Willis, TJ's mother was Black and short-lived father was white, and they both loved him to a fault. Nevertheless, he grew up watching American raciest culture punish his in-love parents for being different races.

Witnessing his parents' hardships caused by race, from an early age TJ promised himself never to get into interracial relations, except that was his identity even if he chose to be black. Then he said it was love at first sight when Asa and he first saw each other. He said Asa could tell me racism has made their love stronger. And TJ told me it has almost broken them up many times, just like his parents. Now living in New York, they could laugh out loud at old stupid Florida redneck fools without fear.

I assured TJ his uncle would say you do not get to choose the hand you are dealt. Then told him my husband and I noticed it is not so easy being LGBTQ no matter our current business here in New York. But we do not punk out about being gay, and when we cannot beat the bigots, we go down swinging.

From his eyes, I sensed a shift to sincerity when TJ said, "You understand, it has not been easy for us. But I love my man and would stand next to him on some gallows with a rope around our necks. It helps me, we live in the leather world with its meaningful values."

Here it was again, and the intake form had a place for it. "How long have you been into BDSM?"

"At the beginning, we were only curious, it was a goof. Now it's how we want to live. Believe it or not, for almost nine years. Asa truly loves and trusts me; I return that love with interest every day. Like I said before, we are better people because of our love. That's our story and it's 100% true, and you better believe it."

"You are much more likeable not being a wise ass."

"Just curious, how did you go from private detective to two PhDs who only takes referrals from other PhD's or MDs? It sounds unlikely, like a rag to riches fairy tale. Whoops, am I being a wise ass again?"

TJ's tale of obstacles loving his man, and how it made them better than their best for each other warmed my heart. So, I opened to him in ways I would normally consider none of his business, even unprofessional and told him Two things happened at the same time, first I'd reached my limit of dead people getting in front of my gun barrel before they expired. Simultaneously, I was made an offer for the computerized electronic security part of my detective agency. It was so large I'd have been a fool to refuse."

What I said animated TJ to say, "Ah ha! Opportunity knocked and you were home. Congratulations! A lot of the success of my artwork was luck and all the sweat, hard work, and sacrifice that made it lucky. Tell me how you got from there to here."

After selling off the electronic portion of my business, I gifted what was left of Queer Queries Detective agency to a longtime employee, Ameli Tsai. That meant I had money and time to go back to school. I completed my education in an entirely new area of interest and could retire my guns. At the same time with the windfall my husband was able to take a leave of absence from his job with the police department and go to law school. So far neither of us has qualms or looks back with regrets.

TJ's face showed he wasn't expecting so much personal background at the first meeting. To recover aplomb after my disclosure, he asked, "Are you going to ask your husband to defend mine?"

I explained, my personal lawyer, MT, is much more experienced than my spouse for TJ's purposes. But before we considered suggesting that, first I needed to find out if the evidence was as open and shut as he thought, and I visited the crime scene. It will speed up the process and would be what your uncle would do.

Looking back in charge of himself by accepting my answer, TJ said he hoped he was not crossing another line. He wanted to know what could be a new an interesting improvement during the mental health epidemic. He said, "To me crazy has been around as long as people and always will be. It's what makes us humans interesting."

I wanted to know, since he had such a strong opinion on the matter, how he thought most clinical mental health diagnosis were treated.

TJ pantomimed, popping pills, then out loud said, "And by joining the Republican Party, and buying an assault rifle. But I think mostly it's pills," then he half-laughed.

Enjoying his sense of humor, I responded with, "You have studied the situation." Then indicated nothing remarkable had been developed in pharmaceuticals for mental illness in almost one hundred years. Most folks wanting to reduce symptoms to be more productive never derive enough benefit from popping pills to achieve their goals.

TJ claimed two out of three points for his team was a sad indictment of psychiatry helping the mentally ill.

I explained mine was one of the few offices in the country where we splice in long strands of artificial DNA into a patient's natural DNA using Crispr. Because it requires enormous amounts of computer power, it is not the first place we go to stabilize mood up to community standards.

Looking confused TJ said, "I didn't even know you can get artificial DNA mixed in with the natural stuff, *and it comes in different lengths.* Is there a Cliff Notes version of what you are talking about?"

I opened a desk drawer and pulled out and held up a handful of female and male custom-made jewelry. Then I showed what we did with AI artificial intelligence, imbedded in the custom fit wearable patient-controlled electronics by pushing buttons or sliding tiny levers.

Looking slightly confused TJ said, "You keep going over my head. But don't stop, I find this is fascinating if just beyond my comprehension."

I explained my PhD in neuroscience psychology and the other one in bio-electrical-engineering came at just the right time. I got in on the ground floor of developing external nano patient-controlled Psycho Tropic implanted electronics. Each device is custom designed with the patient's input at every step. Then once trained and supervised on using it, it is controlled by the recipient for maximum equilibrium.

"You lost me again. Besides batteries how does it work."

"High frequency radio waves."

"Whoops again! I don't understand. Are you saying electronics are implanted instead of chemicals, to help crazies? Wow, that's even too radical for me."

Once again, I explained the century old psychotropic medications never worked for everyone and the side effects for those receiving some benefit required additional pharmaceuticals to deal with tremors, zoning out, sexual dysfunction, and the list went on. Then the medications to counter side effects caused physical reactions needing additional medications to deal with them. On the other hand, what we do has to be precise. Furthermore, all surgery can cause infections and other side effects. So, there are no free lunches."

"Oh, my God, overload, stop already. I'm sorry I asked."

I did not stop as requested and suggested to him many folks with a mental health diagnosis, initially helped by medications, go off the medicine for making them sick in other ways. To say nothing of the many who derived no benefit, ever from pills or injections.

It was clear what TJ was thinking, he kept finger tapping his cellphone and finally said, "So, now you are suggesting playing with something like this cell phone can unscramble a crazy brain?"

"I never mentioned playing with cell phones. But there are apps that encourage that conspiracy theory. A reoccurring ex-president of the United States likes to foster that idea, along with reading books and wind turbines causing brain cancer. You get the gist of it right?"

"No, not at all. I think you are causing me to hallucinate."

Thinking we were still playing around I explained to TJ there are various kinds of hallucinations as symptoms, and in my professional opinion neither of us was having one today.

What he wanted to know felt like a test, I like puzzles, so I played along to see where it was going. Could your creative tear be called deeply depressed struggle with delirium to harm yourself or others. Or could it be schizoaffective hallucinations that interest you, oh, wait, how about schizophrenic terror little green Martian men come marching out of electric wall sockets to annihilate mankind.

"Uncle! I give up, I started this chit chat, so at my request you will stop it right now."

Rather than stop and let TJ boss me around, I explained a person with an illness is more than just that disorder, and they know that, but not why the public is often afraid of them for being ill.

"You could make anyone be paranoid."

I went on to explain if the person with the affliction could just push a button on a pendant, earring, or wristwatch to short circuit the onset of their mental health episode it would keep them in the acceptable normal behavior zone. The symptoms could disappear as quickly as they started, and before chronic disruption and adverse consequences became labels.

Belligerently TJ wanted proof, what I said wasn't all theory.

Never overly shy blowing my own horn, I described one of my favorite success stories about a client with Tourette syndrome. She was barely holding on to her last chance low-level mailroom position at a bank. After customizing an interrupter for her, she was now without twitches and profane outbursts and in line to be the next president of that bank.

Testing my patience, TJ wanted to know how come he never heard about any of what I did before today?

I hit the ball back to his side of the net, saying, "You no doubt learned caring for your grandmother one size does not fit all. With my external interrupter size fittings come in opposition to powerful forces interested in keeping the pills to patients' pipeline flowing with cash. Our opposition is entrenched, rich, and powerful.

"Does what I just explained help you understand why you never heard of what I do for a good living and won't until I am replaced by machines?"

"Okay, Oliver, thank you for the seminar. But what do you do if the patient doesn't know they go into psychotic states, or it happens so gradually they don't notice until it's too late to reverse?"

"You might want to add to your list, the patient enjoys the high from full blown episodes like an addiction overriding what they know better, and their family, social standing, and career require."

"Wow, what?"

"The key is most healing takes place due to the patients' motivation to heal. I never said we have all the answers, it's the patient who controls the limits."

"You've answered my questions and gave more than I wanted and didn't know I wanted. May I call you at this number after speaking with Asa about changing lawyers?"

"Sure, let me write my personal cell phone number on the back of this card. Say hi to your uncle for me when you talk next."

"Okay, and I'll try for an answer from Asa as soon as the jail allows. Are we done I hate to run but have other appointments I'm going to be late for."

"Yes. Let's get together when we have information to share. It was interesting meeting you."

Chapter 2.

An hour and a half after our meeting, Tyrell Joyner telephoned to say his husband Asa Mulroy would accept, sight unseen, MT as his lawyer if he could plead not guilty. However, his current lawyer, Ezra Steinfeld, insisted on being the second chair if the case went to trial. His fee had already been paid and he had a no refund policy.

I telephoned MT using her direct number and asked if she could take on the Asa Mulroy case as a personal favor. She remembered Willis Washington as my best straight friend and one of the good guys at the police department. For my sake, MT was willing to clear a space on her over busy schedule to help Willis' grandnephew. When I explained, the plan was for me to hypnotize Mr. Mulroy and try to recover a blackout memory. MT doubted the jail would be at all accommodating, let alone provide a space without a lot of noisy distractions. But she'd give it her best shot.

Back when I was young during my first job after graduate school, just after completing their new worker training, I walked into a pizzeria without realizing it was being robbed. As I entered the first thing that registered was dodging bullets. Then two gunmen we're dead in front of the required service weapon I vowed never to unholster.

I discovered after the fact those gunmen had just killed four people in their mini crime spree at the old route fifty-two pickup. Being new to the job at parole I didn't know the rules. When the police arrived, they wanted to know did I identify myself as a peace officer before discharging my weapon? I told the truth, there was no time bullets were flying as soon as I walked through the door looking for dinner.

The next week the dead robbers' families filed complaints against me for not identifying myself as a peace officer before shooting to death their beloved sainted sons. I was immediately suspended from my new job without pay until the charges against me and lawsuit were dismissed.

Since I was brand new on the job, was not a union member, and so not eligible for their free lawyer. With no income, no money, and piles of student debt I turned to the free gay services directory and found MT was establishing a private legal practice after five years as an Assistant District Attorney. She was looking for lesbian clients but took me on because new clients were slow in coming. I paid her a one-dollar retainer fee and signed papers that I would pay her $2,500 when or if I ever had it.

At trial MT had me take the witness stand and relive the traumatic events, trying to buy a slice of pizza for dinner while being shot at. She had coached me to say after the live fire stopped, I announce I was a peace officer. The jury unanimously found my belated announcement commendable and me innocent of all charges. The robbers' families were disappointed not getting my head served on a platter and a large cash payout from the civil suit.

Those were the circumstances I first met lawyer MT over ten years ago. Since going back and finishing my education I've had little need for her legal services.

****

The next morning at 10:30 AM, MT phoned and said she had good news and bad. Naturally, I wanted the bad news first, and she told me the jail was not going to let me hypnotize *any* prisoner in jail … their jail, their rules. But the good news was the evidence against Asa looked circumstantial to her. She said there was something off about it, just what she could not put her finger on.

I said I would check it out and go peruse the crime scene. Then closed with, Let me know how Asa Mulroy looks after you see him in jail.

Four hours later I got a call from MT on my personal cellphone. After the perfunctory greetings I keenly asked how her new client Mulroy looked?

"He looks like a sacrificial lamb surrounded by hungry lions, scared, trying to look tough. In my time I have prosecuted and since defended many stone-cold killers, and this sweetheart innocent submissive kid doesn't qualify."

I told her that was good to hear because his husband sounds like a younger, mixed version of my friend Willis Washington, smart, forceful, but down to earth practical with an attitude a mile wide. MT wanted to know what I thought of the evidence. I apologized for getting bogged down at the office and said I was putting my coat on going out the door as we spoke.

I brought coffee and donuts to the old gang I knew at the crime lab, and somehow, they casually left the Asa Mulroy evidence report open on an unattended desk for me to peruse. MT was right, the only place Asa's fingerprints appeared on the murder weapon was not where it could be fired. The rest of the gun was clean of prints. It was a throwaway, mail order, untraceable ghost-gun home made on a 3-D printer.

As luck would have it, the murder scene was a parking garage I knew from the past. Queer Queries had installed close circuit motion activated video cameras when the strip mall was renovated decades before I sold QQ. Looking over the poured concrete ceiling, I saw one last hidden camera's blinking its tiny red light, ever vigilant.

I climbed up onto the roof of my car and copied the serial number on that camera. Then I called the new owners of my old electronic security business and requested the feed from that camera for the last five days. I patiently waited while the camera's security images were located and then downloaded to the laptop in my car.

The only activity of interest to me in those five days, on the security video, was an old silver colored Ford van that drove in. Two men, one wearing all black leather, carried an unconscious naked youth out of the van and laid him down on the cement floor. Then the leather man wearing a mask seemed to engage in an argument with the other guy who was sans clothing. After what looked like a heated verbal exchange, the masked man shot the other guy in the head. Meanwhile, the naked youth didn't move. He was either unconscious or dead lying between them. I emailed a copy of the video to MT and asked if the youth was Asa.

She called me right back and said that was Asa Mulroy in his birthday suit decorating the floor. Did I get anything else we can use? I told her it was impossible to fire the murder weapon from where Asa's fingerprints were found. She said good work, it felt like the old days before I got all academic snooty.

As snooty as I could muster on short notice said, "Thank you. All compliments are graciously accepted and tell the judge I still have my State Electronic Security Certification for court purposes as an expert witness."

MT found a judge who immediately released Asa Mulroy from confinement, on bail, and set a court date. e. He also admonished the police for sloppy work, wasting his time by not finding the hidden video camera I found.

I immediately texted a message for Tyrell Joyner to pick up his husband at MT's office promptly. Then I sent a brief email to Willis Washington, apprising him of recent events, thanking him for the referral, and mentioning, "Oh, by the way, thought you'd want to know, I'm no longer in the private detective business."

That day I drove home content, yes okay, maybe a little too self-congratulatory on how fast *and efficient* I'd facilitated Asa Mulroy's release from jail in a hurry. It was remotely possible my inner self was missing the gritty dangerous private detective life I once lived. I had replaced that life with the safety of teaching and seeing private mental health clients.

Then my mind reminisced to wonder at all the changes over the last few years. One thing that had been consistent over the time was the love from husband Coy. As a couple, we had progressed to look like each other even though there is an age difference.

After graduation we both grew full beards, appropriate or not for our post-graduate jobs. We now didn't often carry lethal weapons, thank God. I knew for sure when I got home, Coy would want every boring detail of what transpired to get Asa and Tyrell back together again. My man was an old softy when it came to romance, and I loved him for it.

On the street we look like an odd couple, me like a mature blond bearded Viking and brunette shorter bearded tough looking Coy, generic white guy. We'd been through so much life and death combat together we often functioned as one knowing the other's thoughts.

I smiled remembering when Coy graduated from the public university's law school. He expected to return to the police department reinstated as a sergeant, but fast tracked up the chain of command. With his new freshly minted law degree and Bar card, he planned to take the lieutenant's exam, then the captain's test, and retire in twenty years with a hefty pension at age fifty.

That is not what happened. At graduation a local prestigious white glove law firm, Hamilton, Hanover, Handicock, and Hoot offered Coy a unique position. All their other staff attorneys were either Harvard or Yale graduates, and everyone brought the firm big buck compensation. The partners decided they wanted to give a little something back to the underserved community they never had contact with.

So, they dedicated one local ex-cop, non-Ivy league lawyer to do nothing but high publicity pro bono work as a public service. Their lofty idea was to sweep up and save innocent people from being railroaded to prison with a guilty plea, their only best recourse.

The partners gave Coy a ridiculously high salary for a recent local graduate law school, former police sergeant, and Army combat veteran. In addition, he was given a small paralegal staff, not held to billable hours and so he brought in bountiful positive publicity at a level advertising money could not buy.

When I graduated with my cognitive neuroscience PhD and bio-electrical engineering PhD, I started teaching in two different departments at two different universities. I understood my work would have to be streamlined fast and good if I also wanted a private psychotherapy practice. The dance I do required keeping three balls juggled in the air at the same time. I taught budding psychiatrists at the medical school, and graduate bioelectrical engineers at the engineering school. Having smart students kept me sharp. I liked that.

Though unique and architecturally distinctive, my old upside-down house was too high maintenance as most one of a kind dwellings are. Especially for the kind of workaholic Coy and my new postgraduate lives became. So, we sold the old digs and bought a new and bigger normal looking home. As it turned out, that was dumb, the bigger house did not help doing laundry, drycleaning, dusting, vacuuming, food shopping, cooking, and general routine cleaning. We needed to go smaller not larger. We should have known better.

Just as we were contemplating selling the oversize white elephant of a new place and moving into a full-service residential hotel, circumstances radically changed for our part-time house cleaner of decades. First her parents died one right after the other after long illnesses. Her grief was debilitating. With her parents dead their Social Security checks stopped being directly deposited in the bank, and innocently or not the bounced mortgage payment notices were sent to the wrong address. Carmen, before transition to Carmine Ganover, was awakened early one morning by the marshals suddenly evicting her into homelessness.

Coy and I took Carmen in, it was supposed to be temporary. She was so deep in grief after her parents' deaths and loss of her one-woman house cleaning business. She had spent too much time doing parental end-of-life care and not taking care of herself and business. Homeless living with partially undomesticated Coy and me Carmen quickly evolved into our full-time live-in housekeeper and domestic-life-skills manager. It happened before any of us realized it had.

Hubby and I lingered over a weekend evening meal of Chateaubriand prepared to perfection and were determined to finish the bottle of vintage Bordeaux wine that complemented the meal. Coy kept asking questions about Tyrell Joyner, Asa Mulroy, and an unlikely murder.

Since I knew nothing more than I already told him, I suggested we invite the young couple to dinner, and he stopped having lunch with his straight colleagues who were making him pushy at home. He liked the idea of dinner guests to interrogate and suggested a week from Saturday. Then he mentioned not seeing adverse effects from his Harvard and Yale lunch companions. So, I slugged his arm a good one and he finally connected an association with my cause-and-effect action.

****

When our two young guests arrived for dinner, Carmen's preparations showed she was finally on her way out of the long dark tunnel of her parental bereavement. I could see our guests were impressed by her elaborate floral arrangements, everywhere. It was too much, we are fags, not florists or funeral home proprietors.

Coy gave me a look that said, "Why did you not warn me?" as Tyrell detached the dog leash from the dog collar Asa was wearing around his neck and said, "Be a good boy. Behave."

Asa Mulroy was six inches shorter and without the well-defined musculature of his husband. In his black leather clothes, Asa looked paltry compared to Tyrell Joyner's musculature molded into his leather form fitting outfit. Personally, I found Asa's wide black leather, silver studded dog collar worn just below his dog snout mask a bit much for casual dinner wear. My bad, the dinner invitation did not mention attire.

Peeking out from under and around his black leather long-billed ball-cap, Asa had curly light brown hair. The same color matched his light brown eyebrows and eyes. Two things were obvious as soon as they entered our house, both men obviously loved each other deeply but, in unusual ways I did not understand. If I were pressed, it looked like a faithful dog and his loving owner.

In adult human context, Tyrell was obviously dominant, and Asa willing subservient. That seemed to be set in stone. Maybe they came by it naturally. For sure they were not putting on a defiant show for our sake, even though I suppose it could come across that way. Why would they put it on, we did not know each other. My interpretation was that is the way they lived, and they did not care who knew it.

Both guests declined a cocktail before dinner and finally after a big brouhaha accepted unsweetened iced tea when Carmen out butched TJ. She said they had to clear their pallet to fully enjoy the meal. Asa practically cowered when his master and our transgender housekeeper went toe to toe. Asa looked like he wet himself, but it did not puddle.

Carmen served a rich flavorful clear reduction soup containing a few strands of long, thin translucent rice noodles, gossamers of carrots, pimentos, and thin sliced filaments of sautéed shallots. The highlight of the meal was a standing crown rib roast, with her fluffy, lighter than air, whipped herb-butter potatoes in the center of the crown of ribs, braised asparagus in cream sauce on the side, and baby arugula, grape tomato, oil cured olive salad, dressed with lemon juice olive oil completed the main meal. The wine was a hardy Chianti Coy and I are very fond of. We have stashed cases in the basement for special occasions. The guests preferred to drink unsweetened iced tea as if it was their punishment. After the meal Carmen served English trifle in balloon parfait glasses and expresso in the living room.

Looking satiated from a meal he could not complain about, Tyrell said to me, "I'd still expect you to hypnotize Asa, first chance you get to find out what's in his blackout."

"Asa, is that what you want?"

Looking first for silent permission from Tyrell, then Asa said, "Yes, sir."

Before I could say anything more to anyone, Coy and Tyrell loudly got into it as to whether Socrates was the father of Western philosophy. I knew Coy was not going to let the difference of opinion die quietly or quickly. I stood, turned, made eye contact, and gestured for Asa to follow me. We walked through the kitchen, where Carmen was busy finishing dinner clean up. Then he and I walked out onto the back deck, and I asked, "Asa, do you really want to try hypnosis?"

"Yes, sir."

"Then remove your K-9 face mask. I'll need to see your eyes and face."

Asa unstrapped his doggy snout face mask. It covered from just below his eyes to conceal his face with a leather dog muzzle just above his mouth. It was a handsome white boy twink face. Then I felt my unmistakable cautious anticipation vibe about to delve into someone's unconscious life. Pushing forward with mixed feelings I said, "Okay Asa, let's prepare you with a relaxation exercise first. Sit in that deck chair and face me, I'll sit here across from you. Now, I want you to take three deep breaths, hold them, then release on my signal."

I raised one finger, and he inhaled. After counting to five, I lowered the finger, and he exhaled. Then I raised two fingers, and he drew in another slow deep breath, held it for five beats and released it as I lowered both fingers. Finally, after an additional long pause keeping my fists clenched, I raised three fingers, and we repeated the exercise.

Asa looked more at ease than when we started, so I said, "Do you have your cell phone with you? Good. Set it to record yourself so you have an exact record of what happens if you can be hypnotized into a deep trance."

"That won't be necessary, sir. TJ trusts you, so I will."

"It is necessary for my sense of security."

"I don't understand. Security? Why? This is your house sir."

"If you can go into deep hypnosis, I will talk directly to your subconscious addressing you in the third person. Most people have no recall of being in a deep hypnotic state since it's happening unconsciously."

"I guess that makes some kind of sense. I don't understand, sir."

I explained that was why most hypnotists leave a post-hypnotic suggestion as proof they were inside. Although I won't make Asa cluck like a chicken or quack like a duck as proof, nevertheless I always leave a tell. Because some folks freak out when they discover they have been hypnotized and have no recall of it. People with very active imaginations accuse hypnotists of all sorts of bizarre goings on while they were in a trance, that didn't happen except in their imagination. I'm just covering my ass by Asa having an irrefutable record. My fingerprints are not on his phone, nor will they be.

Showing slight alarm, Asa said, "What kind of accusations, sir?"

"Could be anything, like I made you dance nude during the hypnosis."

"If that's what you want, sir. I'm sure TJ would give permission, and I don't mind doing that? I aim to please my master, sir."

"That's not the point. I was merely illustrating why I want you to record our attempt to hypnotize you. Stop saying sir. Do you understand?"

With a dismissive look Asa said, "Got it. Give me a second to set up my cell phone to make a video with sound, but just to please you."

"Let me know when you are ready to begin, and please keep your clothes on?"

"Ready, sir."

I told him to sit back in that deck chair, feet on the floor, arms on armrests. "Now relax hands, arms, legs, and clear your mind of all thoughts. Close your eyes, breathe naturally. Good, now for a moment imagine all the muscle groups in your body are letting go by releasing tension into the air. Feel stress leaving you. Good. Now take a big deep breath, slowly in, that's it, now exhale slowly. Wait … now take another very deep breath. Wait … again, now slowly release it with your tension. Now breathe normally and feel the relaxation roll over your body like a warm fluffy blanket. Now you feel completely relaxed as I talk to you. You look ready to start hypnosis." Is Asa ready to begin?"

"Yes, sir, he's ready to serve as a loyal dog."

Speaking without inflection. I softly uttered now Asa opens his eyes. He focusses on relaxing all the muscles around his face for the moment. Then relaxes his scalp, forehead, eyebrows, eyelids, cheeks, nose, and mouth. Asa concentrates on muscle groups around his mouth and lips, making sure his teeth are not quenched. Now he relaxes his chin and allows all those muscles in his face to just let go, peaceably release.

Next Asa relaxes his neck. He feels the relaxation completely taking over and lets go of any stress there might be left in the shoulder area. It feels good to shed the pressure of stress. Asa stays with the feeling of release of stiffness, let it go. He lets go of all tautness imagining his arms becoming very heavy, loose and limp, heavy loose like wet noodles.

Remember to keep breathing normally and comfortably as Asa notices how deep and regular his breathing has become, breathing in, breathing out ... He allows those chest muscles to relax completely. Feel the stomach muscles releasing strain getting rid of rigidity. Now he allows his back muscles to relax those large muscle groups in the upper part of the back. Feel the release go right down Asa's spinal column. Just let it go out and drift away.

Asa allows smaller muscle groups in his lower back to relax. He allows all his muscle groups to relax completely as Asa begins to drift into a very deep fluffy cloud of relaxed being. Let him go, let his mind and body become one, feeling good, now feeling so good he is completely relaxed.

Asa will go deep into hypnosis gradually. I'm going to count from 1 to 20. On each count Asa closes his eyelids then opens them again until they want to stay shut. Allow them to stay closed when they want and allow him to drift into hypnosis at his own pace.

"Is Asa ready for deep hypnosis?"

"Ready, sir."

In flat affect tone I began, "Imagine a fluffy cloud snuggling up to Asa's body in the shape of an easy chair. Imagine this easy chair is a warm and comfortable cloud. It is his personal cloud. Notice how it snuggles up to his body. Now it is going to take him to where he's happy. A place he feels good. A place where he always looks good. Allow the custom cloud to snuggle up to his body and take him to his special place, where he's happy, relaxed, and very, very, very calm.

"Now allow Asa to be in this moment, as I begin to count, and he goes deeper, deeper, ever deeper into hypnosis. Each time I say a number he closes his eyes and opens them again. At some number they will want to stay closed, and he will allow it. Is Asa ready?"

"Ready."

"One, going deeper and deeper into a trance, two, going all the way down deep into hypnosis, three, go deeper, deeper now, four, feeling heavy, tired and drowsy, five, eye lids weigh a ton, six, let go into a welcoming trance, seven, go down deeper, eight, going deeper and deeper, nine, it's like going down stairs steps, ten, so tired eyes are staying closed, eleven, letting go even more, twelve, all the way down he steps into the mind's depths, thirteen, go deeper still deeper, fourteen, follow the stairs deeper down and even deeper, fifteen, Asa is so heavy in deep sleep, sixteen, just let go now, seventeen, breathe naturally, eighteen, Asa feels happy and good, nineteen, he is completely relaxed now, and finally twenty Asa is in deep, deep, deep in hypnosis."

"Asa is safe, protected, and with me. Asa's mind is now open to receiving questions that he wants to answer. In the future Asa will go directly into this deep trance whenever I ask him to close and open his eyes on my count from one to ten, on the number six. Now I'm about to ask Asa questions, he will answer truthfully with what he knows. Is Asa in deep hypnosis?"

"Yes."

"What is Asa's favorite color?"

"Yellow."

"What is TJ's favorite color?"

"Green."

"Can Asa recall what happened just before he woke up on the floor of a parking garage?"

"He was at the grand opening of The Dungeon bar with friends."

"Where was TJ?"

"In Milan, Italy installing one of his mobiles."

"What was Asa wearing?"

"Black leather vest, no shirt, black leather chaps over distressed black jeans, and new black motorcycle boots."

"How long was Asa at the bar?"

"Forty minutes."

"Did he leave with his friends?"

"No."

"Why not?"

"They were busy."

"What were Asa's friends doing?"

"Trying to hook up with other men."

"What does Asa remember before the parking garage?"

"He went to pee. When he came back his bottle of beer wasn't where he left it. Then a stranger handed him the missing beer."

"Did Asa ask his friends to watch his drink?"

"Yes."

"Did they?"

"They were talking with other people."

"Who handed Asa his missing beer?"

"A stranger."

"What happened next?"

"Asa listened to the music and drank the beer. Then he suddenly felt woozy."

"Does Asa often get woozy from beer?"

"No. He never drinks much."

"What does Asa think happened?"

"Someone put drugs in his beer bottle."

"Who would do that?"

"He doesn't know anyone who would."

"What happened next?"

"Asa almost fell down."

"Then?"

"Two guys grabbed him before he fell on the floor."

"Who were they?"

"The man who gave Asa his beer and man standing beside him."

"What were they wearing?"

"The beer guy wore big eyeglasses with black-frames and a black cowboy hat pulled down almost to eyeglass level. He had tattoo sleeves up both arms to his elbows and wore a leather mask."

"How was the other man dressed?"

"He had on all leather gear. It was an expensive looking outfit. Asa didn't pay much attention until that man looked like he wanted to cause harm."

"Harm how?"

"Don't know, he looked at Asa funny, in a bad way."

"What happened next?"

"Asa woke up shivering cold lying on a dirty floor. All his clothes were gone."

"Everything?"

"No. He was wearing his new extra thick white cotton boot socks."

"What did Asa see when he woke up?"

"The other man from the bar was laying up ahead, also with no clothes. He was not moving … bleeding from the head … likely dead."

"Does Asa remember anything else?"

"No. … Yes, a gun on the floor under Asa's hand."

"Did Asa fire the gun?"

"No."

"What one word would describe the cowboy hat guy?"

"Coarse."

"What word would describe the other man?"

"Dangerous."

"Does Asa recall anything else other than waking up shivering?"

"Hearing shouting."

"What was shouted?"

"'I only wanted to give him a light dusting and then a hard fuck. I'm not ready to fuck him yet, put the gun away.'"

"Did the other guy say anything?"

"'You took too long. Your plan was to rape him in the moving van. You went off script, that's not allowed.'"

"Did Asa hear anything else?"

"'Don't shoot.'" A loud noise, pause, feet shuffling, cutting sounds, sounds of running on cement, the car door opens and closes, an internal combustion engine starting and driving away."

"Where are Asa's clothes?"

"He doesn't know."

"When Asa first saw him, what was the dead guy wearing?"

"At the bar, handmade black leather jacket over a black T-shirt, black leather jeans, black motorcycle boots, keys hanging outside on the left, and black handkerchief poking out of left rear pocket. He was wearing nothing at all on the garage floor."

"What happened when Asa became conscious?"

"The police and EMS were there talking gibberish. They covered the dead guy with a sheet when they stopped working on him. There was lots of blood on the floor and their shoes walked in it. The police took photos then covered Asa with a blanket. EMS took some of Asa's blood, then the police put Asa in handcuffs and took him to jail. Asa's brain was foggy, he could not understand anyone clearly when they spoke drivel rot at him."

"Why did they put Asa in handcuffs?"

"His hand and fingerprints were on the murder weapon."

"Had Asa ever seen the murdered man or the killer other than before in the bar?"

"No."

"Could Asa describe the mask?"

"It was just around his eyes, not a good big mask."

"Anything else?"

"No. ... just shadows."

"Can Asa reach any memory between drinking beer and what he said so far?"

"No, only vague shadows."

"This is important, dig deep now, does Asa remember anything he hasn't said so far?"

"He thinks he was in a van. It drove on a street, highway, bumpy road, and highway again."

"What else does Asa remember about that?"

"The van stopped once, and the two men talked about killing someone after raping them. While the van was moving, someone stripped him, and Asa's clothes were put in a green plastic garbage bag. Then that bag was tossed out when the van got moving again along a bumpy road near the highway."

"Now Asa can dig down into memory much deeper. Was the driver the guy wearing the mask?"

"Yes."

"Did that same man also strip Asa?"

"No. The other man did it."

"Did Asa know either man before that night?"

"No."

"Where are the other man's clothes?"

"Asa doesn't know."

"What make and color was the van?"

"It was a silver-colored, old, full size Ford cargo van, in need of an engine tune up. All eight cylinders were not firing."

"Is there anything else Asa remembers?"

"No. Nothing more."

"Try hard for any recollections or dreams about that night? Dig down deep, go deeper, try hard to remember that night."

"Nothing, no nothing, Asa is empty."

Asa started moving around, looking restless. I could tell he had enough for now and said, "Now I'm going to count backward from five. Five, Asa is beginning to wake from hypnosis. Four, Asa is getting ready to open his eyes. Three, Asa is feeling good, relaxed, like he just had a restful nap. He's now almost ready to open his eyes. Two, Asa opens his eyes feeling wonderful, and one, Asa is back. How do you feel?"

"It didn't work, right? I don't feel any different than before you tried to hypnotize me. I am sorry to disappoint you and TJ. Where is my dog facemask?"

"Right there where you put it."

"Oh, okay, right where I put it, thanks. Excuse me, I'll put it on." He said all right sounding, a bit fuzzy then clearly said, "I will take my punishment for failing, I was a bad dog. Please, sir, don't use the cat o' nine tails on me, I can't handle that one yet."

I told him in addition to his cell phone video my laptop was turned on dictation along with its video camera doing documenting. If there was a problem with Asa's cellphone, he could have a printed text and video showing the hypnosis was legitimate from my computer.

Looking a little peeved, Asa exclaimed he did not feel any different, so nothing could have happened. Then he got adamant saying, "I was not hypnotized, so there's no point having records of my failure unless it is to humiliate me. Because I already apologized for letting you down."

Putting my warm hand on his cool arm I said, "Asa, did you know most peoples' favorite colors are either red or blue? Who knows your favorite color is yellow and TJ's is green?"

"Nobody knows that … except us. Who told you?"

"You did, under hypnosis. Before you were hypnotized, you looked stiff and on edge even uptight. That's understandable given what you have been through recently. After hypnosis, you seemed calm, relaxed, and now you look pissed off. Do you still believe you were not under hypnosis for thirty minutes."

"No, not now … sorry I was short with you."

"And lucky you didn't have to quack like a duck as proof."

"Wow, it really did happen without me knowing. Did you learn anything new about the murder? Was I molested during the abduction?"

I explained he had only a little recall from the blackout. I suggested he watch and rewatch the video as it might trigger additional, deeper, post-hypnotic memory. I said we could repeat hypnotic sessions and that might uncover even more of his blackout, but it could take a long grueling time and gain little to show for it. I did not recommend it at this time, he seemed to be making good progress working through his PTSD and more hypnosis might slow his process. I ended with, "Why don't we go back inside and see if our husbands came to blows?"

Chapter 3.

Back inside the living room, the two men sitting on the couch were stoney faced silent. I could read the room, Coy's closed look meant their philosophical discussion had ended in a stalemate, no little triumph smirks on either face. As Asa followed me into the room, Tyrell sternly said it had gotten late, they needed to leave. He stood and addressing me, bossy TJ said, "Thank you for a memorable dinner and uh … conversation," and his body language looked ready to head for the front door.

Speaking to both men, I said, "Don't you two couch potatoes want the results of Asa's hypnosis?"

Meanwhile, Asa walked over and knelt at Tyrell's feet. TJ reached down and gently stroked Asa's long-billed black leather hat covered head and curtly said, "Sit," and Asa promptly lowered his butt to the floor at his master's command.

Making hard eye contact in response to my question, TJ addressed me as if I was a sub subordinate and sternly said, "Since it was at my request, of course I want to know the results. Was he sexually abused? How bad was it?" Then changing to a less harsh tone of voice, stroking Asa's chest, TJ addressed Asa and said, "Was he a good dog for you?"

Put off by the odd human as dog performance and otherwise condescending behavior, I checked myself from impulsively being a jerk. Instead, I civilly related in a neutral tone, "Asa went into a deep trance with little effort, and the blackout was resistant to deep probing. You two will decide whether it's worth the trouble and time to keep exploring a blackout without a high probability of success."

TJ spoke down to me. "So, that's it, all you got for the hype?"

Drawing on intestinal fortitude in measured calm tones I said, "Repeatedly play Asa's recording looking for post hypnotic insights."

As if bullying an incompetent underling, TJ said, "You must know I was hoping for much more than that. I'm very disappointed in you, Oliver."

My dilemma was how to end the evening on a civil note. My mother said always try to be nice, at least at first. I said, "How about I fill *all three of you* in on what I knew from before this evening, and none of you did?"

All three heads turned and looked expectantly at me then the two-standing sat back down in unison.

"Getting Asa released from jail involved a judge allowing me to run the original poor quality close circuit security video of the murder through my customized above and beyond current state of the art photo software package. The shooter's face, mask, clothes, and tattoos shown on my clarified video don't physically identify Asa as the shooter. So far, the police database can't locate the killer or the dead man on their facial recognition software. However, according to the police photos taken when they arrived at the murder scene, their interstate files say Asa is who he says based on a streaking prank he participated in, in high school."

"So, that's how you got him out of jail. As you will recall, that's exactly what I paid you for."

Keeping my emotions in check, I said, "There's more."

"I should hope so."

Wondering why I bothered to be civil, I told those present the police thought Asa was drunk when they arrived. It was because of his lack of coherence and clothing. They had EMS on the scene draw his blood since their breathalyzer registered inconclusive. I got a look at their lab results. They show high levels of caffeine and the date rape drug Rohypnol in Asa's blood when the police arrived. The murder victim had high levels of alcohol and cocaine in his blood. Cocaine often causes impotence and that may be why Asa was not sexually molested by the two older men who picked him. Both the murder victim and Asa's blood drug numbers were high enough to show ossified.

Simmering down a tad, TJ wanted to know if that meant Asa was completely off the hook. I told him not so fast from the hypnosis information the murder victim and perpetrator were unknown to Asa. "But Asa's function in the sequence of events seems too premedicated to be random selection choice. Either the shooter or victim or both chose Asa out of a bar full of leather people, for some reason."

Constantly in charge, TJ snapped, "What reason?"

"We don't know. Could be as simple as he looked like an easy mark. But until we do know, if I were you two, I'd keep an eye out for anything out of the ordinary around you."

Toning it down one notch, bossman TJ said, "Are you saying there is more to this trouble to come?"

"Just a word to the wise, be cautious until the murderer is caught and locked up."

Switching to a little boy pleading tone of voice, TJ said, "Oliver, do you think we need a bodyguard?"

"Don't know, I don't give that kind of advice since I left the private investigation business."

Apparently, Coy had reached his limit of guest's bad behavior and wryly said, "Too bad for you, TJ. Oliver was good at the craft of private detection with fierce bodyguards."

"Right. Then we should be on our way, *cautiously*. Bye. Come, doggy boy." Clearly TJ looked pissed off. I guess he had expected much more from me while I thought he got his money's worth and then some. At least Asa was no longer in jail and charged with murder. That was why he said he came to my office.

TJ and Asa got to their feet. Standing erect, Asa shook himself then leaned his head down, rolled his shoulders forward, and TJ attached the clip end of the dog leash to the wide black leather spiked dog collar around Asa's neck. It looked like such an often-practiced routine it was done automatically out of habit.

Through dinner, that dog leash was folded and stowed under TJ's heavy black leather motorcycle jacket's left shoulder epaulette. It bobbed as he moved. Not being familiar with leather folk close up, that dog leash at the dinner table was a distraction, as much as I tried to ignore it. Every time I think I've mellowed into accepting my fellow human's obstruse behavior, I've not. At least not in my safe space, home.

Up out of my chair, I led our guests to the front door and said, "Bye now."

When I got no response back, I said, "See yah," to their backs.

They exited down our front steps and walkway looking like a young mixed-race man and his man-size domesticated animal on a leash. The waiting driver's face and race were obscured by a black leather motorcycle cap bill pulled down to just above eye level. He/she was completely covered in black leather. She or he left the driver's seat to hurry around and opened the right back door of a new top of the line black BMW parked at the curb. Asa scurried in back and then gave me a little self-conscious wave goodbye. I returned the wave with a slight head bow. The driver closed the back door, opened the right front door and TJ slid in. Then she/he walked around to the left front and drove them away.

Right after I closed the front door behind me and locked it, Coy said, "How could you invite a freak show like that to our home for dinner without at least giving me a heads up?"

"Be fair, Coy. How was I to know they'd come dressed in costume?"

"I thought you met them before?"

"TJ."

"How was he dressed then?"

"Age appropriate, young rich artist."

"Don't be difficult, love of my life, what was he wearing?"

"Black leather cowboy fringed jacket, T-shirt, expensive skinny leg jeans, and cowboy boots."

"Doesn't matter, with those two it's more than just leather coverings. I bet they have a dungeon in their basement where they draw and quarter people for fun."

"For that you need horses, and I don't think the health department allows you to keep horses in basements."

"Ha, ha very funny. You still should have warned me of a freak show for dinner."

"I met TJ at the office for a half hour, other than argumentative he seemed like what you'd expect from a young successful artist. I first met Asa tonight. Although I had previously seen a video of Asa being carried out of a van at the site of a shooting where someone got murdered. Oh, and the police photos of the scene when they arrived, he was laying nude on an empty parking garage floor."

"Is he hung?"

"Better than average for his height. Some might say he's generously endowed with a slight lace curtain overhang. As natural cocks go, he has a pretty one which is more than could be said of the murder victim."

"Interesting mixed marriage. TJ is biracial, which means most probably routinely circumcised as an infant to prevent him raping white women. No wonder they need whips and chains to get intimate."

"You don't know if they need whips and chains. Would you be this upset if they arrived wearing nun's habits?"

"Probably not. Nuns don't stir up my deep feelings I'd rather stayed unstirred."

"Coy, don't you think it's a little strange they arrested and indicted Asa and nobody wondered after the whereabouts of his or the murdered guy's clothes? Or even asked why they weren't wearing any, in the documentation."

"Right, what was the point of his being nude if he was unconscious the whole time?"

"The cops and District Attorney must have been in one hell of a hurry to close this case. I bet they thought it was an easy slam dunk, and nobody would notice how sloppy their work was."

"Oliver, what is stranger than the way these two dressed and acted as first-time dinner guests in our home, is the mystery of some unknown person ham handedly trying to frame Asa for murder. Uh, wait a minute, no, I'm wrong, their behavior as dinner guests was the strangest."

"Why?"

"Growing up we never let our dogs eat at the dinner table."

"So, you are more bent out of shape by our guests' attire and behavior than about a murder mystery with no motive or clues? Coy, old age has changed your priorities."

"I'm younger than you and you're not old."

After meeting with TJ at my office and now seeing him in our home, I thought *Whichever police detective gets this case will have a handful.* TJ had a mouth on him and didn't even try to filter his milewide privileged attitude. Most cops I knew wouldn't take his rude behavior as calmly as I did.

"A penny for your thoughts."

"Those two kicked up stuff I didn't know I had."

"Want to talk about it?"

"No. Not unless it turns into nightmares."

"I'm professionally up to date with leather, bondage, and S&M fetishes. This form of play acting has been around for centuries. It's just not my thing."

"Yeah, I remember some of that from police training. It's not new gay stuff for either of us."

"What's new is it was in our house and ruined a lovely dinner with uncalled for drama."

"Right. Damn right!"

"Okay! How about we try a CBT, cognitive behavioral therapy, approach to mitigate our aversion?"

"If it was *our* aversion, then let's let Sigmund and his disciples rest in peace."

"CBT came along long after Freud snuffed out his last cigar."

"I don't want to know, and don't you write a song about it."

"Oh gee, then what, Coy? Do you want us to dress up in black leather, play bondage games, and take turns whipping each other to better understand?"

"I thought that was how CBT worked."

"Ugh, not exactly." It had gotten late, we were both obviously over tired, quibbling, and neither of us at our best for it. So, I said, "Let's turn in, you have early court tomorrow and it looks like we both have full days ahead all this week."

"I'll only spoon you in bed if we table this discussion until another time."

"You're being mean."

"Oliver, otherwise, it goes against our house rule of *not* going to sleep on an unresolved argument."

"I'm not sure this is an argument. I'm certainly not angry that you refused to dress in dead animal skins and act like a barbarian."

"Wow, now I can go to sleep without worry."

"Just in case you forgot, Coy, I still love you very much just the way you are, even if you hate leather Queens."

"Do I, really? You said no fighting before bedtime Oliver."

"Stating a fact is not fighting. But loving you so much, I won't hold non-inclusiveness against you if you don't join the Republican party."

"I never said I hate leather queens."

"Your body language speaks louder than your words."

"Honestly, I don't know how I feel about performance costume drama at our dinner table. They ruined a nice meal."

"Good night, sweet prince. I apologize for not warning you about what I didn't know was coming to dinner."

****

We both had an over busy week. The first chance to linger over mugs of coffee was after one of Carmen's special weekend breakfasts out on the back deck seven days later. Nevertheless, over the week I could tell something was eating at Coy and he wouldn't talk about it. I knew from experience if we did not hit this head on, it could morph into something much bigger and nasty later. So, with that I suggested we talk over last Saturday's dinner and guests' behavior on the chance it dredged up something. When he made a face I proposed an alternative, we could discuss the mountains or seashore for our next vacation.

Coy looking thoughtful, sipping his coffee said, "Whatever ... No ... I just can't figure out why that freak show on Saturday still bothers me."

"I think it's your inner subconscious cop protecting your conscious self."

"Oh, boy, here we go, unwanted psychoanalysis on demand."

"Those costumes are symbolic of danger and death."

"Maybe we should talk about our different perceptions. Then discuss what's really bothering you and unconsciously may be bothering me too. What do you think?"

"That sounds reasonable for an unreasonable topic. We both witnessed the same thing so our brains should agree on what?"

"I've said it before, the mind and brain are not the same. Coy, remember that internet neuroscience experiment where the exact same sound was played and 50% claimed they heard Laurel and the other 50% swear it was Yanny."

"We are not talking about a sound experiment right now, my man Oliver, okay."

"What about that dress that half the people claimed was gold and white and the other half we're sure it was black and blue. What about that lover man?"

"Are you going to make this all about cognitive neuroscience?"

"No. When you were a street cop was the reaction always the same when you hooked someone up with your handcuffs?"

"Of course not."

"I'd wager some went peaceably, some fought, and even some felt relieved finally to be caught."

"Your point is?"

"On one level we could just dismiss TJ and Asa as bad guests who should have asked to come to our house dressed in all leather and behaving inappropriately as a dog."

"But?"

"Willis sent TJ to see me for help. I feel a sense of responsibility to my old friend who seldom asked for favors while being generous giving his."

"What about your husband ... don't answer that."

"You know I love him more than myself."

"Yeah, I know you do. Maybe this is just a juicy murder mystery set in a costume drama. Now we wouldn't want to miss that, would we? Or let something bad happen to our freaky rude leather queen dinner guests that we might prevent."

"Speaking of which, Coy, it's not like you to call people names."

"What names?"

"Like freaks or you being so sarcastic."

"I'm fighting with myself over thoughts, I don't want to intrude into what you call my consciousness. And I'll admit beginning to rent space in my brain, mind, or whatever. I don't like what our guests stirred up in me."

"You left out interfering with my sleep."

"Just how are my nightmares bothering you?"

"Like mini earthquake kicks, you sleep through, and I don't."

"Sorry, want me to sleep in the guest room."

"No. It might help if we talked about them when you're ready."

"Mmm, to save time, how about telling me what you know about leather queens from your police training?"

Coy explained at the police academy it was all lumped together as domestics' power and control, under the heading of Domestic Violence Police Response. They taught domestic violence is a terminal disease. It starts with harsh words then a light slap and overtime leads to a brutal, violent death.

"That's what I was taught at the university."

"The academy taught first the victim is rewarded for taking violence and pain with extra tenderness and generous gifts. Only after broken bones and hospitalizations does the victim realize they are trapped in a downward spiral to ultimately their cruel death. The gifts and extra tender sex are why when the police are called the victim seldom signs a complaint against the perpetrator, while still fearing for their life. Without a signed complaint, the police can do nothing until it's beyond too late."

Concluding speaking with an "I know better than you" flourish, Coy said, "So, power and control in domestic violence situations is most often terminal."

Half under my breath, more to myself than to Coy, I said, "I doubt that describes TJ and Asa. At least from what I saw."

"I know. You asked me about my training." Coy went on to say he was taught domestic violence can happen in heterosexual, lesbian and gay male relationships. In all three there is also something else, called sadomasochism or S&M. Which isn't domestic violence, but can look like it, but is pretend fun and games for sex. One feature of which is wearing black leather clothing or decorations. Cops are supposed to notice the difference between real domestic violence leading to death and people who dress up and play with simulated power and control for fun to enhanced sexual activity."

"No doubt a fun part of the police job."

"Yeah. Similar, for the harried cop on the beat to tell who's playing games with toy guns from real danger, or domestic whatever nobody wants to sign a complaint about. That's one reason why cops hate domestic calls."

"If I recall correctly, more police officers are injured responding to domestic violence calls than any other part of their job."

"True, thank you for remembering, Oliver. Most of us would rather face a shootout to the death. At least I would."

"I suspect wearing leather as opposed to an expensive business suit and tie, or police uniform is willingly conforming to a different form of regimentation."

"Explain please, love of my life?"

"I went on to explain, some women and men get sexually turned on just from association with leather. It can be imagined some Homer-milquetoast types feel butch, while others protected by superpowers wearing a magic amulet, or shielded by warrior's armor. I'm guessing it is the smell as well as the feel of leather that gets motors running. Just like the smells of being dressed to the nines in a grossly expensive business suit wearing outrageously costly cologne, or the full life and death authority and ultimate power of a police uniform.

"My man, I love you can be so graphic on the spot."

"I don't know if TJ and Asa only use black leather or also SM role playing to augment sex in their marriage. Although Asa did mention a whip."

"Forget them for a moment, what do you know about lesbians, gay men, and straights participating in the freaky S&M scene? That's where my intrusive thoughts are coming from."

"You want to know if they beat each other with or without their leather costumes."

"I said forget them, my understanding is the chains and whipped up pains and such are only a small part of all the weird ritual goings on with dominants and submissives."

"Coy, the textbooks say pain is a level of play in submission. So, most submissives don't require leather, nor necessarily seek to be physically punished. It all can be symbolic."

"How do I keep track of the players without a score card?"

"One way is by playing in their playground. Part of the problem is these esoteric folks are a very small segment of the gay and straight populations wanting or needing maximum extras for ultra sexual satisfaction."

"Oliver, more details please."

"Since you insist, academically I know … uh … you don't want to hear this."

"Yes, I do."

"To become a slave-master a person must start out as a *slave* to learn how to be a slave master."

"What?"

"Consequently, there can be a lot of switching roles back and forth to play their games."

"No wonder I'm confused, it's full of twists and turns."

"I think we can agree what they do is not to everyone's taste. A slave is a true submissive and that is who is always in charge of the S&M scene, no matter what role they take."

"Come on, wait a second, you're telling me even tied up and gagged that person is in control. No way, ha, ha, what a silly notion."

"YES! In serious S&M, there is always a *safe word* that stops play, no questions asked or negotiated. So, even gagged, bound, mummified, whatever, the slave has a prearranged way to communicate they've had enough and it's over."

"I don't think I can believe that. They dress so evil looking. No, I wouldn't *trust* the slave master to stop once they got going."

"All you have to remember is the slave or submissive is always in control. The master in the scene started out as a slave, so knows both roles from experience."

"Well then, I guess if it's a time-tested kind of recreational sex, maybe it's okay. But I don't have to like it or approve."

"You put your finger on something, to play S&M games *trust* is the key word. The same trust people give each other when they fall in love and build a relationship. But in black leather it's without the hearts, flowers, and violins showing."

"What! No chocolates? You know I love chocolate with romance."

"Of course, lots of dark chocolate bon bons and the syrupy music."

"Hmm, … uh, no, … no, I still refuse to understand why anyone would want to be tied up and whipped for love or fun or luscious bon bons?"

I tried to explain most people who like to dress in leather are not into BDSM, a verifiable sociological fact. Furthermore, with or without leather, true BDSM practitioners agree S&M and bondage-discipline are not always synonymous.

Coy complained I was making the subject too complicated to understand.

Trying for less pedantic, I stated, "For many folks, bondage with or without leather was as far as they wanted to go. Being restrained by another person, until they had enough, was their total fun and game. Those wanting corporal punishment don't necessarily want bondage.

Coy's face suddenly showed surprise realizing he knew what I was talking about. "Ah so, it's the same as being a drag queen. Some dress to mimic female stereotypes to an extreme, others just to be outlandishly outrageous, and a few to try and pass as a woman."

"Ha, is this where we break into a chorus from *My Fair Lady*, 'I think she's got it.' Thank you, Jesus, I think Coy has finally got it."

"Oliver, you can't change the subject so fast. I'm not through with this yet."

"Because of your nightmares?"

"No. It still makes no sense. Except, like a drag queen, you could be someone else for a hot minute or two."

"*Pretend* to be someone else." Changing the subject was still in my mind when I explained to Coy probably it was his inner cop's sensed danger. The ultimate test for a really good drag queen was to pass as female among exquisitely dressed heterosexuals at a grand ball. The extra bonus points come from fooling a straight man into having sex with a drag queen not knowing they are male.

"That is not dissimilar from a true submissive whose objective is to manipulate an attractive sex object person into a BDSM scene against their wishes or better judgement. Some folks lose control violently discovering they were conned into something sexual or intimate."

"Oliver, I see how feeling duped is the extreme opposite of trusting."

"Yeah. Think of the adrenaline high running for your life wearing high heels dressed as a woman or trusted up wanting a scary beating as pretend when it turns for real."

"No wonder I'm having nightmares, one of the things I do like about gay sex is its fifty-fifty equality with no predefined gender roles. *Unless the participants agree to define it differently.* Just like you and I have, my vanilla lover."

"Coy, do you think we are missing something by not spicing it up with whips and chains?"

"Not really. It seems like a lot of bother to get all dressed up and go through S&M rituals or drag preparations just to get naked again to get your rocks off."

"Oh, wait, Coy, my man," and I explained the books suggest we were missing an important part of S&M purpose. Theoretically it is to satisfy deep psychological chords that nothing else can compare to, or so those books say. It allows exploration into fantasies of domination and surrender to cruelty and tenderness or contempt and adoration.

"Yuck! Or a cover for those who can't get it up or keep it up or can only enjoy themselves after being punished for the privilege."

"What you said makes it special for those folks just mentioned."

"Huh? Okay, but I wouldn't even know where to start if you wanted to play dress up like a Nazi."

"Then fortunately you are in luck, this is not about us. Some women and men want to know from the onset the role they will play during sex, others get truly excited when there's a struggle to determine who will be top and the fucker, or bottom fuckee."

At that point Carmen brought in a fresh pot of coffee and two clean mugs. I asked her to grab a mug for herself and join us. I sensed she might have been eavesdropping. After graduation, Coy and my time became in short supply and it was our efficient live-in housekeeper, den mother Carmen who maximized our scant time with effective schedules. She had become more a member of the family than just a housekeeper.

Since earning my two PhDs, work responsibilities evolved by necessity into thirds. One third teaching, writing, and committee chores at the Ivy League medical school, one third teaching and ongoing experiments at the public university's bio-electrical medical engineering department, and one third of my time committed to a lucrative private psychotherapy practice. To make it all work I had good teaching assistants, TAs at both universities, and a full-time social worker keeping my private clients happy, and Carmen making it all fit in only twenty-four hours a day.

"Carmen, Coy wants nothing more to do with our leather clad guests from the other night. I on the other hand would like to solve a murder mystery that involved Asa. Do you have any suggestions on how we could reconcile our differences, without bloodshed, and considering your feelings on the subject?"

"Oliver, how about we put it to a vote, yes or no to leather men for dinner? Since you are no longer a private detective and Queer Queries is sadly no more, I suggest you turn your murder mystery over to a working private detective agency. I can give you the phone number of a good one."

"But Coy and I like solving mysteries."

"Your busy schedules have no room for dilly dallying extra curriculars."

"Ah! Where's the fun then?"

"These days your schedules do not allow for fun. If anyone really wants to know my humble opinion, it is nice not to have to clean up after regular gunfights like in the old days at the upside-down house."

Speaking more to himself than to us, Coy nodded and said, "Agreed."

Thinking, *I don't like missing excitement. Although at my age maybe I do though and don't know it.* I automatically nodded my head to the affirmative about absent gunfights. Then to cover my confusion, I said, "Anyway, what is Coy's problem with the leather community?"

Responding to Carmen, not me, Coy said, "They give lesbians and gay men a bad name."

"If you two are going to be like that, I will have to remind you the hate mongers don't need an excuse to parade their transphobia and homophobia during their neo-Nazi rallies."

"Oliver, are you going to gang up against me with Carmen?"

"Let's see what she has to say before we decide."

Carmen watching Coy and I quibbling said, "Okay, Oliver and Coy, you both know there are thin healthy gay women and men who get turned on by the morbidly obese, and in gay vernacular are called *fatty fuckers*. Or the young or even very young ones who find their contemporaries silly superficial and lust for the company of much older sexual partners to mentor them to successful lives. Somehow the older ones have been mislabeled *cradle robbers* when it's the young ones who need to be called *grandfather fuckers*. I won't even mention infantilizing, rubber, golden showers, or scat. Coy, are any of these names worse than leather queens?"

"No, Carmen, we get called a lot of derogatory names. I just don't subscribe to all the magazines."

To keep the conversation civil, I said, "Carmen, does that mean you wouldn't mind entertaining those two leather men again?"

"Well, actually, my vote is kind of split. There was something likeable about the submissive young man who pretended to be a dog when he came to dinner."

With a smirk on his face Coy said, "Like what, for God's sake?"

"He ate all his vegetables and cleaned his plate. I just didn't like his friend's foul mouth attitude."

Surprised at the turns in the conversation I said, "You mean you'd feed them again."

"Maybe brunch …"

Coy abruptly realized I'd thrown him a lifeline and jumped in cutting Carmen off saying, "I could probably handle brunch with those two Middle Ages torture dungeon look alike in costume."

"Carmen, don't you love it when Oliver gets all officious like this? I bet he even thinks I'm the only one with S&M questions." Coy said this good naturally mussing my carefully combed hair.

"Coy, I'm the tranny housekeeper. I already know everything I need to know, and don't get Oliver started or we won't hear the end of it for weeks."

"Are you two ganging up on me again? Just for that, I'm going out and mow the lawn to balance my equilibrium." Oliver said this half in jest.

"DON'T DO IT. The neighbor boy is coming later today for that. He needs the diversion from middle adolescence, and I've already made his after mowing lemonade and cookies."

"Gosh, why do I get the impression there is more interest in the neighbor youth removing his shirt during mowing than me doing it or us solving a murder for that matter?"

Coy not ready to give it a rest said, "If I offer him a big tip, he might bark like a dog, just like a recent dinner guest. Then we could skip a looming brunch."

"Coy, if you get him to wear black leather chaps with nothing on under them, you could get arrested and miss brunch altogether."

"Oliver, some days you are just no fun at all."

Chapter 4.

Reading tea leaves at home it became clear we were not entertaining leather men for dinner or even brunch anytime soon. My husband and housekeeper were merely humoring me by suggesting otherwise. Just as well, TJ's abrasive attitude would be hard to stomach again so soon, for all of us over another *attempted* peaceful meal.

As far as we knew there were no new clues to solve the strange murder mystery that brought us first together. I filed the murder mystery away to the back of my brain until it stopped nagging at me. With so little information available and few people interested in bringing the perpetrator to justice it was not a hard ask of my overworked brain, or apparently the police department. Out of sight and forgotten, the murder victim was quietly classified John Doe after failing to find his actual identity.

Not quite three weeks after coming to dinner in costume, TJ telephoned my office at 10:10 AM on a Friday. He sounded angry and said, "Since you hypnotized Asa, he's having recurring nightmares. Now he's afraid to try to sleep. What are you going to do about it?"

"When you suggested hypnosis, I told you about the side effects. Nightmares were on the list. Hold on ..." I checked my schedule and said, "I have a cancellation at 3:30 this afternoon, bring him into my office then."

"Don't make it worse," and he rudely blew his nose in my ear.

"I don't make promises, but I'll hold 3:30 for you."

"Whatever," and he hung up without a goodbye.

At 3:10 TJ phoned to say Asa was too distraught to travel, and it was my fault. I'd caused the problem, and he would sue me. I told him good luck with that.

I looked up their street address, then telephoned and said, "I'm coming to see Asa. Be home at 3:30."

"Oh, a threat of malpractice gets a house call, well deserved, good. Our home is at eleven Sutton Lane, penthouse #1. Don't talk to the neighbors, they hate us."

"I'll be there in ten minutes."

****

Eleven Sutton Lane had a very small footprint for such a tall building. It was only fifty feet by fifty feet at ground level then the upper floors flared out for many floors and then shrunk back to on the ground dimensions at the very top. The building was vertical for at least 60 floors, but less than half were double wide. From a distance it looked like a giant baseball bat standing on end. The owner had been a baseball star hitter with more money than good taste in architecture.

The building security had three tiers, two-armed guards greeted me outside the revolving front door and asked my business then directed me inside to two more armed guards. They sent me to a reception desk's armed guard, who telephoned the tenant to say I was in the lobby wanting to visit. Finally, I was directed to an exclusive express elevator opening directly into TJ and Asa's residence. There was an over-abundance of security cameras everywhere in the lobby, the elevator bays, and in the elevator cars.

When I walked off the elevator into the leather men's home, I was greeted by an angry looking TJ who said, "I'm surprised such an arrogant prick as you make house calls. I might have to reevaluate your work if I ever get free time."

"Where is Asa?"

"He's upstairs. Don't look confused, stupid, this is a duplex penthouse."

"Before I see Asa, you and I need to talk. You've exhausted free passes with me. Be forewarned, the only reason I haven't slapped you is you were sent to me by my friend Willis."

"Don't threaten me in my own home, security can be summoned in an instant."

"You want to step outside?"

"I'm calling the police."

"By the time they get here I will have slapped you around."

"Don't threaten me old man! I know martial arts."

"Given your malignant personality I'm sure you need it regularly. My housekeeper says you are rude and crude. She has you correctly assessed."

"Listen, jerk off, I paid for your services already, I don't owe you or your housekeeper anything. You don't scare me."

"Before you do that, let me clear up your confusion. You paid my standard initial consulting fee, that included an initial interview. The result was a global assessment, an initial diagnosis, initial treatment plan, and initial prognosis. That's what you paid for, that's what you got."

"Except that was not why I came to your office."

"That is what everyone gets when they see me in my office."

"I was told you were a private detective."

"I'm not responsible for what you were told. As part of your initial interview, I was instrumental in getting your husband released from jail and all criminal charges will be dropped. There was no additional fee for that service, it was free for nothing, with my compliments."

I could see our interaction had taken a turn TJ had not expected. He wasn't still in charge. Stalling for time to get the upper hand back he said, "What diagnosis did you give me?"

Without thinking first I said, "Axis two, personality disorder on the global assessment."

"How many axes are there?"

"Five."

"How come I only get two?"

Why was I entertaining his nonsense and said, "Axis two means you were born with a personality disorder."

"Does that explain why I'm such a successful, rich, young influencer."

"No, that explains why your bad behavior is annoying, and why most people you meet consider you an asshole."

"Be that as it may, I am young, rich, famous, and followed by millions. You are none of those things. So, that makes you the asshole."

"Could be … I've been called worse by better men than you."

"I knew it, you're a racist. I've dealt with your kind before."

"Now cut the fucking bullshit, I came here to see Asa. You TJ are merely an obstacle in my path, get out of the way or get run over."

TJ was clearly not used to being challenged and his face showed it along with indecision whether to call for help to eject me or comply for the sake of his husband, he couldn't decide. The choice confounded his pathology, he stood confused in indecision. He looked bewildered like a little lost boy.

Despite myself I felt sorry for him, my part in it, and said, "Remember why you phoned me, TJ? It was for Asa's sake. That's why I'm here." He'd backed himself into a corner, although much younger than me we both knew TJ was no fighter. I'd been putting men much bigger and badder than he in their place long before he was born. With experience comes competence.

After a full minute staring, considering his options, TJ remembered he had a husband with a problem and concluded he was in an unwinnable predicament with me and said, "Follow me." He turned on his heels and led the way up a short flight of stairs into a sleeping quad with four different size bedrooms. Each room was painted in a different distinct primary color.

In the largest bedroom, the dark yellow one, Asa was sitting up in the middle of a king-size bed which made him look smaller than usual. He was wearing rumpled, unbuttoned, pale yellow silk pajamas, and looked haggard. His eyes looked haunted and showed he hadn't slept recently. I told TJ to take a seat, and I pulled a straight back chair over next to the bed and said, "How are you doing, Asa?"

"I'm not feeling so good. But, Oliver, please stop picking on TJ. I heard you from downstairs. He can't help how he acts, and seldom means it."

"I think TJ and I have come to an understanding for today. However, it is you that I've come here to see. Tell me what's going on that has upset you."

"I never remembered dreams before you hypnotized me and now, I have a nightmare as soon as I try to sleep."

"Tell me the nightmare."

Asa told of being jarred awake from deep sleep by the report from a gunshot, like it was next to him. Then he heard sounds of someone cutting flesh. He knew it had to be cutting off the murdered guy's earlobe. Next the murder was staring at Asa, his bloody knife in hand, then the sound of running. Asa didn't remember seeing any of it because his eyes were closed, but the sounds were so clear in the nightmare it was as if happening right in front of him, again.

"Have you been replaying the video from your hypnosis?"

"You said I should."

"I did. Was there anything unique you noticed about the earlobe?"

"The earlobe had a gold-colored stud earring shaped like the head of a bull."

"Had you noticed it before?"

"Let's deal with the here and now. If you recall, I told you hypnosis deals directly with the unconscious mind. I suspect as a result of what we did, a piece of your unconscious mind is probing up into your consciousness in the form of a nightmare. Playing the original hypnosis recording is helping open the blackout."

"That makes sense. Now what?"

"The question is *What do you want to do about it*? If you stop playing the recording, the bad dream should at least fade. But will resurface again in the future, it seems determined to surface, and sooner or later you will have to deal with it again."

"Oh. Damn."

"Based on this development, I suspect the blackout was your unconscious trying to protect you from the traumatic situation you were unprepared to be in. Now your predicament is, try to bury the nightmare again, or dig deeper to expose all of it. Your choice."

"Is it possible I send it back to where it came from so I can catch a little sleep?"

"Uhm, … we might be able to freeze it where it is for a little while, and I can hypnotize you to sleep for now. But sooner or later, we need to bring the whole memory into full consciousness view so *you can forget it*. Or it will become a chronic problem."

"Is chronic worse than what I'm going through right now?"

"As I see it, your current nightmare is forcing you to know there was more trauma than you were first ready to handle. What's worse, not knowing or knowing?"

"How can I tell?"

"Before the nightmare, you were focused only on what happened in the blackout and your fingerprints on the gun."

"Right after they arrested me, the hospital did a rape kit, and the findings were inconclusive. They said a rapist could have used an unlubricated condom without violence, my muscle tone is not too tight down there. It was another unknowable thing to think about while facing life in prison and a blackout with hidden answers. With life in prison gone, thanks to you, I got a little temporary relief until now."

"The rape kit proved nobody ejaculated inside you without a rubber, and there was no bruising, tearing, abrasions, or lubricant found. Now we all know what they couldn't find. Other than you were found naked, why was that?"

"Now you are making me feel worse ... Maybe they were trying to masturbate looking at me naked."

"Is that how it feels in the nightmare, being stared at, over and over, like it is just happening for the first time each time?"

"How did you know?"

"That's symptomatic of PTSD, posttraumatic stress disorder. What's new is about trying to masturbate."

"Is there no end to all this new vocabulary?"

"There would be little point trying to treat PTSD with your unconscious trauma half in and half out, without trying to surface the whole trauma."

"What do you suggest?"

"Since you and TJ are in a committed relationship living together, and he will go through this with you, let's get his take on all this?"

"I thought you were ignoring me on purpose because you are mad at me."

"And now you know better. What's your opinion?"

"I want whatever makes Asa happy. You tell us, you're the professional."

"Then I say we try to expose the rest of the blacked-out memory, deal with it, then treat the PTSD with cognitive behavioral therapy after."

Asa looked apprehensive and said, "Can I think about it?"

"Sure. But the sooner we address this, the faster you can put it into past tense. Don't look to TJ for answers beyond what he just said, he's the one who first asked me to hypnotize you, and I should have declined."

For some reason TJ felt challenged again, did not hold back and said, "Oliver, my lawyers ..."

Asa cut TJ off with a hand wave, shouting, "TJ, shut your mouth. Oliver, let's do this right now."

"Wait a second, let's ease into it slowly to see how you do. What kind of knife was used to cut off the earlobe? Had you seen it or one like it before?"

"A big folding knife, like used to dress field game. They sell them in hunting supply stores all over Maine, here too probably."

"You said your eyes were closed from the bar until the police came. How would you know the knife?"

"I don't know. But I have a strong feeling I'm right about that knife. Maybe I peeked and don't remember peeking."

"Did you do a lot of hunting growing up in Maine?"

"With my dad, granddad, uncles, and cousins. We all hunted together, until I was a teenager and came out as gay. Then I was not welcome at large family get togethers. I became a persona non grata in my own family and left soon after."

"Do you miss hunting?"

"I didn't like killing animals that much, but camping out with the family was fun."

"Could your memory of a particular knife be mixed in from a different remembrance?"

"I don't know."

"If I re-hypnotize you, you can expect to relive the murder, if you are lucky or unlucky depending how you see it. Do you think if more than one memory was mixed you'd know it?"

"Maybe."

"Are you ready to give it a try?"

"If we can't go backwards and erase time, then let's go forward and try to make the murder a memory instead of a repeating nightmare."

I asked Asa to close his eyes and take five slow, measured, deep breaths. Then asked him to open and close his eyes each time I counted between one and ten. From my previous hypnotic suggestion, when I reached six, he went into a deep hypnotic trance with his eyes closed. With part of his subconscious already poking up into his conscious mind, it was easy to peel back more protective unconscious to the blacked-out memory.

Asa's subconscious told, after he collapsed from being drugged, two men carried Asa into a van, and it drove away. At some point the van pulled off the well-traveled highway onto a bumpy side road. During that part of the drive, the man who was murdered undressed Asa while the other man drove. When the van finally got back on the highway, the driver told the other man to hurry up and have sex with unconscious Asa as planned. The driver said a camera was already set up in the van to film the rape.

The murdered man tossed Asa's clothes out of the van while it drove on the highway. Then he undressed himself staring at unconscious prostrate naked Asa. When pushed by the driver, the other guy told the driver he wanted to wait to have sex with Asa. Because he was savoring the view of who he would soon brutally fuck to death with his big, hard, hungry cock. He said he hadn't expected Asa to be so exquisitely attractive.

When the driver got insistent that the other man hurry up, Mr. Murder Victim said it was his vacation, so he could watch imagining doing the rape as an appetizer to the snuffing out his prize. The van driver told him there were no refunds given. Then the murder victim said he didn't want a refund; he still had a burning lust to fuck Asa to death with lots of blood gushing from his assaulted asshole as he reached lifelessness, but not yet.

What unconscious Asa felt emanated from his potential murderer was a powerful contradictory feeling he not do what he was about to, it was not truly who he was. The rapist was torn between his blood lust and his better self and that made his flaccid cock unfit for battering as much as part of him wanted to do it.

The van driver, frustrated waiting, made a disgusted grunt and took the van off the highway onto a busy access road. The murdered guy complained he hadn't committed the rape he paid for yet. But the driver ignored him and drove them into an abandoned underground parking garage under an out of business strip mall.

The two men carried the unconscious Asa out of the van and placed him down on the dirty cement carpark floor. Staring down drooling at unconscious Asa, the first man, who spoke with a heavy mixed European accent, told the driver he was ready to ravish his prize. He said his mighty cock was now hungry for tight young slave asshole to batter open. Anger in his voice, the driver said the drug was wearing off and the other man had waited too long to fulfill the contract.

Having stripped himself in the moving van, the murdered man was ready to mount Asa from behind with his oversized semierect male appendage. Looking over his shoulder, the foreign sounding man said, "What's the gun for? We won't need it. He'll bleed out as I fuck him to death."

With sudden demanding authority, the driver said, "Move off the boy, I told you, you waited too long. He'll wake up soon."

Looking confused, the foreign sounding guy with a limp dick struggled to his feet. He loudly protested not getting his money's worth while moving away from Asa. At that point the driver fired a bullet into the man's left temple. It killed him instantly and he fell over backward. After kicking the downed man, probably to make sure he was dead, the murderer laid his pistol down under Asa's hand. Then got busy cutting off the victim's left earlobe.

Up until the murder, Asa's impression of the masked van driver was of a wishy-washy kind of wimp with a totally blah personality, if he had any at all. Then just before the murder an icy evil came over him, and he committed murder without remorse. What made the personality change all the stranger was between shooting the man and cutting his ear off, the killer said a prayer.

After amputating part of the victim's ear, the murderer went and stood over Asa for an intense malicious minute. He seemed conflicted, he wanted to kill Asa also, but a strong something held him back.

Then as they heard sirens approaching louder and louder, the murderer ran to the van then stopped. He walked back and stared down at unconscious Asa for another quick indecisive minute, shrugged his shoulders, ran back to the van, got in and drove off.

Then the noisy police and EMS arrived in response to a gunshot auditable alarm. With bright emergency lights flashing, Asa became fully conscious of cops and EMS workers gawking at his body. When they got tired of ogling naked Asa, he was taken to the hospital then to jail.

"Previously Asa told Oliver he'd never seen the two men who drugged him. Is that true?"

"No, the murderer pushed off his mask to cut off the other guy's earlobe with the knife mentioned before." Asa opened his eyes halfway for a quick peek and thinks he saw the killer, or someone who looks like him at the Danger Zone Bar months ago. Asa's not one hundred percent sure."

"Is Asa a regular at that bar?"

"Asa and TJ are not bar people. They miss a lot of what goes on in the bar world. Rumor has it most leather bars are mob connected."

"Then what was the occasion Asa might have seen the murderer?"

"Slave auction nights, the proceeds go for charity."

"Which charity?"

"Educational scholarships for queer BDSM individuals discarded by their biological families. It's local, but similar to the Points foundation nationally."

"Does Asa know the man's name or address?"

"No."

"What does Asa know about him?"

"He's not from around here. When he bids on slaves, he almost never has the money to seal the deal."

"What makes Asa think the man is not from here?"

"He doesn't look local, it's just a rumor he's originally from upstate. I don't know for sure, Albany or Buffalo maybe."

"Does Asa have more blacked-out memory to share?"

"No. Not today."

"Oliver is going to hand Asa a business card with the name and telephone number of an excellent cognitive behavioral therapist, Elliot Page. He/she is also a psychoanalyst used to working with the unconscious mind. Asa will attend therapy sessions with Dr. Page until his PTSD symptoms abate, won't he?"

"Yes."

"Now Asa will be able to sleep without nightmares, and so I'm going to count from five to one as Asa prepares to wake feeling refreshed after hypnosis. Five, preparing to open eyes, four, half opening his eyes, three, opening eyes fully feeling good, two, feeling great, one, completely back from restful relaxed hypnosis. How do you feel?"

"Like nothing happened, again. Otherwise, I feel fine, good actually. I guess I needed the rest. I think I can sleep now." Hugging his big yellow body pillow, Asa rolled over arms and legs wrapped around it ready to sleep.

I was surprised TJ could behave so well, not uttering a single sound while Asa was hypnotized. He really must have read up on hypnosis like he said. But once Asa and I were clearly finished TJ said, "What axis diagnosis does Asa get? I bet it's not as good as mine."

"All global assessments have five Axis. This is not the time nor place to explain that."

"We are legally married, I have a right to know what labels you put on my spouse."

"Not from me today you don't. That's between the two of you and HIPPA. Write up a formal request and I'll have my lawyer look at it, then we'll see."

"I don't mind you telling Asa I'm an axis 2 personality disorder, whatever that is."

"It comes in distinctive flavors. Um I mean varieties. You can pick and choose symptoms online. After you mix and match indicators, you and I can have a little talk about the value of initial diagnosis."

"Oliver, what are you two talking about? Why can't I have a diagnosis if TJ has one? Like he said, we are married. We share everything except his farts."

"Fine, Asa, tell your new therapist Dr. Page my initial axis 1 diagnosis for you is 309.81. PTSD. He'll know what that is. As far as I can tell initially, you have nothing on axis 2. If you want, the two of you can explore the different five diagnostic axes on the internet. As far as I'm concerned, the more patients are involved with treatment the better the outcome."

Looking down at the card I had given him under hypnosis, Asa asked, "Then what can you tell me about this therapist?"

"Before she transitioned, her name was Madelyn. He wears his keys on the left and seems to own more leather clothing than other shrinks I know."

"Oh! I think I'm going to like him."

"Why are you both ignoring me?"

"TJ, I invited you to go online and look up any and everything you could possibly want to know about DSM global assessment."

"Oh, yeah, you did."

"Or you could save yourself the aggravation and focus on, '*I said initial.*' That means based on very little information from first impressions. Got it. I'm giving you an easy out, take it. A thank you is not necessary, or I suspect coming."

"Honestly, I don't get what my granduncle sees in an asshole like you Oliver. You are so hard to be friends with."

"Ask Willis why don't you? I've got a full day of appointments, and I don't regularly do house calls, so don't get used to it."

Chapter 5.

Current events and Coy and my deficit knowledge about BSAM got me thinking where it came from in dress and behavior. The ancient Greeks considered same sex relations superior to the hetero variety for their time. Then due to practical necessity, the ancient Romans deemed homo and hetero sex of equal value for the thousand-plus years Rome dominated the known Western world. After Rome, most of the Dark Ages, people had sex with whoever, wherever, and whenever they liked, without judgment other than from the religiously insane.

I had recently read in the gay press that homosexual bars across the developed world today were in decline due to cellphone hook up apps. From the mid-1800s till the 1970s, gay bars had been relatively safe places to socialize for gay women and men. During that period, the three modern religions went on a campaign of deceit and hate against gay people to keep their followers inclined to reproduce a lot and thus multiply tithing religious wealth power by outnumbering each other.

In ancient times, fertility cults used orgasm as part of their rituals and were much more popular than the new strict religions that exploited sexual development with abstinence, except for breeding. But as the three modern religions continued to wane after the mid-1800s, they needed a hook to snag new converts and keep them defined one from another in opposition to competition.

Two of the three modern religions used the Abraham sex negative body image, slave marking circumcision, to diminish interest in sex and brand their male parishioners for life. The five books of the Jewish Torah are the Christians' Old Testament. Christians added Jesus for a New Testament. Then Islam came along and incorporated the Jews and Christian books into its Quaran. For most of these Gilgamesh plagiarizing modern religions, fasting from food and sex, while giving ten percent of income, was supposed to guarantee followers direct first-class access to heaven.

The religious nuts tried and failed to stamp out homosexuality in the developed world between the mid-1800s and 1973 using their bogus medicalization of sex as a weapon for discrimination. During that time of religions persecuting gays, organized crime, the mob, paid off the authorities to keep gay bars open for business and relatively safe for their officially oppressed customers.

Then the American Psychological Association removed homosexuality as an illness in its DSM in 1973. Consequently, the rest of the world also stopped suppressing individual's free thinking, artistic expression, and basic human rights. Due to the change in nomenclature, New York City gay bars went from 100% mob owned to 100% gay and lesbian owned in a small amount of time after the Stonewall rebellion.

In retaliation, the fundamentalist Christians and Muslims exported their homicidal hate-discrimination against free people to desperate, hungry, Africa. At present twenty of the fifty-eight African countries have laws with long prison sentences or death by capital punishment attached for all their children's right to exist if born gay. It does not speak well of Africans' character, for being willing to sacrifice their gay children to please white evangelical benefactors' western superstitious beliefs.

Killing their own to grab a few greedy handouts was selling out their own traditional culture, and as shameful as colluding with slavers was. It also distracted us from solving the problem of hunger on the continent of Africa in a world that produces more than enough food for all humans.

Reportedly, worldwide the general gay bar scene is in decline due to social media's efficiency and other artificial intelligence helpers for hook ups. But the specialized bar scene is holding their own in changing times. For example, bars known to allow prostitutes flourish. As did establishments catering to the heavy set or specializing in older affluent clientele with their much younger admirers increased as the population aged. The same growth was true of bars that cater to the leather set, BDSM, motorcycles, cowboys, rough/raunch, race explicit, and admirers of esoteric taste in sex.

Calling it research, and to humor me Coy accompanied me on a tour of local leather bars. It was further proof of the affection and love he showed me every day, sometimes against his better judgement. I always tried to make my quirks interesting for him.

Not to stand out as tourists too much, I bought matching, pocketless, black leather vests. To complete our leather bar tourist outfits, we wore black leather vests over new plain white T-shirts, well-worn denim jeans, and scruffy old work boots. Admiring our grungy look in the mirror, I suggested we attach a holstered sidearm to our outfits for butch effect. Not because I expected trouble, but rather since we had licenses to carry them. I told my mate they would distract from our looking out of our element on the leather boys' and girls' turf drawing unwanted attention.

Trying hard to appear nonchalant, I showed a still photo I had made from the video tape of the murderer and Asa's abduction. I had made it with the perpetrators masked raised, showing three quarters of his face. None of the barmen, barbacks, and patrons at each watering hole we visited knew him. Several bartenders said maybe they had seen him on busy nights but could not say for sure. All agreed the man in the photo was not a regular but dressed like one.

When we left the last bar, the Trench, it was late, the sidewalk and street outside looked like a ghost town. As we headed back up to my car a pickup truck screeched up, out of nowhere cutting us off on the sidewalk. Three men jumped out from the pickup's bed. Two more leaped from the truck-cab. They were holding baseball bats, golf clubs, and one was swinging a length of heavy metal chain. I looked at Coy and said, "What are your druthers, love of my life?"

He already had his pistol in hand, so I drew mine. In a loud voice I said, "You boys have your affairs in order?" At that point the largest member of the group rushed at me waving an aluminum softball bat at head level. I shot his left knee out and he went down falling forward like a 300-pound sack of (expletive deleted). Whoops, I meant cement.

The man swinging the heavy chain over his head aiming it in Coy's direction fell over backwards when my husband fired a shot hitting the man's right shoulder joint. My man had timed his live fire to coincide with the momentum of the chain going behind the queer basher. Gravity and momentum can be a bitch in a fight. Between the force of the 9-millimeter slug hitting his front shoulder timed to the centrifugal force of the chain pulling him back, oh, my. The man left his feet, flew up backwards, and sailed a few yards in the air. He landed in a head over heels heap with the chain somehow wrapped around his arms lying in the roadway.

The other three men froze in a mid queer bashing tableau. Taking advantage of the momentary cessation of assault, I said, "You want to take your friends to the hospital or wait for the police and see if our accurate shooting continues? The army taught my husband to shoot straight. I just do it to piss-off thugs like you. Want to see some more shooting?"

Without conferring or comment the three uninjured bashers lifted their fallen comrades into the bed of the pickup truck and sped away in the direction of the hospital. While we were collecting ourselves, two things happened almost at once. Patrons and staff from the bar we had just left poured onto the street at the sound of our gunfire. And a police car emergency light flashing sped right up to us responding to an auditable gunshot alarm. We barely had time to tuck our guns away in their holsters.

Coy gave the arriving officers the license plate number of the pickup truck. I had had the presence of mind to cellphone record the queer bashers attempted assault showing them waving blunt instruments with intent at us. The arriving police officers watched my video and checked our conceal carry permit licenses and shared they had been looking for our perpetrators and sped out after them. Meanwhile, several bar patrons and a bartender who heard our shooting jumped on their motorcycles parked out front and sped off chasing the pickup truck. I suspected the hospital emergency room was going to have a busy night.

Looking at a long workday in a few hours, Coy and I headed home, rather than watch how the queer basher's night concluded. Carmen had not just left snacks out for our return; she had waited up and mothered us like only a male to female transexual can with concern. Naturally, in return she wanted every detail, how our search for a murderer failed and why we had discharged our weapons.

The snacks were good, they hit the spot. I always like to eat something after a fight, probably to make sure all my organs were working. Although technically, tonight was a one-sided gunfight, because softball and golf were never my sports.

What was chilling was the two to five ratio and potential plight of a single unarmed patron leaving that bar at the hour we did. I thought, *Next time I should shoot to kill to protect the public.* That thought triggered a deeper reaction, *Huh, I wonder if that means I'm already over my aversion to killing so many of my fellow citizens?*

In her usual motherly way, Carmen decided to catch the uncatchable murderer with only a few clues and lack of apparent official interest. So, I suggested she design a simple flier using the black and white grainy photo I made of the perpetrator from the parking garage digital closed circuit security video. Carmen was good at making mundane interesting, and liked her cooking, she never disappointed on fine details. Her flier was eye catching and invited a response without being frightening.

When I showed her finished flier to Chucho, he was very impressed and said, "This poster *will* get responded to, only the responses may all be BS. Tell you what, I have a string of home visits scheduled for downtown today. How about I post Carmen's fliers where it will do the most good?"

"Where would that be?"

"Several leather bars are downtown as is the Gay Community Center with bulletin boards on every floor and the lobby. Then after my home visits, two of those small urban parks on the west side get cruisy late at night. I could staple flyers to trees with the most used condoms on the ground around them."

The first question Carmen asked of the anonymous flier telephone callers was, "Where'd you get this number and why are you calling it?" That is how she separated the kooks from the seemingly genuine information callers.

Coy or I, depending on who could be pressed into service fastest, prescreened follow up interviews. To be interviewed callers had to be willing to give a call back phone number and be recorded face to face in a quiet back booth at a downtown coffeeshop during their slow time between lunch and dinner. There was no way to know how many legitimate witnesses we lost through Carmen's direct in your face approach. On the other hand, Coy and I probably missed out on wasting a lot of time doing dozens of fruitless interviews. I will call that fair trade.

As luck would have it, Coy got all three telephone responses to the flier that netted something interesting to pursue. Brett Franklyn, Mike Snyder, and Nordune Visnue all had tales to tell not too dissimilar to Asa. My forays were either no shows or bogus with desperate need for ongoing mental health services.

Five years prior, Brett was supplementing, any way he could, what his single working mother could provide for him and his siblings to eat from her two jobs. When he was younger, he'd taught his siblings to shoplift food.

The car sex started his last year in high school, one day a teacher kept him after class to discuss his academic future. Consequently, Brett was running very late to get home to do childcare so his mother could get to her second job on time. He had been warned hitching rides was inviting kidnapping, but it was a long walk home. The first driver to pick up Brett gave him money to do what he had planned to do as soon as he got in the bathroom at home. The driver just wanted to watch as Brett did nature's bidding, surprised to be paid for his new favorite hobby.

At some point forward his mother had to know extra money was coming into her home feeding her kids Chinese takeout and other fast food she could no way afford. Brett became careful disposing of food packaging materials before his mother got home. What he could not hide was the children were all gaining weight.

The confrontation with his mother that Brett dreaded over the kids becoming chubby never happened. Between working two jobs and grabbing a double shift, when possible, she still barely covered their rent. She just did not have the energy to push Brett for the truth. He was probably stealing, like his father, and she would know about it soon enough. Each of her kids had a different father and getting any of them to keep her rent paid was a failed undertaking.

One day afterschool Brett was hitchhiking when two men offered him a ride. He thought it odd one man was wearing a mask. That man, the driver offered him much more money than his regular fee. His sibs had developed enormous appetites and ramen noodles were no longer enough for them. When his little sibs were very hungry their eyes seemed to grow big and accusing.

The men who picked him up offered $100 if Brett whipped the man without a mask, *light dusting,* they said nothing heavy until that man was turned on enough to fuck Brett in the ass. He had never had anal sex before or knew how to prepare for it. But the masked man, who was only going to watch and record for posterity said Brett would like it, everybody did.

When Brett asked why he wore a mask, the man said so Brett could tell the two men apart. He said the important thing was they would give Brett a brand new $100 bill and drive him home after the sex. Brett was skeptical until he saw the $100 bill. It was new and would buy a lot of Chinese takeout for his hungry sibs. They drove to a Won't Tell motel, and the driver already had a key to room eighteen.

Not having any clothes on was not too weird for Brett because the maskless guy also got naked right away. Hitting the man with the braided black leather whip, even just lightly, gave Brett a feeling of power over an adult who asked to be whipped.' It was a powerful first-time experience for Brett and kept his dick rock hard. Then the whipped guy rimmed Brett with a long slippery tongue and that was another first the teenager liked.

Brett had to hold himself back from cumming from a long jigging tongue up his shit shoot. Taking the guy's cock up the ass was the distraction he needed to prevent cumming too soon. Getting it in the backdoor was not as bad as Brett imagined it might be. Once the guy was deep inside him, he screwed slowly and easily. Brett's ass muscles loosened and then his body did not mind being penetrated. But it was smelly, and he did not like that. The next time he would take a shit first and shower.

Just as the maskless man started to huff and puff cumming inside Brett, the masked man put a thick braided black leather cord around his neck and garroted him. The maskless man came gyrating wildly as he attempted to breathe, air sacks in his lungs started popping like firecrackers in his chest. During the wild gyratory death throes, the mask slipped off.

Realizing what was happening, Brett slipped off the spurting dick, grabbed his clothes mixed in with the strangled man's, and ran for his life as fast as his feet could go. But not before getting a good look at the murderer.

Brett found a service alley, nearby up the street between two out of business stores. He dressed in a hurry behind rows of empty dumpsters, found the dead man's wallet in pants brought along unintentionally. There was money enough in the wallet for Brett to feed his siblings and stop turning tricks for a month, $375 buys a lot of noodles or fried rice. Then he tossed the man's clothes and wallet into two different empty dumpsters. Took a cab home, shaking with the realization of a man murdered while fucking him, and if he had not run away him too, maybe.

When by necessity he returned to strolling for johns after school, he kept an eye out for the killer. He felt sure it would be his murder if he ran into the man in the poster again. Brett had nightmares for years reliving the man dying on his back, in his ass.

At the interview Brett told Coy he has never gotten over the man on his back dying in orgasm. He said, "It was as if he parked his soul inside me before he died, and I never even knew his name."

That five-year-old event was so traumatic Brett could only tolerate oral sex or hand jobs with his wife, and they wanted to have kids if he could ever get beyond what happened to him in high school.

I was surprised Carmen was not put off by the recording of Brett's salacious rendition of an encounter with our masked murderer. It was Coy and Chucho who felt Brett's story was unnecessarily visual.

Brett's story indicated to me we probably had a serial killer on the loose and nobody had connected the dots. The new information changed my impetus to solve murders.

****

Coy said Carmen's next find, Mike Snyder, gave off an ominous vibe. He was not threatening to Coy but wanted to find and kill the murderer. Mike was a physically self-assured big guy who looked able to handle himself in any violent altercation. He was over six foot six inches tall at maybe three hundred and fifty pounds, with medium complexion, dark brown hair and eyes. Mike carried himself and dressed like he was streetwise but not *of* the street, a notable distinction.

A few years prior while in college, Mike worked street outreach for a business association's nonprofit community self-help violence prevention project. The project's mission was to get homeless women and men into substance abuse rehabilitation and permanently housed. To achieve those lofty goals Mike and his partner Big Jim had to get known by their clients to gain trust.

The two men gained trust by defusing violent situations, exchanging clean injection needles for used ones, providing healthy snacks, and bringing a nurse or physician along when appropriate. Much of what Mike's program did was against the law, but the police looked the other way for the sake of good deeds being done.

While establishing rapport with new clients, he and his partner noticed an increase in overdose deaths. Then rumors started about a man handing out free heroin, but only to those most strung-out in need of a fix.

Supposedly the man would assemble five addicts desperately hungry to get high in a shooting gallery and give each a glassine packet of powder. He told the dope fiends one of the five free packets of heroin was also a hot shot that would kill the user. Nevertheless, all five used the Russian roulette white powder and watched one of their number go into convulsions and die as they nodded out into drug fueled oblivion. The killer always videoed the death party.

The police did not want to believe someone would waste their time killing junkies who they believed were working hard at being dead by their own hand with drugs. So, Mike and his partner made it a priority to find the killer.

Tipped off to his whereabouts by street people, Mike's partner Big Jim, had a run in with the filmmaker who was handing out free heroin at the time. When Big Jim approached the man, he pulled a gun and shot him in the gut. Mike right behind Jim broke the gunman's arm and took his gun. The shooter managed to escape while Mike attempted to revive Jim.

The killer has not been seen around homeless drug users since. That was a few years ago when the free hot-shot heroin stopped. Rumor has it the filmmaker took his gruesome death dealing show on the road to different cities.

Mike said, "Your poster means he's back in town. Not to worry, I plan to make him dead as soon as I find him. Just tell me where to locate the son of a bitch."

"Do you know how many heroin users were murdered by this man?"

"There was no way to know at that time. Homeless drug people didn't get autopsied. The Jane and John Does of that time got cremated right away and their ashes dumped into a common grave no muss no fuss."

****

I created Queer Queries to function in thirds, highly technical electronic unmanned security, armed men with and without big dog bodyguards, and sophisticated covert investigations of all sorts. No matter how well I planned, one third was always too busy, one third doing about right, and one third too slow to justify its costs.

Most small enterprises called what I had *feast or famine* and where possible cut off their losses. In my experience operating in the red means not in business for long.

After a break for more education, my new enterprise, surprise *surprise,* is in thirds, research, teaching, and private psychotherapy practice. The new problem with the old feast or famine cycle was no short legs, so *no lean time* to adjust wobbly stool legs.

There was no time flexibility with teaching, schedules were set in stone, even during vacations and between sessions there were meetings, required planning sessions, and report deadlines up the wazoo. With research of different kinds, there was constant ongoing accountability justifying or running after funding.

I really expected my private practice would give me a measure of control to breathe, it did not. It filled up quickly and appointment slots stayed full, and a waiting list had to be added. With foreboding, history seemed to be repeating itself and going against the point of going back to school.

I was seriously thinking of stopping new intakes and closing my most lucrative and interesting third, to stave off burn out. Teaching the least profitable and researching the next least did not take as much out of me as the constant challenges of one-on-one private practice. Something had to give, I was not having fun anymore, and one man alone cannot be expected to fix a mental health worker shortage.

Then Carmen got another scary call from her poster and was sure it was important to follow up. Right that instant, since I was busy up to my eyebrows, Coy made time to placate Carmen. She arranged for him to meet Nordune Visnue to be recorded at our favorite coffee shop for that purpose. Coy's initial impression of Mr. Visnue was a thirty something man of average height, weight, and extremely uptight. His light brown-amber colored eyes looked ready to flee the first chance his murky gray complexion got.

Coy also busier than he wanted to be and having been the recipient of more bull shit from Carmen's poster than I, said, "It looks like you don't want to be here. So, why are you?"

"How I got to this, here, right now is a long-complicated story. Shall I just tell you the little I know about the man in the mask, or do you require the whole maquilas?"

Coy the ex-cop assessed the mostly bald, thirtyish, pale, gray skinned South Asian anxious man in front of him was telling the truth. On the other hand, Coy the new lawyer sensed the man had more to tell than he wanted to reveal, "How about you talk, I'll listen. Or I could tell you a joke."

"Tell me a joke."

"Right now, in mainland China the big joke is to request *Bai Ren Fan* at totally inappropriate times and places."

"I don't get it."

"*Bai* is white, *Ren* is people and *Fan* food in Mandarin. For Chinese to request White Peoples' Food at a fancy banquet in China gets a big reaction. My husband speaks Mandarin."

"That's not funny."

"For most Chinese White Peoples Food is a salad or a cold sandwich. Food they wouldn't normally want to eat."

"It's still not funny."

Bushy eyebrowed, amber eyed, Nordune Visnue did not notice when Coy click record on his cellphone lying unnoticed on the table. He spoke of being raised in a Christian fundamentalist family until at puberty he discovered he was bisexual. At first, he secretly celebrated being doubly blessed by experimenting with both genders.

Then when he learned in church it was the opposite of a blessing. He tried praying the offending side of his nature away. That did not work. He fought the hardon urges for other boys and usually failed. Then even after masturbating he felt miserable cumming for cumming.

After high school Nordune joined the Navy, not to see the world but rather to straighten himself out or die trying. While on his ship a really mean ambitious ensign caught Nordune with another sailor's cock in his mouth. It was on a part of the ship's deck where everyone knew mutual sexual activity was common for stress relief, no big deal, no labels attached, usually no worry.

To make an example of him, Visnue was given a dishonorable discharge, and the ensign a promotion. Back home his family, longtime girlfriend, and pastor said he was a communist sympathizer, and spawn of the devil for engaging in same sex, sex.

Discarded by his family, friends, church, and the military, Nordune migrated to a big urban center, found a maintenance man job. Churches he gravitated to maligned him for choosing to be half a queer rather than 100% for God. A therapist he later discovered at church advertised she did outpatient conversion therapy on the cheap. She only took cash, no insurance would accept her lack of credentials.

Right from the start she said he needed discipline and thought the black leather BDSM set might help him eliminate his bisexual urges. She told him it was a logical choice and clearly, he needed a female slave master to beat Nordune's perversion proclivities out of him.

Nordune was confused, he thought the basic training he received in the Navy was all about his learning discipline. He completed that training right on schedule, without any issue. Nevertheless, he wanted to fix himself since most people are either straight or gay. With his therapist's firm belief and encouragement, he started reading the BDSM ads online. Only one ad caught his attention, it was different from the others, light bondage, light pain, sex only if you beg for it, NEWBEES WELCOME! Not a true submissive, apply anyway, you might learn a thing or two.

After a brief telephone call explaining what Nordune wanted and God required from a bondage and discipline hiding session, the dungeon master suggested they meet in person for authentication of intent. They met at the Pits, a biker bar that allowed gay people on the three slow nights a week, if not too fem acting and willing to service the regular patrons.

The dungeon master Nordune had phoned and said he always wore a face mask as part of his BDSM persona. He seemed older and was built large around the middle. His assistant was about Nordune's age, with a high reedy voice, foreign accent, willowy build, extremely docile manner, with a full head of curly bottle-blond hair. The three were not at the bar long before the dungeon master suggested they try Nordune out in their playroom, as a compatibility test.

Nordune followed the other's car to a bleak derelict section of abandoned factories. They parked behind a row of neglected warehouses and entered a nondescript drab gray four-story structure. The dungeon master led them upstairs to a third-floor chain locked heavy steel door. Then things happened fast.

The master took Nordune over to a hanging grid made of heavy weathered ropes. The kind used on the sides of tall sail ships early in the last century. The dom told his new slave want-to-be Visnue, he would be tied spread eagle to the rope web by other ropes. But the rope knots would be loose, easy to get out of if necessary, so, no safe word needed. Visnue did not say anything, trying to figure out if he should stay or leave. The slave master's assistant, Miss Fey, deftly stripped Nordune naked, with caresses and mouthing his body all over. Meanwhile, Visnue was told his task was not to yield to his body's wants during the test. The discipline was under no circumstance could he cum, until told to, otherwise the punishment could be more than he could bear.

While the master continued explaining, the assistant seductively stripped himself out of his own clothes while Nordune watched and listened. Miss Fey and Nordune's eyes locked, the master tied a knot around Nordune's left wrist and said, "See how easy it is to get out of that."

It took little effort for Visnue to free his wrist, so he let the Dom tie him spread-eagle to the abrasive sea weathered web of thick ropes using thinner, soft cotton ropes to bind. Meanwhile the assistant did an erotic Dance of the Seven Veils without veils, keeping his eyes locked on Nordune's. Miss Fey's best trick was to go from flaccid to rock hard without touching himself. Only stimulated by air, Miss Fey's member went quickly to an impressive girth and length.

It started out as the dungeon master said it would, except the knots were tighter than they were supposed to be. The assistant Fey was good, first he touched Nordune all over, everywhere, but ever so lightly. Next his fingers were like a feathery butterfly landing here or there randomly.

At some point the staccato touching turned into gentle rubbing, then it became insistent, and Nordune wondered if that was all there was. Most guys can give themselves the best hand jobs. It occurred to him he was about to get very bored. Then mouth and tongue titillation started finding new nerve endings in the nether regions of his body. The dungeon master had pulled up a chair and was watching and recording video. Nordune wondered if being watched and digitally documented while being serviced was part of the initiation or just plain perversion.

Then he was finally distracted as the dungeon assistant got remarkably serious, ass and cock sucking. From that point forward, he constantly brought Nordune to the edge of a pinnacle, then just before going over into orgasm he would distract the newbie slave with unexpected tactile delights, like tonguing between his toes, or the arch of a foot. Once Nordune understood the game, he used the time between build up to loosen the ropes that were tied too tight as opposed to what was promised and demonstrated.

Nordune realized, with a shiver, his body could not hold back much longer. If he was going to face unbearable consequences for failing, he might as well enjoy shooting a big load of cum first.

He decided to relax into what started as his most memorable orgasm despite witnesses watching him and consequences coming for cumming. Then the mask guy got up, came over, leaned over the busy cocksucker's back and said to Nordune, "Assistants must be replaced from time to time to keep the dungeon vibrant." That said, the master reached under his assistant's bobbing chin and slit his throat ear to ear with a common box cutter while Nordune blasted pent up cum down the cutthroat gullet.

The cocksucker felt the sting from his mortal wound. He instinctively turned, lunged forward onto the masked man. At the same time, he grabbed the cutting weapon. In the struggle for the box cutter, the mask was pushed off and onto the floor. The slave master's face was revealed to Visnue for the first time. Still spurting cum, Nordune freed himself from the rope web, and ran at breakneck speed, naked, to his car, and escaped into the night in terror.

Nordune Visnue had not seen the dungeon master's face again until he happened upon Carmen's poster stapled to a tree in a rendezvous spot inside a late-night park. When asked, Nordune said he had not seen any media account of the assistant's murder. Then he sat back in the booth and said, "That's it, all I got." He got up and left the coffee shop without looking back.

Chapter 6.

Following the weeks since Coy's interview with Nordune I started paying attention to what I'd been ignoring. For no physical reason I could ascertain from cause and effect I was experiencing unbelievable crippling back pain with growing frequency. Using old tried and true home folk remedies, it was not getting better. Fearing the worse, I got my middle-aged carcass medically checked out. When the medical boys could not locate a physical problem, they said to get thee to a shrink.

Alas, I am a credentialled shrink and supposed to know stress when I see it. As a private detective, mine had been a high stress life and that's one reason I changed careers. Not wanting to admit what I had tried hadn't worked I added stress by taking a day off from work. My plan was to think about the meaning of nonphysical sacroiliac pain, drink beer, and shoot pool.

I rediscovered an old favorite watering hole from my halcyon undergraduate days. I happily, surprised it was still in business, doing well, and nothing seemed to have changed. Then noticed *except my back pain was suddenly gone.* Like it or not closing new intakes for my private practice became an obvious solution to my progressively worsening aching back.

****

During one of our routine case review I picked up Chucho was out of sorts about something before he said, "Oliver, what happens to me? Now that you're planning to close intakes for your private practice, did you forget to give me notice to look for another job?"

Putting the form I was checking down, I thought *there was proof I was over extended* and said, "I didn't mean for you to find out from overhearing a phone conversation, Chucho. Listen, old friend, I've got you covered. Don't worry about your job, my cash reserves from selling Queer Queries guarantees your salary."

Looking me hard in the eye, like he never had in all the years I've known him, said, "Oliver, I hope you don't expect me to just sit around here doing nothing once the current crop of patients no longer needs us."

"Of course, not Chucho." Saying that I felt guilty as sin for being so inconsiderate.

Uncharitably there was a hard edge to his voice when he threw down his pen and said, "Then with no new clients coming in, what will I do besides twiddle my thumbs?"

For the first time in years, our roles as supervisor and supervisee were staring us right in our face. Working together we'd shared our clients unimaginable human suffering and despair. I wanted our old relationship back and said, "You know us, there will always be exceptions, unavoidable concessions. But for the moment, my back needs a break from being too busy to think or feel right. If you're worried about being bored, we can always find some a special project to keep you busy."

Picking up the pen he'd thrown down while softening his tone, Chucho said, "I could resign or if you'd rather, how about instead of me working 7 hours a day, five days a week, like now. I work 12 hours three days a week and complete all the same work."

How could Chucho do that in my office? I had already explained to him in our field there is no such thing as working from home. The labor laws required him to come into the office to have a coffee break, meal, snack, and nap or I'd be severely fined as a bad employer.

Chucho explained his plan to me, the way it's been is he comes in at 9 AM works on reports and other documentation until 10 AM, sees clients or worked the phones till 3 PM, and finish the day doing more paperwork till 5. With three 12-hour days, instead of 5, 7-hour days, he'd start work at 8 AM, doing paperwork till 9 AM. Then he would see patients or work the phones until 5:00 and finish up the day with documentation and or do reports until 8 PM. With a three-day workweek I would get an extra hour's labor unpaid, with his complements.

Sitting back in my desk chair impressed with what he'd devised I said, "Clearly you have thought this through. I have no need of a free hour's labor; I'll pay for it."

"That's not necessary, boss. Consider it my contribution to our modernizing."

It occurred to me *I think I'm going to like this new an independent thinking Chucho.* "Since I'm disrupting your work life with my changes, it's only fair that I at least try out your idea. Just out of curiosity what will you do with extra free time going from a five-day week to three-days."

Sitting up in his chair, twiddling the pen, in his old collegial tone of voice spoke evenly, "When I overheard you were shutting down new intakes, and anticipating you being the good boss you've always been. Not wanting to be a burden, I looked around. You have always treated me fairly." Then he sat back and was quiet.

"Extra time, spit it out Chucho." Huh, there was our roles as supervisor and subordinate, had I been ignoring all these years?

"I applied for a part time social work position at the gay senior citizen, public housing authority building on 117th Street near Second Avenue."

Once again, today, my free-thinking employee bested me. "I didn't know they had special gay senior housing, there or anywhere."

Chucho gave me a look that said, "Where have you been?" Then he went on to explain, it all started when Trump tried to kill constitutional democracy and that allowed half the states to pass anti LGBTQ Laws to actively discriminate against their queer and transsexual citizens. As a result, the other half of the states, to fight overt mounting injustice passed laws to protect their citizens from an out-of-control bigoted conservative Supreme Court. One extreme seems to have germinated the opposite.

As Coy often wryly says to me, using his words said, "Don't hold back, tell me exactly what you think."

"I am trying without digressing!" Then ignoring my sarcasm, Chucho painstakingly explained in New York City one positive result against bigotry was a gay senior Housing Authority building in each borough. Unfortunately, each building has a waiting list longer than the average seniors' life expectancy, to get a safe, nice, affordable apartment. It is only a gesture, but still better than those new signs down south and Midwest that say, "We reserve the right to refuse service to niggers, spics, chinks, queers, trans, gimps, old-farts, mud people, or if we don't like your look, under the authority of law."

I was vaguely aware of discriminatory laws enacted in the South and Midwest, late at night by their Rightwing legislators. I'd been invited to speak at several professional conferences that were moved at the last minute to less bigoted geography. I wasn't knowledgeable just how overt public accommodations to discriminate in red states had become.

Chucho continued clarifying, the building on 117th Street is quite nice. It's twenty stories, eight small apartments on each floor. At ground level and basement, it connects to a big four-story Community Center facing 116th Street. The seniors in gay housing can use the community's Senior Center and swimming pool even when weather outside is bad. The connecting elevators between gay senior housing and the Community Center are locked between 5:00 PM and 9:00 AM and all weekend.

I was feeling twinges of guilt and peeved at myself. Carelessly, I had taken a loyal employee for granted, my selfish bad. Hoping to improve I said, "I'm sorry I didn't handle this transition better. Your new job sounds nice, when do you start?"

Shifting from on guard to our usual collegial tone, smiling Chucho said, "When I inquired, the old part-time social worker there said she's postponed her retirement until I came aboard. She was one of my favorite adjunct professors when I was in graduate school. A direct answer to your direct question is, I can start at your earliest convenience."

"Is the first of the month too soon to make the transition to your new work schedule?"

"That is perfect. Thank you, boss."

****

After two weeks adjusted to our new work schedule, and being *back pain free*, I asked, "Chucho, how is your second job going?"

"I like it. Working with LGBTQ senior citizens is like hearing living history from those who suffered it. I never knew how lucky my generation of queers have it."

"Then I'm happy for you and them."

"Oh, by the way, I have a message for you. Do you remember a guy … a retired homicide detective actually … what was his name? Oh, yeah, Jack Warren?"

"Most assuredly, I'm curious what's he doing in gay senior housing. We all thought he was straight."

"That's all news to me. According to the building's records, Jack and his husband of fifty-two years moved into the gay senior housing shortly after it was built. Jack's husband Trevor died eight months back, and now Jack has just been diagnosed with a debilitating terminal condition. The docs give him a short time left to live."

"Chucho, do you remember Darrell Wayne's parents' murder? Jack Warren was the lead homicide detective on that case. He retired right after handing it off to the feds."

"So, that's where I know the name from. He says there is something he needs to ask you. Can I tell him you will be in touch?"

"Most assuredly, I'm curious what he's doing in gay senior housing we all thought he was straight."

"Given how he cruised my crotch, and his husband, Trevor's, reputation as a letch and both were the longest serving co-presidents of the tenants' association, he is as straight as a three-dollar bill. Trust me those seniors would have eaten Jack alive if they thought he was straight and trying to get over on gay anything. There isn't that much out there for our people. They get very protective of what little there is."

"Spoken like a diehard social worker."

"It takes one to know one."

****

The following week I juggled my schedule to accompany Chucho to his second job. I got the cook's tour of the gay senior housing complex and ended it at retired homicide detective Warren's home. Jack's small but cozy apartment was tidy. We had no sooner sat down, and Jack put the kettle on to make tea than Chucho's cell phone rang, and he had to leave.

Jack was hardly recognizable. He had shrunk and wrinkled a lot from the fit, vigorous man I once knew as a no-nonsense cop. Now he walked stiffly using a cane, and his balance seemed a little wabbly.

Although small the LGBTQ senior apartment was clean, neat, and showed a couple made it homey. There were framed pictures of Jack and another older man, they looked very much in love. Content, like older people look after years together.

There were also photos of children bearing a family resemblance to both the older gentlemen.

Not knowing what to expect or why I was there I said, "Chucho says you wanted to see me. What can I do for you Jack?"

"Oliver, okay, I suspect you have questions for me first."

"You haven't changed all that much detective … fine. I guess old habits die hard, so I'll go first."

"That was my plan."

"Back when I was a parole officer, everyone I knew thought you were straight. Were they wrong? Did you have a wife, children, and minivan back then?"

"Right to the point, eh? What your generation does not understand is how hard it was to come out for my cohort. Anybody who wanted a full life had a beard marriage one way or another. Noël Coward, a famous songwriter of my generation, wrote a song about it, 'Down in the Depths of the Ninetieth Floor'."

"Jack, I can't imagine living my life to please somebody else's rules. How could you share yourself with people you loved who loved you back, pretending to be someone else?"

"Ah ha! I see the founder of Queer Queries hasn't lost his holier than thou judgmental attitude looking down on us lowly mortals."

"Everyone said you were an honest cop, how could you be in the closet?"

"It's a good thing I've gotten too old to slap you around. So, I'll tell you. Back in my day what we had to share with those who loved us was a full take home portion of our incurable mental illness, incorrigible criminal destiny, and an afterlife burning in hell for eternity. Who in their right mind would want to share all that with people they loved? Society expected everyone to reproduce, live in a nuclear family, or be perverts with no opportunities."

"You had me and your colleagues fooled. I wonder what that says about us as investigators?"

"You all saw what you expected to see. If I'd come out as a young copper, I wouldn't have lasted a hot minute on the job back in my time. I liked being a police officer."

"Those were hate filled circumstances, a lot like today in half the states trying to undo our small gains for equality as humans. Uh, so, what happened to your show family?"

"Margo was a lesbian. We went to high school together and were best friends. In our way we loved each other, just not how society wanted. For the sake of both our careers the marriage of convenience served its purpose. My husband Marty and I mixed our sperm to be inseminated into Margo whose career required her to have children. She and her wife Abigail often double dated Marty and me for big showy events. All our kids turned out straight, raised by four queers. I am the last of the four and believe it or not really enjoy my grandchildren and hope I have enough time left to see my great grandchild expected in a month."

"Jack, since I don't know what to say, that won't sound judgmental, what is it you wanted from me?"

"I had a stash of cold cases I worked whenever there was down time on the job. After I retired, I didn't stop looking even after the department couldn't find the killers with the whole force."

"I remember at your retirement dinner the brass gave you a lot of praise for locking up serial killers. They said you caught more than anyone ever. Their ha ha joke was you never let a cold case get cold."

"Oliver, okay, it's touching you remember bad jokes told in my honor. I thought one day I'd write a book about those successes and the ones that eluded me for almost a decade after my retirement. Now the docs say I don't have much time left, so I want you to find me a ghost writer to finish what I started."

At the moment I was thinking *I don't need any extra stress these days.* "Why me? I don't know any ghost writers."

"You were a detective, you can find me a good one, and you are the only PhD I know. Congratulations, you win."

Why did I find it so hard to say no to people? "Hold on, cowboy, I think much of my reputation was hype. I was just lucky a lot."

"I know about lady luck, she smiled on me too, along with all the perspiration that came with the luck. As my kids like to say, 'been there done that.' I have seen your work."

"Sorry I'm too busy."

"Okay, if you are too busy to find me a good ghostwriter, just take my files from my hand to yours, and do a quick read and then be awed by my professionalism. That is glory enough for this old worn-out copper."

Somehow, I just couldn't say NO. "I'm already awed by you Jack."

"Sure, but with your usual diligence … maybe I missed something. You would find it if anyone could, and more importantly know what to do about it."

Looking for no without saying it, I said, "Wait, what happened to writing your book?"

"Could be there are already enough books on murder. Do this for me and I can go to my grave in peace."

"Don't leave us Jack."

"The prostate cancer I had for years recently decided to metastases to my nuts and elsewhere below the belt. My time is about up."

I didn't know this guy well but genuinely felt for him in that moment. A moment we'd all face if someone didn't shoot us first. "Sorry to hear that old friend. Anything I can do?"

"The oncologists want to castrate me to maybe buy a little more time on earth. I said no, being a eunuch was never on my agenda."

His decision was consistent with his reputation. "You thought this through."

"Everyone I really cared about is buried in their graves. It's my time, I'm ready to join the party."

Could it be my feeling uncharacteristic emotion for this man were interfering with my ability to say no? "Sorry to hear that, like I said before, I'm over busy as it is. Otherwise, I'd gladly pitch in for you."

"We can always find time for a friend's dying request."

Still trying to say no and failing. "Whatever time I could scrounge up wouldn't do your hard work the justice it deserves."

"Oliver, I did not want to get threatening. If you don't do me this one favor, I'll come back and haunt you at night. If you send me to my grave a hungry ghost, you will get *no uninterrupted sleep,* that is a dying man's promise."

Before I could think of a tactful objection, Jack got up and wobbled out of the room. He returned right away and put four thick to overflowing accordion files on the table between us. I could see in his eyes most of the material he collected was on his own time, and it mattered greatly to him that it was treated with respect.

The questioning expressions showing on my face, got back a self-assured look that said he knew once I sank my teeth into something I did not let go without results. That was true. I remembered Jack used to tell the detectives he supervised, "After death you can catch up on all the sleep lost on the job."

Damn it, what was I supposed to do? Jack and I were never close during my time running Queer Queries, before or since. What little official interaction I had with him was around Darrell Wayne's parents' murder, and that was not much. Nevertheless, here was a fellow human asking me to get busier than I saw as possible, so he could rest in peace. I adamantly do not believe in ghosts. However, who was I to deny Jack the peace after death he asked from me. It seemed life liked to throw me curved balls.

The first chance I got, when Jack looked tired and was polite, I stood, shook his hand, and left with two overstuffed accordion files under each arm. I stopped by Chucho's little office off the lobby. He was with a client, and others were waiting to see him. So, I left without saying thank you for the grand tour. Jack Warren's four bulging accordion sided manilla files made it into my car's trunk without dropping to the ground and creating a snowstorm of various size bits of paper.

****

Between seeing patients, I sneaked peaks at Jack Warren's forty years of extracurricular investigations. Three of his four accordion files were the relevant materials on cases he successfully closed despite major obstacles. They would be ideal for someone ghost writing a true crime murder mystery book. Jack had locked up more murderers and serial killers than anyone had even heard of. I taught at two universities, surely an English professor at one of them would know a good reclusive ghost writer interested in murder.

It was the fourth accordion file that was going to barter for my sleep. The contents at first glance were loose or dead ends at best, not connected to any main thought thread. Except, if I looked hard enough, maybe there could be something.

This caper started out as a group endeavor, Willis, his nephew TJ, Asa, Carmen, Chucho, Coy, and now guys responding to the poster. To make Jack's work more than an unaccompanied solo sonata that I did not have time to tease out, I would need help, lots of help.

Coy and I still loved doing things together and Carmen had become our loyal family's matriarch. If more hands were needed, I knew a few if I called, would show up. Like it or not Jack Warren's story was pushing my routine work that paid the bills aside for a pro bono project.

****

English professor, Dr. Victor Jacoby, at the Ivy League University where I also teach gave the words frumpy and rumpled meanings. His once *white,* now *grayish* button-down shirt was clearly not drip dry. In fact, it was so badly wrinkled, all over, it demonstrated unfamiliarity with the concept of a hot flat iron making fabric smooth. That his socks did not match was undermined by one black penny-loafer and the beige colored moccasin.

Dr. Jacoby was a short, plump, older than me man who won a Pulitzer Prize in poetry a few years back. I'd never met the man but was told by faculty I know well and respect that the good doctor was the best source for the help I sought. When I arrived at his office for hopefully an impromptu meeting, there was a line of four students already waiting ahead of me.

Ten minutes after his posted office hours, the good professor showed up. He pulled me out of a line that had grown to seven students waiting patiently outside his office door. He showed me inside and shut the door behind us. The room was much larger and grander than the small office I occasionally use at the university only when necessary.

Looking around the dusty environs of the esteemed professor's office, every horizontal surface, including the floor, held stacks of books, journals, or other printed material. There was an open space about two feet by three feet between a lonely straight-backed chair facing the professor's massive desk, hidden under stacks of printed matter, and his highbacked desk chair on the opposite side.

He stuck out a pudgy paw for a shake and said, "We have never met, Dr. Kulgul. What can I do for you?"

"Nice to meet you too. I was told you could give me the name of a good ghost writer."

"Show me the contract proposal."

"I don't have one."

"What's the proposed payment plan?"

"I thought the publisher would handle all that."

"Oh! You have a publisher lined up. Good."

"No. I only have a police homicide detectives forty years of meticulous notes."

"Sorry, I can't help you. You came here unprepared and wasted my time. Why don't you look online." Then he shouted, "Next!"

"Wait, can you at least give me names of local ghost writers who might be flexible?"

"You come here not ready, used up my time, and now you want a favor. That's uncivil, even rude."

"I'm not one of your students. A little professional courtesy is in order and would be much appreciated."

"Oh, … maybe I was a little short with you. Nevertheless, two PhDs seems grossly excessive. What do engineers and psychologists need the highest degree for, twice? It sets an unnecessary bad precedent. What is it you want again?"

"An old colleague of mine just learned he's dying. He gave me the notes he's been compiling for the book he'll never get to write. It was suggested you would have a list of ghost writers interested in putting their names under his."

"All right, fine, do you have his power of attorney with you?"

"No."

"Why for the gods' sake are you wasting my time? Didn't I say there is nothing I can do for you?"

"Can you recommend one of your students to ghost write for a share of the profits from the book?"

"Ah, profits! You are a dreamer, aren't you? No wonder you need two PhDs. Do you know how many books of poetry I've published? Profits indeed. Did you know Walt Whitman self-published all his poetry? He even set the type by hand."

"You're right we're wasting each other's time. You're a stuffed shirt and reputation is overrated."

"Um, possibly there is something … Hmm, your visit may be auspicious. How do you feel about quid pro quo?"

"I'm listening."

"I have a student who could be perfect for you if he agreed. Be forewarned, he'll need special handling by you to get him moving. You interested?"

"I was raised to believe something is better than nothing. What's the prognosis he'll work with me?"

"You know our students are the crème de la crème, and Len Lym was head and shoulders above his classmates. He was a journalism major, perfect four-point zero grade average, editor of the school 's award winning newspaper with great job prospects after graduation."

"I'll take him."

The rumpled professor said, "Hear me out first." Then he detailed, second semester his senior year, last year, Len Lym and a student photographer were covering a Black Lives Matter protest downtown. Things got out of hand, ultimately the police and demonstrators clashed violently. Len was knocked unconscious, and the student photographer was killed in the melee. Len was in a medically induced coma and hospitalized for three months. He lost all his last semester's class work, property and naturally couldn't graduate.

"I'll still take him."

Ignoring my comment, Dr. Jacoby continued to clarify. When taken to the hospital emergency room a small lymphoma was found on Lym's left prefrontal cortex while imaging his head trauma. Surgery without incident removed the growth as soon as he was admitted to the hospital. Then because of his age, and to be on the safe side, he was given chemotherapy for that specific cancer.

After recovery he was given physical and occupational therapy. The medical boys say there is absolutely nothing wrong with him physically and discharged him to a homeless shelter for young adults. Hospital psychiatrists say Len has PTSD from his head trauma, losing a semester's academic work, not graduating, and it has been suggested he and the photographer killed by the police were more than just best friends. The university's psychiatrist says he is also deep in bereavement, from all his losses on top of his PTSD, in other words he's an emotional mess.

"Professor, you said a year ago, what's he been doing since discharge? I've heard those young adult shelters can get very rough."

"Now he's a busker. Earning his keep, such as it is, from tips playing music and singing downtown during rush hour outside the commuter bus station. Other students say his original music is dark or sad and he'd make more in tips singing peppy happy upbeat songs. The word is his 'Oh, Danny Boy' will make anyone cry."

"Is there a runner up student? Perchance do I get a second choice?"

"No, it's a lot like life, take it or leave it. But you might want to hear me out first, before rejecting Len Lym."

"If you say so, Dr. Jacoby."

The frumpy professor alleged Len was not the same student he knew before his head encounter with police batons. That his spirit had diminished or was gone. Nevertheless, with Len's input a few of his professors cobbled together five special independent study projects so the boy could be awarded the baccalaureate degree he had earned and thus get a decent paying job.

This morning the faculty Committee on Students sent all parties concerned a memo rejecting the plan. They offered Len Lym an alternative. Because of his previous exceptional work, they felt independent study would lessen the value of his Ivy League BA. They suggested he write an acceptable, for them, master thesis, and they would award him both undergraduate and master's degrees. It's a stodgy committee, seldom this generous, so said Dr. Jacoby.

"Who would call the shots on the master's thesis?"

"I have already been assigned to be his graduate advisor if he accepts the committee's offer. As unprepared as you were coming here, from what you say, your friend's true crime murder book might make a perfect thesis for a journalism student special circumstance master's degree."

"It sounds like a win for the student, a win for the English department, and Jack Warren gets his book. My husband says I am a sucker for pathos. He is usually right about most things."

The rumpled professor gave me an odd look and then said, "Ah hm uh ..."

"So, I will buy in. Dr. Jacoby, what is my next step?"

"Husband huh ... I have a cat ... they are similar in their ways. Both become feral without enough attention."

"Sage advice. What is next?"

"What is next indeed. I was just informed about the faculty committee's offer for Len. Let me talk it over with him. If he is interested, I'll have him call you. Oh, look at the time, I am running behind. It was nice meeting you."

"Likewise."

****

The student Leonard Lym called my office the next morning. Chucho set up a meeting time for the following day. I wanted Chucho to sit in on the initial interview anticipating he would be the go between with Jack Warren in gay senior housing and homeless Leonard Lym ghost writer. In theory my back would only have to be involved if a problem arose, yeah, I know, many others have suggested my imagination is overactive.

Mr. Lym arrived fifteen minutes early for our ten AM appointment. Chucho was on the phone, so I did the greeting. Like many East Asians, Mr. Lym looked younger than his years, and stood about five feet ten inches tall, at maybe 130 underweight pounds. He appeared clean and neat for a homeless person.

His thick black hair was cropped from around a bowl. He had bangs in front above abundant eyebrows, long eyelashes, and brainy looking dark chocolate eyes. His slightly flared nose, full lips, and other facial features fit together perfectly into my idea of a classic East Asian attractive face.

Below the chin, a thin light gray cotton T-shirt showed Leonard's underweight swimmer's muscle structure. His gray gym shorts' covered butt flowed down two well-built thighs, legs, with an attention grabber crotch bulge, not huge but noticeable in front.

In my younger days, I thought it would be interesting to explore the forbidden fruits of rice queens. But alas, I never had the chance or time. Nevertheless, I obtained two years of so-so Mandarin in high school. My guidance counselor thought Mandarin might perk up my otherwise ho hum academic record, and truth be told

I found it a challenging diversion from regurgitating humdrum standard uniform schoolwork.

Leonard Lym was checking out the waiting reception area he had just entered as I walked over and said, "Mr. Leonard Lym? Hello, I am Oliver Kulgul, Dr. Jacoby spoke very highly of you."

He seemed timid taking my hand but met my grip with equal strength. "Call me Len, everybody does."

Smiling I said, "*Len, ni chi bai ren chi fan ma?*"

"Are you inviting me to lunch? Isn't it a little early? Why do you speak Mandarin to me?"

"It's a joke circulating in mainland China these days that my husband tells constantly, even though nobody laughs."

"Oh. You have a Chinese husband."

"No, he is *bai ren,* white. If you ask me white people's food does not compare to Chinese food, it is just faster to make. But hey, that is only my opinion."

"I am ABC, American Born Chinese, white people's food is mostly all I have ever eaten. Anyway, there are things we need to talk about in English, if you are going to consider me for ghostwriting in English."

"If you have no objections, I'd like to invite my associate to join us."

"Will I be out of line asking right off, how much money do you plan to pay me and how often?"

"So far, I'm not feeling put off by that question."

"How much then? Dr. Jacoby had no idea. He usually knows everything about everything."

"The man you would be writing for is terminally ill and Chucho's other job is social worker where the writer lives in gay senior housing. Oh, here he is now. Chucho, this is Leonard Lym. He likes to be called Len."

The two young men eyed each other up and down as many males are inclined to do greeting strangers and then they bumped elbows. It is an artifact from our recent pandemic I had yet to assimilate. Their generation seemed to have adopted elbow or fist bumps instead of the handshakes that projected masculinity for my generation.

I explained to Chucho that Len wanted to know how much he would make ghost writing for Jack Warren. Chucho surprised me speaking right up as if rehearsed, "We have not seen any samples of your writing, and you have not seen Jack's notes you would be working from. Don't you think it is too early to negotiate a price? Shouldn't we all see if we can work together first? The man you would be writing for is dying, that may or may not be an obstacle for you. Learning his exact finances for this project may be difficult, his husband died, and I know he managed their funds."

From the startled look on his face, Len clearly was not expecting someone close to his own age to be so blunt and to the point. Chucho looked and carried himself much younger than his twenty-six years.

I jumped into the conversation before it went south and said, "Len, is money your only concern in ghost writing a book about a life solving murders?"

"No. But I have never done that before, and I do not want you two to take financial advantage of me because school credit is involved and I'm homeless. Listen, I need money to even consider doing what you want."

Maintaining his dominant position Chucho said, "How much to get started?"

Len explained while he was in the hospital for three months his possessions and his deceased best friend's things were lost or stolen. After months in the hospital Len was discharged homeless because no family or friends could be located willing to take him in.

Ever since the hospital he had been couch surfing at acquaintances or in strangers' homes. In other words, he does not have a physical place to ghost write a large project. In addition, his computer along with prized electronic keyboard, and most everything else he owned was lost when possessions were removed from his dorm room. Consequently, as much as he would like to try ghost writing to complete his formal education and then get on with his life, all the problems seemed insurmountable since being homeless was a taxing full-time job.

I gave Chucho an inquiring look and he said, "Those problems do not sound insurmountable to me. Make a list of what you require. After you meet Jack, I will start getting what you need together for you."

"Huh, are you both and the Jack Warren guy on board with saving me from the streets? Dr. Jacoby thinks I have become feral because I cannot bathe every day."

Chucho looked at me and I nodded. They both watched my reaction, and Chucho said, "First you meet Jack Warren. If that goes well, you take a look at his notes. If that doesn't stop you, I will arrange housing, a computer, and a small stipend to live off until a fair price for your work can be negotiated by people who know what they are talking about."

"You gentlemen have me at a disadvantage. It is my hope you will be fair, not exploit my inexperience, and current life circumstance. I will give you my best work if treated fairly."

I felt a need to contribute to the conversation and said, "Do you have anyone you trust besides Dr. Jacoby to bring into negotiating a fee?"

"What's wrong with Dr. Jacoby?"

"Nothing. It is just, he is already involved. You will feel less vulnerable with someone else you trust by your side talking money."

"Dr. Jacoby said *you*, Dr. Kulgul, have a husband. Are you and Mr. Nascence married?"

"No. As far as I know Chucho is available?" I winked but it did not get the jocular response intended to lighten the mood.

Instead, Len frowned deeply and said, "Humph! I do not have anyone beside Dr. Jacoby looking out for me. Anyway, Mr. Nascence mentioned this Mr. Jack Warren I'd be writing for lives in gay housing. Furthermore, his husband oversaw their finances. Aren't you two going to ask me how I feel about working for gay people, or if I might be?"

Chucho the ever-ready social worker said, "As far as both of us go, if you and Jack Warren can work together what either of you do in private is none of our business."

"Don't you two even want to know why I have no family to help out or stand by me negotiating a book deal?"

To reenforce Chucho I said, "No, not necessary, nor our business."

"How do you know I'm not an American Nazi or gay hating White Supremacist Christian Nationalist?"

"You're not white."

"My Black, Brown, and Red classmates treat me like I was."

Chucho spoke right up and said, "How do unenlightened white people treat you?"

"Like I was Black or Brown, and in Indian country Red."

Chucho said, "Yup, the bigots hate you just for existing as much as they hate us for being alive."

"I suppose."

Feeling left out of the conversation I said, "Tell you what, if someone bothers you let me know and I'll have my husband sue them for you, or in a worst-case scenario, I'll shoot them."

"Dr. Kulgul, you make everything into a joke."

Chucho perked up and said, "He's not joking."

"I thought he was."

To get us back on track I said, "Like you, Len, this ghostwriting business is new to us. So, anything you need to take on this project express it to Chucho or me. That includes anyone bothering you. We want to hear about obstacles because this endeavor is all about granting a dying man his final wish."

"Then I hope I'm the man for such an important job."

Lightening up the mood a little, Chucho said, "How about we learn together as we go? My boss and I only want to help. Len, you ready to meet Jack?"

Looking not sure, Len said, "Sure."

I gave Jack Warren a call and he said, "Come on over."

The three of us took Chucho's van to the gay senior housing building. The whole trip Len looked sulky and did not respond to small talk intended to lighten the mood. However, when Len met Jack, instantly a noticeable change happened. It was like a light switched on behind their eyes and they put on open welcoming faces. It was like Len became someone else. Somone I did not mind being around.

I knew from Jack's over 40 years with the police he was used to meeting all sorts of human beings about trouble or in trouble. He had an innate way to put them at ease. He was a born people person. But why Len immediately opened to Jack, compared to the chip on his shoulder with Chucho and me at our office, was a mystery or a level of chemistry I had not studied.

The meeting went better than I could have expected between the old dying man and the fresh face homeless young person. It went so well, when there was a lull, I suggested we all go out to lunch to celebrate. It would be my treat.

As Jack was switching to his portable oxygen tank to travel, he suddenly got dizzy and had to sit down. After an awkward pause, he said, "You men go on without me. I need a nap and will skip the meal. Enjoy your lunch and thank you for coming to visit."

Back in the van, I asked Len if he had a favorite restaurant for lunch and he said, "Now that I met the author, I would rather look at his notes than eat."

Chucho already driving toward the office said, "How about a compromise? While you pour over Jack's files, I telephone for delivered takeout. Near the office we have Thai, Chinese, or Korean."

Looking at me, and winking with a little smile Len said, "*Wo xi won chi bai ren fan.*"

Chucho threw me a questioning look, so I said, "Len is going Mainland on us and wants their latest fad; white people's food."

Looking at Len in back through the rearview mirror, Chucho said, "That food is heavy with carbohydrates, not healthy at all. I know a particularly good Latin American restaurant in the area and their lunch specials are fabulous."

"Do not quibble boys, since we are eating on my dime let us order from the diner across the street from the office. They may be Greek, but they make decent white American food and okay empanadas."

Lunch was a little greasy but nutritious. Len was clearly hungrier than he had indicated and ate everything in sight. All his food and what we did not want of ours. With him so thoroughly enjoying himself there was little room for conversation while we watched in awe his face feeding.

After lunch, each of us got busy installing Len in the vacant office in our suite. We moved file boxes out of the way and stacked them in the hallway, thus making his work room as comfortable as possible on short notice. When that task was completed, Len asked to use a computer to go online and Chucho installed him at our receptionist's desk.

Len quickly downloaded samples of his writing, printed them out, and handed them to us to peruse. He was an award-winning student journalist. His writing showed clear thinking and precise use of the English language. His was a good match to Jack's no bullshit style.

As the end of the workday approached, I stuck my head in Len's door and said, "Let's have a brief meeting."

When he nodded his head yes, Chucho and I dragged chairs into the rather barren looking excess office. Except the top of the oversize desk was covered in the contents from one of Jack Warren's accordion files. Looking confident and comfortable working, Len said, "You know I could bring my sleeping bag and put it over there in the corner. Then I would be all set to work longer hours. Having a purpose makes me happy. I waste so much time these days standing in lines to get tickets to stand on other lines for food, carfare, or a bed."

"We have a commercial lease for this space which means the heat goes off 8:00 at night and doesn't come back until 8:00 the next morning except for the weekends when it's off both days. All the leases for this building are specific about no living."

"I would be very discreet, nobody need know I was sleeping here."

"Chucho, do you have any better idea for temporary housing Len?"

"Sure, just off the top of my head a couple things come to mind. There is a youth hostel not too far from here, he'd have to sleep in a dormitory with strangers and shower with them."

"All hostels charge a fee and I'm flat out broke."

"We could cover that until something permanent showed up."

"I'd rather rough it in the office for the sake of a little privacy. The homeless get no privacy."

"Okay then, in a pinch you could use the sofa in my place. It opens into a comfortable double bed. I have both cable and streaming on my TV and could clear off a couple of shelves in the refrigerator which is mostly empty anyways. With my bedroom door closed you would have as much privacy as you want."

"Do you live close to the office?"

"No, but the advantage is if I'm not coming here to this office, I have to drive by it going to my gay senior housing office, so you have a ride to and from here no problem." Then Chucho gave me and inquiring look and said, "Boss, do you have any suggestions?"

"I would have to run it by my husband first, but we do have a guest room at our house and what might interest you Len, a 7-foot grand piano. The house was built around the piano to give its sound great acoustics."

"Is your house close by this office?"

"It's not a bad bike ride to here from there."

"And you have an extra bicycle I could use?"

"I could get you a commuter card for the city's rent a bike program. There are bike parking slots near the house and others downstairs and with the commuter card it's not that expensive, I'll be happy to pay for it."

"Do you and your husband play the piano?"

"Average four hands mostly Baroque. Our housekeeper is good, she spends about an hour a day while we are at work practicing new material. She is no grand concert artist but is very good. Here let me give him a call." I whipped out my cell phone and had a one-minute telephone call with my husband.

"Dr. Kulgul, what did he say?"

"If you promise not to parade around wearing black leather you may stay with us."

For no reason I could fathom Len started to cry and quickly covered his face with his hands. Then the only indication of what was happening was his shoulders moving up and down as he silently sobbed. Feeling uncomfortable watching this young man crying, I went out to the reception area and filled a paper cup with ice water from the 50-gallon spring water dispenser. I sometimes get mixed contradictory feelings seeing attractive grown man cry. I guess I am one of those guys that it's easier to throw a punch than shed a tear.

When I returned, Len was blowing his nose into a tissue from a newly opened box Chucho must have given him. I am a shrink; we buy tissue boxes by the case load. Feeling emotional monkey see monkey do, I handed the cup of ice water to Len and his red rimmed eyes thanked me."

Chucho and I exchanged a look that showed he knew my position on adult men crying for no reason. Watching us but not understanding Len said, "I am so ashamed I embarrassed myself in front of you both. I am not usually such a crybaby."

"What do you suppose triggered the tears?"

"I don't know."

"Too bad, if you did you might avoid future unwanted public crying jags. Not that I mind or it's any of my business."

"Okay I lied. For me a homeless guy being invited to stay in someone's home is a big deal. That is why I lost control and humiliated myself in front of you."

"Oh, I sense there was more to it than that. But I've been wrong before and will be again, so I better keep my mouth shut."

****

Carmen took to Len immediately and the two enjoyed playing piano pieces for each other. Coy came home from work just before we sat down to a nice weeknight's dinner. After the meal Coy volunteered to take Len back to the youth shelter to collect his things and they could get to know each other better. While they were gone Carmen told me she got a good vibe from our new house guest, and I told her I did too.

Chapter 7.

Right after handing over files and random notes about his life's work to me, Jack Warren told his medical team to stop aggressively treating his geriatric maladies and change to palliative end of life care. Then Jack met Len Lym and something unexpected clicked, Jack's will to live revived. At first it was subtle, then after Len phoned Jack several times with questions and comments, it was not so subtle. Friends and neighbors commented that Jack had reengaged in activities he had been shedding. From my periphery point of view, it looked like Jack and Len were working together more as a collaboration than ghost-writer and principal author.

Jack's medical team apprised Chucho, gay senior housing and senior center social worker, after stopping aggressive medical treatments by weening him off all ongoing aggressive medications, Jack's prognosis changed. He went from short time left to live, to longer life, amount unknown for his advanced age and cancer without treatment. He was switched from an oncologist to a hematologist for research's sake. On his own to magnify the positive changes, Chucho suggested Len regularly meet with Jack, face to face, over lunch at the senior center.

What evolved over a few weeks was a regular scheduled Monday and Thursday lunch. Those days always had the best menus. What soon evolved to repay the seniors' kindness for a free lunch, Len played music during lunch-meal cleanup. That is until a small crowd gathered around the piano in the center's lounge. Then Len would turn it into an impromptu community sing along for a half hour or so. The seniors loved the new post-lunch activity.

Chucho and the residents in house nurse documented for their allied medical team, meetings with Len had a positive effect on Jack's overall terminal health condition. In addition, the Senior Center nutritionist mentioned, in general, the members' attitudes and probably digestion improved by enjoying music after lunch. Meanwhile Coy and Len's Relationship developed independent of his and mine, his and Carmen, or his and Chucho.

Coy called in a favor from his law firm's expert on copyright law and publishing, Hortense Abogado. She drew up an ironclad contract for Jack and Len to sign and publish the ghost-written true crime documentary style book. Hortense also recommended a literary agent friend who would be good at finding them the best publisher to do justice to their work.

On the home front, in their spare time, Len and Carmen became piano buddies sharing pieces of classical music and playing duets. Both also encouraged Coy and I to spend more time at the piano. Consequently, about once a month we had a kind of Sunday afternoon soiree taking turns playing piano for each other and then a few select friends were invited to join us. There is nothing like a deadline to stimulate chamber music.

It was interesting to me how Len had a dynamic relationship with each of us independently, but when we were all seated around the dinner table Len was the quietest among us and had to be laboriously drawn out into casual conversation.

That was what I anticipated discussing with him when I put my head through the open office door where he was working. I smiled, and before words could come from my mouth, Len said, "I know what you want to ask me about."

"So, you are a mind reader among your many other talents."

"You want to know why I am not more forthright and speak about my family and background."

"I do?"

Clearly, Len needed to unburden himself and I accidentally stuck my head in when he was most ready to spill the beans. As he told it, his best friend Connor, student news photographer died from head trauma, as Len was head bashed by the police covering a demonstration. The two young men had known each other from their diaper days.

They lived down the block from each other and their mothers took turns watching the two boys grow up. When puberty hit Len confessed to being in love with Connor, who admitted to being hopelessly heterosexual. As these star-crossed events usually go the boys did not have a fist fight or promise never to speak to the other again in this lifetime. Instead, Connor suggested it would be okay for them to fool around sexually, if neither were dating someone else with serious intention. After all the boys had learned to masturbate together and played in a garage band that included an irregular circle jerk after rehearsals.

Apart from breaks while Connor was going steady with one girl or another, the two best buddies had friends with benefits sex right into college. During Connor's heterosexual affairs of the heart Len explored casual sex with gay classmates and learned new tricks to teach Connor when he was on the rebound with a broken heart.

Len's words flew out of him in a hurry. When he stopped talking at me, his face showed relief from unburdening himself of pent-up emotions held back too long. Making direct eye contact he said, "That's what you wanted to know right?"

"I would be lying if what you just shared did not explain the big chip on your shoulder. Which I did not come in here to ask about. I am sorry for all your trials and tribulations."

"Thank you."

"That is not the reason I stuck my head in your door. I just had an appointment cancellation and hoped for some casual conversation about how you are doing here and at home."

"Whoops, I guess I gave you a lot more than you were looking for, sorry about that."

"S'okay."

"Well, so far Jack's book is going better than I expected. All the music in your home feels soothingly therapeutic to my frazzled nerves from death and violence. You and yours couldn't have been kinder to my emotionally wrecked self, thank you."

"Are you busy? I was just checking in, want me to leave you to your work. "

"I am fine if you want to talk. After I unloaded on you just now you must have questions. Or do you want me to pack and leave your office and home, good riddance to bad rubbish?"

"Nobody I know wants you to leave us. It feels sad to me that your first love object was not able to fully return your feelings. I wonder how common that is."

"Yeah, according to the gay and straight student alliance at school, most gay guys first serious love attraction is with a straight guy who panics."

"It figures since we are socialized in isolation our coming out is protracted and without social skills. That can be dangerous."

"At least I had the courage to tell Connor the truth and he cared enough about me to go against his nature for my sake."

"For both your sakes. Have you visited his grave since you got out of the hospital?"

"A lot happened while I was in a coma for months. That's one reason why I don't know or can't find out whether he is buried in a common grave on Potters Field or somewhere else."

"I assume there's a good reason you haven't asked his family about that. But Coy and I can probably find out where he's buried and possibly improve the views from his real estate. If that is something, you want?"

"You have done so much for me already. It is too much to ask for more."

"That's not how I see it. But while I'm making offers without knowing the full story, I'd be remiss if I didn't also offer my services for reconciliation."

"Thank you. But you should hear the rest of this story before you offer to give me your car."

"Sorry, under no circumstance can you have my new car, we are inseparable, attached at my hip to the drive chain."

The rest of the story was on their first vacation home from college, they yielded to nature's urges after the long drive. Then Len's bedroom door was yanked open while he and Connor were in bed doing the nasty. His father said he heard disturbing sounds, flung open the door, and saw more than he wanted to. He threw the two-college men out of his house, with their clothes going on to the lawn after them. He told them never to return until he was dead and buried.

When both boys tried to speak with their mothers, they were cruelly rebuffed. The family's pastor and spokesperson told them in no uncertain terms were they allowed the smallest drop of mother's love. They were dead to their whole biological family and church congregation because of being an afront to God in all his magnificent loving glory for the chosen few who could keep it in their pants. All future birthday and Mother's Day attempts at contact were refused.

After months in a coma, because Len was not related to Connor, the hospital refused to say who picked up Connor's remains. Then the city morgue refused to say, for privacy, if Connor's ashes were mixed in with the other destitute ashes making up the common public ash grave.

I told Len to say the word and Coy and I would find the grave for him. He said thanks, but no thanks. It did not matter anymore and was better to only have good memories of Connor. Then a tear rolled down his cheek telling how all their stuff was stolen from the school dorm rooms they were assigned.

I handed him a box of tissues as he said there were a lot of photos of Connor and him at every stage of their lives. They were banking on them for old age. Blowing his nose, he said see why I was not comfortable sharing my sad and disgraceful life story.

"Len, I'm curious about something. Just now you said all your possessions were stolen, and Dr. Jacobi said you were surviving as a busker. Which is true?"

"I can play most musical instruments, not too bad. I'm a natural fast learner. I borrowed musical instruments from friends and strangers. Guitars for the most part because there's a lot of them out there. It was a challenging way to make a buck because many borrowed instruments were of poor quality or badly maintained, or both."

"That certainly sounds like a tuneful way to survive homeless on the street."

"It was if you did not mind missing meals. Sad songs make people feel sad. If I played peppy tunes, the tips would be better but if I were not in the mood the music sounded inauthentic, insincere. Listen, I would rather you did not tell anyone I know what I just told you."

"You have my word. Then, to change of subject to why I came in here in the first place, how is the book going?"

"These first three file folders practically wrote themself and Jack added a lot of richness in answers to questions as they came up. But this fourth file folder is a mishmash, as far as I can tell, of unconnected chaos. Jack insists we included it to balance all his well-documented successes."

"Is there anything you need help with?"

"I don't think so. At least this far."

"Leaving no stone unturned, have you spoken with Carmen about her killer's poster mission?"

"No. Why would I?"

"It appears to me what she is doing has a large dose of unconnected chaos involved or at least doesn't seem to fit any obvious pattern I can see."

"If you think it might help, I will speak with her. I have organized Jack's fourth file chronologically, geographically, situationally, by garb, colors, and by random loose pieces that don't fit anywhere, so far nothing connects."

"Does garb include black leather clothes?"

"Yes."

"It never hurts to get a fresh pair of eyes on a problem. Like you Len, Carmen can be amazing ... why are you crying?"

"Sorry, so sorry, nobody has paid me such a compliment since Connor died. I was not prepared to hear praise. I have been living so low down I feel unworthy of kind words. But please, nobody can know how bad it has been, or I am a crybaby."

****

After serving Coy, Len, and me a scrumptious Sunday breakfast Carmen said, "We need to have a family brainstorming meeting."

Rubbing my satiated tummy, I said, "Why would that be?"

"Len and I have found a peculiar link between my poster boys and Jack's chaos file."

Coy said, "To do with wearing black leather."

"How did you know?"

"Lucky guess..."

Knowing where this was going, I cut Coy off, saying, "Carmen, what should be on the meeting agenda ..."

Coy cut me off saying, "Ugh! Leather queens again, my man is obsessed."

Making a sour face Carmen said, "Coy Goff, Esquire, stop badgering Dr. Oliver Kulgul, or no dessert for you after dinner, and tonight's is your favorite."

"Carmen, if Oliver is so clairvoyant, we do not need to consult experts from the wearable leather world."

All through this verbal bickering an expression of mixed confusion with interest flitted across Len's usual placid face. In preparation for a neckache, his head turned from Carmen to Coy to me and back and forth as we poked each other in family fun.

Then Coy just watched Len watching Carmen and me jawing at each other and said to Len, "Prepare yourself for a black leather brunch. It will be coming soon. Do not look worried, proper attire will not be required."

Declaring an armistice with Carmen, I told Len, "Pay no attention, Coy, as usual, is showing intolerance for a small esoteric faction of the gay community. You can wear whatever you want."

Wiping her hands on the spotless starched white apron she always wore serving food Carmen said, "Oh, what a good idea, how about brunch a week from Saturday?"

Before Coy could counter her suggestion, I said, "I'll see if the leather boys are available."

****

Depending on point of view, as luck would have it, TJ and Asa were available for a brunch brainstorming get together. Initially TJ thought it would be a big waste of his valuable time. Then Asa said matter of factly in his subservient voice they would attend and asked what they should bring. I suggested their knowledge of gay BDSM could be useful along with any new recollections from his encounter with murder.

I reminded Carmen with six or more for a sit-down meal, she agreed to hire help. As always, she objected saying, "The brunch could be buffet style, then extra help would be unnecessary."

"Cleanup is never on a buffet and brainstorming was your idea, your presence will be needed."

"Okay, Oliver, I'll see if the neighbor boy Randy is available for serving brunch and washing dishes Saturday. If he is busy, I do not know where I'll find short notice extra help to put up with what Coy calls a freakshow."

Neighbor boy Randy Webber started showing a lot of rage and getting into trouble with the law shortly after puberty hit him. His parents, both successful fiduciaries, had replaced his lifelong nanny up to that point with a series of tutors. Their good intention was to prepare him, ready or not, for legacy admissions to the Ivy League his parents had graduated from.

A series of counselors and therapists were no help getting Randy under control, until a family court judge finally sentenced the boy to either weekly music lessons or six months in juvenile detention. If music was chosen the judge would spot check the boy's musical progress. She let it be known she preferred German polka music played on the accordion with a happy beat.

The Webber's living next-door to us had often complained about loud piano music emanating from our house. They were not expecting music to help their seemly incorrigible only child. Consequently, Mrs. Webber asked Carmen, our housekeeper, to give her son piano lessons on her day off. She paid Carmen the going rate for music instruction in the neighborhood, but said she anticipated her son would fail at music."

Out of neighborly concern, Carmen had already been giving the lonely sullen boy odd jobs, like mowing our lawn, pruning hedges, and cleaning the roof gutters. Like his parents, Carmen had low expectations of turning Randy's brooding fury into beautiful music. Consequently, she selected modern German composers for him to express his rage and learn to control it. It wasn't just that they were German composers, as much as he loved their pointillistic music abstractions, and the wide-ranging dynamics fit his moods. Then like a powerful circuit was finally engaged, Randy's antisocial behavior dissipated into contemporary serious music and devotion to his music teacher who lovingly expanded his musical horizons.

Then somehow Randy learned Carmen had started out life as Carmine which may or may not been an additional factor in his new love of new European music. What caused a domestic disturbance was when Randy asked his parents if he could legally change the spelling of his first name to *Randi*. Initially they would not hear their pride and joy boy wanted to be a girl.

Fortunately for us, the Webbers took their wrath out on the judge and not us. The judge had a family meeting where she laid down the law to Randy's parents. Making serious threats against the possibility of their future freedom of movement if Randy's antisocial acting out got worse. His parents were shocked to be threatened with jail because their progeny would not behave and accept his gender at birth.

Then the judge asked the fifteen-year-old teen to remove his shirt. She complimented his teenage male developing physique and got him to agree not to radically change anything until his body was finished developing at age twenty-five or thirty. Her part of the compromise was to recommend a famous drag queen she knew to give Randy powder and paint cosmology lessons, wig lore, along with female fashion tips for men.

Randy arrived early to help Carmen prepare a sit-down brunch for six. When he helped serve the food his eyes popped out of his head when he saw TJ and Asa in full black leather drag. I could imagine there would be new black leather in Randy's wardrobe since Asa looked close to Randy's age. I insisted there be no talk of why we were together until brunch-breakfast was over and all the eating, drinking implements were cleared away.

****

I set up six canvas chairs in a circle on the deck with little folding side tables to put drinks on. When we were all assembled, well fed, and mugs of coffee or tea at hand. I said my general plan for the day was for us to decide whether what we had fit together or not, and if not why to exclude it. First Carmen then Coy would tell us what they found out, then I'd do a brief police update, open for questions, comments, and Len would be our scribe for the day.

When I asked if anyone had additional agenda items or objections, TJ strongly objected. He demanded to know why the murderer who abducted Asa wasn't caught yet. I told him that was the whole point of our sharing what we knew so far, so we all knew what was happening to catch the culprit. TJ's head shook no, disappointment showing on his face as he sat back morosely in his seat.

Carmen spoke next, saying new poster contacts had dried up. But a few of the original callers had called back and were contemplating giving her the information she wanted to verify them, and even were thinking about sitting for an interview. She said, "Do not get your hopes up. But one or more may turn into something worth pursuing."

Asa said, "Why don't we put the poster on social media?"

Carmen replied, "The internet is international. Right now, we think what happened to you, Asa, was local."

"Oh, I see, that makes sense."

Next Coy told the group about his recent recorded interviews with Brett about what happened to him five years ago after school, Mike's experience in a drug shooting gallery four years ago, and Nordune's explorative involvement with BDSM three years back. Brett, Nordune, and Asa all reported a masked killer, dressed in black leather, with tattooed forearms.

The five of us listened politely, not showing any reaction. When Coy finished, he asked for questions. When none were forth coming, he polled the group wanting to know whether they thought his three cases were related to Asa's experience.

A draw resulted along age lines, Carmen, Coy, and I voted yes. Asa, TJ, and Len voted no connection. Since the U.S. Constitution was currently under attack by a reoccurring president, we'd become hyper democratic about voting. Just then Randy came out onto the deck with a pot of just brewed delicious smelling coffee and refreshed everyone's mug of coffee. While he was busy Carmen said, "Randy, how would you vote?"

When the boy finished what he was doing he tried to give Carmen a blank stare. Caught off guard, Randy said, "How would I know?"

"You know. I saw your shadow eavesdropping in the kitchen doorway. It's okay because I know how lonely it can be alone in the kitchen when people out here are talking. There is no right or wrong answer you vote yes, or you vote no whatever is your opinion."

A look of embarrassment traveled across Randy's face and then was washed away by Carmen's kind words. The boy carefully looked from one to another of us, shrugged his shoulders and said, "I vote yes."

I looked around cautiously and said, "If the no's do not object, I think Randy should bring out a chair and whatever he'd like to drink from the fridge and join us."

Since we live in a post-truth or truth decay world, speaking fast I said, "For age balance's sake I will only vote to break a tie, if we even do any more voting. My contribution to today's meeting is slight, we don't know the name or identity of the perpetrator or the murder victims. The police department is already classifying Asa's ordeal as a cold case for lack of information. Does anyone have questions thus far?"

TJ had been paying attention after all and spoke up with his usual authoritarian bossy style. "Was a dead body found in the motel room mentioned five years ago?"

"I went back over the cop's call logbooks from back then. The motel wasn't mentioned that month, but a badly decomposing John Doe body was discovered nearby. The medical examiner determined the cause of death was strangulation by a braided object. Flies had eaten off the victim's face and his fingerprints were not found in any data base, so without a missing person's report to connect him to, he was cremated, and ashes placed in the Charles Dicken's common human ash pit."

Carmen glanced around the circle and asked, "Am I the only one curious about the missing two years between Asa's attack and the previous one? It seems to me that is the key to whether these murders are connected, yes or no."

There was a pause, you could almost see the little wheels turning round in people's heads. Randy fidgeted on his chair sure he had the right answer and finally said, "Those two years were Covid-19 pandemic isolation, most everything was closed."

TJ clearly not sure what to make of a precocious fifteen-year-old, said, "Or in prison, locked away in an insane asylum, or dead and it was somebody else with bad taste in masks."

Len looked up from his note pad at no one in particular and asked, "Do any of you think the killer was a junky? If he were, that could explain the missing two years, he was in recovery or relapsing."

Speaking to Len, Asa said, "Is there anything besides the time gap that makes you think the killer was a junky?"

Glancing down at his note pad Len said, "He was handing out poison heroin in a drug users' squat spot. I would not know how to do that, would you?"

"No, I would not, that is unusual. You are right." Asa said this seemingly drawing himself back inside himself.

Coy caught the young men's exchange with interest and said, "When I was a new police officer learning the culture, where, what, and how of hard drug use, at least for me, it was like going into another dimension. Now discovering gay BDSM at my age it feels very similar."

Speaking to his note pad, Len said, "According to Mike Snyder, his maskless killer knew his way around that scene. What we do not know is how, why, and is he, our killer?"

"Huh, maybe the drug killer was not involved with the other murders. I read somewhere drug users are disorganized individuals and what is keeping me confused is the well-organized how and why of the guy we are after." Carmen said this with the authority of a regular ladies' magazine reader.

Being the reader of scholarly journals myself, I could not let her comment go unchallenged and told the assembled I had recently seen a pie chart that surprised me. It showed forty percent of the pie never tried hard drugs, twenty percent tried them and did not like them, twenty percent were functioning addicts for decades, and twenty percent are defined by increasing drug use in a downward spiral to death or sobriety.

TJ, ready to show me up at any chance, said, "How could anyone do accurate street level illicit drug use research that was provable?"

"Mike Snyder is not the only do-gooder working to improve the lot of less fortunate than himself."

"Ah ha, Dr. Kulgul, always ready with a quick retort, no matter what, provable true or not."

Coy, my husband and defender, feeling heat turned up expounded, on the street I had to learn a lot more than I wanted to know or they taught us about drugs at the police academy. The same thing became true after Asa was attacked and I had to discover details from the hidden gay world of BDSM, which we are all delicately avoiding talking about today.

Meekly climbing down from his high horse, TJ said, "It's not the same, or either or. It's different for different people."

Len looked up from his note taking and he and Randy exchanged a look that seemed to say, "Now what are they talking about?"

Carmen, seeing Coy and I in couple mode versus irritated TJ, intervened by asking a question I knew she knew the answer to. "Did they find a body in Nordune's case from three years ago?"

"No. But the area he described is next to the river."

Len then asked Asa and me, "Did the masked guy set up a cellphone tripod to record that murder? Or could you see any other preparation from the security images?"

Asa said, "Until hypnosis, I thought I was mostly unconscious until the police came, and the masked man was gone. Now, I don't recall a tripod."

Noting Len and Asa were locked in to exchanging a lot of eyes contact, I said, "Two of the buildings' security cameras covering the area had died of old age, so we don't have a full view of the scene. From what the one working camera shows no tripod is visible. That doesn't mean one wasn't there. Why?"

"A tripod could connect some loose pieces from Jack Warren's notes. Or I may be grasping at straws."

We discussed what we knew so far, *two* of three of Carmen's witnesses matched Asa's story. Before adjourning, Carmen and Coy decided they would revive the poster campaign with a new poster showing the man in his mask again. I suggested my search area for John or Jane Doe who died from suspicious circumstances be expanded to statewide and ten years instead of five. To accomplish that I said I would invite Chucho to join our merry little band. Len wanted to invite Jack Warren via Zoom to our meetings and TJ said he was hiring a private detective to help.

Chapter 8.

After the brunch munchers disassembled, Coy walked TJ and Asa to the front door, Carmen and Len headed to the piano, Randy took his kitchen chair back inside, and I stayed on the deck to reflect on the meeting.

I had just folded and stowed the six canvas deck chairs under their tarpaulin and was turning to fold the side tables when I discovered Randy was already doing it. I said, "You don't have to do that, brunch is over. Don't you want to go back home?"

"No."

"Won't your parents worry?"

"They are in Chicago."

"Then who's looking after you?"

"I'm almost sixteen, I can take care of myself and don't need a babysitter."

"Is that so."

"I've looked after the house when my parents are away on business since I was 12 years old. Dr. Kulgul, why are you looking at me like that?"

Just then Coy slid open the glass door between the house and deck, sweet Mozart four hand piano music wafted out and he said, "Oh, there you guys are. I just walked TJ and Asa out the front. They had a uniformed chauffeur waiting in a brand-new luxury car. I thought we we're going to invite their chauffeur inside."

"I completely forgot. Next time, if there is a next time, let's ask Carmen since she won't forget."

"Oliver, what is that expression on your face?"

Randy spoke right up and said, "He was about to lecture me about needing adult supervision."

"What are your parents for?"

Holding my husband's eyes in one of our private looks, I said, "They're in Chicago."

"Randy, you do know I'm a lawyer, right?" Randy nodded his head yes to Coy's question. "Do you also know in this state *people under the age of eighteen* are required to be *supervised at all times by people over the age of eighteen?*"

"That's okay, I'll be 16 in just a few months, and we don't have to tell anybody."

"I guess Oliver didn't mention to you he and I are mandated reporters."

"What's that?"

"Required under law to report any incident of child abuse or neglect. If we don't the penalty is loss of our licenses, hefty fine, and five years in prison. You are a nice kid but not worth all the work I put in to pass the bar exam. Randy, do you see the problem?"

"Nobody is abusing me."

"Without adult supervision it's called neglect."

"Holy shit, DISASTER!"

I put a hand on Randy's shoulder and said, "Maybe not, can you telephone your parents and ask for their permission to stay at our house until they return?"

Looking apprehensive the teenager said, "Where would I sleep?"

"We have an unused fourth bedroom, it shares a bathroom with the room Len is using. To give you a lay of the geography there are five toilets in this house."

Randy took out his cellphone and started to dial and I said, "Put it on speaker and record. Do you know how to do that?" The teen nodded his head yes and continued to dial.

After a brief pause, he said, "Mom, I need your permission to stay over at the neighbors until you come back."

"Why Randolph? You know I don't like those people. I must continuously remind them to close their windows and doors when they play that big piano. We can't come home right now, we're in the middle of a very big deal. You will be fine on your own, you're a big boy."

"The child welfare police say I'm not allowed to be alone, and they will arrest me without adult supervision."

"The housekeeper is there until six. I TOLD YOU NEVER TO ANSWER THE DOOR WHEN WE AREN'T HOME, DIDN'T I? Didn't I SAY THAT?"

"The judge says if I get into trouble again, she is going to put me in junior jail, remember?"

"Randolph, I think those men may be homosexuals. They may try to molest you if you stay over there."

"Mom, you told me I was gay when I was eleven."

"Ugh, that was just too much wine with dinner. We already talked about this many times. You'll explore *that* when you are much older and not living with your father and me. Why did you bring it up again?"

"I didn't, you did."

"Here talk to your father."

"Rand, why are you upsetting your mother? We've talked about this behavior before son, you must stop getting on your mother's nerves."

"Father, I need your permission to sleep over at a friend's house until you come home. Can I please?"

"All right, make sure you lock all the windows and doors, and stop upsetting your mother."

"Bye, Father."

"Bye, Rand."

Randy clicked off his cellphone looking chastened and said, "My father says I can stay, if your offer is still good. I wish you didn't hear all that. It was embarrassing."

Coy and I exchanged a couple's commiseration look. He shut down in situations like we just created. I was torn between encouraging Randy to talk about his right now feelings, and not making a bad situation worse for a volatile young man, so I said, "How about I walk over to your place with you and help carry your clothes and other stuff needed until your parents return?"

Glumly he said, "Only if you want to."

"Let's go."

At first, we walked in silence with our heads down. Then Randy lifted his head looked at me and said, "Can I ask you a question, Oliver?"

"Yes of course it's covered under your first constitutional amendment. Whether I answer, is also covered under my freedom of speech."

"Adults make everything so difficult for their kids."

"What's the question?"

"You heard my parents on the telephone they expect me to be a virgin until I graduate college and leave their home."

"It sounded like you agreed to that."

"How could I know what I was agreeing to? I was only 11 years old and just starting to jerk off."

"If you and I are going to be talking about sex, I would be more comfortable if we use the academic terms rather than vernacular."

"Great. Now I get a vocabulary quiz on top of everything else."

"Consider it a fringe benefit." We shared a little smirk that lightened the mood between us.

"Ha ha, just so you know I have studied human reproduction from library books and the internet, so I know everything there is to know about sperms and eggs getting together. My question to you is how much is the right amount to jerk off and what it's considered too much?"

"How about we use the word masturbate instead of jerk off?"

"That's the story of my life, the adults control the narrative."

"Do you like chocolate cake?"

"Of course, everyone does."

"Imagine there's a freshly decorated luscious looking chocolate cake sitting on the kitchen table and it would be okay for you to take one slice. However, if you ate the whole cake there are consequences, like upset stomach, vomiting, diarrhea, and all the angry people denied a piece of cake because you ate theirs."

"What does chocolate cake have to do with masturbation?"

"First tell me what you know about masturbation."

"Ugh! My father says I should do it as seldom as possible to avoid blindness and insanity. Most of the boys at my school do it morning, noon, night, and every chance in between. So far none of them have gone blind."

"At the possible expense of making your most knowledgeable subject more complicated, have you ever baked a chocolate cake?"

"No."

"There are many different recipes for making a chocolate cake. Also, if you are missing one or more ingredients you can make substitutions. Like I said before you can share the cake or eat the whole thing yourself with consequences."

"Now I don't even know what you're talking about."

"I believe you began this talk of biology with sperms and eggs uniting. Then you morphed into belief systems versus common sexual practice for one. Obviously, my chocolate metaphor was not getting any traction with you."

"Hell, what did I expect talking to a PhD about low down earthy real life. Wait, did you say sex for one? Mmm, interesting, but why?"

"I suspect you are denying your biological needs for other people's religious, political, or power and control beliefs."

"Does sex for one have other names?"

"Self-pleasure, solitary-sex, you'll like this one, *playing the organ*."

"Does it cause blindness or make you go mad?"

"No."

"Biologically, what's the purpose then?"

"To learn how to prepare you to introduce your sperm to an egg or occupy alone time."

"I don't understand, it was murder, then chocolate cake, now solitary-sex."

"Pleasuring yourself to learn what you like and do not, is one way to instruct an egg donor for your best outcome, when the time comes. Knowing what works for you is a good jumping off place to learn what pleases them. If they are pleased with you seconds and even thirds may be offered."

"But why bother?"

"It is a numbers game. If your goal is to mate your sperm with someone else's egg you will need repeat performances to score."

"Why would that be I wonder?"

"Females are fertile one day a month. Males are fertile twenty-four hours a day every day. Do you see the problem?"

"Keep shooting until the target is hit. Mmm, I like it, repeat performances are required, yeah. So, if the receptive partner did not like how it went, no more chances."

"I think you understand, it's mutual."

"How was I supposed to learn that?"

"Be born into a sex-positive country. Oh, look, we have arrived at your house. You will probably just need to bring socks, underwear, a toothbrush, and a video game or two. You can always come back over here if you forget something you want."

Randy was quick throwing what he expected to need into a backpack then said, "I think I'm ready. Will you and Coy answer any questions that come up when I am self-exploring?"

As the teen walked around securing his home against intruders, I said, "I can only speak for myself. Sure, I'll answer questions, if we keep the vocabulary on an academic level."

Giving me a little pretend lude smile Randy snickered, "Rats, which means no show and tell or actual physical hands-on demonstrations." Then we exchanged deep genuine heartfelt smiles showing shared closeness for the first time.

"Correct. Your mother already expects us to molest you. I hope you know we would never do that, and anyone who did would damage your development. You understand?"

"Got it. My father's cockamamie belief in dick blindness and crazy has retarded my personal growth by four years already. I do not want to screw up my chance to get it right."

We walked back to my place lost in our own thoughts. Instead of going to the front door, Randy went to the side of the house where Coy and I had hung two swings from the century old oak's strongest limb. He dropped his backpack on the ground and sat on a swing seat. I took the other plank swing seat. When something was bothering one or both Coy and I, we would swing out here until we thought the problem through.

After a few easy glides forward and back, in a gentle voice Randy said, "Oliver, have you ever worn a woman's dress?"

"The opportunity never presented itself. Why do you ask?"

"Isn't it every gay guy's dream to dress like a woman sometimes?"

"No. Not mine. Coy never mentioned it either. What is up with that question Randy?"

"To annoy my parents, I told them I was going to change the Y in Randy to I and eventually my gender. They told my lawyer, and he told the judge and now she wants me to meet with a drag queen. I am sure that person will want to put me in a dress, and I don't know how I feel about that. Maybe I went too far this time."

"Are you even sure you're gay?"

"I'm not sure but I heard mothers always know."

"Tell that to the judge or have your lawyer tell her."

"Can't you tell? Do I walk and talk gay?"

"What do you think about when you masturbate?"

"I start out thinking female egg donor snatch, but when I really get going it switches itself to a pretty dick I have seen in the shower at school. That makes me gay right?"

"Maybe, but the only person who will know is you. At your age it is expected you will try different things to find out what you like, and not. To complicate the matter what you like today might not suit your mood tomorrow."

"Isn't that the definition of schizophrenic?"

"No. I recently saw a study that showed the majority of gay men in college identified as straight and most straight college men identified as bisexual."

"That sounds crazy. Sometimes I wonder if I'm crazy too."

"I think normal adolescents and the certified insane share a few similar symptoms. After spending most of a day with you, you are not nuts."

"You say that like you know, with authority."

"I've got the credentials to back up what I say."

"Lucky you, I don't know what I should do. Isn't that stupid not to know at my age?"

"Think about it, there have been a lot of changes in you recently, and you can expect more over the next ten to fifteen years. Give yourself a break."

"How do I do that?"

"Just keep it simple, lower your expectations. Nobody expects fifteen-year-olds to rule the world."

"Easy for you to say, what if I'm queer?"

"At my house we will love you just the same straight, bi, gay, or a-sexual, as long as you keep doing an excellent job mowing our lawn."

"I wonder if you were a failed comedian in a previous life."

"When I was your age, with early teenage seemingly insurmountable problems, my high school counselor said, 'What'll it matters in 100 years?' I almost slugged him for saying that. If I had hit him, my life would have turned out a lot differently, and in hindsight he was right."

"What I do know is seeing those two guys in black leather at your brunch today got my imagination going down in my underwear as to what they might get up to in private. Those thoughts kept my dick hard the whole time. Do you think I'm a pervert?"

"If dressed the same and one were female, would you have had the same reaction?"

"Good question, I don't know."

"That's what adolescence is all about, learning what's all right or not, with you. There are adults who are damaged and exploit innocent young people because they think they can't compete with other adults on an equal level. You must avoid them at all costs."

"Thank you for all that character building. It's getting a little chilly, maybe we should go inside."

"Let's."

Chapter 9.

Back in the house, Carmen was in the kitchen getting dinner ready, Coy and Len with game controllers in hand were fighting it out on the video game screen. Randy and I plopped down to watch the others battling. The phone in the entrance hall rang and Carmen came out of the kitchen drying her hands with her everyday work apron and answered it.

After a long interval of Coy and Len's gamer gunfire and explosion sounds, Carmen came into the living room with a troubled look on her face and said, "That call was in response to the poster of Asa's perpetrator. He has just had a run in with the guy we're looking for and sounds very upset. The man does not want to involve the police, he is undocumented but is scared out of his gourd. I said one of you would be right over."

"I'll go." Coy got stuck with most of the other poster boys. "Where is this one?"

"Behind the junction truck stop on Interstate Route 86 at exit twelve."

"Oliver, let's do this one together."

"Okay. What do you say armed or not?"

"After that leather bar research, I think better armed than sorry."

"Can I come too?"

"Sorry, Randy, maybe next time. Why not see if Carmen can use a hand in the kitchen? Or if you feel up for video combat, possibly Len needs a competitor on the battlefield."

****

I kept my car at exactly five miles over the speed limit, accelerated through every yellow light, and got to the truck stop in eleven minutes. We found Mr. Javier Torres cringing behind dumpsters near the backdoor of the diner's kitchen.

Clutching a burner cellphone and copy of Carmen's poster in one hand for dear life. Torres looked thirty to thirty-five, with hard-lived lifelines around mouth and eyes just beginning. He was maybe five foot six inches on a good day, at around 120 pounds wringing wet. He had straight thick, dark longish brown hair, bushy eyebrows, over intense light brown eyes. Most probably, his was normally an angelic, but now terrified looking face. Wearing no clothes, in his other hand he held a greasy dirty cook's apron up to cover himself. The man was sweating profusely, beads of sweat covered his trembling body head to toe.

Just as Coy and I walked up, a big burly cook came out of the rest stop diner kitchen's back screen door, scowled at us, and took the burner phone from Mr. Torres' hand. The big guy, dressed in chef soiled whites, including a white paper chef's hat took a protective stance between the naked man and Coy and me. Hand on my gun butt I said, "We're here to help." Not getting any reaction I moved so the diner chef could see my mouth and repeated, "We're here to help."

The cook read my lips, eyed us up and down, grumbled, turned, and went back into the kitchen. I started to wonder why a hearing-impaired guy needed a cellphone when mine vibrated and a text appeared on the screen from Carmen. After retrieving a blanket from my car's trunk to cover Javier, I indicated he sat in the back seat. The man was trembling uncontrollably with sweat pouring off him. He looked shaken to his core.

Javier told us when a kitchen worker found him next to their garbage dumpster, the kitchen crew went looking for the murderer and the van was gone. At that point I went into the diner and soon came back with trucker coffee for each of us. Using sign language, the cook with a paper chef's hat indicated to the cashier my coffees were on the house. I nodded a thank you and he returned it with a nod back. He looked more relaxed, less protective inside the diner.

Surrounded by two armed men, Coy and me, sitting in my car sipping coffee, Javier stopped shivering. I recorded Mr. Torres's account of what just happened to him on my cellphone. Not allowed a work permit, Javier was stuck between under the table, off the book's work from exploitive employers who cheated workers or to panhandle. Panhandling money was more dependable but dangerous with immigration agents or the police looking to deport all undocumented.

Another new clue in Asa's criminal case, Mr. Torres was begging outside a pool hall on skid row when two men drove up in an older Ford full size van. The driver offered him money for sex. Javier told them he is not usually a sex worker, but was famished, knew his wife and kids had not eaten in a while, and was desperate to get money to feed his family.

When they got down to negotiating who would do what for how much, Torres categorically refused to be fucked in the ass. But agreed to give the other black leather man half and half. He would get an enthusiastic hand job finished by mouth. The driver, whose face he could barely make out from under a cowboy hat pulled down close to his eyes, and large frame glasses. That guy was only supposed to watch and record the sex but not get too close or touch. He lied.

They agreed on a price of one hundred dollars cash. But the driver insisted Javier take a shower first. Vehemently the other black leather guy did not want Torres to bathe first. He said the smell was part of the turn on. But the driver overruled him after a furious argument.

They drove out to the truck stop, with the stink-loving guy grumbling like a disappointed child. Mr. Torres got wet and clean while the other two men watched him scrub. The driver paid for Javier's communal trucker's public shower. Then the driver guy put on a mask after the three climbed into an empty, unattached, truck-tractor's trailer.

Right away the black leather guy stripped Mr. Torres out of his clothes, then dropped his leather gear on top. Finished undressing them both, that guy put Javier's hand on his long, hard sausage, and literally fucked his fist like mad, staring at Torres like he was something out of the ordinary to eat for dinner.

As he got into his hand being fucked, Javier went with the flow and worked the guy's loose skin all the way back then forth over his dickhead and played with his big balls in his other hand until ready to pop. It was a job, he was working. He needed the money. His family was hungry. Imagining seeing the one-hundred-dollar bill again, Javier went down on his knees and took the guy's member into his mouth. He hated doing it, but they say on the street only the idea is hard to swallow.

Disgusting himself, Javier mechanically bobbed his head back and forth. Just when that man started to breathe like into an orgasm, the masked man moved behind him. Then he stuck a needle into each side of the leather guy's neck from behind.

Shooting spunk, smelling like bleach, then ammonia the leather guy went into convulsions and collapsed on top of Torres on top of both their clothes. Javier struggled to get out from under the big older man and tangle of clothing. Then in sheer terror he ran for his life.

Javier Torres took Coy and me to the parked empty long haul truck trailer. We found a fiftyish looking dead guy who had vomited on top of crumpled black leather clothing, which was on top of Javier's twisted well-worn threads buried beneath barf absorbing into fabric.

There were two hypodermic needles stuck in either side of the dead guy's neck. On the floor near him were a used pair of clear rubber gloves. A plastic bottle of store brand household ammonia and a white jug container of the number one selling laundry bleach stood on the floor nearby, out of sight.

Coy and I rechecked the truck stop but the vehicle that brought Mr. Torres was most definitely nowhere to be found. While Javier scrunched down in the backseat of my car, hidden under a blanket, Coy drove away. Meanwhile I called the police, and when they arrived showed them the dead body. I told them I had gotten an anonymous tip from a poster and gave them a copy of it.

I had to stick around and answer police questions from various ranks of officers scribbling notes. In the meantime, Coy drove Javier to borrow clothes from a cousin. Then they picked up the Torres family at a tent encampment of homeless people living under a highway bridge. Coy drove them for pizza and got them back to the encampment before their stuff was stolen.

We had agreed not to tell the police about Javier because he believed he and his family would be deported back to Honduras where a gang would kill them. Our agreement was he would cooperate with us, and we would keep his family safe. Coy was owed favors by pro bono lawyers who helped undocumented families. The Torres family would be moved to the top of the list to keep our favors coming.

The most immediate problem was keeping Javier and his family where we could find them. The homeless encampment was under constant threat of being raided by immigration. If they end up in custody or back on the street, we might lose them and any help they might be to solve the serial killer case or receive what we could provide for them.

Police officers checked the security images at the truck stop entrance and saw my car with two people in it arrive and then leave with just one person driving. When the police were finally done asking me questions, I telephoned Coy, and he drove my car back to pick me up. When he arrived the police wanted to know what he knew and why he had left. Whereupon Coy showed them his courtesy card identifying him as a former police officer. He told them he had pressing attorney client business but was back now for their questions as a concerned citizen.

His first question to them was did they have an ID on the killer's van? They were working on it, but the license plate was obscured, and the side logos appeared to be removable magnets, so not reliable identifiers. In other words, like in Asa's case, they had nothing and with little prospect of getting more.

****

Back home over Carmen's boiled dinner of beef brisket, mixed potatoes, cabbage, carrots, and horseradish sauce, Coy and I related Mr. Javier Torres's encounter with the masked murderer. When the story was over Len asked, "Is it common for serial killers to escalate killing?"

"I don't know but I sure as hell will find that out for you."

After an appropriate time to digest, Carmen served a scrumptious dessert platter of homemade cannoli, some shells dipped in chocolate and some plain. Both had the same cheese-chocolate-chip filling. The waistline busters were delicious, and nobody ate just one.

"In these cases, was both the murder victim and killer wearing black leather?" Randy asked this looking like he was not sure if he should.

"We have only one taped image of the killer and that is how he is dressed. Mr. Torres was not. Asa was decked out in full leather gear, but they stripped it off him. Then they threw his clothes out of the moving vehicle in a plastic trash bag."

"Maybe we should go look for it, there may be clues in the bag."

Timidly Randy asked, "Then was Asa the only eyewitness wearing leather?"

"No. Nordune wore a black leather headband, wrist guards, and top harness. Three of the five witnesses had no leather other than a belt. We still do not know the actual number of murders with or without a witness, so we do not have any answer to your question."

"Do you think the ones that got away were there only to witness? From what you said some thought they were next to die and ran. What if other witnesses were killed and ended up as John Doe buried without their own name."

"Maybe, Randy, we should get you a junior detective badge. But seriously, so far, the witness's role was to watch, distract, and run away with or without the promised money, except for Asa who was too drugged to get away."

"Teenagers are never taken seriously. It's that damn narrated 'Peter and the Wolf' story Prokofiev set to music. Its marked us all as unreliable."

After looking lost in thought for a minute Len said, "Mike Snyder's drug story doesn't fit with the rest of them."

Possessive of her poster's finds, with an edge Carmen said, "Why is that?"

Shrugging his shoulders looking defensive Len said, "Black leather wasn't mentioned at all, every witness zonked out or dead from drugs, and the murderer wasn't reportedly wearing a mask, or tattooed sleeves."

We looked at each other with facial expressions that said, "Huh, why didn't we see that?" If Mike Snyder and Asa Mulroy were not part of the same setup, do we still have serial murder or was it just a collection of coincidences?

Looking drowsy, Len said, "If you will excuse me, Chucho is picking me up early tomorrow and I need to shower. Goodnight, everyone. Carmen, dinner was great as usual. Thank you so much."

It was a bit early for me and Coy to turn in. However, when opportunity presented itself, we cuddled, so naturally we wanted to head for a shower together and forementioned intimate clinching. But we were not alone. Then Carmen gave us a knowing look and bustled off to the kitchen.

After a few uncomfortable pregnant minutes, Randy said, "I think I will turn in too, tomorrow my parents will be back and that will be the end of my junior detective fun. I had better get a good night's sleep to prepare. Goodnight, and thank you for another great meal and sanctuary from the child welfare police."

****

The next day Coy sent one of his investigators out looking for the trash bag with Asa's leather outfit in it. She found it on her first try. The bag had been knotted closed, so the contents were protected from the weather. The police didn't know where to look since they hadn't wanted a transcript of Asa's hypnosis, since it was inadmissible in court.

I checked with my friend at the medical examiner's office and was not surprised to learn our latest John Doe expired from simultaneous, intravenously ingesting bleach and household ammonia. Once again, the police were not seeing a connection between these cases as we did. They didn't want to know we called it serial murder, since they didn't.

It was not one of my days to be in my own office, but the university was having a class free day for students. I had final reports on aftercare follow up to catch up on in my private practice. For today any students' cellphone calls would be answered there instead of on campus.

As soon as I walked in the door, I could feel something was up in my private healing place of business. Whatever it was permeated the whole physical space like a bad smell. Even though the air had an odorless negative presence, it dampened the whole atmosphere.

Len walked out of the office he had been using looking ruffled and said, "You don't have to say anything I'll just pack up my stuff and head to the shelter. Thank you for everything. As usual, I screwed it all up."

"Huh?"

"Oliver, I am so sorry I know you gave me every chance. Honestly, I do not know how it happened or what I should have done to stop it. I want to say it was nature that took over me. Or more likely I am just not a good moral person."

"What the hell are you talking about?"

"Didn't Randy tell you?"

"He had gone home by the time I left this morning. What is going on with you, Len, you really look upset."

"I certainly owe you an explanation. Except, I am embarrassed to even tell you what happened."

"For God's sake just spit it out. I hate drama first thing in the morning without more coffee."

"I was taking a shower before bed last night and wanking. That combination often defeats my usual insomnia at bedtime. Randy opened the door, came in, and said he needed to use the toilet to pee. I turned my back to him and said, go ahead. While I lathered, I noticed him stop making splashing water sounds, then no zipper up, or flush sound.

"Looking over my shoulder at the mirror, I noticed he kept staring at my butt in the shower and playing with himself. Then he changed to openly beating his meat hard and looking at me harder. His face was a lust mask.

"I turned to confront him, but the situation had me more roused than before he entered. I was in no condition to scold anyone. He moved closer to the shower checking me out. Then nature took its course, and I found myself mirroring what he was doing. Long story short, watching each other's face, we shot our loads onto the glass shower door, simultaneously hitting the same spot, him outside, me inside, with the water running to cover our grunts."

"You shouldn't waste water during the drought."

"Then Randy cleaned up his mess on the glass door with toilet paper, flushed, and left the bathroom looking sheepish not saying a word. I am so sorry I know he's under eighteen and somehow, I should have stopped what happened. I think I am destined to be a loser all my life. I will go, you don't have to throw me out."

"Did you touch him, or he you?"

"No and no. I am not attracted to Randy. Believe me since Connor was killed, I've had zero interest being with anyone."

"Then chill out, nobody died since Connor."

"There has to be consequences for my part."

"Fortunately, we have a lawyer in the family in case Randy or his parents want to make a big deal about his sharing a bathroom."

"You deserve better from me."

"Randy knows where the other bathrooms are in my house, they all weren't occupied."

"Why didn't I just keep my back turned and ignored him?"

"Because you were already self-pleasuring when he walked in on you. The textbooks say one way you will know your bereavement is over is when sexual interest in others returns. As near as I can tell you are still grieving."

"Truth be told, I don't ever expect to stop grieving for Connor. I loved him."

"That is on you. In the meantime, you and I have an agreement that you will finish Jack Warren's book and get your degrees. And you will *not* let anything sexual happen between you and Randy until he's of age if you can help it."

"Absolutely."

"Did you feel like Bruce Wayne with horny Dick Grayson lusting after your body?"

"Batman and Robin never got my motor running."

"Ah, a comic book deprived childhood, how sad."

"The Green Hornet ruined comics for me."

"How'd he do that?"

"With interchangeable East Asians."

"Mmm, do you mind explaining?"

"In the beginning the Green Hornet's faithful chauffeur sidekick Kato was Japanese with secret Japanese fighting skills. Then when the United States locked up all west coast Japanese in internment incarceration camps Kato mysteriously became Korean. When the comic book radio show was revived for television and movies decades later Kato became Chinese Bruce Lee."

"Well, if it is any consolation the Green Hornet's theme music was 'Flight of the Bumble Bee.' Bumble bees are not hornets, green or otherwise, and hornets resent the misrepresentation and kill bees."

"Huh, gosh what did I expect discussing comic books with a Ph.D."

"Give yourself a break, we are not in competition."

"Once again you are not kicking me to the curb, which I deserve for not stopping Randy."

"Listen, Len, this is the second time you have been ready to cut and run from our agreement. What can I do to keep you around to finish what you started?"

"Ugh, don't know."

"If you have not noticed, it's important to me, Jack Warren gets his book read out in the world, and you receive the credentials you already earned. What will it take? Name your price."

"I think I'm defective with major character flaws."

"Well, no disrespect intended, I do not. Do me a favor, consider these real-life events learning experiences. That is what the rest of us do. Now get back to work, and do not waste water it's a precious diminishing resource in this time of global warming."

"Lately every time I hit bottom you lift me up, will you shadow me all my life?"

"No. I am already married. By the way, your contribution to the Asa Mulroy case last night was the first break we have had. Thank you, Len, for another job well done. Don't argue with me, I'm always right."

Carmen telephoned my work at three fifteen and said the neighbors wanted to meet with me and Coy. She sounded guarded, so said, "I can be home by five thirty, I'm not sure about Coy."

"I'll call him next. See you later, boss."

****

I pulled into the attached garage at exactly 5:25, and Coy drove in no more than a minute or two behind me. When we entered our living room, Mr. and Mrs. Webber and Randy were sitting on our couch. The Webbers looked angry, not an unusual demeanor for them. Poor Randy looked uncomfortable squeezed between his parents. Coy took his easy chair and I mine and with big put on smiles we said in unison, "Hello, neighbors."

Just then, Carmen came out of the kitchen and said, "Would anyone like a drink? It's cocktail hour."

The Webbers all nodded no. I said, "I'll have a scotch over ice with a twist. Coy do you want a beer?"

"Beer sounds good, was in court all day. I earned it."

As Carmen was leaving the room, Mrs. Webber said, "We don't want Randy over here ever again. To make that point perfectly clear to you, we had our lawyer draw up papers you can understand."

She stood, tried to hand me trifold papers, but Coy snatched them out of her hand as she poked the papers at me.

Giving them a cursory look, then throwing back his head laughing, Coy said, "Oliver, look they took out a restraining order against us. We are not allowed within one hundred feet of Randy."

"Mmm, now what should we do about that?"

"Would it be overkill if I prepare a lawsuit, contact child welfare, and have my investigators compile Webber's travel itinerary without Randy since he was twelve? I could have that done before lunch tomorrow. Oliver, how much should we ask for?"

"You mean pain, suffering, defamation of character, and punitive?"

"Yes."

"I won't take less than nine hundred fifty million dollars, but a billion seems a bit excessive."

Mr. and Mrs. Webber looked at us askance, and after an awkward moment, she said, "You two are not only fags, but you are also criminal fairies, we will see you in court. Our lawyer is Harry Hoppingstock, the giant slayer, do you know him? He is exceptionally good."

Coy had an amused look on his face when he said to me, "My firm recently beat old Harry in a big civil suit. His client unnecessarily lost his shirt."

"What is your paltry law firm called, Mr. Know-it-all Smart Aleck?"

"We are sometimes called the Four H Club among peers. I head up the criminal division at Hamilton, Hardcore, Handicock, and Hoot. I'm sure your lawyer has heard of us we regularly beat him in court."

Mr. Webber looked to be experiencing sudden gastrointestinal upset and said, "Does this have to turn into the legal proceedings of the century?" I could see his wife was digesting what Coy said and suddenly caught her husband's look of indigestion.

"You could withdraw your order of protection and save my paralegals and investigators unnecessary work tomorrow morning. Then we'll be appreciative not to need a new lawn mowing boy. I think we could call that even, right Oliver?"

"Sounds fair. But eight hundred and fifty million is as low as I would go for punitive damages."

"We only want what's best for Randy."

"Randy was this order of protection your idea?"

"No! The happiest I ever remember was at your house, getting piano lessons and helping Carmen out. I can be *me* here, I feel valued."

"Randolph, how can you say that and play that awful, Arnold Schonberg, Anton Webern, and Alban Berg, twelve tone music? These degenerates have corrupted your mind to something awful."

"I like that music; it makes sense to me. I know it's not for everyone, but I like it. We were German generations ago. They speak German like we used to."

"See how you've been corrupted *again*, just like with the nannies?"

"You said all that turmoil was their fault."

"It was, if they were any good it wouldn't have gotten so out of hand."

"That was just after you told father I am destined to be gay. That was long before we moved to the new house. Mother, nobody corrupted me, if I am damaged I did it to myself, and you said as much."

Mother and son were escalating their battle with increasing volume, pops looked on impotently. We heard Chucho's van drive up, and seconds later Len walked into the house, kicked off his shoes and started to walk past the living room to say hi to Carmen in the kitchen. What stopped him at the living room door was hearing Randy's counterattack at his mother.

The two young men exchanged a loaded look I could not unpack without reference to my earlier conversation with Len about extracurricular activity involving the shower.

Then Randy stopped speaking, staring at Len with intent, and I said, "Len, why not grab a side chair? This might interest you our neighbors seem to want Randy removed to a group home by child welfare for their neglect."

Just then Carmen arrived pushing a rolling cart with our drinks and snacks, she said, "The snacks are savory or sweet, all homemade with healthy nutrition in mind." She handed me my drink, Coy his beer, and placed the snacks on the coffee table in front of the couch, and then said, "Len would you like something to drink?"

Shaking his head no to a drink, Len looked confused and finally said, "Why does Randy have to live in a group home? I've heard they're rough places." He was thinking, Randy has been helpful uncovering serial murder, why send him away?

The three Webbers were conspicuously silent, so I said to Len, "His parents are about to face child welfare charges of neglect and psychological abuse."

Mrs. Webber spoke right up, "*We are not*, you have blown this all out of proportions."

"You come to our house with an order of protection and now accuse us of blowing it out of proportions, what universe are you living in?"

Mrs. Webber was building up a full head of steam to blow a gasket, loudly voice her distain for the fags next door and their evil ways corrupting her son. Mr. Webber spoke in an even tone at normal volume and said, "Muriel be quiet." She looked stunned like he'd slapped her. Then he said, "What's needed for us to get back to ignoring each other?"

I could tell by the way he answered Coy had been waiting for the question when he said, "Start by withdrawing your complaint and take your brood to a family therapist I know. She'll make room for you if Oliver asks."

"What about Rand?"

"He keeps mowing our lawn and studying piano with Carmen. We won't increase his piano lesson fees beyond what we pay for his mowing."

"Rand, what do you with the money they give and all the money I give you?"

"I send it to Ukraine to fight the invaders."

"Damn it, Rand, we've talked about this, your mother has investments in Russia."

Carmen gave me a look that could only be interpreted one way, so I said, "Would the Webbers like to stay for dinner?"

"Oh, no, we couldn't do that," Muriel Webber spit-it-out like a hypersonic rocket.

"I'd like to stay. Carmen is a fantastic cook."

"No, Randolph, you are coming with us, understood?" She said this like it was the law.

Randy looked disappointed and reached for one of Carmen's healthy snacks a few feet away.

Muriel pushed her son's hand away saying, "Behave yourself! We have reservations, you'll ruin your appetite. Why must you constantly drive me to distraction?"

I saw a little boy's expression of despair float on to mid-teen year old Randy's embarrassed face. He became the image of defeat going into complete and total dejection. I thought based on my professional training, that is what hopelessness looks like.

Randy's mother saw it too, modulated her tone slightly, and said, "Randolph, it's for your own good."

"Sure, it is what *you* want. Forget about bratty me, I'm going to live in a group home to show how much you care."

"You weren't bred for such a place. Do you know the music of Ricard Wagner?"

"I've heard you play bits and pieces but didn't really pay attention. Why?"

"When I was in college, I liked him a lot. Maybe I could introduce you to his music, he spoke German and is loved by the German people. His music is where the composers you like came from. What do you think … then can I get a hug?"

"You never wanted to do anything with me before. Do you know Brahms, Beethoven, and Bach?"

"Not as well as Wagner, but I'm willing to learn, maybe you could teach me the 'B' German composers." After saying that the mood between them seemed to shift from combative to shared purpose. An imaginary needle moved to maternal positive filial mother and son collaborative endeavor from child abuse and neglect. They stood. exchanged a hug and looked ready to leave. So, Mr. Webber also stood and looked odd one out, then caught the mood and awkwardly created a group hug.

When the clinch broke heading for the door, Coy handed Mr. Webber the order of protection his wife had tried to poke me with and said, "I'll check with the court tomorrow that this has been withdrawn. If not, we'll file multiple complaints against you with the same court. Nice seeing you again. Bye."

I walked the Webbers to the front door and waved to them on their way next door. The look of anticipation on Randy's face was worth all the bother that put it there. Mothers and sons are entitled to a special bond, and they seemed on their way to forging one.

Chapter 10.

My plan to look at John Doe cases, up to ten years old and statewide proved impossible. If Jane or John Doe did not have a missing person report to link a body or were the victim of an obvious homicide with witnesses, they would be ignored and then callously buried in a hurry when no one was looking. What paperwork I could find, if any, was spotty and a major challenge to get a copy.

Most little towns and villages had miniscule police departments when they existed. Counties had some version of an elected county sheriff with a deputy or two, often working part-time. For the most part the sheriff department's paperwork was shuffled off to other county departments' clerical staff. In rural parts of the State, which comprised most of it, the state police responded to 911 calls. The state police are very good at investigating traffic accidents and doing spot safety stops. Their criminal divisions usually covered several counties with not enough resources. All the above did not want to be bothered with the likes of me and made that abundantly clear on the telephone.

By telephone I did find two victims in Buffalo, New York, that might be relevant. An anonymous hysterical 911 telephone call claimed to have just witnessed a murder. Anonymous complaints are gotten to eventually by the understaffed police. But only after complaints with verifiable names and addresses are checked out. Eventually the police found a badly decomposed, bound with ropes, male nude body in a hot spring.

It took so long to check out the 911 call and find the body, the caller's recorded tape transcript was lost in a paperwork shuffle. At first the medical examiner ruled the case a suspicious death because a rag soaked in an unknown liquid's remains was found tied over the victim's face. Then for reasons unclear, the retired and since deceased medical examiner clearing his desk before retirement ruled the case a suicide.

Six months later another bound male nude body, again with a mysterious cause of death was discovered in the same hot spring. This time was found by hunters. Motion activated cameras were attached to trees around the spring and the mysterious dead bodies stopped showing up.

A year and a half went by before the city found and hired a new coroner. In the meantime, many cases, some high profile, required immediate attention. The built up of waiting autopsy cases used up all available morgue cold storage space and two refrigerated mortuary truck trailers. In order to make room and stop renting trailers, the second bound John Doe and all other John Does were ruled suicide based on the one previous case. The only thing helpful for us was the time frame for these two cases fit between Brett and Nordune.

I also thought I had struck out in Albany, New York until a newbie police clerk not trained yet to give people like me with questions the bum's rush off the phone. She mentioned they might have something, but I would need to come in person to find out what. Learning from Buffalo, I did not wait and phoned the small Westchester County airfield. I had them wheel my Cessna out of the hanger and gas it up ready to fly.

Online I filed a flight plan and reserved a rental car for when I landed. The question of whether to take a gun or not popped up. Since graduating into a new peaceful life, I got used to leaving my guns at home, until recently Coy and I went leather bar hopping. Ah, hell, he would say better safe than sorry. Lucky me, I had a tailwind for the flight and got to Albany in record time.

When I arrived at the Albany police headquarters, the helpful clerk had not survived her probationary employment period. However, to get me out of his face, a bored desk sergeant directed me to see Al, an old cop soon to retire. After forty years doing street patrol, Al currently ran their property room. The sergeant said Al was the precinct's memory and knew every case ever worked during his time. Supposedly, he was more accurate than a dozen filing cabinets.

When I went down to the dusty basement, Al's domain, he was busy checking in evidence from a detective, and a uniformed officer was waiting to see him. Before leaving to grab lunch, I noticed the top third of a half empty hip flask size Jack Daniel's showing in a partially open drawer.

I took a long lunch, figured Al had to eat too. Then I checked my messages, returned some, and stopped at a liquor store on the way back to Al. It was three o'clock by the time I saw Al again. He looked bored, so I said, "Hi, any chance you can spare me a few minutes?"

"Sorry, fella, I don't talk to reporters, it's not good for my pension."

"I'm not a reporter. Here's my card, I'm a psychologist."

"The same applies to egg heads."

"That's too bad I heard a lot about your remarkable memory and was hoping we could share a drink about it." Saying that I pulled a liter size bottle of Jack Daniel's Tennessee whiskey out of a brown paper bag.

"You did come all this way, and I don't suppose you brought glasses. Since that Covid-19 thing I'm not keen passing a bottle back and forth."

The liquor store tried to give me a couple of clear plastic cups with my purchase. With my usual tenacity, I pointed out for the price of a liter size Jack real glass glasses were necessary to properly savor the fine elixir. Then magically they found two new, heavy weight old fashioned crystal glasses to give me free of charge. Good old Al was a man from an era that appreciated hefty lead-crystal glassware over thin flimsy plastic.

As the liter of hooch slowly diminished down our gullets, Al told me a tale that would dress up the last chapter in Jack Warren's book. Less than a year ago a naked teenager walked into the precinct saying he was a party to murder. He was so agitated an ambulance had to be called and the naturalist was supposed to be transported to the Albany State Psychiatric Facility.

For proof the teenage nudist was a kook, a patrol car was sent to the location he mentioned to document his involuntary commitment to a mental hospital. Instead, the police found another naturalist mummified to a chair with duct tape. Almost every inch of the exposed man had been taped to the chair.

Mummification appeared to start with the victims legs taped to the chair legs, then his arms taped to the chair arms. What killed the victim was his mouth and nose were taped close. What would never be known was whether the man's left earlobe was removed before or after his demise.

Following a few minutes searching here and there, Al produced nine color eight by ten photographs of the mummified man. There were three full body shots from different angles. Also, a closeup photo of the victims uncovered genitals, he had just had an ejaculation onto the tape, another closeup photo was of blood seeping out from under left ear tape. These photos definitely looked like proof a serial killer was on our hands.

One photo showed scuff marks the chair made during the victim's death throes, and three closeup photos of discarded adult-size leather clothes and also teenager-size normal cloth garb. DNA evidence identified the clothes to either the mummified victim or the teenage nut the police intended to be sent to hospital.

I asked good old patrolman Al for copies of the photos. He explained copies had to be requested through official channels. As I reached for what was left of Tennessee Whisky, moving ready to leave, Al said, "Sorry, fellow, rules are rules, there are no exceptions."

Ready to leave without the bottle I came in with, I asked, "So how was this case closed? Any chance I can talk to the crazy kid?"

"The naked nut case jumped out of the speeding ambulance on the highway and was hit by six cars before you know, being pronounced dead."

"Any chance you remember his name?"

"Hold on … oh, yeah, Norwood Haverstraw. He was a local boy, born and reared."

"You wouldn't have an address by chance?"

"I can look it up … Here you go."

"Al, this case has to be one of the strangest you've seen."

"No. I got better, but you'd need to bring a bigger bottle of sauce."

"That's a date, but for today how was the mummy case closed?"

"It's still open along with other cold cases not likely to ever get closed."

"I bet it got a lot of attention from the superstitious."

"At that time rumors flew around this place. Some said beware, black leather men means we are dealing with devil worshippers. Others here said it was all just nonsense. Most were skeptical, and you know there are always a few crazies in any group looking for fanciful rubbish. Any who, nothing unnatural happened, that's all I know. Drop by any time it was good to see you."

"Likewise. Thanks for the help and take care."

****

I drank too much alcohol to fly home. I phoned Coy and said unless he felt like a long drive, I would be spending the night in Albany. He was expecting a late night at his office on a problematic case. So, resigned to a night in Albany, I walked over to a not too low-class looking hotel. It was near to the precinct, couldn't be too disreputable. After a shower and sobering nap, it was still early. I located Norwood Haverstraw's address in reference to where I was by rental automobile GPS.

The address Al had given me was for a detached bungalow among rows and rows of look-alike houses. A drab looking, unkempt economy station wagon was parked in the driveway. The name on the mailbox at the curb was Glen Gardner. I pushed the lit buzzer button and after an appropriate pause the door was opened by a youth. He was wearing a three inch plain black leather dog collar and matching jockstrap and nothing more. I asked, "Does Norwood Haverstraw live here?"

The youth's facial expression changed from sunny to stormy and he said, "One moment, sir," and he turned shut the door, but first making sure I saw his perfectly sculped adolescent ass.

I could hear muffled male voices in conversation. One tone was strong and stern, the others sounded wimpy whiny. I imagined they were talking about me standing outside. Then the door was yanked open by a barefoot man about my age, height and a lot more weight. He had a shaved head, chestnut brown eyes, big hooked honker nose, and a full brown shaggy beard. The bear of a man was wearing a black leather vest over a hairy chest, beer belly, and black leather shorts on hairy legs. His big body spent more time working out at the gym than I regularly did.

"Did Norwood Haverstraw live here?"

"He's dead."

"I know, the police told me." The man started to close the door, and I said, "You can talk to me now or when I come back with a search warrant."

Puffing up an over developed chest ready to fight he said, "You are no cop!"

"No. My husband is a lawyer, and we are working on a case Norwood may be related too. What's it going to be, me now or a bunch of hetero cops later?"

"FUCK! Come inside and make it quick." With that said he stuck his head out the door to see if anyone was watching, right, left, and straight ahead.

I entered the living room of a modest three-bedroom bungalow just as four youths around the same age as the one who greeted me at the door scurried out of the room. All four adolescents were dressed the same, wearing only jockstraps and dog collars. The room smelled like teenage boy, bodywash soap, and leather. Startled, without thinking I said, "What's going on here?"

"Is that what you came here about?"

Regaining composure, I handed the man my card and said, "No. Sorry. I'm Oliver Kulgul, what can you tell me about Norwood Haverstraw?"

"He was a confused young submissive who couldn't keep his pronouns in order. He had movie star good looks, a big dick, and mayhem followed him everywhere he went."

I could feel this guy was looking for a fight, and said, "You kick him out?"

"The other kids voted him out. I'm surprised he didn't come back; they usually do after a day or two back on the street. Now he's dead and buried and we'll never know why. That's all I know, and you are ready to go."

Considering how I would handle it if this guy tried to throw me out of his house physically, I stalled for time. Thinking, *I shouldn't have drunk that much alcohol with Al,* I said, "Besides gender confusion, did Norwood have mental illness?"

"What's it to you, bud? He's dead."

If I could keep him talking, I might get useful information. But I was not looking for a fight. "I'm working on a case involving a serial killer who murders BDSM doms while an innocent sub watches." I handed Glen one of Carmen's posters and said, "Norwood called 911 before he showed up naked at the police station. He was agitated and jumped to his death into speeding traffic."

"That sounds like Norwood, he was a performer without a lick of common sense. Are you sure there was a murder? Nobody mentioned murder."

I could feel that got him hooked and said, "After Norwood's accidental death, the police found a murder victim where he said they would."

Looking over Carmen's poster, Glen said, "Holy shit! The police didn't tell this part. Wait a minute, serial killer, we haven't had any unexplained missing people up in these parts that we didn't know about."

He was hooked, now to land him. "If this one fit, two more probable in Buffalo, and five that we know about in the city. There could be more. The murder victims are all classified as John Doe, but don't fit homeless nomenclatures."

"What you are saying is very troubling and the leather community needs to be warned."

Back on track, sounding professional I inquired, "If you don't mind my asking, what kind of facility are you running?"

He looked me up and down deciding whether to try and throw me out. Noticed my shoulder holster under my jacket and said, "These kids are throwaways. They showed up at one of Albany's leather bars offering to sell their asses. We attempt to keep these underage persons safe and prepare them as best we can for a BDSM life. The police look the other way except when they drop off a jailbait leather punk want-to-be."

To keep him talking I said, "Oh, this must be one of those unofficial underground social services that take over when the tax paid public systems don't want to know or care."

"Something like that. The BDSM community has muscle, dentists, physicians, and lawyers. Before one of our throwaways gets too comfortable here, they get free dental work, complete physical checkups, and they're verified not returnable to their biological home after show of force of different kinds. Some people should not breed, know what I mean?"

I felt the information spicket was now open. "What you do sounds expensive."

"Yeah, well, when we need a little extra cash for the boys, a bar will have a raffle. For need of a lot of extra cash, they have a street fair. Beyond that, the mob helps with extreme problems, when asked nicely."

Ah ha, now we had a new player in our case. "Even with the mob from the bar scene involved, I'd imagine, from time to time you still get overloaded. Do you have any other funders, maybe from overseas?"

Glen started getting fidgety. He was obviously having more conversation than he was comfortable with. He took a calming breath and said, "June, Gay Pride month the boys pour in off the farms to party like there's no tomorrow. Then we have to go hat in hand and ask the Church to help us out with overflow beds."

Watching me closely, he saw I saw his silent *but* and said, "We only use the church in serious emergencies they're not too Christian except for those priests who can't keep their hands off our boys."

To get back to what I wanted to know I said, "Up here in Albany, the State Capitol, which is more powerful, the mafia or the Church?"

"You're asking questions you should know better than to ask, no matter where you come from. We're done talking. That's the door you came in."

To deflect the bum's rush, I said, "I'll take it the big problem with the Church is unasked for laying on of hands blessings."

"Listen, it's hard to teach these boys discipline with adults around them who don't follow rules. Like you for instance."

He was moving like we were going to have a throw down. So, I said, "I'm impressed you take the kids development seriously. Most teenagers are in turmoil about following guidelines."

"It's time for you to leave. Don't be impressed, the gay community is as ignorant as straights tolerating leather folks at every age."

He was shifting me toward the front door as I said, "And the religious are equal opportunity exploiters, gay, straight, girl, boy, God's representatives sexually molest all equally. If you want to remain healthy forget the mob and Church were in this conversation."

Clearly, I had overstayed my welcome. "Do you know who Norwood was in contact with just before his death?"

He lunged hands up to grab me. Automatically I did a sidestep. While he was momentarily off balance, I tripped him then pushed him down, hard. Leaping up off the floor, he flew at me. I was not where I had just been. With little movement I was right behind him, and then had him in a sleeper hold. My arm around his neck from behind. "Let me repeat myself, do you know who Norwood was in contact with just before his death?"

His windpipe constricted by my arm, he wheezed out, "No one here could, the boys voted him out … he was killed … let me go."

I lessened the pressure on his neck ever so slightly, and he croaked, "Out on the street, *I already told you.*"

I let him have just a little bit more oxygen and he gasped, "They come back right away with a promise to follow the rules, they are cold and hungry. Norwood never came back. *You are going to be sorry you messed with me.*"

Unintentionally, I had injured Glen Gardener's pride, my bad. I sensed I'd pushed that as far as I should have risked. So, I said, "Never mind, obviously I've come at a bad time. No hard feelings, fella." Then I squeezed the armbar sleeper hold for him to get some rest and he went out unconscious asleep.

If nurtured along, or at least not antagonized further, the place could be a future resource for someone else. But I had just burnt that bridge down. Walking back to my rental car, I reflected on an ominous feeling when handing him Carmen's poster. Could he be mob connected, work for the Church, or was I being paranoid because he thought he could bully me in middle age.

****

Reviving old private investigator habits, I spent the rest of my time at the State Capitol handing out Carmen's poster to bartenders and barbacks working that city's leather bars. As a whole, the upstate BDSM bar workers were friendlier than their downstate cousins. But when all was said and done, the results were the same, a lot of maybe absolutely nothing was for sure. Professionally I was forming an unseen opinion that our murderer's personality, even when present decked out in full leather, did not leave much of an impression on others. Naturally, an opinion, my license, and a two-dollar bill could only buy a little bullshit in today's Albany economy, just like back home.

The last stop in my leather bar trolling was at a tavern named S&M, short for Sid and Murray's place. It was bigger than the previous hyper masculine watering holes visited that night. I would guess in a previous life it had been a horse barn. Entering at the narrow end of a large rectangle there was a bar on either long wall or a narrow stage at the back of the other short wall. Four young, well-built go-go boys gyrated on the small stage at any one time. A quick reconnoiter of the busy bar indicated a short hallway with restrooms on one side of the stage and another longer hallway with doors closed together on the other side.

Standing around, outside the second hallway were easily a dozen males dressed like the gyraters up on stage. A performer would give a sign and be relieved by someone standing around waiting to dance. Then the relieved guy would disappear down the hallway of many doors with a bar patron for fifteen minutes. Since all the dancers were only wearing jock straps, I wondered where they stashed their proceeds from dancing tips and whoring fee.

The differences in jocks could not have been more distinct. It ranged from high gloss black leather to flat-matte black suede, studded with silver or gold or not, they came in every shape and size imaginable. Some guys wore pretend jocks, no strap under each ass cheek to support their nuts. Instead, they had only one thong strap going from the waist band back straight down their ass crack, over their bottom hole, to secure the genital pouch. While others were wearing even less, G-strings with no strap below the waist for any illusion of hernia prevention at all.

Wasting time watching what was not for me, I realized it was time to get out of there. As consciousness from moving, pushed away the stupor, breathing tobacco smoke breath mixed with alcohol breath, the question became, what do I do about the three men cruising me. I was not so zonked as to think they wanted me for sex, which would be an easy brush off. So, I wondered what *was* their game?

I took PI evasive action just outside the bar's front door where people were standing around smoking and talking. Blended in, until I could stealthily maneuver, unseen, to the quiet street and my parked rental car. Found, a nearby dark recessed doorway and I merged with its shadows across the street from my rented wheels.

Sure enough, minutes later the three men in question came around the corner. I could see flashes of reflected streetlight from knives they held openly in hand in a side sweeping motion. They were ready for something sinister. I unholstered my forty calibers, cocked the hammer back and pushed off the trigger safety lock. Since Coy and I started getting serious on our serial killer hunt, he started carrying a gun again, every day. In this situation I had to admit my husband was right, better armed than sorry.

When the three knifers moved several car lengths beyond my vehicle, looking. I stealthily left my hiding place and walked to my car, a half block behind them. At my rental chariot's door, I pressed the ignition key-fob that unlocked and rotated out the side mirrors. When the car made a noise indicating it was ready for me to enter, the men up ahead stopped and looked back around.

In a clear loud voice I said, "You looking for me?"

Three a breast the men turned and came at me knives swishing side to side extended in front of them.

I shouted, "Stop! I'm a peace officer! What's this about?"

They stopped on my command and the middleman said, "You must have pissed somebody off or owe them a lot of money."

"You've got the wrong guy. I don't live around here."

"You're Oliver Kulgul, right, handing out tacky homemade posters cluttering up Albany? Shooting us would be too extreme even for you, we don't carry guns."

Then they moved fast, like synchronized swimmers the three came at me marching in step, now sweeping wider extended knives in front of them. I did not think, self-preservation took over and shot to kill. Just like at the gun range shooting paper targets left to right. The first two men went down with one shot each, eliciting a grunt, thud, pistol report, and then they crumpled. The third man got to almost an arm's length of me when my semiautomatic discharged a second bullet into his body on its own. That second shot obscured any sound he might have made from the first. It's an annoying characteristic of semiautomatics that they sometimes fire a second bullet when only one was requested.

I checked, these three were not going to answer any more of my questions. I knew I did not owe anyone any money and I had been pissing people off since I was a child, but not so much they would want me knifed times three. I liked Carmen's poster and did not consider it tacky, that was not grounds to send a hit team after me.

When nobody showed up after my waiting twenty minutes, it occurred to me I had left copies of Carmen's poster with the police, liquor store, hotel, group home, and in every Albany leather bar. After waiting long enough I concluded there was no gunshot audible alarm in Albany, and the police were not coming for a while. So, discretion won over valor, no matter how over the top the scene before me, and finally I was sober enough to fly out of town.

Chapter 11.

Leaving Albany, New York, the sun was peeking over the eastern horizon, my small plane bucked a stiff headwind, and then ready or not I dealt with heavy rush hour car traffic to work. I just made it to my first class at the medical school on time. Not as prepared as I like, I used a Socratic method and let the students ask me questions for a change and it turned out to be a good class.

During my lunch hour I toiled to make a bushel basket full of emails, and phone messages disappear. It helped me disregard guilt I had overindulged in straight whiskey with Al and the attempt on my life in Albany possibly as a result. Even when I was a hard-working private eye, I didn't chain smoke cigarettes and guzzle whiskey as the image implies. Now as a prestigious university professor it wasn't a good look. One phone message, from someone named Ariana Bruschetti, turned into a game of telephone tag. We finally connected person to person by phone at the end of the day.

Come to find out, she was a police detective just assigned to the truck stop murder. Nevertheless, I was on guard it might also have something to do with three dead men in Albany. I decided not to tell Coy about hit men after me upstate yet. His anxiety on top of mine would be overloaded. I needed to understand what was going on so we could face it with a unified front, not commiserate I *should* know better than overdo it with booze.

Bruschetti wanted to go over my statement at the crime scene and 911 call. I preferred we did it over the telephone to save time on both ends. The matter was settled when she said her boss required us to have an in-person face to face interview at the precinct house. I was familiar with inflexible protocol, and she sounded too new to know her way around it. Then with a sigh of relief I remembered Albany was out of her jurisdiction.

Eventually, we agreed on a time the next morning and I would bring Len along to see the precinct where the stories he was ghost writing were initiated. Less than enthusiastic due to his last brutal encounter with the police, Len had not figured out how to say no to me. Usually, most people do not find me so intimidating unless I am holding a gun. My mother told me to always be nice, and I try when that seems like the best course of action for not working up a sweat and wrinkling my creases.

****

Len and I arrived precisely on time and were told to take a seat and wait. As police officers ambled, walked, and rushed by us, Len's body language grew tighter like a spring about to violently sprung. After fifteen minutes of tightening tension waiting, a tall well put together woman in her forties collected us from the waiting area saying, "I'm detective Bruschetti and you must be Dr. Kulgul and you, Mr. Lym, biographer of great police officers. Nice to meet you both, please follow me." She spoke in a deepish, Lauren Bacall-like breathy voice and moved with authority.

We followed the detective to a drab gray interview room. She was a natural sandy blonde with hair bobbed in back, piercing green eyes, minimal makeup was capped off by a medium shade glossy pink lipstick. The detective wore a honey-colored-silk-blouse, expensive looking denim jeans with a stainless-steel S&W semi-automatic holstered on her right hip, chrome handcuffs hanging in back, and pink running shoes on big feet completed her outfit. I noticed besides running shoes in my size she also had large hands, she kept her nails short, and the nail polish was the same pink shade as her lipstick.

Once we were all seated, the detective read a transcript of my 911 call and my statement to the responding police officers. She then asked, "Is there anything you want to add to what I read?"

"No. That's it."

"How about we stop wasting each other's time and you tell me what the hell's going on?"

"Do I need my lawyer present for this interview? You told me on the phone I wouldn't, now it seems you are accusing me of something."

"I don't think you need a lawyer to answer a few simple questions unless you are involved in the crime. I know of you from an interesting history as told by older colleagues. I'm not accusing you of anything other than forgetting information I need to solve a murder. To be frank, okay, Oliver, I've got nothing to go on with the truck stop murder and your name is also associated with Asa Mulroy's abduction and that associated dead end murder. It's another case that makes no sense and has no clues."

"I'm not sure what's being said about me these days around the precinct house but back in the day when I was running Queer Queries, I provided a lot of on-the-job police officers and retired cops per diem moonlit work. I've always had a good relationship and cooperated with the PD."

"I've heard that, and that's why I need you to help me solve these cases."

"May I call you Ariana? Just so you know, I'm not comfortable being bait if you are going fishing. What makes you think I know more than I said?"

"Under the dead body you brought to our attention, we found male clothing in two different sizes, not sold domestically, and DNA doesn't link either to our database."

"I didn't know that."

"But the black leathers belonged to the dead guy, whoever he was. We have no missing person's report or any other identifiers. We don't know who, or why, the "how" was bizarre, and your housekeeper has a poster of someone I'd like to talk to. Do you understand why you are a person of interest to me?"

"If I'm a person of interest, I want my lawyer present. In the spirit of cooperation, how about Len tells you what little we know about those two murders, until you accuse him of something, and we both stopped talking without lawyers to hold our hands?"

"Clearly, we have gotten off on the wrong foot. There are people around here who hold you in high esteem, and photographs on the wall out there of Jack Warren receiving awards. In that spirit I'll go along with your suggestion, Dr. Kulgul, reserving the right to ask either of you questions with or without your lawyers breathing this room's limited oxygen. Is that acceptable?"

"Len, would you like to tell the nice police lady what little we know about the two murders that interest us all?"

From his body language, Len clearly did not want to speak to the officer or anyone. Nevertheless, he mumbled, "If we're held to only those two murders, we don't know more than you do, officer."

"Without jumping to conclusions are you suggesting there's more than two?"

Len looked over at me wanting permission to tell what we knew. As we'd previously discussed, I nodded my head yes, so Len said, "We think a serial killer has been operating around here for at least five years. It looks like the killer somehow connects with dominant S&M men wearing black leather and scoops up a submissive to witness the killing. Wearing a mask, the murderer has used a different location and method to dispatch each victim. As far as we know, except for Asa Mulroy, the unsuspecting witnesses escaped fearing for their lives and not telling the police."

"Are they trying to get caught? Why have a witness present left alive?"

"We haven't figured that out yet. But no witness has come forward who spoke to cops. Though the killer doesn't look to be trying to be caught as hard as we tried."

"Why have you been withholding this information?"

Len took the challenge, and his journalistic persona showed itself. "The only thing we know for sure is after the fact. What happened to Asa Mulroy in the parking garage, and less about the truck stop killing. Far be it from us to speculate on all the variables and make your difficult job harder."

"That is so kind of you to want to make my job easier. How many dead, unidentified doms are you speculating?"

"Oliver has reason to believe seven or eight. Four or five from Carmen's poster, and two in Buffalo, and one in Albany."

"Damn."

"I'm trying to work in what we know so far from Jack Warren's notes. If I can make connections, the numbers could be higher."

"At what point would you say you're withholding information from the police?"

Looking bullied and not wanting to say, so Len said, "We were not going to bother the police until we had concrete information and provable numbers. Now we are in a Catch-22 you made by calling us."

"How did I do that?"

"If we tried to share what we had, we'd expect to be told not to bother the police without concrete facts. The public knows you're overburdened solving crimes. So, Detective Bruschetti, we are not withholding anything, you called us, and we are not as prepared with facts as we would want to be."

"Quite a good story indeed. Your concern for our workload is touching. The problem is my bosses expect immediate results from me. Most likely failure based on what they gave me to work with. What else do you know that I don't and should?"

"We can only document the killer's collecting left earlobes from Asa Mulroy's case, the truck stop murder, and a mummified case in Albany."

"Now that's something new, tell me more."

Len looked uncomfortable being roughly interrogated, so I spoke up and said, "Someone said, a picture is worth 1,000 words, you can officially request the nine glossy color eight by ten photos of that Albany crime scene."

"That helps me. Thank you."

"Len and I don't know if the Buffalo Police Department has photos of their two hot spring murder victims' ears. The hot springs destroyed much of the body's outsides. You could find out what they have, we can't."

"I only know Jack Warren by reputation, but what you've spelled out so far sounds like one of his famous cases. Before I can go forward with the investigation *you both started*, I need to check with the brass to see if I'm the detective they really want to work with you. With your reputation and what you've done so far, I'd expect the bosses to assign favored detectives to work with you."

"Your frankness is starting to grow on us, Detective Ariana Bruschetti, right, Len?"

"Be careful what you wish for. My partner and I are called the local freak show. That's why we are always assigned unsolvable cases."

"How come we haven't met your partner? I understand how things are supposed to work around here."

"He's out on a different assignment."

"Let me guess, you are only expected to do the paperwork on this case so it can be moved to the cold case pile. And this looks like a case you could sink your teeth into if given a chance."

"Sounds about right, and a good cop wouldn't be so transparent."

"If you think you can work with us, so far we like your honesty, right Len?" He nodded his head yes and I said, "I may have a few strings to pull."

"I'll be honest, what you described looks like a juicy nightmarish case from where I sit, and not like what we are usually assigned. So, you can expect our brass to assign a hot shot or nepotism to question you next."

"But would you work it given a chance?"

"My partner is out finishing another lost cause case as busy work. That's what we get, dead end chores." With a shrug of the shoulders she said, "Thank you for coming in, I'll pass what you said up the line and they'll either bury it or assign it to detectives being groomed for success."

"You didn't answer my question. You up to solving a case like this?"

"Listen, you know a person could build a career on something like you described, even with few breaks. But the powers-that-be around here don't have that in mind for me and my partner. Thanks for the cooperation, I appreciate it, let me show you out."

"Wait up a second, why are you and your partner called freaks?"

"Not that it's any of your business but I'm a transwoman and my partner is a transman. And as good cops as anyone in this building. Yes, of course we'd love to work the cases you described, but I don't believe in Santa Claus anymore."

****

Detective Ariana Bruschetti telephoned my cell the next afternoon to say the police higher ups had assigned her and Detective William Marin to solve my hypothetical serial murders. She was told the prospects of her success were small, but the case handled well could give her career a boost out of her usual sludge assignments.

She and her partner wanted to meet with Carmen and discuss telephone responses to her poster. I relayed the detectives' phone numbers to Carmen and suggested she photocopy her notes. When I returned home from work, Carmen and the detectives were just finishing what looked to be a cordial field visit.

Detective William Marin was maybe five foot eight inches tall, solid 220 pounds of muscle, and bone crushing handshake. William shaved his head, so deep brown eyes peered out of a smooth black coffee complexion over pug nose and full lips. He was wearing a tailored Forrest-green blazer, tan slacks, and dark brown wingtip shoes. I assumed the jacket bulge under the left shoulder was a holstered sidearm. I liked Wiliam right away, he made direct eye contact when he spoke. Smiled, when I met is grip, but in a friendly not challenged way. He gave off a good vibe.

When the cops left, Carmen made me a drink without being asked and said, "They think you had something to do with being assigned this case or rather cases. Did you?"

"I talked it over with Coy and we agreed somebody else's nepotistic wunderkind in our lives could be annoying. Len and I liked these two right off, but not how they were treated by the police department. Coy knew who to call without making a fuss. Carmen, you have endeared trans people to us."

"Remember, trans folks are just like everybody else. We come good, bad, and mostly indifferent. Speaking of that, why didn't you ask what pronouns they prefer?"

"It didn't occur to me. I'm still unlearning passe political correctness from my youth."

All parties accepted that Len was trying to link Jack Warren's old police files with our miscellaneous related murders. Consequently, he reluctantly became our family's point person, and the police granted him a level of cooperation seldom seen. Which was ironic since his beating and Connors death Len wanted as little to do with police officers as possible. Three days after being assigned to the truck stop murder Bruschetti and Marin with Jack Warren's suggestion and then supervision authorization, brought in the FBI to look for possible related serial killings in other states.

They based their request on the photos from Buffalo hot springs murders that were gruesome but not totally inconclusive. Although there were no photos taken of the body possibly related to the murder Brett Franklyn witnessed, one of the responding cop's notes noted a left earlobe was gone and it appeared cut off rather than eaten by rats.

I imagined the FBI on a national level would run into the same photo shyness from dead John Does I ran into trying to expand our little local search statewide. It took them less time than I would have guessed to find twelve more victims with missing left earlobes in states bordering ours, along with Toronto, and Quebec, Canada. Once given a heads up, the Royal Mounted Police produced five more possible one ear lobed missing unsolved dead John Doe doms.

What was maddening about these cases was there was so little to go on or link them. Three were in Toronto and two in Quebec were close but not close enough to a match. Pennsylvania had two in Philadelphia, one in Pittsburgh, two in Scranton, maybe most likely, maybe not. There was even an unlikely case in Vermont, and another one located in New Jersey, all with too little to go on to be a good fit to be our serial killer.

Frustrated, the FBI put together an international task force to capture our serial killer on the loose. It included our state police, surrounding states' troopers, and the Canadian Mounties. The task force put out a scary flyer suggesting going to BDSM bars could be hazardous to the patrons' life expectancy. It was a generic yellow, bureaucratic looking, police advisory poster. It was nothing like Carmen's heart felt sincere warning poster. I heard nothing about my Albany self-defense shooting.

The local police were obliged to continue investigating the murders of local citizens. With added attention Carmen continued to receive calls from her poster. We decided to continue to follow up what we had started in order to see it to a logical conclusion before any required final handoff to the authorities.

With the help of one of Coys paralegals, the Torres family was expedited through the asylum-seeking process and Mr. and Mrs. Torres were given temporary five-year work permits. An investigator working for Coy connected the family with a four-season organic farm in New Jersey. As it happened, the farmer needed farm labor skills the Torres' had.

The farm provided low rent housing for its workers, and they were encouraged to have small truck farms to feed their families beyond damaged produce the farm cannot sell and gives them as a fringe benefit. A big yellow school bus picks up the children in the morning and returns them in the late afternoon. The farmer treated his laborers fairly and in return they worked hard for him.

As part of an earlier arrangement with Coy in return for the work visas, Javier Torres (the truck stop witness) met with the police. He was embarrassed about the gay sex for money, so did not want to but finally said, "A deal is a deal."

Coy set up a meeting for Mr. Torres and Detectives Bruschetti and Marin to tell of his being an uncooperating witness to a murder. The arrangement stipulated Coy would be present during the interview due to Javier 's raw emotions since the murder he witnessed closeup, and fear of authorities.

New information from the meeting was that the murder victim had picked Javier to be solicited to participate and the killer preferred someone else. He surmised the driver wanted a clean real gay person, but the victim had some level of control in the dispute. Otherwise, Mr. Torres said, "I don't know anything. I never saw them before, but thought it was kind one wanted me to get clean. That one said cleanliness was next to godliness. I could hardly stand my strong body odor, but the victim liked it as much as the killer hated it."

Coy discovered from Bruschetti's questions at the interview when panhandling was not enough to feed his family, Javier would sketch tourists on weekends in Central Park with a borrowed sketch pad and pencil. That led to his agreeing to meet with a police sketch artist.

When the police sketch artist completed the memory drawing of the murderer, Mr. Torres said, "That looks a lot like him. But if you give me a piece of drawing paper and a pencil, I can make a better one."

Completed, both the police sketch and Javier 's looked like the same person except the second drawing had quite a noticeable, stand your hair on end demonic expression. Comparing the two drawings Coy said, "You put a blemish on the evil man's left cheek that's not on the police artist's drawing."

"I forgot to tell him, the pencil in my hand remembered. Anyway, that's not a blemish. By blemish you mean like a pimple or something small, right? No, it looked to me more like a dark purple birthmark that goes from cheek, down his neck, to under his shirt collar. I thought that was why he kept putting that stupid mask on."

Coy said you could almost feel an electrical jolt go through the room at hearing the new information revealed flatly. Feeling the air quality change from his words Javier said, "Oh, that reminds me, the bad man walked with a slight limp, like maybe one leg was shorter than the other."

Detective Bruschetti wrote faster than the others in the room, finished writing and said, "Anything else you can think of that would help us get this bastard?"

"No. But if you can keep the sex part out of it, it would mean a lot to me. I'm ashamed I did that. It's not like me to be so desperate. My kids were getting skinny, I was worried for their health."

Placing a comforting hand on Javier's shoulder, and in a reassuring voice, Detective Marin said, "We should be able to redact or obscure that. In any case our notes can only be read by our boss. Don't worry we'll look out for you you've been a great help."

Transcripts from their interview and both drawings netted high praise from their supervisor, Lieutenant Vega. Asa Mulroy identified both drawings as the murderer he saw. The FBI did something it rarely did and complimented the local officers for their diligent police work while the case was ongoing. When no one was looking, Coy snagged photocopies of the police drawings for Carmen to make a revised poster.

Meanwhile on the home front, I noticed no indicators of life, and a for sale sign on the Webber's property next door. When I queried Carmen, she said, "Rumor has it, they are getting a divorce, but it has nothing to do with loud piano playing from over here. The other neighbors' domestic help say Mrs. Webber has been carrying on an affair with her secretary, and the two women want a more permanent living arrangement."

"Do you know what happened to Randy? I've been meaning to ask about him since not seeing him around, and our lawn looks scruffy."

Carmen went on to tell me a reliable rumor had it Randy had been staying with one or the other grandmother for the last two months, and not adapting well. Currently he was being housed by the family court. His parents were duking it out based in friends' abodes. Neither one was paying their mortgage out of spite toward the other, because the downpayment was both their moneys. Those for sale signs are from the bank, and the only available lawn service company does a half-assed job while charging a ridiculous amount.

Speaking right up I said, "God, I hate gossip."

"Its domestic help rumors of the highest quality. Household workers do more than clean, food shop, and cook."

"I've heard the younger ones of both genders spread their legs for the male householders of all ages."

"See, now that's an unreliable rumor. I feel sorry for Randy though, he never received the love and attention every kid deserves. Do you think his parents could turn him into a serial killer? It would really be a shame. Randy, was making such wonderful progress with modern piano pieces."

"Randy, serial killer, I think that's an over estimation. However, my colleagues are split about serial killers. Half believe nurture is responsible, the other half say psychopathology is innate with no exceptions. Then again, they seldom agree on much."

"What do you say, Oliver?"

"Nurture to become a serial killer, nah, that doesn't sound like his wimpy parents. Anyway, I prefer to treat every case as unique, it's simpler that way and makes them all special. Carl Jung wrote, 'No matter your expertise, treat every human as a fellow human.'"

"Understatement or whatever, I hope Randy is going to be all right. I see a lot of untapped good in that boy."

"Carmen, if you did a survey most people would say their parents screwed them up. That's why the Objects Relations people replaced Sigmund Freud with Winnicott's 'Good Enough Mothering.'"

"What's that to do with Randy?"

"If Randy continues to love twelve tone music, he has a readymade 'Good Enough' community willing to accept him. That's an antidote to parental neglect and abuse."

"How's that?"

"Modern music aficionados tend to be intellectuals and intellectuals tend to have a high tolerance for other oddballs."

"As if I didn't already know about odd ducks." She said this with a quirky little smile which seemed to imply I might be a member of the oddity tribe.

"Keep me posted if Randy needs back up with his ongoing family court adventure. I'd hate to see him lost in the juvenal injustice system. That could permanently screw up his future."

****

True to his position as the family's unwilling point person with the police and knowledgeable if unenthusiastic informant, Len facilitated a meeting with Jack Warren at his small apartment. Present were Warren, Bruschetti, Marin, and himself. The on-the-job police brought Jack up to date on recent case developments. Marin and Bruschetti seemed in awe of a department legend in their presence, and Len kept his head down and took notes.

Towards the end of the meeting, Len postulated that he had been working under the assumption that the killer used a different method with each kill. With the new influx of cases from the FBI there were a few cases with similar kill methods. Len wondered if anyone had a new hypothesis.

William Marin, after giving it a thought, said, "From what we have, the methods are similar but not the same. So, your original theory might hold, either way it's bizarre. But with so many unconnected diverse bits and pieces, does it really matter?"

Len said, "I need more details of every kind. Back up what you just said with an example that would help me."

"You know this already." Then Detective Marin went on to explain the suspected case in Toronto had the death blow coming from a hatchet to the front of the head. Whereas in Syracuse the death blow came from a hatchet to the back of the neck.

Another example would be in Asa Mulroy's case, the victim was killed by bullet to the temple and in the suspected case in Philadelphia the murdered man died from a bullet to the cheek. It could be the killer is running out of different methods, close but no cigar. It is doubtful this could be a fruitful line of inquiry with so little to go on.

Watching three people much younger than himself quibbling, Jack Warren said, "Then with so many unconnected bits and pieces of information, which make no sense, if I were you, I wouldn't rule out anything at this stage of your investigation. Don't ask me why, but I still like my original idea the victim chooses his method of death. I just can't prove it yet."

Marin and Bruschetti nodded their heads yes, Len continued to scribble on his fool scrap pad, and Chucho came in to say it was medication and then nap time for Jack.

Chapter 12.

A bug bit Len and it energized him to the point of being manic. It became hard to be around him for more than a minute. After a week of his bizarre frantic energy, I asked for a family meeting to discuss a calmer home life. Len knew the meeting was about his recent behavior and insisted Bruschetti, Marin, and Jack Warren be present for his big reveal.

Coy and I had not seen the detectives in a while, so as much to accommodate Len, they were invited. I reserved a small conference room at the Ivy League university where I taught, and Len was an independent study graduate student. A time all parties could manage was finally agreed to, which turned out to be like herding cats for Chucho. Present at the meeting were Len, Coy, Carmen, me, Ariana Bruschetti, William Marin. And Jack Warren via Zoom with Chucho at his side.

Before I could say anything, Len wasted no time and projected a slide from a PowerPoint presentation he had constructed. He stated, "I know this isn't why we're having this meeting, but it might just break the serial killer case wide open, indulge me. Do any of you recognize this once-a-year publication?" The slide showed a cover of *The Leatherman's in Guide.*

Since nobody did, I asked, "Len, what's going on?"

"You'll see, this next slide shows the preorder form for the periodical. Reservations are now being taken for the next issue." Len went on to show the address was an oscillating website, sometimes in, India, Denmark, England, Philippines, or Finland. The next issue will be published from Holland, using a printer in Belgium, and the publication was printed only in the English and German languages.

Stirring a tad, William said, "Okay, that sounds suspicious unless they're having an identity crisis."

Len kept describing, the next issue would cost $175 a copy. "Last two years it was $125 for a copy, before that it was $95, then $75, and $65 the last year I could find any record. They only print the prepaid number ordered then disappear for a year." He thought business must be good or they are refining their client base by what they are willing to pay.

His body language matching his words, Coy said, "You've piqued my curiosity, how soon do I need to send a check?"

Len said, "The cutoff date for orders is October 15th to have the annual in the customer's hands on October 31st."

Exchanging a quick smile with Coy, I said, "I'll bite too, what do I get for $175?"

"Articles on BDSM life today, fictitious (hopefully) snuff stories, photo spreads, buying and selling slaves for real, and cryptic ads from subscribers."

Looking around the room, William said, "What's this have to do with us, and why does a once-a-year periodical cost so much?"

In command of the meeting, Len said, "Be patient all will be revealed by the end of my slide presentation."

With a wink Coy said, "If you say so. I thought the hay day of magazines was over decades ago."

"When I showed the ad for the periodical to Jack Warren, he somehow got me old copies of several BDSM magazines. Most of them went out of business years ago, not this one."

Not knowing who he was dealing with, and a nod to Coy, William said, "Good man, Jack! What else can you get us?"

"My foot up your ass as you extract yours from your mouth." Without thinking first, Jack said this automatically as if he was back doing his homicide detective job.

Still in charge, Len said, "This third slide is of an ad I found buried in the back with other strange to me ads from that old 2020 issue of *The Leatherman's in Guide*."

The pointed-out ad was in a bold, unusual typeface surrounded by a thick black ink frame. That set it apart from all the borderless ads printed in Currier New or Times New Roman type. Another thing that made it stand out from the other ads was how few words were used.

Still using his boss voice Jack said, "Len read the ad out loud to us."

"Yes, sir detective Warren." Speaking loudly for emphasis Len said, "If you can afford it, we'll make your darkest fantasy a reality. Discretion guaranteed, with irrefutable proof we made it happen. You receive the only existing recording of your unique event for inclusion in your time capsule."

After pausing for the words he read to sink in. Len spoke in his normal voice and said, "An autonomous website address in Staten Island, New York, U.S.A. completed the ad. I found the web address service was only to connect the ad with a $500 application fee for the $50,000 three-day service offered. Am I the only one seeing a possible connection to our murders?" A sharp temperature drop seemed to chill the air as faces around the room looked stunned.

Abruptly realizing I missed a cause and effect, I humbly ask, "Len, is this why you've been so worked up lately?"

"Yes. But reserve judgement whether I've found something significant until you consider all the slides." Then he projected the fourth slide which showed a ten paged application, and a paid receipt for $500 attached.

Astonished, Coy could not hold himself back and loudly expostulated, "Wait a minute! You paid $500 just for an application? Why? You're homeless, where'd you get the money?"

"Jack found it. Take a look at the first page in the box top left. It says, 'The Unique Leatherman's Once in a Lifetime S&M Adventure costs $50,000 in advance for the lucky privileged, selected few.' Down here on the lower right in very small font it says the $500 nonrefundable application is to determine if the dark fantasy is achievable in memorable style and suitable to be recorded for the applicant to keep in their personal time capsule."

My outlook for the meeting shifted noticeably. Enthusiastically I did not care who noticed and said, "Now I'm getting a big hint of what got you excited this week." My attitude about the subject of the meeting shifted from adversary to colluder.

Coy, picking up my bandwidth, said, "You and Jack think this is related to our serial killer how?"

"If you thumb through the application, you see in slides four to eight, there is lots of open space to write out your fantasies and answer long, highly personal questions."

Coy's body language supported what his mouth said, "It's not like any application I've ever seen. 'Preferred method of killing, first, second, third choice.' Damn! Who wants to know that?"

Len postulated, "I suspect it's the way one application is chosen from another, and the fantasy vacation is constructed. But look at these last two slides of check lists. They're all about serious harmful torture, and I highlighted this one, What is your harshest method to snuff out a sub you've decided is not trainable and deserves a bad end?"

What we were thinking was showing on everyone's face. So, I voiced it and said, "Len, you are saying there are people paying $50,000 to be killed in a predictable way of their choosing. How did you fit this together with what we know?"

Without missing a beat Len said, "Oliver, remember Asa Mulroy said the murder victim and perpetrator had an argument, because Asa was supposed to be viciously raped in a moving van? That mattered to the driver, but not the murder victim."

Coy jumped back in, he had caught Len's enthusiasm for solving part of the mystery. "Yes! I thought that strange at the time, but everything about this case is weird."

It was my meeting, I had called it, so I leaped back into the conversation. "Remember when Torres said the Dom with him got turned on by his unwashed stink? His taking a shower was at the other guy's insistence, and they argued about it like it was something important going against a script. I see a pattern."

Looking up from scribbling notes, Detective Bruschetti said with skepticism in her voice, "Hold on a second, boys, you guys are suggesting there are people willing to spend $50,500 to travel to live out a dark sexual fantasy and die by their own design."

Meeting Ariana's eyes with his own, Len said, "They don't expect to be killed. The plan is for them to have a sexual release with a sub they picked out, and then snuff him out afterward. Jack and I think the sex may be optional. Because even strange sex can be purchased anywhere in the world. But the kill is the main taboo part of this rare adventure. That could explain the arguments both Asa and Javier witnessed."

With skepticism gone, Ariana said, "Believable variables … to this unbelievable scheme. Huh, son of a bitch, in a bizarro esoteric way, it's a big game safari to hunt forbidden human quarry wearing black leather."

Jack Warren spoke from the Zoom screen and said, "Except the prey is supposed to be a submissive human not the hunter. I imagine that's an unwelcome and unexpected twist for the murder victim. It certainly has kept us off track until now."

Ariana glancing up from her notes again, looked over to Len and said, "Spoon feed me, I get this application and send all this money, what do I get?"

"I'm just guessing for much of what I am about to tell you. All the victims are from outside our country. They're here on tourist visas. If an application is approved, a means of self-erasing correspondence back and forth between the patsy and perpetrator is employed in cyberspace. They take the time to move at the mark's speed to refine what is required for the patsy to have a perfect dark evil vacation."

Overanxious I said, "Len, cut the background, tell her what she gets for her money."

"After the initial cash outlay of $50,500, all future expenses have been paid forward. Then they are attractively chaperoned at every step, no cash or credit cards sully hands to add to the illusion of royal personhood. The mark is tricked into thinking they're a king or rockstar, not a common knave on an exclusive naughty sex snuff vacation. Think of it, the mark is totally pampered expecting to live out his darkest fantasy, taking another's life, without consequence. It's pure irony." Len said this proudly like a college student answering an unsolvable problem to win praise.

Ariana, scratching her head, said, "It seems complicated, there are so many ways for it to fail. Tell me again how a killer could establish rapport enough to lull a victim to his predetermined choice of death. Spell it out for me … it seems like … such a reach."

"Remember I'm speculating, going simpler is hard with so little to work with. So here goes, the mark is met at the international airport by good-looking black leather clad driver, greeter, and videographer, then treated like royalty. They'd know the mark's likes, dislikes, and wishes in advance from his application and subsequent communications. As requested, the stooge wrote out his vacation fantasies for his killer."

"What a sucker, go on."

Len said, once the mark clears customs, his legit documents are exchanged for a set of phony identity papers as mentioned in previous correspondence. The phony papers encourage the pawn to think they're somebody else. He'll feel safe because, before leaving home the patsy was informed his original documents would be returned just before boarding the plane going back home, nothing to worry about.

His audience captivated, Len continued talking. So far, his story was good, fit what we knew sort of, and he spoke with authority. The next step the mark is taken in grand style, complete with stretch limousine and chauffeur to a boutique hotel favored by the leather-motorcycle crowd. The grandest suite in a place like that would not break the bank but would impress in a grunge way. Then the mark is wined, dined, and given a night tour of the local leather scene. Keeping him busy and video graphed at every step keeps the illusion of celebrity real, and he's never alone to reconsider what he's about to do.

Then next day a different good-looking guide and videographer take the victim on tours of special interest for him. As stated in their application and discussed in correspondence prior to the trip, the tour is custom designed to please the patsy. That night a different attractive leather man tour guide shows up for a second look at bars or clubs of interest

Ariana asked Len, "Where is the killer getting the people he is using to lead the stooge around? I wonder how large a conspiracy we're looking at. Who all could be participating, this is not how serial killers work."

Len answered her with, "I'd guess he or they hire *different* unemployed actor-prostitutes, and videographers conforming to the mark's stated taste. They show up as greeters or tour guides don't know any more than they were told, report what they observed to get paid. So, every word the chump speaks is treated as newsworthy and furthers the illusion he is a very important person. If each piece of the scam is unconnected, it's easy, fast, cheap, and the killer is less likely to be caught.

"Huh. What else do you surmise?" Ariana was scribbling notes at full speed.

Len Lym explained the third and last day of the victim's life. First, he meets the masked man to realize the murderous dark fantasy. The killer shows up for his first face to face meeting with the chump. The killer has field reports and videos since arrival from his per diem paid actors-prostitutes and camera men.

"Go on, Len, this fiction has gotten interesting, based on so little factual information. How do you explain the old Ford van?" William Marin asked this to support his partner.

"Asa recalled an old silver full size Ford cargo van from Oliver probing his blackout, and it showed on the security video."

The old van after the stretch limos is a reality check for what's coming and keeps the sap off balance. It indicates the fantasy phase of the vacation has ended with a search to find the suitable sub supposedly to sacrifice. The van creates a gritty scene to complete the victim's idea of a final dastardly deed. With an unknown twist at the end, or at least that's my guesstimate from what we know.

"Why not stick with the rental limos and skip the grungy old van disrupting the illusion they built?"

"A limo would standout, be noticed out on the kill, and easy to trace and track, one van among many, not so much. Also, the van makes it seem genuinely authentic. It's a sharp contrast to how the mark was treated up to that point and keeps him off balance for introspection, and all the easier to kill."

"You haven't mentioned the sub yet. Most of what we know is from them. What makes no sense to me is 'Why bring a witness to murder?'"

"It's because the submissive doesn't have a clue to what's really going on. Some are picked at random and drugged, and others negotiate a fee for sex. Any vibe they gave off could not be ominous. The sub not knowing what is going on keeps pressure on an already emotionally over stimulated Stooge to prepare himself to kill an innocent. Thus, making him all the easier to murder."

Looking dubious, Coy said, "Now that's quite a tale built from a magazine ad and bits and pieces of files."

"It's only what I could cobble together from unconnected bits from Jack Warren's file and all your collective notes or from Carmen's poster boys. I know it looks like a lot from so little."

"You have built quite an elaborate story from few facts. Then again, this whole nightmare case is circumstantial, I mean other than concrete dead john doe bodies." William said this while getting up and pacing.

"What's bothering you, William?"

"I don't know … for instance on what do you presume they are big breakfast eaters?"

"Oh, that's easy, coroners' reports on our two local victims indicate they had eaten a big breakfast not too long before they were killed."

William wasn't ready to let it go and said, "Do you have proof they stayed at the same hotel?"

"No. What I have is, motorcycle black leather welcoming boutique hotels don't ask a lot of questions or check documents carefully. The best ones, I checked, provide a big elaborate complimentary breakfast to its patrons, it distinguishes one from another."

Ariana jumped in coming to her partner's assistance saying, "If what you surmise is true, why bother with getting phony identifications? Good ones are expensive and not hard to spot. If the mark is to be killed, papers don't matter."

"The first thing I learned when I became homeless was it's hard to keep anything with no safe place to put it. Since ID is essential for services to survive on the street, a cottage industry grew up providing close enough documentation on the cheap."

"But why bother?"

"Correct documentation is vital for international travel. I already said the document change at arrival was a tangible way to manipulate john doe into believing they were living their fantasy. With different identity papers they could imagine having different values and character. To be someone unacceptable back home, a ruthless killer, and to have that they only had to give up the security of their true identity papers in a foreign country."

I sensed the mood in the room shift. Suddenly it felt more inclined to attack Len rather than his hypothetical explanation of events, with so little to go on leading to the killings, so I said, "Whose got a different version they'd like to share with us?"

Carmen, who had been the least animated of the listeners present, looked down at the conference room table and filled the silence with her voice, "If nobody has a better story, what are we going to do with Len's theories? Can everyone please focus, this isn't a game,"

Ariana and William eyed each other then he said, "Good luck getting $50,000 from the police commissioner. He's threatening layoffs again."

Ariana patted William's empty chair for him to sit down then said, "We may be able to prove part of Len's hypothetical."

"How?"

"If they're clearing international airport arrivals there is a record. If their visa expires before they leave, there will be a record of that. If they don't check out of their hotel, or someone else does it for them, there may be records, we can find out."

Sliding into his seat again, Marin said, "That sounds positive like needles in haystacks, ha-ha." Catching a disapproving glance from his partner, he said, "Uh so, this wasn't a complete and total waste of time Ariana found us busy work."

After a long look around the room during the uncomfortable silence, Coy said, "I like hopeful better than positive, but let's not get too ahead of ourselves."

"Yes, Coy, hopefulCoy, hopeful is good." Carmen said this looking maternal.

With his hands folded on the table, Len placidly watched the conversation go around the room. When there was a lull, he said, "Well this went better than I expected."

Coy had been watching me closely and said, "Let's take a week to think about it. Then next week see if there are any other scenarios to explore. Oliver, can we get this room again next week?"

"I don't know about this room, but I can definitely get us a conference room at this university. Coy is your suggestion leather queen avoidance?"

"God forbid, no. I'm being lawyerly. I for one didn't come to this meeting expecting things to move this fast. You know me, time is necessary for complete digestion before I vote for anything."

After the meeting Len reverted to his old way of being around our house. I did not at any point need to bring up his being in hyper drive. My behavior conformed to the theory we are all nuts some of the time, but only a few push the limits often enough to warrant an official mental health diagnosis.

****

One week later I was able to snag a slightly larger conference room on the same floor with better window views of the campus. When everybody invited was present, close to on time, I nodded to Len who said, "Part two, welcome. Who has a variation on last week's theme, please raise your hand to speak."

When nobody raised their hand he said, "Okay. Does anybody have anything at all to say about last week or something new?"

Jack Warren via Zoom said, "I think it's too early in the investigation to remotely consider undercover. Don't."

Ariana Bruschetti glanced around the conference table and said, "Since last week, I wasn't comfortable doing nothing, waiting for more bodies to pile up. William and I got access to international air passenger's arrival immigration forms and crossed check them with expired tourists' visas. We are waiting for conformation from Croatia from a morgue photo we sent of Asa Mulroy's John Doe."

"Do you have any clue who he was?"

"More than likely Mr. Nevin Hojo, local small businessman, age fifty-three, no wife or children, left for a short vacation to New York, and never returned. His current where abouts there, here, and everywhere are unknown according to what we can find out so far."

"Anything on the other guy?"

"It's too early for his paperwork to be processed by Washington. We expect something soon. "

"Is that it?"

"Hope springs eternal, a possible trip to Zagreb, Croatia for one of us would be nice this time of year. I'll send post cards."

"With luck, either Mr. Hojo or the other guy left a computer or correspondence from the killer laying around. Who knows they may have even talked about vacation plans to New York with friends or coworkers. That is the local police working hard for your taxes."

I could gauge the room temperature go into a lull. I was already scheduled for a too busy day and running late for it, so I said, "If there is no new information, all those that favor continuing this independent investigation at a future date raise your hands … and that is unanimous. Jack, do you have a thought to send us on our way?"

Jack moved closer to his computer's camera and said, "What Ariana and William are doing is how I worked cases; slow and steady, keep at that."

That evening after dinner, for I forget why, Coy and Carmen decided to play the Handle organ concertos transcribed for piano four hands Coy and I often played. Oh, I remember, it was about his messing up embellishments. I was out on the deck in our old wooden glider chair ruminating on the masked killer's complex mode of operation. Normally quiet, Coy and I would sit gliding back and forth holding hands. Even after all these years, we enjoy the nonverbal closeness watching the sunset in our old wooden glider chair for two. There was a shared comfort in touching, gliding, and seeing the day turn to night. I missed him while he was with Carmen.

Len came out onto the deck and silently stood by the railing next to the glider.

"It's a nice evening, temperature is just right, and the deep sunset colors are exceptional … Is something on your mind?"

"Oliver, I didn't mention this to the others for fear of adding confusion to an already confused mess of speculation."

"Tell me."

"It's the $50,000. Think about it, that number and the application fee screens out most interested working people looking for this kind of thrill. For the very rich they could almost ask any amount for such a unique esoteric short vacation. Except, the very rich would want to talk with satisfied past customers, do other research, and be missed when murdered away from home. Somebody cleverly figured out an amount, not too much, not too little that could draw lone modestly successful suckers to their death."

"Ugh, Len I wouldn't mention what sounds like 100% complicated speculation. You already have us lost in our imaginations. Wha else is on your mind?"

Making hesitant eye contact, he said, "Okay, first Randy made me feel like I betrayed Conner's memory with that shower stunt. Now it's the police stirring up contradictory emotions in me. They put me in a coma, killed Connor, and currently are helping solve these murders to finish Jack's book."

"I see your dilemma."

"I even like Ariana and William they seem like good people. But I just can't get past it was the police that turned my life upside down. I guess I'm screwed up. I don't know how you put up with me, Oliver?"

"Take ownership, nobody made you feel anything. If you don't like thoughts that led to your feelings, don't let them hang around. As told to you before, I like having you around in my home and office with your East Asian esthetic and added benefit of getting Jack Warren's book published before he passes."

"It's just so upsetting to think, what was, what is, and how little I do about any of it."

"What did I just say? Evict those thoughts without return postage."

****

As time slogged along with no new John Doe bodies attributed to the masked killer, Len got his hands on another old *The Annual in Guide,* then two more issues. Three of the four back issues (counting the one Jack provided first) had the same ad from the killer. The year 2029 didn't run an ad. Thinking about it, given the number of murders we knew about, did it matter if he ran an ad every year?

Ariana sent me a detailed email, the local PD didn't have funds or inclination to send her or William to Croatia, but the FBI had an agent in the neighborhood and would check out Mr. Nevin Hojo's home and associates. In the meantime, our second John Doe was also known as Klaus Walhiemmer of Basel, Switzerland had drawn the attention of Interpol. Interpol had a small but growing file of Europeans who went on vacation to the United States and vanished. However, the powers that be here in our police department decided to keep what they had classified as a local matter, individual, and unrelated go any other murder. It was simpler that way.

Chapter 13.

Carmen received a poster phone call wanting to be anonymous. The caller was from a teenage drag queen student at the Yonkers High School of Fashion Design. With Carmen's motherly relentless persistence, the youth revealed his name, Roger Dunn, was underage, and lives in Yonkers near the New York City boarder line. Roger called Carmen because he saw her latest serial killer poster while cruising in a section of Van Cortland Park in the Bronx. He wasn't sure which police to contact, the Bronx Police, New York City Police, Yonkers Police, New York State Police, or his favorite choice, no police.

Roger saw the poster was in a section of the park where sex goes on after midnight. He was much younger than eighteen and not supposed to be in that part of the park at any time. Except, he looked older and really enjoyed receiving and giving blow jobs while wearing full drag and cosmetics late at night.

The afternoon after seeing Carmen's poster, Roger, a precocious youngster, saw the serial killer from the poster's drawing through a fabric shop front window. That man went into the post office right next to Roger's favorite Yonkers fabrics store.

The boy said he got discounts on material sold at that store. But it could only be used for his dresses and gowns, and in exchange for doing alterations for store customers after school. He boasted on the phone to Carmen of his being an excellent seamstress, and the old queen who owns the store can no longer sew due to arthritic fingers.

Seeing the poster in the Bronx Park on a slow night cruising for sex, then the man again the next day in Yonkers. Being all boy in a dress naturally Roger had to follow the killer into the post office to be sure it was him. The man looked the same as Javier's poster drawings while he checked inside his P.O. Box number 1217. Roger Dunn was a lonely boy, who responded intuitively to Carmen's maternal nurturing powers information collecting.

At the end of the phone call from Roger, Carmen telephoned Ariana with the sighting location. William Marin and Ariana Bruschetti arrested Myron Acker at the main Yonkers post office on their first stake out at that location after Roger's call. Mr. Acker refused to talk other than to ask for a lawyer.

In the meantime, while being held, Myron Acker was picked out of lineups as the murderer by Asa, Brett Franklyn, Nordune, and Javier Torres. Mike Snyder said he had never seen the man before. The security footage of the murder Asa Mulroy had been present for was not a perfect match, but damn close. To cinch the identification, Mr. Acker had a birthmark from his cheek to chest and one foot shorter than the other.

Myron Acker continued to refuse to say anything other than he wanted to talk to his attorneys. Ariana and William obtained a search warrant for Mr. Acker's home. His neighbors claimed he had no friends they ever saw and suspected him of being a recluse. A search of his tiny, tidy studio apartment turned up black motorcycle boots, the left sole an inch thicker than the right, well-worn black leather chaps, black leather jacket, cowboy hat, oversized eyeglasses, and a handmade leather Lone Ranger or Zorro mask. No specific links to any one of the four murders he was accused of were found. Also, no keys to bank safety boxes or storage lockers were uncovered. He did not own a computer, and only ordinary correspondence was found.

Mr. Acker lived simply in a rapidly declining section of Riverdale in the Bronx. He lived on the MTA bus line to and from the Yonkers City line route. Because of his clubfoot he was issued a disabled half fare bus pass. He apparently lived on Supplemental Security Income called SSI, received monthly Food Assistance Stamps, and had a savings bank account in the amount of $239.45. Other than Medicaid, he had no other resources.

The Deacon at Saints Peter and Paul Roman Catholic Church of Riverdale, Ernesto Diaz, was reluctant to speak to the police. He said he was newly assigned to the church. When William brought out his hand cuffs, as if to manacle Diaz for not cooperating, Ernesto said, "Monsignor O'Keith is the only person authorized to supervise Mr. Acker."

"Now you don't want to obstruct this murder investigation, do you?" Officer Marin said this in an officious sounding tone of voice looking grossly serious.

Gulping down anxiety Diaz said, "No. I don't. Please stop waving those handcuffs around. It's, it's annoying."

Ariana let her ignored presence be known by speaking with police authority. "Somebody around here knows when the monsignor will return."

Feeling intimidated from two sides, at his workplace, Ernesto meekly croaked, "Try the rectory secretary."

Putting a reassuring, calming hand on Diaz's arm detective Brucshetti said, "As far as *you* know, what does Mr. Acker do here?"

Based on previous experiences, Deacon Diaz felt sure if he called for help from his offsite church supervisor, about threatening police officers, he'd be told you handle it. So, with reservations showing he said, "Myron sets up and arranges chairs in the church hall for the nine twelve-step meetings held there every week. He also cleans up and, folds and puts away all the chairs each night. Then every morning, he takes the folding chairs out, opens, and arranges them. Oh, Myron serves at Mass if an altar boy or girl doesn't show up."

"How much does that job pay?"

"Mr. Acker is not a church employee, he is given a monthly lunch and carfare stipend, not considered income that would affect his means tested public benefits. Other than that, he's an introspective man who keeps mostly to himself." Ernesto said this through clenched teeth thinking he was about to be arrested and sent to prison for he knew not what. But where he came from you didn't argue with the police and live to tell about it.

****

The arrest and indictment of Myron Acker was what Len needed to complete his last ghostwriting assignment. It solved the last murder case. With Jack Warren's approval the final manuscript was submitted to the publisher. Two weeks later Chucho brought Jack to the publisher, where they met Len and reviewed cover art for the book. Jack and Len finally decided on a book cover design they both liked. As Jack was preparing to leave, he slumped forward, his complexion turning gray. Emergency medical technicians arrived soon after being called but were unable to resuscitate Jack. He was pronounced dead at a nearby hospital after hours trying to revive him.

It was later discovered Jack died from an embolism rather than his many geriatric maladies. In response to Jack's demise, the police department decided to give him a grand send off by breaking out the bagpipes and black and purple bunting. As it happened the mayor was up for reelection and so decided to give Jack a graveside eulogy. If that was not grand enough since Jack had been a marine the Marine Corps was sending an honor guard in full dress uniforms to fire a twenty-one-gun salute over his gravesite.

I did not know Jack well but well enough to know he would not appreciate all the fuss. He was the kind of low-key guy who radiated power through silence, or a haymaker knockout punch to the jaw. That got me thinking about what he told me, due to homophobia as a youngster he was forced to live in the closet for survival's sake. Despite those obstacles, Jack had a full life with acknowledged accomplishments.

It occurred to me that Jack could not object to being outed since he was dead. I would never out a living person, but the dead give up many civil rights. So, I decided to up the ante, it was time to bring him out of the closet. I ordered a large quantity of rainbow flags and bunting to enhance Jack's final send off.

Coy felt as ostentatious as my contribution to Jack's funeral was, it did not quite measure up to bagpipes, the mayor, and the Marine Corps in full dress uniforms firing rifles twenty-one times to scare off evil spirits and playing taps on a bugle. On reflection I realized Coy was right. So, I paid the gay men's chorus to come and sing "Why Me Lord?" by Kris Kristoferson at Jack's gravesite.

"Why Me Lord?" would confuse the hell out of any cop or Marine homophobes staring at rainbow flags and bunting in and among the black and purple. Jack's kids and grandkids gave me permission for the music as dramatic irony. Surely if Jack had a problem with my contribution to his memorial service, he would have sent me a sign from beyond.

I realized some of my reaction or maybe most of my response to ignoring Jack's sexuality was from my disturbing discovery as an adult the attempts to change my favorite American poet Walt Whitman's sexual orientation for heterosexual preference. In elementary school, like my peers nationwide before and after, we memorized Whitman's "O Captain! My Captain!" in honor of slain President Lincoln. To further certify Whitman as the country's first and greatest poet, his book of poetry *Leaves of Grass* was a must read for students.

When the fundamental religious White Christian Nationalists fascists discovered Whitman's love letters to and from his male lover, the Philadelphia trolly driver. They wanted all trace of the letters destroyed and the poet impressively and publicly heterosexualized. In response to the misinformation campaign gay academics brought out Whitman's tantalizing homoerotic poetry and the religious nuts wanted Walt neutered. When the religious crazies could not have Whitman's nuts, then they wanted him erased altogether. With so many shopping centers and villages named after the famous American gay poet the extremists had to seek out weaker victims to bully.

Living in mid-1800s America as an openly gay man, Walt knew how to handle prejudice, he self-published his poetry. During his lifetime Walt most likely had no way to know how heteros were trying to erase homosexual art and history from antiquity going forward. Anyhow, old Walt was too busy nursing injured Civil War soldiers to acknowledge homophobic bigots' futile buzzing around like irritating gnats.

Jack Warren was given a respectful funeral worthy of the hardworking man whose life was dedicated to keeping the public safe. His adult children with their progeny in tow had given permission and thanked Coy and I profusely for showing the world Jack's hidden side.

****

Carmen in her not too often used subtle-assertive way was lobbying for a party to celebrate her poster's success capturing a serial killer. She said, "How many housekeepers in this neighborhood are responsible for capturing a notorious serial killer using a poster and teenage drag queen? I'll tell you, only this one, that's how many, and a party is in order to honor that fact."

Coy voiced a point of view that Myron Acker did not fit any serial killer profile he ever heard of in history. A wake party *was* in order to commiserate Len unsuccessfully defending his master's thesis at orals examination. That was supposed to lead to his graduation and didn't. For my part, I threw cold water on the idea of any party as being too soon after Jack Warren's passing.

Carmen said she could wait, Len was too morose to talk, and Coy said he could feel in his bones the case was not over. In my heart of hearts, I knew we were overdue for a grand party before I was called to task for my recent gunplay in Albany. It was coming just as soon as discovered.

The next thing to happen was a lawyer flew in from Boston named Seymour Pottercrock to represent Myron Acker. Pottercrock was famous as a Harvard criminal law professor who had written twenty-four books on hair splitting legal fine points. In his early days the distinguished university professor had been known to get Boston Irish mob boys off from serious murder charges with a slap on the wrist.

Since teaching at Harvard, his main work has been keeping Catholic priests out of prison for sexually molesting altar boys and girls. Seymour Pottercrock had a reputation for never losing a case no matter how serious the crime and convincing the evidence.

Understaffed and overworked, the District Attorney's office knew it did not have the resources to mount a fight against Pottercrock's delay tactics. Instead, it used an "if you cannot beat them, join them" response. So, the D.A. also tried to drag out going to trial for as long as legally possible.

The judge assigned the case implied the prosecution *and* defense were delaying going to trial in hopes Mr. Acker would be shanked to death in jail. The jail staff reported that was a real possibility since he was friendless, universally disliked, and did not play any games his fellow inmates enjoyed.

****

Carmen put an extra special weeknight meal on the table. She did not have to say she was lobbying for a big celebratory party; her actions said it for her. In contrast Len Lym wore what he was feeling on his face, and it was not party attire. As was my wont I asked, "What's up with you, Len?"

"At the oral defense of my thesis, two of the four graduate committee members returned my work unsigned off on. At the last minute, they require a different ending, which was supposed to be decided before. I'm glad Jack isn't here to put up with this bullshit."

"What's their problem?"

Begrudgingly, Len spoke his defeat and anger in a half tone voice. "Except for the last serial case, all the others ended with a conviction and prison sentence. As things stand right now, it will be a long time if ever before that could happen, for Myron Acker."

Coy looked sympathetic and said, "Something about that damn BDSM case has stuck in my craw too. Len, how about we go see if the Monsignor O'Keith is back from vacation and if he is, talk to him."

Trying to be funny I said, "If you are going to ruin Carmen's party planning, I want to know why."

"Not ruin, postpone, to make legitimate if you must know."

"Why?"

"Because Acker doesn't appear smart enough to be an international serial killer mastermind. The guy's barely literate. Despite concrete evidence the pieces don't add up. Who is paying for one of the most expensive lawyers in the country to get him off? Our boy Myron doesn't have those kinds of bucks that we know about."

Throwing an arm over Coy's shoulder I said, "If no one objects, I'd like to tag along with you and Len. I love a mystery." What I did not say but thought was *I need distraction from worrying about Albany mob hitmen with knives.*

"Oliver, the more the merrier." My man said this tickling me under my arm.

****

The secretary at Saints Peter and Paul Church rectory gave Len an appointment time we all could manage. At eleven thirty AM, Monsignor Thomas O'Keith smelled like he'd ingested a lot more alcohol than ceremonial wine delivered for breakfast Mass. He was at a florid level of intoxication greeting us haughtily in what once was the church pastor's large office, and said, "What is it you men seek from me?"

I knew he'd most likely either get very drowsy or belligerent, so I said, "What can your eminence tell us about Mr. Myron Acker's academic background?"

"I don't know who that is. Why are you bothering me with such trite hokum?"

Coy, no longer with the police, lost his tolerance for being lied to his face and said, "He's the man you supervise unfolding and refolding chairs for twelve step meetings."

I could see Monsignor Thomas O'Keith had reached a juncture in our interaction, use his lofty position to order us out of his office for catching him in a lie, or drowsily slouch into an alcohol driven nap. Just then his eyes closed involuntarily, and he began to snore softly sitting up at his desk facing me.

Quietly, not to disturb the sleeping man, I and my companions left the office and went in search of the rectory secretary. When found again, where we had left her at the rectory entrance, she apologized saying, "Sometimes the Monsignor's behavior is intolerable. Let me see if Deacon Diaz is busy." With that said, after pushing a button she spoke softly into an intercom on her desk. Then made eye contact and pointed down the hall waving to the left.

Mr. Ernesto Diaz's office was small but adequate for four full-size adults. He gave each of us a firm handshake and said, "The police have already been here, and Mr. Acker is in jail."

Since I'd invited myself along, I spoke right up, "We wonder if you might help us."

"Call me Nesto, everyone does" Then he silently shook his head no, as we relayed our encounter with the Monsignor. He finally said, "I doubt I can be of much help, but promise not to fall asleep. What do you want to know?"

Halfheartedly Len asked, "How long has Mr. Acker worked for this church?"

"Let's see, I've been here less than a year, he was on the job when I arrived. Hold on, let me look that up." Saying that, Ernesto got busy clicking away on his desk computer's keyboard. "It says he's not an employee, he receives a stipend for five years, and before that eight at Saint Pats. He must have done something bad to get demoted from midtown Manhattan to up here in the Bronx."

"How long has the Monsignor been here?" Len asked this keeping us on track with why we came.

"It might be faster for you if I just tell you what little I know about Saints Pete and Paul and those two gents."

"Sounds like a plan."

"This fancy Riverdale neighborhood started to fall into decline with the church following right behind about nine years ago. Then about five years ago, the big shot Cardinal in Manhattan stopped trying to save Peter and Paul's. The church secretary, Mrs. Hollihan, is the last of the workers who remembers when this church was a viable part of an elegant thriving, wealthy Bronx community. Myron Acker was transferred here when the archdiocese gave up on saving this church."

So, they did not think I was sleeping too, I asked, "Nesto, do you know why Acker was transferred here?"

"Not a clue. This was said on guard, ready to hold back.

I could see from Deacon Diaz's response he was weighing just how much to tell us. "We could research what we need to know online or you could save us the time and answer a few more questions and forever be in your debt." First the Catholic School had to close for lack of pupils who could afford the tuition. Then there was no need for the convent. Someone at archdiocese level sold those properties right away, almost as if they had buyers waiting. The school is now a rental storage locker independent business, and the convent was converted by the Protestant Community Charity Society to a nonsectarian home for unwed mothers willing to give away their babies. Then Monsignor O'Keith was sent here two years ago to close the church, and formally di-sanctify it. In its next incarnation it will be a warehouse for imported African artifact replica plastic trinkets.

"How long have you been here, Nesto?"

"Less than a year since the archdiocese found the monsignor's alcohol abuse impairs completion of the Di Sanctify assignment."

Coy spoke to himself mostly. "How hard can it be to go out of business in a failing Bronx neighborhood?"

To take over the narrative Ernesto said, "If I was left alone to do it, a couple of days. But someone high up in Rome keeps throwing stumbling blocks in the way, always at the last minute. While here in New York the Cardinal and a few of his higher ups are in a hurry to see Pete and Paul sold."

"That sounds enigmatic even for the Catholic Church." No one ever accused me of keeping my opinions to myself.

"If that's not enough trying to find new homes for *NINE* distinct twelve-step meetings at different times every week, and *they must be conveniently located geographically near the old meeting place* is no small feat."

"You have my sympathy." I said this to keep his frustrations talking.

"Oh, good, thank you. Then there is trying to keep the monsignor out of the drunk tank and in court when the court wishes. Just because his license was permanently suspended *for life* and *car impounded*, doesn't deter him from driving in traffic. He radically maneuvers in and out of traffic flow in vehicles borrowed without owner's permission, while severely impaired by alcohol."

Now his work frustrations were threatening to shut down his information flow, so I said, "Your job sounds like the story of Job in the Bible. Tell us more about it."

"Okay so, finally, his holiness the Cardinal needs Myron Acker's services here and there and everywhere from time to time, but not too often. and that means I must do his duties as well as my own without advanced notice and for how long. Got the picture, chaos without warning but only often enough to be disruptive. Have you heard enough of my trials and tribulations?"

Coy arched his eyebrows at hearing O'Keith was still driving while drunk and said, "Not quite, would you say the archdiocese is helping or hindering closing this church?"

Looking at Coy with renewed interest Deacon Diaz said, "I regularly ask myself that same question. The answer always comes up BOTH. Someone downtown had to know O'Keith was not able to do the job when they assigned him. He didn't start drinking at Peter and Paul, he had years of practice. To me it often feels like a secret tug of war between strong forces at the archdiocese and the Vatican."

"Oh, my you have our sympathy."

Appreciating having his toils and troubles heard the Deacon not even a priest seemed to let down is guard and relax saying, "Then for background, do you want to hear a little relevant gossip?"

"Of course."

"Supposedly, there is something funny going on with the money from selling church real estate region wide. Rumor has it there are several surreptitious clerical investigations going on around Pete and Paul. I've heard from a good source at least one of them is from Rome. Oh dear, I wonder have I said too much?"

"No, not at all Nesto, but do you know why we are here?" I said this to bring the conversation back on track.

Probably feeling lighter after having just vented his spleen Ernesto said, "You don't think Myron Acker is a serial killer. Guess what, neither do the DA investigators who keep coming around e. I could testify he doesn't have the smarts for it."

Scribbling notes without looking up Len asked, "Why do you say that?"

Looking from me to Coy the Deacon said, "God forgive me for saying this, but old Myron is barely dull normal. Serial killers are supposed to be intelligent. I've heard that's how they get away with their crimes for a long time."

"And yet, four eyewitnesses picked him out of a line up, there is video security footage showing him doing murder, and articles of clothing in is apartment support the video and eyewitness statements." I felt we'd gotten what we'd come for and needed an ending.

Clearly the good Deacon was not ready to say goodbye now he'd open up to us. His new friends at a lonely job. "If I don't write out detailed step by step instructions, Myron will screw up even a simple job. I swear the man has so little memory he'd forget his head if it weren't sewed on."

Obviously, Len was not ready to leave when he said, "Nesto, how do you explain all the evidence against him?"

Encouraged to keep going Ernesto pontificated, "Either he has a smart identical twin nobody knows about, or he's got somebody pulling his strings micromanaging his behavior like the secretary and I do for him here on the job here."

Coy watched our verbal exchange as a bemused expression flitted across his face and he said, "You'd know about puppet masters and such things, right?"

Pausing to think first, Ernesto said, "Not necessarily. If he had been born in an unwed teen mother's home like our old convent is today, they separate twins and send them to different families. I know nothing about puppetry using people, it doesn't sound like a good thing."

Like a dog with a new bone, Coy persisted, "Deacon, do *you know* about BDSM in black leather? I've heard many of the religious are practitioners.'"

"It's consensual sex, like play acting, or psychological psychodrama, or role playing. Those who do it, love it, but not my idea of fun sex. Then again, I'm celibate and without experience, no judgement."

Coy had to let it go, instead he said, "It's not my idea of fun, but lately, I think about what they do a lot."

Shifting to his minor cleric role the Deacon said, "When thoughts like that come to me, I give them up to God. What about them bothers you?"

"Giving total power over to another person is not normal for me." Saying that Coy gave me a wink.

Coy had hit a nerve with the lesser church man who said, "I respectfully disagree with your imaginings. To make a submissive feel safe, secure, and cared for in a BDSM relationship, much self-sacrifice and testing are required of the dominant to prove trustworthiness for the sub. To reach that level of deep intimacy both dom and sub mutually agree on the limits and respect them. Then the sub is affectionately rewarded for expanding those limits."

"And you know this how?"

"I have my ways."

Put in his place Coy meekly asked, "Do you think it possible for a BDSM scene to go wrong and be lethal?"

A little too quick with an answer Ernesto said, "I've read an unschooled unsocialized submissive picking an unsuitable unwilling playmate who takes murderess offense at being manipulated, sure it could become lethal, or thrilling beyond imagining."

Keeping at it, Coy asked, "Do you think Myron could have that kind of sex life? He didn't take a vow of celibacy to be a handyman."

Reverting to his chosen role as a minor religious practitioner Daiz said, "What's your opinion about that?"

Coy the ex-cop was ready and replied, "We're human beings and biology is a powerful force. For some stronger than willpower."

"Good answer." It was said like a churchman trained to be a teacher.

"Is celibacy a problem around here, along with the obvious alcohol abuse, and accused murder?" Coy would not let go of his bone chewing.

Apparently, Deacon Diaz had decided to stand toe to toe with Coy and explained, "Every year the Church loses a few from religious life. I hear it was a lot from Peter and Paul's when we had the convent here."

"Hmm, that's interesting."

"Not really, those that quit for a sex life are not a problem. They took a vow, it didn't work, they moved on, no hurt no foul, and they can keep their church pension. The Church sees that as transitions. Celibacy is not for everyone, especially if the vow was taken young."

Looking surprised Coy said, "Now that sounds mature."

The Deacon was bonding with my husband like he didn't get enough meaningful socializing, and said, "Women and men who think they can live two separate and distinct lives causes the Church big problems. And at a time, fewer and fewer are choosing a religious life over a secular one."

Coy on topic said, "Really, that's the Church's biggest problem these days?"

Huh, they were bonding toward friendship, the Deacon said, "No, situational pedophilia is bankrupting the Church. It spends considerable resources to screen out pedophiles from entering the seminary. It is those trying to live a double life who lose their moral compass and possibly their soul intent on being someone else, other than who they are. They rack up tremendous legal bills."

What he said sounded familiar. Looking for new insights, I couldn't hold back from having a new friend too and asked, "How would *you* fix it?"

Ernesto seemed happy to tell us. "Let women become priests and all priests marry whoever they love almost as much as they love God. It's an easy quick fix for a huge problem, which will never happen."

Coy was back saying, "Makes sense, why not?"

Deacon Diaz was more than happy to edify us, "Relinquishing power is an alien concept for very old men who have a short time to be alive in beautiful Rome as princes of the Church."

Taking charge Len said, "Change of subject, if Myron's fancy swanky lawyer gets him out of jail, will you welcome him back to work?" He apparently got a different answer than expected based on facial reactions.

Our friend the Deacon said, "Of course, this is the United States of America, he's innocent until proven guilty. Not guilty he can set up and break down chairs."

I'd heard enough. "I for one have a long busy day ahead and must rush off. I don't know about my friends. Thank you for your time and insights." As I got up to leave and shook Mr. Ernesto Diaz's hand, my housemates did the same and we left together.

****

Dr. Jacoby, working behind the scenes, twisted arms. He was able to convince the last two graduate committee members to sign off on Len Lym's master's thesis, after their vociferous refusals. He convinced them the oral defense went as perfectly as adversaries ever did and the student had no control when or even if the latest case would come to fruition. Len *had completed* his task as it was initially refined by the committee, they were guilty of changing conditions too late to count. But of course wouldn't admit the later part.

Around the time Jack's tome was completed and accepted by the publisher, he changed his will to include Len his ghostwriter. Len had thought he would get Jack's old classic car and fifty percent of the book profits. At the reading of the will, Len found he was included along with Jack's children in sharing his entire estate. Which included most of Jack's husband's estate, which was considerable.

Unexpectedly a moderately wealthy college graduate, Len still decided to stay with us rather than live alone and lonely for the time being. He insisted on being allowed to pay for his room and board. We left it up to Carmen and Len to decide on the matter. Together they chose small esoteric trans or gay charities for him to give a monthly charitable contribution, and Carmen took him shopping for a new wardrobe.

****

After two uneventful months, life went on as usual. Myron Acker's case had not progressed beyond distant court dates regularly postponed at the last minute. Furthermore, we still had not had a celebration party or plans to celebrate Len's graduation. Sitting down to a pleasant weeknight meal of home-corned beef brisket, cabbage, and mixed root vegetables, Coy said, "Guess who called me out of the blue today?"

"I give."

"Randy Webber. He's in a fix again."

Not welcoming a dinner conversation digression during a luscious meal, I dutifully asked, "What's he need a lawyer for?"

"His grandmas couldn't keep up with him. So, the family court adjudicated him PINS, a person in need of supervision. You'll never guess where they sent him."

I wondered if Coy was ingesting too much caffeine. "Then husband, tell me."

"Supposedly the only placement that could be found was at Cardinal Tommy Diddlysquat Group Home on Staten Island. Randy says the home is fifteen dormitories of twenty boys each. The residents' ages are twelve to eighteen, sleeping in huge unheated rooms. He said violent boys' prey on the weak of every size."

A sad remembrance popped up from long ago, when I worked as a parole officer, *That place was always a scandal of unreported abuse from neglect.*

Coy was on a mission and said, "Randy says on a resident's eighteenth birthday he's given a one-dollar bill, a sugar cookie, and a single use Metro card, along with a happy birthday referral letter and address to the nearest homeless adult men's shelter."

To share in my man's enthusiasm, I swallowed my wish for a pleasant meal and said, "All these years later, sad to say, nothing changed except the name of that soulless place. Many of my parolees claimed their life of crime started there."

"Why can't it be reformed?" Len said this knowing his naivety was showing.

Without forethought the answer to his question escaped my mouth before a fork full of food could stop it. "At election time the candidates promise reform, then forget after the voting is over. What does Randy want you to do, Coy?"

"To help him escape a fate worse than death and come help Carmen, mow our lawn, and live here with us. He was pitiful on the phone." Coy said this with his caring peeking out from behind his words.

With my empty hand gesture asking for more information I said, "Randy. Pitiful?"

"Like he's terrified for his life. But he didn't say that. Rather, my words, he sounded emptied of a will to live." I could tell my man had been moved.

Trying to deflect from where this was going, had gone, I said, "Where are his lovely rich parents during his hour of need? His parents who hate us for playing the piano."

"Oliver, be nice. You like Randy. At present, his father lives in Singapore now and his mother in Krakow and apparently, they have trouble remembering they had a kid."

Looking for an ally I asked, "Len what do you think?"

He surprised me sincerely saying, "I'm willing to find another place to stay for the kid's safety. It wasn't that long ago I was homeless. It is a terrifying anchorless existence. But I will miss piano four hands with Carmen and these great meals with both you kind kibitzing gentlemen."

I was on my own, and it was true, *I did like Randy,* and contradictions come with graduate degrees for me. "You've been through a lot, Len. Why should you have to make sacrifices just when your life has gotten stable?"

His sincerity showing Len said, "Randy is no fighter. The adult shelters are hellish, I can only imagine what fears he's going through."

He'd given me a way to save face. "Len, if we all agree to rescue him, do you think you could keep his underage lust under your control?"

"Oliver, before I had nothing to lose. Now, thanks to Jack's jack I don't want to lose my future for a little slap and tickle meaningless, underage sex."

"Carmen, come in here, we are taking a house vote on more work for you. All those in favor of offering Randy sanctuary from Cardinal Diddlysquat Group Home raise your hand ..."

"That settles it, in the future we'll need another place setting at dinner. Coy, how long will it take to get him through the formalities?"

"Let's see, a little bribery, a few threats, prayers to the Virgin, I'd estimate tomorrow this time should be about right."

"That's my man hard at work, with the Virgin's help."

****

As Coy forecasted, using extra procedural methods, Randy came to live with us the next night. Through hook and by crook Coy had gotten us listed as a one-time emergency teen foster home for a special needs teenager. He used my credentials to receive the special exemptions from years-worth of bureaucratic forms, interviews, home visits, and years of red tape bumbling.

Chapter 14.

When Randy arrived to live with us, he looked like an abused wet dog cowering with his tail between his legs. He had lost the sparkle in his eye, was nothing more than skin and bone with a frozen besieged, dismal facial expression. The soul crushed look in his eyes was that of a pardoned man moments before his execution. He was nothing like the mischievous teen we had once known. Carmen immediately set to rebuilding self-esteem with small chores and fattening him up with his favorite snacks as rewards.

After dinner, the first week of our new housemate's rescue from the Catholic Group Home, Len and Randy spent up to bedtime talking seriously out on the back deck. Coy, Carmen, and I left the young ones to commiserate undisturbed while we read or watched one or another streaming movie classic.

By the end of the second week, having reached his well-meaning amateur level psychotherapist saturation point, Len suggested once a week Randy could clean and dust my office in exchange for a little *real* professional psychotherapy on the side. Instead, I called in a favor, making a referral to a colleague-friend who worked exclusively with teenagers with problems outside the normal orbit.

Shooting hoops before dinner at the end of our fourth week with Randy in residence, the boy stumbled into Coy. He fell and badly scraped-bruised both his knees. Propping him up, Coy half carried him inside the house for first aid.

Len and I continued to play one on one basketball until he said, "I feel a need to unload on you a confidence I swore not to share. I feel stuck in a quandary about it."

"Tell me about the quandary without revealing the confidence."

"Let's say, hypothetically, something so bad happened to a friend of mine he's thinking about committing suicide."

"Get him to a shrink."

"He already has a therapist but won't talk about an emasculation issue that he believes ruined any future he can have."

"Don't journalists have a code of ethics that includes if they find out a person is contemplating harming themselves or others, they are required to report it to the authorities?"

"We do, but at the expense of betraying a friend's confidence. A friend emotionally hanging by a thread already. Does your hypothetical friend have means and opportunity?"

"Yes."

"Why does Randy want to kill himself and not tell his therapist?"

Len said Randy was repeatedly raped at Cardinal Tommy Diddlysquat Group Home, and witnessed other boys raped before and after his turn. Then after the assaults victims were told they can never be real men, only substitutes for women.

"Now Randy is too ashamed to tell his therapist. He likes the man like a father and does not want to spread his disappointment of a bleak future. Randy felt he already failed his parents, teachers, and Len with that shower incident."

I suggested for the time being we all be very vigilant and not leave Randy alone, and I would have an off the cuff chat with my friend, his therapist. Once we felt Randy was safe, I would ask Coy to take a hard look at this group home with me to see why the staff was not intervening.

Looking relieved, Len said, "If you plan to kick ass, count me in. I survived the men's shelter system using the martial arts moves I learned as a kid. I had a lot of practice before being invited to live here."

"Before we let things get physical, let's use our educations to see what we can see."

****

The problem was greater than we all suspected. Randy had already tied a noose and was only waiting for all of us to be out of the house to kill himself in the garage. In the nick of time my colleague got the teen to reveal his plan to end his life.

He talked Randy into voluntarily agreeing to spend a short time in a private psychiatric hospital. Randy agreed only if we would visit him regularly so he could know we hadn't abandoned him. We all went as a family unit, with a picnic, every weekend, rain, or shine, and convinced him he was valued by us.

In the meantime, with the help of state legislator acquaintances. I instigated a case-by-case review of the group home's professional adherence to the state's mandated nutrition, health, clothing, staffing, and record keeping. The home was deficient on all counts, and Medicaid started an investigation into fraud. Apparently, they were using a post-truth recordkeeping method popular with a disgraced American reoccurring President they idealized.

The reasons the home got away with wrongdoing for so long was they were the only placement for hard-to-house older male teens, and the wilds of Staten Island was an inconvenient location for monitoring. The States Department of Education suspended the homes' license pending further investigation.

Then the State put in place monitors until all their recommendations were completed and then would require new monitors be assigned after the mandated corrections were carried out and boys allowed back. The archdiocese decided to fight the State Education Department over the loss of its cash cow.

On his own Len started research for a three-part national magazine exposé. With little effort he found homeless young witnesses hustling on the street willing to talk for a warm meal. They reported overcrowding, intimidation, extortion, police and nonpolice involved violence, unreported ongoing sex abuse, and unexplained deaths as regular events at the Diddlysquat Group Home.

My review of the group home uncovered more and more noncompliance, and Coy's team started talking impaneling a grand jury. The Cardinal himself yanked strings and the pushback against our simple inquiry without a plan zoomed vertical.

We should have known it is what happens with interference in the flow of a lot of money intended for the poor but first go to wealthy pockets for skimming. Unexpectedly, the city's Child Welfare Agency's appointed chief administrator came out on the same side as the bad guys, and their group home from hell. Child Welfare had not developed any other place to put difficult teenage boys and enjoyed quiet under the table cash for resupplying aged out residents.

Right on cue parish priests stirred up their congregations' weekly sermons with misinformation that the Catholic Church was under attack by Godless queers attacking the most pious Catholic group homes and its work for Father, Son, and Holy Ghost. Monsignors descended on City Hall every other day and twice on Thursdays; Bishops were swiftly deployed to the State Capitol one after another to continuously disrupt legislative schedules. The Cardinal himself, with all his grand pomp, went to Washington D.C. to lobby the president.

Ultimately, all New York Roman Catholic clergy were directed to work toward the Cardinal Tommy Group Home be restored to its previous funding levels, census, and operation method, without outside interference. To make sure the message was heard in high places, the Church's highest paid lobbyists descended on Congress in mass to twist arms to go against the local and State agencies charged with enforcing rules, regulations, and bringing the group home into compliance.

Cynically, the reaction to our humble inquiries was so grossly mismatched it brought to mind hunting hummingbirds with howitzers. The Church trained all their big guns, top to bottom, on needy elected officials hungry for campaign contributions and votes. While all our probes were with regular civil servants, not dependent on elections or public opinion to keep their jobs by enforcing legislative mandates.

The tabloids love exposes, and the grownups' news media was obliged to tell all sides of the story. Talk radio and cable TV news pundits spun the story of overcrowding, coercion, fraud, and regular repeated sexual abuse to fit their usual particular political position about what is right and wrong with the world in general, the United States, and local politics in particular. For once both sides of the partisan media came out on the same side against an unnamed big greedy bully, the Church.

Commercial-free nonprofit community media discovered and made an expose of when Tommy Diddlysquat was first assigned Cardinal of the New York Archdiocese he tried to change the names of everything to his name. He thought that was one of the perks of the job. Then alms parishioners revolted and demanded the original names be brought back. Except for Saint Augustine Group Home which remained the Cardinal Tommy Diddlysquat Group Home since the residents and staff had no voice to protest the new name in the wilds of Staten Island

The deeper Len dug, the more dirt he uncovered, like the archdiocese's involvement with the home was not just from afar. Initially, it was said they only managed money coming in from different funding streams and then made operating expense outlays. In truth they had their hands and fingers in most day-to-day operating decisions. For example, how often the boys could change their bed linens and underwear.

Len discovered with the generous private and public charities funding the Group Home the boys should have been royally pampered rather than eating Oliver Twist's mid-1800s watery gruel. What especially did not make sense to Len was why so much of the public taxpayer money intended for boys' care and feeding was mysteriously being directed to places other than the Home. Deeper digging found much of the money ultimately went to certain select African countries, antigay religious-political organizations, yet the why could not be explained with believable facts.

Over dinner one evening Len said, "The three articles I contracted to write about the Cardinal Diddlysquat Home could easily turn into another book. If only I could find out what's really going on. I already learned the African connection to the home's money isn't sanctioned by the Vatican and is causing no end of internal controversy they won't talk about."

Contemplating a class action lawsuit, by court order, Coy obtained copies of the home's logbooks. Looking them over he decided his team needed to explore in detail the strange anomalies between Group Home's reports of accidents and the hospital's version of the same events.

An example of a logbook anomaly, on such and such a date the Diddlysquat Home reported resident X had slight bleeding and was sent to the hospital by ambulance after being injured playing soccer. On the same date the hospital record showed a patient with the same name and address was brought to the hospital by ambulance from Tommy Diddlysquat Group home hemorrhaging a lot of blood.

The patient required sutures to close internal anus tears. It was determined the boy's injuries could only be caused by violent unlubricated rape, and not from normal anal fissures occurring from defecation. Surgery under general anesthesia had to be performed to stop the excessive bleeding and prevent sanguinarine.

The hospital social worker's notes asked how the boy could have sustained internal anus injuries playing soccer, when the Home did not have a soccer field. When no believable answer was given, the social worker telephoned the home's administrator. The administrator acknowledged awareness of the soccer injury but refused to give any answer as to where, how, or why. However, he was adamant the Home had a budget line for a soccer field, only funding had not yet been secured due to other priorities.

As required of all mandated reporters, the hospital social worker reported the incident of apparent child sex abuse to the State hot line designated for such matters. One week later the social worker was telephoned and told by someone claiming to be an Albany hot line administrator to fill in the soccer accident location as *unknown.*

When the administrator was queried by the social worker, she was told the usual rules did not apply for Catholic group homes since they had special papal dispensation covered under papal infallibility and the Vatican was a sovereign country. The phone conversation ended when the administrator said, "Lowly social worker, you are not empowered to engage in international relations. For God's sake know your place, woman. At best females are second class beings in the Bible."

For expediency's sake, searching for the serial killer and free labor with inside information, Coy assented for Len to accompany his investigators on interviews of ex-group home residents. Those who had aged out of their eligibility and were now residents of the adult homeless shelter system. Len knew how the homeless shelters operated. He had lived there and was close to the interviewees' age up and down. In addition, thanks to Randy, Len was knowledgeable of the group home's rape parties involving residents. Accordingly, the interviewees were not rats for divulging forbidden secrets to an outsider.

Len felt a connection between Myron Acker and the Cardinal was just beyond his grasp as he pursued an unlikely avenue. He made a conscious choice to follow the less likely thread than the obvious one laid out frustrating the police.

It was a surprise to hear a hush hush hint of a rumor. Cardinal Tommy his holiness himself on occasions was present to watch certain high holiday rape parties. Apparently even virulent homophobic Diddlysquat occasionally enjoyed a voyeuristic penchant for witnessing up close and personal the facial anguish showed during violent rape.

Ostensibly, the Cardinal's type of preferred victim to see deflowered was slightly built light blond, blue-eyed boys forcibly ravaged by big dark ugly rough-cut brutes. However, after many serious attempts Len found it impossible to prove the rumors the Cardinal was present during the crimes. One reason could be the Cardinal's choice of victim was a rare resident at the group home. Most of the boys were from an opposite demographic.

Nevertheless, with the new information revealed, Len got busy exploring the Cardinal's history before being assigned to lead the New York Archdiocese. And most especially his personal relationship with Myron Acker and serial BDSM murder. Len found it close to impossible to accurately document the Cardinal's involvement beyond common rumors.

Through studious research, Len discovered the Cardinal had been written up as a virulent homophobe from his earliest days at seminary. After ordination he was considered a highly intelligent, promising new priest with limitations. Then after many parishioner complaints his conservative bishop wrote up Diddlysquat for preaching bigoted hate from his church's pulpit to stir his parishioners to violent antigay rights protests and gay bashing.

To prove he'd not learned his lesson, Tommy was arrested and fined for organizing and leading an antigay murderous mob. Then he was fined for protesting drag queen's right to exist and arrested again as he blocked the doors to a clinic known to help transsexuals and provide abortions. In court it was shown all his street protests were without permits. No parade permit was a serious offense against the city's tax structure, and court ordered gesture toward inclusiveness.

In rebellion against the authorities for *fostering* drag queens, transsexuals, and abortions, he was fined again for each of his offenses against public decency. Outraged, Diddlysquat spontaneously attempted to violently disrupt a grunge bar named the Broken Axel. He heard in confession the bar was black leather gay BDSM on Tuesdays only, and leather queens practiced nonviolence.

What wasn't known to the new priest was the Broken Axel was also a motorcycle gang hangout twenty-four, seven. The gang, Demons from Hell, took umbrage that a local parish priest was harassing their Tuesday black leather gay pets with benefits.

The motorcycle gang from hell did not practice nonviolence. As a result, the new rotund reverend was beaten, stripped naked, tarred feathered, then tied to and dragged behind a motorcycle through town. Then well feathered Diddlysquat was dumped unceremoniously on his church's top step. In his letter of reprimand and reassignment to a small out of the way parish father Tommy's bishop complained bitterly of the rigorous labor involved removing tar from church granite steps.

Father Diddlysquat's new church, Saint Hortense's, had a small but active evangelical group. To compete holistically in the marketplace for parishioners some Roman Catholic congregations had small and separate evangelical groups who got hysterical on cue and spoke in tongues for release. The mother church neither encouraged nor discouraged its own holy roller type activity while putting down Pentecostals as unsightly primitives.

However, when Saint Hortense's evangelical members complained, Father Tommy got much too extremely crazy violent when speaking in tongues against gay people, he was rapidly transferred again. He was sent to Saint Agatha, a small urban black ghetto congregation. They had been requesting an African American or African priest for years.

Saint Agatha did not have an evangelical group. The new priest, who was the only white person at Saint Agatha's, lasted one month. Congregants wrote furious letters to their bishop stating Father Diddlysquat was culturally insensitive and most likely racist.

The new priest forbad as unacceptable nutrition, slave food such as collard greens, sweet potato pie, ham hocks, and chitlins for the Church's Sunday late mass, potluck suppers. When queried live on air by a community radio reporter about his dislike of slave food. Father Tommy said it reflected badly on slaves' benefits from slavery, a popular anti reparations notion of the day among certain white people.

Between stints doing administrative busy work at one archdiocese or another the hard-to-place parish priest was repeatedly promoted out of the chaos he created. Cardinal Diddlysquat's meteoric rise, at a young age, from small town midwestern priest to monsignor, and to bishop. Then finally to cardinal was over senior men, more qualified, and deserving. But far less troublesome for the Vatican maintaining a homosexual double standard for its clergy.

Cardinal Tommy's first and current assignment was a result of Vatican reaction to the death of previous flamboyant Cardinal Spillseed. Within the gay community he was called our outrageously dramatic stage door Cardinal. The old Cardinal had dozens of dear friends among stage and screen actors and enjoyed partying hearty with them. Spillseed made sure several grand old Catholic Churches welcomed LGBTQ worshipers the same as all others.

Initially Cardinal Spillseed was replaced by a conservative, nongay, no fun, all business cardinal. The new man O'Conner did not leave much of an impression trying to tactfully impose the Vatican's conservative double standard after Cardinal Spillseed's spectacular New York flamboyant archdiocese. Because the new man was not a well-organized administrator of double standards. He was declared boring, and a failure compared to his predecessor.

It did not take the archdiocese and Vatican long to realize there is no such thing as balance in love hate homosexual double standards. The Churches with large numbers of out gay parishioners had grand pageant Masses with the most glorious organ and choral music. All their church ceremonies became elaborate, visually colorful spectacles, incense heavy, perfumed with abundant fresh cut flowers worthy of the early European Renaissance. Then the mostly straight Catholic Churches became green with envy with their wimpy plain Jane services.

When the new Cardinal Diddlysquat was assigned deceased Cardinal Spillseed's turf, the first thing he did was cast-out all gay worshipers and organizations from church property. Many different protestant denominations, and Jewish synagogues welcomed the newly disenfranchised gay Catholics to worship in their accommodations.

The archdiocese and Vatican were not at all happy having large numbers of parishioners and their tithe money driven out to worship with the protestants and Jews. On the other hand, Rome knew they definitely did not want the new Cardinal at the Vatican, which was the only way to restore what he had swiftly destroyed. With no alternative, they heaped more and more responsibilities and administrative work on him to try tone down his antigay violence. Instead, he found time to use his new larger megaphone to preach his intolerance toward others, hate against homosexuals, transexuals, abortions, and it was rumored to steal with impunity.

Tommy did not just abstractly hate gay women and men, he sincerely wanted everyone of them dead and would have bloodied his own hands to kill them personally if he could get away with murder free and clear.

Consequently, even the most conservative popes knew Diddlysquat was too extreme, but there was little they could do to contain him that they had not already tried. Nevertheless, the Vatican like most of Italy does not take kindly to being robbed. The Italian Church required vengeance.

Whenever there was a new American civil rights law to protect homosexual citizens, the gay press and *in the know* straight press would go out of their way to get the Cardinal's reaction to the legislation for balanced two-sided reporting.

First, Diddlysquat would give a diatribe against gay people and their parents for producing them. Then mention as his life's work how much he contributed to antigay rights social action. Second, Cardinal Tommy Diddlysquat would praise certain African countries, "he loved" that had kill gay people and their family laws. The Cardinal said the United States could only receive God's love if it moved forward with their own kill homosexuals and their families' laws using Africa as an enlightened example.

Adult media was quick to publish the names of the twenty countries, out of a total of fifty-eight African nations. The twenty were paid by Christian Fundamental Fascist to eat their gay children by law in order to receive God's love. Cardenal Tommy Diddlysquat was known to be the biggest cash contributors to capital punishment for the crime of homosexuality and producing such unacceptable progeny. The Vatican had no record of any contributions for Diddlysquat's public executions by unusual entertaining methods of death prescribed as amusement.

Uganda had been the first country to enact "Kill Gays" laws. To prove their veracity doing God's work to their rich white benefactors, they immediately set to arresting blood kin and planning public executions. When their neighbors saw the consequences to new antihuman rights laws was Christian National Fundamentalist Fascist cash, and lots of the cash. Naturally, they joined in wanting blood money for their leaders' pockets in exchange for their fellow citizens' gay children's gruesome death to show love of God.

The United Nations, successful humanitarian minded governments and NGOs withheld most aid to the twenty blood-lust-driven African countries until they stopped killing their citizens for existing. In response Christian Fundamentalist Fascist increased their contribution by an equal amount withheld. They also complained bitterly it was unjust they were being discriminated against for doing God's work in Africa.

Not unexpectedly, pressure at home to back off trying to repeal African "Kill Gay" laws started to be forcefully applied by Republicans. Coy advised the partners at his prestigious mostly Republican law firm the work they hired him to do could get ugly in house mixing American religion and African politics to execute innocent Africans. He was given a green light and assured, if necessary, he could expand his team with democrats. Even the oldest fuddy-duddy partners loved a good internal fight.

While the exposé at the Cardinal Tommy Diddlysquat Group Home was simmering away, headed to a full rolling boil in all the media, Randy Webber returned to live with us from the psychiatric hospital. Efforts to ease him into the family's extracurricular serial killer capture activities proved ineffectual. Rather than try answer his remedial questions at the dinner table, *every night,* we asked Carmen to keep Randy up to date at the piano. To his credit he controlled himself not to react with noticeable fear and loathing to information hard to hear given in private.

The next Thursday evening shooting hoops, two on two in front of our garage, twilight descended into night. Randy and I were beating Coy and Len by a lot. That was not how it usually went so I asked the two losers what was up with them?

Slapping Len's butt, Coy said, "My basketball partner has become preoccupied with unpaid work."

"Len, is that true?"

"Sorry to say yes. My research on the nightmare group home and Cardinal from Homophobia Ville has stalled out my writing. I've hit a wall writing just as a magazine deadline looms. I've never had writers block before."

"It might help to talk about it with your overeducated functionally illiterate housemates."

Randy instantly piped up and said, "Don't forget me. I'm not over educated yet so I can be an objective listener too."

Looking at Randy Len said, "Now I understand why Jack Warren believed staying in the closet protected the people he loved from society's disgraceful vehemence against his being born gay. What I don't get is why history is repeating itself with Florida's 'Don't Say Gay' laws, and book banning and burning in twenty-five other backward states. It seems to be1938, all over again."

Not knowing when to keep my trap shut, I said, "In history it's always been two steps forward and one back, that's called progress."

"Okay, I can accept that. But what I can't get my head around and write about is the malicious hatred of someone like Cardinal Tommy Diddlysquat, and his fellow American religious nuts. They finance destitute Africans to pass "Kill Gays" laws to sacrifice their own children for handouts. Where's the bigots' profit for their part in the hate? What's their motivation." Len's face showed what his words meant.

Running my mouth unfiltered I simply said, "Not all mental illness is found in the DSM or its *Diagnostic Criteria Supplement to the Manual.* What exactly about this is so bothering, you've dealt with anti-Asian discrimination your whole life? You're familiar with mass-psychopathology."

With vigor Len vented his anger. "I take it personally that people who never met me want me dead. I mean how sick is that? Don't I at least deserve a chance to give them a good reason to exterminate me? If they asked, my parents would give them a reason, but they want my parents dead for having me."

Even though every question does not require an answer, I could not resist a rhetorical one and said, "Aren't all gays the proxies for their hater's self-hatred? They don't need a face-to-face meeting to want every gay or transperson to suffer pitifully and then die horribly for being what they loath and fear about themselves as a public purging."

"If the Cardinal ever tasted my homestyle fried rice and sweet and sour shrimp, he'd think twice about wanting me killed."

"Len, don't bet your life on it, that guy is lightyears beyond pathological."

"Is that your professional opinion, Oliver?"

"Sorry, I'm not allowed an opinion since I never met the man professionally."

"Don't be sorry. You wouldn't like him and I'm sure it would be mutual. Knowing you, you'd probably kill the bastard, and then I'd have to defend my husband on a murder charge." Coy said this jokingly, but facts of late revealed that he was not far off the mark.

To change the subject I said, "Randy, why are you looking so morose? Nobody insulted your taste in piano music. That's our usual default. What's up with you? Don't say writers block, Len took that one."

"During the worst of the bullying abuse at that group home, I got through it without crying or begging by saying Hail Marys to myself over and over while wishing I was dead."

Grabbing the basketball and trying and missing a three-point shot, Coy said, "Good for your self-worth!"

"Except now you guys are saying the Church that helped me swallow the torture, wants me dead too. Come on, guys, what should I think about that? I mean how am I supposed to feel beyond being a sad sack victim?"

Catching the ball on the rebound and dribbling away from Coy and Len, I said, "Randy, if prayer works for you use it, use it all the time. Life is full of circumstances beyond our control, prayer is a good way to deal with good and bad situations."

"You're right, Oliver, even I noticed that."

I passed Randy the ball saying, "My young friend, just because Cardinal Diddlysquat is a hatemonger doesn't mean all clergy are. Thirty-eight of the fifty-eight African countries don't have kill gays laws."

"Big deal."

Grabbing the ball out of Randy's hands, Coy passed it to Len and said, "It is for the people who don't have to be afraid their governments will kill them just for being born." It was pure luck Len made a three-pointer while dribbling then stopped in the fading twilight.

"Huh, the internet on my phone says organized religions are in decline all over the world, especially among young people. Maybe Cardinal Diddlysquat and his pals are the reason?"

Looking thoughtful, Coy said, "Randy I'm sure there are a lot of reasons."

"Like what, Coy?"

My man ever ready these days with answers said, "Lately, the U.S. Congress is polling in the single digits no doubt a result of working only for the rich and powerful. The same is true for the Supreme Court's place on public opinion polls. I suspect organized religion has also lost touch with its people's needs and wants. But hey, I'm only a do-gooder lawyer."

Being closest to the garage electric switches, I said, "Hey, guys, want me to turn on the outside basketball lights to continue this sloppy one-sided game and feed the mosquitos our blood, or should we go inside and see what Carmen made for supper?"

"Yeah, I'm hungry. Whatever she's making sure smells good."

Coy grabbed and sat on the ball said, "I hope it's not Hungarian goulash again. It tastes good but I don't like the name. The leader of Hungary is such a fascist pig."

Ever ready to contribute my two cents to my man's opinion, I said, "Don't eat the leader. He looks very unappetizing, gristly, ugh!"

Randy continued to look troubled and said, "Do you guys think too much was asked for wanting same-sex marriage?"

The kid hit a nerve, and I couldn't hold back, "No! We only wanted what everyone else had, to live openly with the one we love. By denying us a means to respectfully express our love makes that love forbidden sex and an object reason to treat us as different than the others, and thus justification to hate, brutalize, and even kill us."

To lighten the mood from my anger, Len said, "Can any of you imagine loving that sad story Myron Acker or twisted Cardinal Diddlysquat?"

It was almost completely dark when Coy said, "Nope. Nobody could, let's go see what Carmen has been up to before Oliver ruins my appetite with heavy politics."

Coy tossed me the basketball and I opened the garage door and went in to stow it with our other adult toys. Returning outside I found Randy waiting for me and said, "I thought you went in to wash up with the others."

"I have a question?"

Draping an arm around his shoulders I said, "Shoot."

"Will you answer truthfully and not just tell me what you think I want to hear?" Then he leaned into my body for butch male contact.

As we walked to the house, I said, "I'll try."

"Did I sound girly telling you guys I prayed while being raped?"

"Why even think that?" That said I ruffled his hair with my other hand.

"The bullyboys told their victims that pleaded, begged, and cried to stop being little girls and take it like a man."

I stopped, stepped back, put a hand on each of his shoulders, and made direct eye contact. "The next time you take a shower check between your legs. I have high confidence you'll find you are one hundred percent man there."

"Ha ha, and what should I do with what I find there?" Twisting out of my grasp Randy gave me a fun laughing poke.

Playfully putting a finger to my chin as if thinking, said, "Prayer might help you get past temptation to use it frivolously."

"What happened to egg sperm practice?"

With a light slap on the butt I said, "Too much practice could ruin your game."

"Not sure, I think a bigger, better man than me would plot to get even."

My arm draped on his neck again I said, "Trust me, Randy, I've been around long enough to know. You don't have to dwell on retribution, whatever pain those bullyboys caused will come back on them with a vengeance many times over."

Snuggling against my body like a cat, he said, "You sound so sure … I hope it is true." With that said he put an arm around my waist.

"Trust me, good deeds are rewarded, and bad ones cause suffering sometimes in unimaginable ways." We were walking again, almost there.

"Oliver, thank you, that makes me feel better. Let's go wash for supper. I could eat a horse."

Chapter 15.

Detective Ariana Bruschetti called my private cellphone. "Any chance I can pick your brain and bounce some ideas off you?"

"Officially or otherwise?"

"Unofficial, informally, but it includes dinner in my home with my wife and cat."

"Can I bring my husband?"

"Is he housebroken?"

"Usually."

"Then he's allowed on the condition any mess he makes, you clean up."

"Let me check with him on dates and get back to you."

****

We settled on a date and time, and I said, "What can we bring besides a roll of paper towels?"

"What's the paper towels for?"

"In case my husband, Coy, is not in a housebroken mood."

"Just bring a big appetite, we have paper towels. Furthermore, with your permission, I'll swat him with a rolled-up newspaper if he misbehaves."

Ariana's wife, Jennifer Vinnecova, was about her age, height, weight, and had a similar appearance. Their posture and walk made me think they worked out together. We were told by them they had been misters and misses before Ariana's transition created misses and misses. That they loved each other was obvious from the amount of touching and how they deferred to each other.

Jennifer was a nurse practitioner at the university's health center where I taught graduate bioengineers one day a week. She had bright dark blue eyes under light brown hair worn in a medium conservative cut. Both women were barefoot wearing jeans and tank tops. Arianas's was white with a small police department logo and Jennifer's was logo-less light pink. How comfortably they were dressed was in stark contrast to Coy and me wearing dark business suits and ties.

Their home was clearly ruled by the house cat Murmur. A large, shades of gray, Himalayan tabby, who appeared to have an initial aversion to strangers, or at least Coy and I. Then due to her curiosity she got stroked and liked it enough to purr in a deep Himalayan voice. It seemed Murmur's role as home ruler was to greet us, check us out, accept stroking, disappear, and then watch us go out her front door with pompous regal dismissive authority.

The meal they served was straightforward, no-nonsense vegan, nothing like Carmen makes with meat, poultry, or fish. To start they served a tasty homemade caponata still warm from the oven, and baby arugula, grape tomatoes, oil dried olives, salad, with avocado oil, roasted garlic, lemon juice dressing. The main course was delicious homemade mixed grain over-stuffed ravioli in a clear reduction sauce flavored delicately with fresh parsley, sage, rosemary, and thyme sprigs. They served crunchy from the oven, beer batter dipped onion rings, broccoli, and cauliflower flowerets as a side dish. After a needed pause, dessert was a lovely warm peach cobbler with a whipped vegan topping and coffee.

Jennifer and Coy cleaned up the after-dinner things in the kitchen. Ariana and I sat on a couch making small talk in their modest but comfortable living room. Making eye contact, Ariana told me she completed ROTC in college so graduated as an Army second lieutenant. After six years in the service, she attained captain's bars with no future promotions possible if she transitioned, so she left.

Interrogating prisoners was one job she was good at in the service. When she was first assigned to military intelligence, they had her shadow an FBI expert in interrogation. He wrote the book on getting valuable information without intimidation. The man always got results, never made threats, or used coercion, or even raised his voice.

To show interest in our small talk, I said, "Wouldn't expect that level of sophistication from military interrogation."

She went on to tell me, she was told to watch and learn and learned a lot. It was slow at first, just sitting staring, nobody talking, but once you learn their favorite brand of cigarettes and candy bar, you are on to finding out about their families and after that they are yours to learn almost anything you need to know.

"Sounds less messy than waterboarding."

Ariana showed sparkle to my remark saying, "Definitely." Then more tranquil said, "Here's the thing, I passed the Myron Acker serial killer case on to the district attorney some time ago. We have conclusive concreate evidence of his guilt and they are just sitting on the case. Since I'd established a relationship with him, when I have other business at the jail, unofficially, I visit him too."

"And?"

Animated again she said, "I'm convinced he couldn't have committed those murders by himself, and his lawyer *will* get him off free and clear with no future trial from double jeopardy."

"What can you tell me about Mr. Acker I don't know?"

After a pause to collect her thoughts she said, "In his youth, Myron tried to be 'Limpy,' a mixed martial arts fighter off the books for quick cash. That's why he has those tattoo sleeves, as part of his 'Limpy' trademark. He was an embarrassing dud."

"That sounds brutal."

Looking thoughtful, she then said, "I suspect he was never very bright and too many blows to the head didn't improve cognition. The man has practically no short-term memory or any imagination. He is probably capable of committing murder but not without someone guiding his hand at every step using a cheat sheet."

"Possible murder by cheat sheet, is that the question you asked us to dinner to answer?"

I could tell she had been waiting for me to inquire after the invitation. "No, but close, is it possible for him to kill someone while under hypnosis?"

"Ariana, dinner was lovely, we thoroughly enjoyed it. Sorry to disappoint, I don't have the answer I think you want. Studies over centuries show it's impossible to get someone under hypnosis to do anything they wouldn't ordinarily do. You said he is most likely capable of committing murder, so why bother hypnotize him?"

"I think he needs help to guide him."

"If he couldn't kill on his own without help, studies say he probably can't kill. But we know he can, we've seen him do it."

Making a face she uttered, "Ugh, right."

"It sounds like your issue is with the District Attorney. Did you speak your complaint?"

Slight anger showing, she said, "Yes. They said buzz off and mind my own damn business."

"That's crude."

"I'd hate to see Myron walk on a technicality. We have concrete proof on video and four witnesses and yet if I had to testify under oath, he is not capable of doing what we can see he did without detailed help. It's a paradox."

At that point our spouses joined us from the kitchen with a freshly brewed pot of home roasted coffee. Jenifer asked her wife, "Is Oliver any help. Did he earn his supper?"

Ariana exchanged an intimates look with her wife and then said, "Not yet. But I want to keep trying."

Coy gave me a look and I shrugged my shoulders.

Jenifer watching Coy, and I closely then touched her wife's shoulder, gave her a peck on the cheek and asked me, "Is it possible the BDSM aspect of these murders allowed Myron to do what Ariana says he couldn't do on his own, without sadomasochism."

Coy's body language perked up and showed he wanted to know that too but kept quiet.

Making eye contact I addressed Jenifer's direct question and said, "No. Ariana would have found that out in her interrogations one way or another. She knows what she's doing."

"Why couldn't it be that simple?"

Taking Coy's hand in mine I said, "My guess … murder of a strangers needs a deeper wiring than random dress up for sex play. One thing these murders have in common is they're not simple even if Myron *is* following a script."

Coy jumped into the conversation and said, "What you call BDSM should really be called BLBDSM. Wearing black leather with or without bondage and discipline or sadistic masochistic anything is a big turn on for getting off sexually, just by itself. Myron seems to be missing the point, but in the end his victims aren't."

Playing tag team off, Coy I said, "For many, wearing black leather has the same or better effect as using sexual enhancement drugs. But murder is never like dress up fun play. After an extensive computer search, we couldn't find any connections with serial killers, professional assassins, and wearing black leather."

"Huh. Wearable drugs, what will they think of next?" Ariana said this while pouring us each a fresh cup of coffee.

Ever ready on the trigger Coy said, "Insertable ones."

As if correcting a student, Jennifer nurse practitioner said, "Wrong. We've had drugs in suppository form for years."

Coy gave my hand a squeeze, he was going to change topics and said, "I just read a scientific article that said straight males buy the majority of dildos, worldwide. Those dildos to penetrate male butts is piloted by their girlfriends or wives before the men can perform in the saddle, during straight missionary sex. Imagine that?"

Glancing at the ceiling silently asking for divine intervention Jenifer said, "How could anyone prove it? Don't answer that, no need-to-know gay guys come equipped with natural dildos, and lesbians prefer vibrators. What were we talking about before?"

Still hand holding, I said, "Clinically it could be argued that some practitioners of BLBDSM *can only* enjoy sex while wearing sex enhancing, black leather adornments."

"Well, that's definitely not for everyone." Jennifer sat back looking satisfied she had put an end to a subject that had not turned out as she hoped.

Coy holding on like a bulldog said, "BLBDSM participants must give their consent to participate. As, far as we know, none of Myron Acker's victims consented to be killed by him."

Jennifer took up the challenge and was back in the fray saying, "BLBDSM as sex enhancement is not normal in anyway, right?"

I tag teamed in for Coy and said, "Would you like my personal or professional opinion?"

"Professional. That's why we made you dinner."

I was getting bored and said, "The literature says, if it's by mutual consent and nobody is being hurt against their will, there is no diagnosis."

"Okay, then says you, there's no problem. But there should be."

Without a gap Coy instantly said, "To Oliver's point, I imagine most people are turned off rather than turned on by ritualized sex, and maybe that's a detraction. But not a problem for those who like it."

Still trying to end the topic with a win Jennifer said, "I can't imagine where such crazy ideas come from."

Always one to try and pick up on social cues, I told those present, in the early days of the three modern religions, Jewish, Christian, and Muslim, they were oppressed from the outside by the prevailing culture of that time. Then once they became established, they oppressed from within those with different points of view. The torturers and executioners of religious martyrs dressed in black leather while applying their trade. It was to strike fear and compliance in religious followers, and to keep their regular clothes clean from blood and gore. Cognitive Behavioral Therapy says one way to handle fear is to identify with it to demystify the feeling.

Jennifer was done trying to get a win.

Seeing what was going on between Jennifer and me, Coy told us it is well documented in the Southern United States during the time of slavery slave children played mock slave auction while being sold as slaves at those auctions. The younger kids probably didn't know what was going on. For the older children who did know it was a way to symbolically have some imagined power and control by identifying with the slave owner.

Jenifer took Ariana's hand, mirroring Coy and me and looking at her said, "Hearing that breaks my heart." The two women silently acknowledged having the same feeling.

To wrap up his point, Coy said, "Like many others, our country has done some good *and bad things* here and elsewhere in the world. We tend to only celebrate the good and are encouraged to forget the bad."

To take the heat off Coy and calm the conversation, I said, "My people immigrated here from Scandinavia promised free fertile farmland in the upper Midwest."

Jenifer supporting Arian said, "Vacant farmland, really, how unusual."

Figuratively speaking, Ariana took the relay baton from her wife and said, "Cowboys and Indians in pulp periodicals, movies, radio, and TV plays are always portrayed, cowhands good, Native Americans perpetually bad. For the most part the opposite was true."

"How do you mean, Ariana?"

"European adventurers immigrated here, stole the Indigenous peoples land, killed their women, children and old folks, and the buffalo their main food source. Once the Native People were forced off the lands they farmed, the U.S. government ran ads in Scandinavia 'Free Farmland to very white people only.'"

Seeing how uncomfortable Coy and I must have looked, Jenifer tried to mollify and said, "That was way back in olden times. We learned from our mistakes after interning the Japanese Americans during World War Two."

Ariana was on a tear and finished the thought she had been building to by saying, "Tell that to stateless Palestinians for the last seventy years after having been indigenous there for millennia thanks to European occupiers once again. History is repeating itself with Indigenous Semitics being accused of being antisemitic by European occupiers of natives' lands."

It had been a pleasant evening until it went south politically, so I said, "Oh, look at the time we have to go."

Realizing she had gone way off the reservation and then to try and put Humpday Dumpty back together Ariana said, "Oliver, could you teach me how to hypnotize Myron Acker?"

With leaving on my mind I asked, "Why? It sounds like you've already gotten all the useful information you needed for your case."

"Correct. But I'm no longer working on it so don't have the luxury of time for interrogation. He's holding back something I can just feel it."

"Hypnosis has been around for hundreds of years, Ariana. There are tons of books on the subject. Tell you what, I could recommend a few, if you want."

"Oliver, I was thinking it would be faster if you did it or taught me. It's only for one case that I'm technically not even working on. I know I sound like a broken record, but it would be a shame to let a serial killer go free because I couldn't bring it to conclusion. So far, I have a perfect record thanks to your help."

"Truth be told, I seldom use hypnosis in my private practice. Something about exposing another person's most inner thoughts feels too intrusive to me. If our innermost self is not safe from prying eyes, what is?"

"Don't make me beg, Oliver."

"How about a compromise, I own an excellent book of hypnotic inductions. I could loan it to you, permanently. It should be worth the homecooked meal, collegial conversation, and pleasant evening."

"All right, I'm game."

Seeing my other hostess withdrawn, left out of the conversations, I settled back down and said, "Jenifer, I want to apologize for monopolizing the after-dinner conversation with shop talk. "

"As a nurse I'm not used to being the exposed center of attention. It feels awkward."

"I feel we've been rude with shop talk. What can I do to earn your very excellent dinner?"

"I've heard you have a private practice as well as teaching. As a nurse practitioner, when the student health center becomes like a ghost town, at finals time, I often think I'd like to open a small primary care practice or urgent care storefront. Would you encourage my deranged thinking?"

"Sorry, I've just capped my waiting list to downsize my practice. I'm not the right person to talk to about this."

"You sound like the perfect person."

"I was on the verge of burnout when I pulled back. It's hard to say no to people in pain and easy to remember when business was slow, and the rent and payroll was due."

"Um, ah, I think I see."

"Spreading ourselves too thin effects the quality of what we can do."

I became distracted by Ariana and Coy talking intently, right next to us, about military procedures. He had been an NCO trainer before we met. When my drifting attention was back, Jenifer had noticed my distraction with irritation. As quickly as I could fake it, I started a commiseration about recent changes in administration policies at the university where she worked full time, and I part time.

She was having none of it, making stern eye contact Jennifer said, "Ariana is still working that Myron Acker case she already turned over to the DA. Are there ramifications, could she even get in to trouble?"

"She's crossing lines of sorts; it could even be seen as blurring hierarchical boundaries."

"That's bad."

"Sure, Jennefer, Ariana could get in trouble big time. But you can hardly blame her, a bizarre serial killer like this one comes around once in a career. Then it got stuck at the DA's office."

"Is there anything I can do?"

Responding to her concern I said, "Our problem isn't Myron Acker, we've got him, for the moment. It's his unknown puppet master, who choreographs premedicated murder using him with the victim's help, we don't have. What we need is a confession implicating all those involved."

"This case is too much, and I will blame her if she loses her job."

"Why? It's a whale of a once in a lifetime crime case."

"We're saving to buy a house and have kids. She froze her sperm before the transition surgery. It's not getting any younger nor are we. What is she thinking?"

They both had asked for my professional opinion. One on one I asked Jennefer if she was familiar with transference and counter transference from psychotherapy. She shook her head yes. So, I explained counter transference occasionally causes good therapists to lose prospective and their jobs every year. She indicated she knew that. Then mentioned the Myron Acker case is way out of the ordinary and has fascinating counter transference hooks. I let her know if it were me, I'd try to snap Ariana back to reality to keep her job. But Jennefer should keep in mind the case is a big one probably with big shots in high places trying to block us.

Then Coy pointed to his watch, which meant the hour dictated time for us to leave. Before we left, we received kisses on cheeks and an invitation to, "Come back real soon."

****

Unexpectedly Deacon Nesto Diaz telephoned to inform me Myron Acker's apartment was just scheduled for clean-out and to be painted. A trash dumpster would arrive early the next day for the contents. The church was anxious to prepare the apartment for a new tenant. He mentioned the police and church big wigs had searched through it many times. However, if I wanted a final look, he had the key. I thanked him for the kindness of thinking of me and made an appointment to go see one last time. and then got an emergency phone call going out the door.

On short notice Chucho agreed to take Len and Randy visiting Len at the office for homework help. They left immediately for my appointment with Deacon Diaz. They arrived, only a little late, Nesto and Chucho hit it off speaking in Spanish. Meanwhile Len and Randy went through the thoroughly searched apartment looking for anything missed in unlikely hiding places.

Told he was looking for secret compartments, it didn't take long for Randy to find one behind the bathroom in-wall medicine chest. When he pulled the cabinet completely out of the wall, inside he discovered a surprise. Handwritten, loose leaf papers and envelops all helter-skelter were hidden between the wallboard studs. Randy called out and then proudly showed Len, Chucho, and Diaz the wrinkled papers he'd found behind the unanchored wall inserted medicine cupboard.

Chucho and Len determined the crude scribbled handwriting on creased paper loose sheets matched Acker's scattered around in the apartment in clear view. The postage cancelled envelopes addressed to Myron Acker's Yonkers post office box were from the same computer inkjet printer.

What was written on the loose sheets didn't make sense at first, then by luck Len linked a sheet to the murder Asa Mulroy had been accused of. Then wading through often barely readable misspelled and missing words, with horrific grammar proved to be step by step instructions for drugging Asa, raping him in a moving van, and then a stranger's murder by gunshot to the head as the victim intended for Asa.

On even closer examination of the other loose papers, they found a handwritten instruction sheet detailing the murder Javier Torres witnessed. That got them searching with much more interest. Then they found cheat sheets of sorts for murders we previously knew about and several nobody was aware of. It was another irrefutable link tying Acker to his crimes.

My old contacts at the District Attorney's office had dried up years ago. As a last resort, rather than bother Coy who was going through a busy time, I telephoned Ariana. and let her know what had been found hidden in Myron's apartment and asked her to pass them along to the district attorney's office.

In a manner of speaking, we put our heads together talking over the phone while I emailed her copies of Acker's handwritten recipes for murder. She said up to that point from her repeated jail visits she knew enough about the murderer's childhood and biological family to write his biography, but nothing about the murders until what I was just now emailing

Ariana revealed Mr. Acker checked most serial killer boxes if they had a form with boxes to check. The killer had suffered extreme social deprivation from poverty since birth. To start with he had a poor self-body image born with a clubfoot. Additionally, he had been physically and or sexually abused at home, at church camp, in school, the boy scouts, and in young adult prison.

After a youthful offender indeterminant prison stay for attempted armed robbery with a toy gun, ego diminished young adult Myron took his internalized rage to mixed martial arts octagons for cash fights. Unfortunately, he was not technically a good fighter and was often savagely beaten. Which further lowered his already low self-esteem. On some level, he believed he deserved to be punished because he had developed a taste for torturing and killing stray house pets and captured wild animals and birds.

At present Ariana was sure Myron was holding back information he guarded like a steel vault whenever she tried to probe it. Otherwise, the two had established a close relationship where he would answer all her other questions, no matter how personal. In return he had every creature comfort the jail allowed Ariana to provide an inmate.

Since the lawyers were elaborately stalling to set a trial date as far into the future as humanly possible, the main jail planned to move Myron to their annex number three. It was their furthest jail-annex out of town in the boondocks. That would make visiting Mr. Acker much harder, but not impossible. Ariana suspected with less visits the prisoner might value them more and become more talkative.

While in the main jail, the accused serial killer was kept in isolation for everyone's protection. The annex he was slated to go to had no single cells. Myron preferred to keep to himself and have segregated treatment. The very idea of two-man, four-man cells, dormitories and all using the same communal showers at once made Myron uncomfortable bordering on psychotic.

Emailing completed we ended our pleasant morning phone conversation when my next appointment for the day arrived. I hoped Ariana would receive some brownie points for giving the district attorney additional evidence against Mr. Acker and repair their relationship.

****

When Ariana tried to give the district attorney's office copies of papers Randy Webber found, she was told in no uncertain terms to buzz off again, she was to have nothing more to do with the case. It sounded to me like the DA's's office was stressed to the max defensively facing an unbeatable defense attorney. Ariana took the rude behavior personally, though she knew better decided to show Myron copies of the found papers. She thought she knew the risks.

Ariana telephoned me to report what had happened and what she intended to do about it. I said, "DON'T!" And once again, I reiterated the dangers of counter transference to a long career.

She said she knew she was putting her job with the police department at risk but could not let a serial killer go free without acting. I was at a loss for what to say, I had seen too many promising young psychotherapists lost to other fields by countertransference. Finally telling her I would find a way to get the papers where they needed to go and if she was tired of being a police officer resign. I wanted no part in her being fired, personally I knew she was a good cop.

Ariana said, "Not today. Goodbye," and hung up."

With fifteen minutes to cool off, Ariana telephoned and said, "I'm sorry I bit your head off. This Acker case and how badly it's handled since I passed it on has me going bananas. You've showed me friendship and deserve better than how I was just now."

"All is forgiven. None of us want to see it end badly or your career self-sabotaged. I'll pass along the found papers to higher authorities, don't worry about it."

She abruptly changed subjects without commenting on what I said, and at her suggestion we did a quick review of what was known, or thought we knew. We agreed the opportunity for the murders came from magazine ads in a once a year highly specialized international publication. By self-selection the chump patsy had above average income but not too much to be missed if disappeared. Others were not dependent on him for income.

The victim unknowingly dictated the means of the murder. But our big unknown was motivation for such elaborate, protracted, detail choreographed, expensive murders. Committed by a murderer with cognitive deficits and little to no short-term memory, it just did not jive.

Was BDSM just an easy way to skewer wealthy victims, or to draw negative attention and shame for naughty esoteric sex? Or was it somehow related to the prurient interests of Mr. Acker's puppet master, or something unknown to us? Also, it did not appear Myron profited from the killings that required large amounts of money to change hands from start to finish.

Two uneventful weeks passed quietly, hardly being noticed, since we were busy at work. Coy and I did not complain, when our lives get mundane, we cuddle more at home. Then one Thursday afternoon, at about three PM, Ariana Bruschetti phoned my office. She was upset and said Myron Acker had gotten extremely unhinged at jail annex three after seeing the hidden pages from his apartment. He totally freaked out and needed to be restrained. Later he told his jailers to take Ariana's name off his approved visitors list.

She said he seemed to change before her eyes into someone she had never met when he saw the papers. Ariana said, "Talk about Dr. Jekyll and Mr. Hyde. I saw him metamorphose right in front of me and wasn't prepared for the transformation."

Without forethought, words tumbled out, "Are you alright?"

"Only shaken a bit, I'll survive."

In an even guarded tone I inquired, "Does the DA know what you did?"

"No. Nobody knows except for the murderer. Myron wrote the jailers he was taking me off his visitor list because I wouldn't give him head after promising."

What she said and the way she said it changed the mood, so I said, "I thought you said he was against all sex except for procreation in the missionary position."

"That's correct. He did it to punish me, to get even for my crossing his imagined invisible line I didn't know about before traversing boundaries."

What she said brought reality back with a vengeance and I said, "We did talk about you putting your job at risk, right?"

"Yes. Thanks for caring. I'll be fine. I'm working on a new angle, getting a visit with his cellmate Patricio Gelatinous, but it's iffy. He's a slippery character."

Again, my mouth working without brain connection, I said, "Anything I can do?"

"Not unless you have connections to a country willing to take Myron's deportee cellmate that isn't Turkey or Greece."

It felt like Ariana was playing with me and I said, "Excuse me?"

"Patricio is from Cypress. Our Homeland Security has him on hold to send back. His lawyer claims he's an active Cypret separatist and Türkiye sent assassins to Cypress to kill him and that's why he says he's here."

Why did it feel like we were going around in circles? "Send him to Greece."

"Greece is less than enthusiastic about a more independent Cypress. No country wants him because we've labeled him a terrorist. By the way, he's also being held for felony attempted murder here. Don't ask I don't know yet."

"Duh, is that what makes this guy special." I said this wondering *Why does this case have so many obstacles to make it simple?*

"Well, add to that politically this isn't a good time to be undocumented for any reason."

My other phone line lit up and I heard my next appointment enter the waiting area so said, "Sorry, got to go. Good luck, keep me posted."

****

Three days later Ariana telephoned to say, "I've got good news and bad. What do you want first?"

After thinking, *OH, NO, NOT AGAIN SO SOON,* I said, "I'm having one of those days where nothing is going right. Good news please."

"Patricio loves the lawyer you recommended, MT aka Mac Truck. He says he'd marry her if she wasn't already married to a woman."

Thinking, *I have never known MT not to get positive results,* I said, "What's the bad news?"

"Patricio has been released from jail. All felony charges against him were dropped and nobody will say why."

I was not expecting to hear that and said, "Where does that leave your extra-curricular attempts to get fired from your job?"

"On orders from the Department of Corrections administrator, after a big shower brawl, Mr. Acker will not have another cellmate. Unless overcrowding becomes too big an issue."

Trying to think of a polite way to end a nothing burger conversation, my mouth unconnected to my mind said, "Did you get anything from Mr. Gelatinous before he was let go?"

"There wasn't much to get. According to Patricio, Myron's only other visitor other than me was the Priest who comes to jail once a week to provide confessions, and mass. It seems, Myron always wanted to serve at mass as an altar server."

Nature calling, so ready to end the chat I said, "And now you want to talk with the priest, right?"

"Well, since he's a different priest from the one at the main jail, I'm working on talking with both clergymen. I'll let you know if I find anything of value. Bye for now."

While Ariana continued to put her career in jeopardy working on a case no longer hers to work, on my own I tried to save her job and phoned Deacon Diaz based on what she said about Myron serving at Mass in jail. After checking his computer, it showed Myron Acker had attended every religious ceremony held while he was a non-employee at Saints Peter and Paul Church. Acker's religious devotion practice included serving at Mass, especially for the very early morning or late-night services.

****

The next day Esmeralda Nascence surprised me with a telephone call. We had not spoken in months or years. Esmeralda is Chucho's aunt, handy with a gun or knife, and met her wife MT through me.

"Hey, Esmeralda, what's up?"

"My wife asked me to call you, she thought you'd be interested in something I turned up. "I'm all ears. When I did a background check on Patricio Gelatinous, he's not a Cypriot separatist as he claims. His main source of income in Cypress is as a killer for hire."

"You know this how?"

"It seems Gelatinous is listed on a hitman bulletin board on the darknet. I checked with a couple of bad characters I know and it's true Patricio was a hit man."

"Was?"

"I met with him. After a little physical persuasion, come to find out, Patricio was hired for Myron Acker to have a fatal accident in jail. Then my wife got him released before his kill contract could be satisfied."

"Where is he right now?"

"Gelatinous had an unfortunate accident himself. Either he fell or was pushed out of an open window on the sixth floor, Russian style. Right up to the very end with me he claimed not to have subcontracted his hit. So, I think for now your suspected serial killer is safe. But so far, we don't know who killed the killer hired to kill your serial killer. Not to worry, I'm working on it."

"The Russians would know it must be six floors or higher to assure a kill out a window. Esmeralda, I appreciate your diligence. Any idea who hired Myron Acker?"

"No. He might not have known who employed him. You know how the darknet works."

"Thank you, Esmeralda, I doubt Myron was using the internet. Do you want to talk to Chucho, he's in the next office."

"No. He has my telephone number. I got to go, bye for now."

I telephoned Ariana with Esmeralda's news. She was in the field on a case, so I left the word I called. For some reason, having a need to pass the new information along, I phoned Coy. He was unavailable in court, and I left a message to call me back. Chucho seemed to be on a long difficult telephone call, so I stuck my head in Len's door and said, "Guess what?"

"What."

I told Len what I had just heard from Esmeralda, and he said, "You going to tell Myron?"

"Don't know how to get on his approved visitor list."

"Make it anonymous to the press. So far, this story has gotten very little main media attention."

"Maybe it's too complicated for public interest without the rich and famous or celebrities sullying themselves."

"Or BDSM and black leather make the public queasy."

****

That evening just before dinner I was about to tell Coy about the Acker case's latest revelation when the landline rang. Ariana called to return my phone message and to say Myron Acker was dead. It seems while preparing to transfer him back to the main jail, someone got the idea he should have a shower first. Apparently while in the shower he slipped on soap and broke his neck. Since she was in the field closest to jail annex three, she got the call to stop what she was doing and investigate.

On the surface the death looked like an accident. But nothing in this case had turned out to be what it appeared. It was plausible the death was just as it appeared, a straightforward slip and fall in a wet shower room. Except, I used the occasion of her phone call to say there was at least one hit out for Myron's life we knew about.

Then Ariana said, "Hmm, there were no witnesses, which seems rather unlikely in an overcrowded jail that only allowed showers twice a week." Myron had told her when inmates hear showers running, they automatically line up first come first served. That is because not everybody gets wet and clean even twice a week. "Conquer and control through body odor."

Ready with a quip I said, "That's one way to break a man's spirit."

"Um, naturally in the name of prudish discretion, there are no security cameras in the shower area to show what goes on in there or what happened."

Quick on the trigger, I said, "Check to see if there were any staff or inmate cellphone or other videos taken. It's a long shot but if someone wants to get paid, they'll need some kind of proof."

Naturally all the confiscated cellphones turned up zilch proof of murder, it was a jail.

Chapter 16.

Months went by, life went on with little notice other than the usual mundane frustrations. Then Randy turned seventeen and we were all talking about colleges for him, *except him*. Each household member lobbied for a different university and a few of us, and his parents, had connections to grease the admission process if that was something he wanted, *he didn't*. Despite being extremely bright our youngest household member respectfully did not see a college education in his future.

Randy believed going into the military as an enlistee would restore his stolen sense of masculinity from being repeatedly raped by bully boys in the group home. The rest of us felt otherwise to the point that Coy detailed for Randy the hardships of basic training and difference between Noncommissioned Officer versus Commissioned Officer's life and privileges from rank in any branch of military service. Finally, to cap his sincere college recruitment try, Coy explained GI means General Issue, expendable cannon fodder in other words, like pawns in a chess game.

A decent chess player for his age, Randy told Coy sometimes the pawn can checkmate the king.

When I had a chance to talk with our boy alone, come to find out, he had seen a recruitment poster that said the Army would make a man out of him. No matter what angle I approached his poster belief, Randy had fixated going into the military without his usual privilege would restore his sense of self and manhood. Even though I often joked about being over-educated, it was just possible our young house guest knew what was best for him and we should get out of his way.

Randy's father resurfaced here in the States again. He had made another fortune while in Asia and wanted to reconnect with his son on weekends when he was not too busy with business. His first contact with me was to say, "Stop giving my son pocket money. I've given him a prepaid debit card with a $75,000 limit. He no longer needs your charity."

"For your information Randy earns the walking around money he gets from me. Earning his spending money seems to have improved his character and he thinks twice before frivolously letting it go. What he needs is to hear you love him."

"Don't tell me how to parent my son. Too much pampering spoils children."

"Just a word to the wise. Randy was traumatized and needs healing."

"With all due respect, mind your own business. He knows I love him I just gave him a debit card worth an average workingman's annual wage."

After stalling and thoroughly searching, again, Ariana could find no excuse not to close the Myron Acker serial killer case as an accidental death in a jail shower. Len's articles about the Acker BDSM murders won him awards and interesting job offers. He went to all the interviews, even those out of town, but was not ready to leave his status quo freelancing and living with our family as a permanent guest.

One late Saturday afternoon as sunset light began to stealthily dip below the far distant horizon, the air temperature commenced to drop, giving more notice night was on the way. Wearing light jackets Coy and I were gently swinging on the swings at the side of the house. It felt idyllic, no big emergencies weighing us down, we were content being an old married couple, not talking as another day turned into night before our eyes.

Randy came around the front corner of the house looking anxious. Len was following several paces behind him wearing a more inscrutable demeanor than usual. Coy said to the interlopers, "Ah Tweedledee and Tweedledum looking shaken and stirred. What's up boys?"

Randy stood at attention in front of our now stilled swings and said, "You know that teen al-anon meeting you guys like me to go to after school on Thursdays?"

"Yes."

"Lately they are talking about twelve steps making amends. So, I thought I'd try it out on you two. It's supposed to make everyone feel better and forgive."

"About what?"

"I lied to you about where I went last weekend."

"Why lie?"

"I figured you'd say no."

"RANDY, have I or Coy ever said NO to you about anything?"

"Not exactly, but you both always add conditions or concerns or some deep think that seems to mean no without you saying it."

"Well then, forgive me for looking out for your best interest. I'll break *that* bad habit *right away.*"

"Are you going to let me make amends or what?"

"I don't know. Coy, do you think I can handle this level of honesty without screwing it up?"

"Right. Well maybe if we both just listen and don't say anything. Oh, but wait, aren't there usually hugs, kisses, and such, as part of making amends."

"Don't forget firm handshakes."

"I don't know if I can handle all that without saying a few toastmaster words that might be misinterpreted as no."

Just as I was about to pile on to Coy's teasing Randy, Len looking serious spoke up and said, "Trust me, you are going to want to hear what Randy has to say."

So, instead I said, "Tell us, Randy. All kidding aside, I'd like to know what's on your mind."

"Last weekend I told you I was going to spend time over at a classmate's home playing video games. The truth is I was over at Asa and TJ's playing video games not approved for anyone under eighteen years old."

"Did the games rot your brain or cause any measurable damage?"

"No, of course not. I had brain rot from an early age," Randy giggled as he said it.

Quick on the trigger, Coy said, "See what happens with too much association with you, Oliver?"

The best defense is to be offensive, so I said, "Not that it is any of Coy or my business but how did this underage meet happen?"

"I ran into Asa at the game store in the mall. We chatted and he invited me over for lunch to play their latest greatest adults only game box and one thing led to another."

"Uha, did you get into BDSM with them?"

"NO! Well? Not really, but I did have questions about it."

"Without getting too deep into your personal business, did you do more than ask questions?"

"TJ put a pair of handcuffs on Asa. He liked it. So, I let TJ put a pair of handcuffs on me."

"How was that?"

"If you must know it was a major turn off. It reminded me of being arrested and then going to court wearing real handcuffs locked behind my back. But without my family's lawyer there to get the charges dropped. I told TJ I'd yell my head off if he didn't take them off."

"How did TJ and Asa take your not wanting to play with them?"

"Not playfully, ha, ha. Disappointed actually, I could tell they wanted more. I wasn't ready for a visit to them."

"How so?"

"I could see they were both hard under their clothes. With my hands cuffed in back, I was defenseless, anyone could do anything to me. All I could do was bite or spit. I panicked."

Looking thoughtful, Coy said, "I wonder if there's room in Randy's schedule for kickboxing lessons."

Resisting the change of topic, I asked, "Do you still have BDSM questions?"

"No. I'll learn discipline and pain in the army or practicing the piano, thank you very much. Carmen just introduced me to Franz Liszt's music, it's hard, but worth it. After what happened to me in that group home, I never ever plan to have sex with anyone again, and I mean it. It was so disgusting; I won't do that again in this life."

"Randy, I'm sincerely sorry things did not work out how you hoped. Do you want me to stop showing interest in your adventures and only hear what you want to share?"

"I'm not sure, I don't think so. Anyway, none of that is why Len wanted me to tell you about what Asa and TJ are doing."

Coy had been watching my interface with Randy away from kickboxing and then decided he approved and reinserted himself into the conversation. "Tell us, suspense is killing me."

"TJ found this weird, once a year magazine. They think Asa's abduction might have come from there. I feel close to Asa, he looks my age and isn't that much older. Also, what happened to him was like what happened to me in the group home. You had to experience the helplessness to understand how it fucks with your head."

Seeing the conversation going all over the map, Len said, "TJ and Asa read my three articles about Myron Acker. Remember, I interviewed Asa for the first article. When they saw an ad like I mentioned TJ answered it with $500. Now he's corresponding with someone who's not the late Myron Acker. Randy thinks the situation is heating up with them."

"This sounds familiar. Didn't TJ try something like this before?"

"No. He talked about trying it and was talked out of it by the cops. Now he feels ignored by everyone. He thinks he's a star and thrives on attention."

Randy eagerly waiting to jump back in for some limelight said, "TJ and Asa have hired bodyguards for each of them."

Len to answer Coy and me, said, "To conclude my last article I wrote, 'Maybe, maybe not the murders stop with Myron Acker's death.' We'll only know in the future if I have to write its sequel."

"Hmmm."

"Oliver, from your meetings, I surmised you and Coy and your detective friends think there is more to this story than I wrote."

"A little mystery adds spice."

"You all think there's more than one lone killer, right?"

"Making a not too smooth transition, and without looking like a couple of old maid nosey bidi-bodies … what do you think Coy, and I do about TJ. You know this case better than anyone."

"Because you ask me, I'd give my detective friends an anonymous heads up."

"Saying what?"

"TJ and Asa maybe getting into something potentially dangerous that we all agreed was too risky for any of us to undertake."

"They'll ask for details."

"All the previous victims were middle aged men into BDSM. It will be hard for TJ to fake the age difference, which it sounds like he's planning to try."

"Ha, what do you guys think of having brunch with the leather boys and our favorite lesbians for Carmen to observe and nudge appropriately? Her point of view is unique for this case."

Len looking relived to be off the hot seat said, "Okay, if we make Randy wear one of those cute waiter's aprons. Ouch! Randy, you don't have to punch me. Just for that I'll buy you a waiter's apron myself and bet you wear it without anything on under it …" Len and Randy started play fighting.

"Stop fighting, boys, or the adults will show you how it's done."

" … the bet is still on."

"Come on, gang. it's getting chilly out here and something for supper smells good."

****

After hearing it was related to her favorite serial killer sleuthing case, Carmen was happy to plan and execute a vegan brunch for ten or twelve people. If Randy agreed to help serve and do the cleanup.

I telephoned Ariana Bruschetti with the first invitation to brunch for the coming Sunday next. In addition, I asked if her old partner William Marin, would be interested in joining us. She said no. Both Ariana and William were credited for solving the Acker case. As a reward William was now teaching LGBTQ sensitivity and advanced hand to hand combat skills at the police training academy and Ariana was now a member of the prestigious homicide unit Manhattan South.

Along with her invitation, I mentioned what we weren't supposed to know about, as to what TJ and Asa were up to. While Carmen planned the meal's recipes and shopping for out of the ordinary ingredients, I telephoned an invitation to TJ and Asa.

I could feel TJ's hackles go up over the phoneline at my invite. I suspected he was expecting a dress down from me for putting Randy in handcuffs. Since his uncle Willis Washington and I were best friends for decades, the friendship came with limited family member privileges. Calling TJ out was one privilege we both knew I could use with his stern uncle's backup. Only he did not know the ulterior motive for the invitation.

Chucho called about a business matter, and I knew he had given up on romance after his motorcycle accident left him impotent. So, I invited him to brunch with us. He agreed if he could bring Deacon Ernesto Diaz. It seemed his self-imposed celibacy and Chucho's inability to get hard was a match, and so they were kind of dating. They held hands, kissed, cuddled, and that was better than nothing, so he said.

Once an invitation is extended, good manners say it cannot be taken back. So, I quit while I was behind and invited them to brunch too. I told Carmen the exact number was unknown but the more the merrier.

****

Carmen outdid herself presenting us with a grand brunch that looked traditional, and she could easily explain all the plant-based substitutions she used to make it look otherwise. The bottom line was if I did not know better, I would not have guessed those fluffy scrambled eggs in an earlier rendition were tofu, same as the soybean vegan breakfast sausages.

TJ and Asa (doggy boy) had arrived in three cars, a lead car, a follow car, and their usual luxury car in the middle. Before their driver opened a car door for them the other car drivers walked around the outside of our home, guns out, looking for God knows what. I went outside and invited the five men inside to brunch. TJ explained only he and Asa would brunch, the three drivers had to stand guard duty outside my house, for what was not explained.

It was so subtle how Jennifer Vinnecova brought up the topic of serial killers and Myron Acker (God rest his soul) not fitting the loner type image, and what could it mean. A more diverse group would be hard to imagine. Ernesto knew Myron from day-to-day work, Len had a journalist's thorough understanding of the case.

The group of brunchers enthusiastically chowed down on vegan breakfast food while drinking champagne, club soda, mimosas, Bloody Mary's, Harvey Wallbangers, and screwdrivers. To no one in particular, Ariana casually mentioned Myron Acker might have been a member of a large syndicate of ruthless killers. The consortium could have been determined to eliminate middle aged BDSM aficionados one at a time and scare off young converts in the process.

Jennifer picked up on her theme openly speculating, "If it is a large international crime organization, as we suspect, it will be next to impossible to entirely root them out. Especially if they are aligned with international White Supremacists or Neo-Nazis organizations. The local police are thinking of asking the public for help since several killings happened on our turf and we have local Nazi gangs."

I watched TJ and Asa closely as the two woman nonchalantly spoke to the table about serial murder, Nazis, and White Supremacists. The complexion of both young men dressed in black leathers instantly drained of blood to look like spent vampire food. Meanwhile the women chatted about their work with nonspecific serial killers. Then TJ interrupted Jennifer and said, "What kind of help?"

"Any information from the public may put police in touch with the killers and their gangs. You see the way these murderers operate is very clever and an average citizen could easily be snared and killed before they knew what was happening. The police have been working against these thugs for a long time now. Ariana and I know their sneaky tricks."

TJ abruptly looked gut punched on top of drained of blood. Never having met TJ, Ernesto Diaz was unaware how disconcerted he appeared and cut him off.

Nesto spoke directly to Ariana and Jennifer saying, "What if it was not Nazis or White Supremacists Christian Nationalists, but rather a small group within a larger group within a huge international religion, all hiding in plain sight? Then what could you do about it?"

"Then the cops would really need extra outside help from people in the know." Jennifer said this glancing at Ariana.

Ariana listening closely to her wife said to Deacon Diaz, "Can you be more specific?"

"All I know is whispered gossip that would be impossible to prove or even explore further."

Glancing from Ariana, to Ernesto, Coy asked, "What are you all talking about?"

Deacon Diaz, his face showing he had spoken without thinking, reluctantly explained the Roman Catholic Church held an official position against homosexuals, while ignoring the many gays working in the church structure for gay civil rights. As a revolutionary countermeasure, there are supposedly, unofficial antigay clergy element raising money and actively working against gay rights in this archdiocese, nationally and internationally. Within that antigay cluster is a smaller group of priests who take part in homophobic homicide as God's work, or so I've heard. Part of the rumor is officially the Vatican is unaware of the internal conflict, and unofficially trying to restore balance without letting it be known what they are doing.

I should have taken a picture. Except for Ernesto, who was talking, the rest of the table looked stunned open mouth. Some brunchers appeared so startled they were still showing food recently masticated at his suggestion the Church was behind the BDSM murders. It would be hard to prove that dead Myron Acker was only a replaceable dupe in a grand church conspiracy.

Looking flummoxed Len said, "I don't understand the why? I can see a head biting its tail, but the middle fighting both ends, that's new to me."

I couldn't hold back and said, "Len I've been told you'd have to be raised Catholic. Apparently, there is a history of the Church going against its and its parishioners' best interest."

In further than he intended, Ernesto expanded, this is only hearsay. It had been suggested the killer priests and monks joined religious orders to cure their homosexual desires and when that didn't work, they actively tried to eliminate their source of lust. Because of the Ten Commandments, the religious are not allowed to take life like everyone else does. So, the priests and monks use proxies to do the actual death dealing.

"And how could they do that?"

"Len, I don't know. But Myron told me he was an avenging angel sent to earth to do God's work eliminating gays. When I showed surprise, he said he was given that information from an irrefutable high Church authority."

"Authority, what authority?"

"I thought he was crazy and didn't ask." Ernesto mumbled this wishing he'd kept his mouth shut.

Ariana chimed in showing she'd been paying attention. "Huh, okay, what about all the money changing hands. Greed has a way of infecting criminal hate group dogma, even big religious conspiracies?"

Ernesto, uncomfortable sitting on the hot seat, gave a quick response, "Can you imagine a better money laundry than the collection plate at Mass on Sunday. Rumor has it after skimming profits and funny fund-raising go to support countries in Africa with 'Kill Gays' laws, but not in any way the Vatican would approve such things."

"So, no need to mix up greed with vows of poverty when engineering killing fags to please the gods and feed starving Africans."

A relevant thought occurred to me to bring back what was known and said, "Has the archdiocese sent a replacement for Myron yet?"

"Yes. That was the whole point of clearing out Myron's apartment. The archdiocese seemed to know Myron wasn't coming back even before his lawyer."

"What's the new guy's name?"

"It would be un-Christian and unkind to call Jimmy Jordon a dim-witted idiot, so I won't. But you get the general idea."

"A duplicate?"

"Yes, he's a lot like Myron needing his work instructions written down exactly if the job is to be done correctly."

Ariana was still back one step and asked, "Who at the archdiocese would know about homicidal homophobic groups within groups in the Church hierarchy?"

"I wouldn't know, that's above my humble pay grade, I'm not a priest."

"Do you think the Cardinal would know?"

"He's the head honcho and supposed to know everything."

"Do you know anyone trustworthy at the archdiocese who might help us explore this line of inquiry?"

"Let me think on that. If they find out I've been blabbing, I could be reassigned to Siberia without snowshoes to go barefoot in the snow and ice."

Doggy boy Asa, looking for approval from TJ, got silent permission from a head nod and said, "As more of a goof than anything else, we've been corresponding with an anonymous someone on the computer. At first, we thought it was just an expensive BDSM fantasy game. But now it is getting real. Would the police be interested in looking at what we've been doing without us getting in trouble?"

"You betcha, let's set up a time and place to meet." Ariana said this casually not showing the boys were playing a dangerous game.

Before I hardly realized it, the brunch was over, and the group was dispersing in several directions. Ariana had put her head together with TJ and Asa, all three had their pocket calendars out and then wrote on their phones. At the same time Ernesto Diaz and Len seemed to be having a deep conversation.

Coy and Chucho followed me out onto the back deck for a breath of fresh air. Inside, Randy was giving out coffee, tea, and other drinks, while still wearing his new short-black-waiters-apron Len had bought him for this occasion. Having won the bet, he was fully dressed under the apron.

Leaning back against the deck railing, Coy said, "We got more than we bargained with this vegan feedbag."

"For sure, it was definitely worth the price of admission to eat all that healthy health food while gleaning new crime solving information."

Just then Ernesto joined us and said, "Are your brunches always mystery cracking intriguing?"

"No. This was our first foray into vegan breakfast food. What did you think of the eats?"

"I don't mind missing meat and fish and eggs, but I do miss butter on my bread and cow's milk in my coffee. I was referring to the murder mystery game you played."

"It wasn't a game. As you know we found a real serial killer, your coworker. Now he died or was killed, whatever. And now it seems we may have another. Welcome to our house."

"Thank you for inviting me. Is that live piano music I hear?"

"Yes. It's either our housekeeper Carmen or her helper Randy. Wait, that's Scriabin, it must be Carmen. She plays really well."

"It was nice seeing you guys again you have a lovely home. Thank you for inviting Chucho and me."

"Come again Earnesto. We enjoyed having you visit. Let me walk you out."

Chapter 17.

You would think after brunch revelations of a church sponsored antigay murder syndicate, the next weeks would be rich with more expectations, they were not. Life seemed to go back to more or less as usual, mundane, work, home, sleep, repeat. The thank you notes we received for the Sunday brunch, after indicating appreciation, requested a repeat but with live music at the center. That got Coy, Carmen, Len, and I talking of reviving our old Sunday afternoon chamber music soirees.

The police commissioner made sure his edict reached down to the lowest ranks, that the Myron Acker case was closed and would stay closed. Police resources were too limited to waste on old, closed murders that reflect badly on the department and Corrections' competency. The old timers at the police department said the commissioner's message, content and style indicated he was under profound pressure to bury the case from high up the governmental food chain. That started Ariana and I on a telephone reassurance consultation at least once a week.

William Marin had a State Trooper friend, Donna Sims, to who he expressed doubts they had seen the last of BDSM serial killings. When introduced to Donna, I inquired if there were any new and interesting criminal doings in or around Albany. She said, "No, just the usual house and garden mob hits."

Using Williams suspicions and my inquiry results from both locations, Donna convinced her bosses the Buffalo and Albany murders might not ever get closed. She lucked out, it was a slow time for them and was given a free hand, but with limited time to settle the cold cases.

Donna and her partner set up twenty-four-hour surveillance in twelve-hour shifts and put a tracker under Jimmy Jordon's old pickup truck. They quickly discovered other than opening and closing folding chairs for twelve step meetings and going to every mass, the man did not have much of a life. His one variance from that schedule was to drive to the Yonkers Main Post Office to check his P.O. Box during his lunch break Tuesday, Thursday, and Saturday. Occasionally he received a manilla envelope along with regular junk mail.

Chucho mentioned that Deacon Diaz said a new fresh faced direct from the Vatican acolyte to the Cardinal's archives looked to be a bit of a wild card. The new friendless padre might be approachable for covert activity, if approached delicately. The newbie young man with an independence streak a mile wide was Father Amporo, Rodrigo Amporo.

The new guy was supposed to be a computer whiz kid originally from Chile, South America. He was tasked with computerizing all the old paper records in the archdiocese's basement. A more boring job for an energetic young priest was hard to imagine, unless one had a reason to search for something untoward. I mentioned the new priest's name to Ariana as a possible ally.

After a month of nothing new going on, the state police command said unless something happened soon, their assets might be better used elsewhere. In other words, they were getting busy. Then surveillance lost Jimmy Jordon for six hours. Dressed in a new, off the rack sleek, black leather outfit costing more than six months' stipend fee (in lieu of salary), he took a cab to a car rental agency.

Jimmy picked up a pre-rented luxury car and immediately ditched his police tail. Six hours later he returned the rented car to the agency, took a cab home, and then drove to his church twelve step job in his old clunker of a pickup truck. He was dressed again as usual, in everyday, worn out, out of date thrift store clothes.

That evening, smelling smoke and hearing a fire detector alarm scream, a neighbor called the fire department. When the firefighters gained access to Jimmy Jordon's new home, they found he'd burned sheets of paper in a large aluminum cook pot on the kitchen table. By the time he let the fire department inside his smoke-filled apartment, all the papers and a large envelope had turned to ash, and the newly painted white ceiling turned dark gray.

When the Assistant Fire Chief in command of the fire scene asked, "What's going on here?" Jimmy said, "The paper shredder hasn't arrived yet."

"Why couldn't you wait for it?"

"I must destroy paperwork as soon as the task is finished."

The Assistant Fire Chief said, "Then I must give a desk appearance summons for having a bonfire on a kitchen table in a fully occupied apartment complex *without a permit*. Fella, if I were you, I'd come up with a better story. Unlike myself, those fire court judges don't entertain fools with kindness."

Three days later a large, nude, John Doe body was found in the woods. It lay on top of highest quality BDSM black leather vest, wrist-forearm protectors, pants, chaps, motorcycle boots, found by a homeless game poacher. The body's hands were secured behind his back by black plastic handcuffs and a clear plastic bag tightly sealed over his head with industrial grade gray duct tape.

No identification was found on or near the body and black leather clothing. At autopsy it was discovered John Doe had had an ejaculation just prior to death by asphyxiation. DNA from saliva not belonging to Mr. Doe was found all over his penis. Fingerprints and DNA databases could not identify John Doe, or the saliva provider.

The autopsy put Mr. John Doe's time of death within James Jordon's missing six-hour time frame. Mister unknown victim's left earlobe had been removed through a slit in the bag postmortem. That meant the only missing link to a previous pattern of serial murder was a young BDSM novice participant-witness to the death.

Our little family mobilized for an additional murder; Carmen set to making a new poster inviting information on the latest John Doe murder. Len said he had already put tear sheets up on bulletin boards in leather bars. Donna had been generous in sharing undercover photos of Jimmy Jordon for a poster. Listening to our dinner conversation about the latest serial killing and what we could do, Randy said, "I could show you where the group home boys say the best place to sell your ass is. Want to take a look there for your missing person?"

In the spirit of demystifying Randy's posttraumatic events, I said, "Sure, why not. Anyone else up for an after-dinner drive?" It had just occurred to me the smell of Carmen's arts and crafts materials made me feel uncreative.

Coy and Len joined Randy and me for a go-see look-see. It was still early but there were already many boys and college age men out on the stroll earning school tuition, lab fees, and books, or at least that is what they said. We drove around the area twice, parked, and decided our empirical field research needed face to face on-foot interviews.

Randy chose to talk to boys his age, Len took the older age group, and Coy and I lurked in the shadows in case our lads needed physical support. Both Len and Randy asked anyone who would stand still and listen if they had recently witnessed a murder. Both were batting zeros starting a conversation. It did not take long for them to look discouraged though they pressed on.

Just then I saw a young guy try to pry open my car's trunk with a small crowbar. Without thinking, I grabbed him and his prybar from behind. I had him well subdued when Coy and the others walked over and surrounded us. Without a preamble, Coy shoved the state police surveillance photo of Jimmy Jordon in front of the guy whose arm I had tightly pinned behind his back.

The car burglar want-to-be I was holding tight, turned white as a sheet, and stiffened more in my grasp at the sight of the photo. Then to escape my grip, he repeatedly squirmed hard left to right trying to slip out of the grossly oversized black leather jacket he was wearing.

My housemates witnessed the kid's reaction and without any discussion, joined in securing him with their hands.

Then Randy said, "How much you want for the jacket you're trying to get out of?"

"Shut up, it's not for sale."

"Too bad!"

"If it was you couldn't afford it."

"It's four sizes too big for your scrawny punk ass."

"Fuck you."

"How about I trade you my nice warm comfortable goose-down coat, just your size, for that thing that swims all over you and you are trying to escape from?"

"Don't be a stupid asshole, it's too big for you too. Anyway, like I said it's not for sale."

"Why not?"

"It has sentimental value."

"Feel it, my coat is so soft and cuddly warm."

"Shut up! Why do you want my jacket, we're the same size."

"I know cops looking for a jacket like that linked to a murder. You keep it they will think you did the murder."

"I didn't murder nobody."

"Out of the goodness of my heart I want to help you out. I was jammed up myself recently."

"Oh, wait, right, I saw you before. You were getting plowed at the Diddlysquat home. Yeah, you were jammed all right, jammed up the ass."

Not having heard the word used in that vernacular for decades, out loud more to myself than anyone I said, "Plowed?"

"Yeah, stupid there, getting his oats up the ass. Let me go or I'll tell the police you all tried to take advantage of me."

"While you were out having a stroll up and down a prostitution area?"

"Take your hands off me!"

"Did you plow my young friend?"

"No. I could have if I wanted. He was an available floor mat for all comers at Diddlysquat."

"Why didn't you partake and plow him?"

"He's not my type,"

Randy had heard enough hard to hear insults hitting close to the truth and said, "No, it was because you were too busy dropping your pants and bending over for any bully who'd halfway glance in your direction. Admit it, you liked it."

"See, that's why this coat is too good for a snitch punk like you, tattle tale."

"Suit yourself, SKUNK RAT!"

Coy, Len, and I had been watching Randy's spontaneous performance trying to manipulate the guy wearing an oversized motorcycle jacket. As the exchange of words appeared ready to completely stall out and from training I was about to intervene. But at the last possible moment, I checked myself and swallowed my words, as both young men exchange a long look best described as shared shame and humiliation. Wordlessly the two showed on their faces a depth of degradation from being repeatedly raped while others watched waiting for a turn to extract status from helpless victims embarrassed dehumanized condition.

Uncomfortable watching a shared disgrace commiseration, I said, "You guys hungry? I saw an all-night diner around that corner."

Over the years Coy and I have found food often lubricates conversation in situations about to go silent, like we were witnessing. As it turned out, our new friend said his given name was Junior. Although, he refused to give a last name, but snarfed down a cheeseburger deluxe and chocolate shake in *Guinness Book of World Records'* time.

Sitting back in the booth looking full and redeemed for the moment, Junior said,

"Okay, what's this all about?"

"Do you know the man in the photo my husband showed you?"

"Yes. You saw I did."

"Did you see him put a plastic bag over another guy's head?"

"Not exactly, but I think that guy in the photo did it. The bag head looked dead."

"You didn't check to be sure."

"No. I split out of there as fast as I could go not to get dead too. And I don't want to talk about it."

"If you tell me the whole story, I'll buy you a tasty slice of pie, your choice, with a scoop of ice cream on the side. Yum."

"There's not much to tell really. I am working my corner, and two older gents roll up in an expensive big car. One is tall and built big like a brick-shithouse, and the other short and roly-poly fat. The driver was the fat guy in your photo. He says he'll give me a $100 bill if I do half and half with the other guy while he records it. The passenger was the big guy, huge, this is his coat I'm wearing."

"How did you come to have it?"

"He gave it to me. I'm no thief."

"Is this your crowbar?"

"Anyway, the car driver said his passenger wanted head and then my ass to finish. I said my ass costs a lot more than $100. He said how much? I say more like $1,000 for such fine tail, and since I'm not a porn star $5,000 to be filmed doing it."

"You definitely sound like a professional."

"I am. I'm very experienced. These days you get what you pay for. That's a law of nature."

"Oh, I see, then how much did he offer?"

"He was a cheapskate, wanted to know what he could get from me for $100. I say, for only $100, the best you get is a half and half hand job with a finish in my mouth. The driver and passenger talked for a couple of minutes, then argued. Finally, the driver said get in the car, it was a top-of-the-line German auto. I think it was black and was cozy warm inside."

"What happened next?"

"I don't like to think about this part."

"The sign says pies are made fresh every day and baked on the premises. To check their quality, I'll have a piece of the blueberry I saw when we came in here. It's calling my name. Now do you want to hear what pie choices my friends will order and why or finish your story and eat pie with ice cream?"

"Okay, so, we drive to this cheap, low heat motel somewhere, and the driver sets the scene. I'm told to strip, and the passenger guy leaning against the wall pulls out a huge natural cock. He's watching me undress and playing with himself. Then he strips and there is this awkward moment, then I remembered time is money, so gave him a nice steady two hand handy.

"I can see he is really enjoying what I'm doing, while he watches me do it. I know my business. We were making hot sex eye contact, and I kept licking my lips letting him know what was coming next. All of a sudden, he stopped me, I thought maybe he didn't want to cum too fast. But instead, he takes off this jacket and gently puts it around my shoulders, like a lover might do.

"Normally I don't allow kissing with johns, but his coat was so warm and cuddly, I let him tongue my mouth. After a minute of that we go back to what I was doing for him. It did feel drafty-chilly there and the jacket was so warm inside, and it showed me *he liked my technique.*" Then Junior went quiet and seemed to get lost in his memory.

"And?"

"Then the driver says give him head now. Soon after I'm going down on the passenger's big thick dick there's a scuffle between them while the guy's cock is way down my throat. I can't breathe. They sort of got into a foot shuffle for a minute. Then somehow the passenger guy's hands weren't holding my head in place any longer and I could breathe again."

"Where did his hands go?"

"I don't know, maybe behind his back. After a minute, I guess, he liked my mouth because then he starts to cum down my throat. Except I could feel something else was going on. It felt different and not in a good way. I'm experienced having sex with men, something wasn't right.

"When the passenger finished shooting sperm into my insides and I rock back on my heels to catch my breath, I saw the plastic bag over his head and hands behind his back. It was creepy, he had this eerie surprised, terrified look on his face. I could tell it wasn't bliss."

"What happened then?"

"I got dressed, the driver gave me my money, and he pulled out this gravity knife. So, I took off like a bat out of hell. He didn't chase me, he was too fat to run anyway. Looking back over my shoulder, the driver was kneeling next to the dead passenger guy who was now laying on the floor."

"And?"

"$100 doesn't last long around here, and I'm back on the street."

"May I see your jacket?"

"You can look, but it was gifted to me. It has memories. Here!" Saying that, Junior twisted himself side to side out of the grossly oversized black leather motorcycle jacket.

"Look, guys, this jacket says handmade, and the other inside label is from a Swiss leather shop. Junior, sooner or later this jacket is going to get you into all sorts of trouble you really don't want. Swap coats with Randy and we'll deal with the police and keep your part to a minimum. Or you're on your own."

"How old is the down coat?"

"New this year and that shade of blue really sets off your eyes."

"All right, my life is complicated enough. Trade, even Steven. Though I did like the guy who gave it to me. But because he got his final Jollys in my mouth it's mine to trade. Wear it in good health."

"Now that's a nice cheerful outlook."

"Having a full belly brings that out of me. But you know what … something like that never happened to me before and won't again. It gives street hustling a bad name and scares off clients."

****

Meanwhile in another part of town Deacon Ernesto Diaz, the landlord's representative, was notified of the date and time tenant Jimmy Jordon had a court hearing regarding an indoor bond fire without a permit. Chucho apprised me, I let Ariana know, she told William, and he advised Donna of all the latest developments. He also told her of having the John Doe's jacket in police custody and communicating with an exclusive leather shop in Switzerland to identify the victim.

Jimmy Jordon arrived at the courthouse right on time for his court appearance. His business there was established by showing his desk appearance summons to the court officer standing at the metal detector. Then he was told to walk through the magnetometer and go to a courtroom side chamber. He wasn't expecting state police detective Donna Sims and city detective William Marin to be waiting for him.

Mr. Jordon, an unattractive scraggly fifty-year-old, was shorter than average around 5'5", and weighed maybe 280 pounds. The fringe around his bald head was thin-straight-mouse-brown with a smattering of gray mixed in. He waddled into the side chamber, saw the two cops sitting there and said, "Is this about the fire on my kitchen table?"

"Yes."

"Nobody told me I needed a permit."

"When we get through chatting, you'll go to court room five and tell them that. For the moment we'd like to know *what papers you were burning and your recent movements.*"

"Why do you want all that?"

The two detectives showed their badges and Donna said, "At the moment you are a person of interest to us and the fastest way not to be is to cooperate."

"I'm not supposed to talk about the papers."

"Why not?"

"They are directly from God to me, not for everybody to see."

"Which is easier for you, we arrest you now or after you see the judge?"

"Arrest me for what? I didn't do anything wrong. I'm innocent."

"Then you tell us why we are sitting here."

Abruptly a guilty look washed over Jimmy Jorden's face, and he mumbled, "Uhm, well, I guess nobody will mind if I tell you about the retreat. That's recent time and movement, right?"

"Let's see."

"It was upstate in the mountains. That's what you said you wanted to know, and that's all that happened."

"Tell us about it and we'll see if that gets you off the hook or booked."

Jimmy appeared indecisive. He had been schooled to ask for a lawyer in situations like he found himself. What was bothering him was he might also need a lawyer after he saw the judge. He suspected asking for two lawyers when he was so new on the job might be too much. They might fire him for needing two.

Jimmy decided to try and tough it through, took a deep breath and said, "After Covid-19 wiped out the nursing home I worked at, it was sold. The archdiocese said we would all get new jobs somewhere else, and everyone did but me. Then after interviews with priests, monks, whatever and the Cardinal himself. I was told if I went on this religious retreat to be retrained, I would get a new job."

"What was your nursing home position?"

"I did everything, helped out where needed, even called bingo sometimes when nobody else was available."

"But what was your job title?"

"Janitor's assistant."

"How long did you work there?"

"Thirty-two-years, but they didn't believe in worker's pensions or other benefits. I was what they call a full time parttime worker off the books with a daily lunch and carfare stipend instead of salary."

"What job training did you get on the retreat?"

"For my current job at Saints Peter and Paul Church, I set up and break down their twelve step meetings and help out where needed."

"Huh, you went on a retreat for that."

"No. There was a lot more to it. We fasted, didn't sleep, and they gave me elixirs to help with my spiritual awakening. I was shown how to overpower bigger stronger men. It really worked; God spoke directly to me. It was amazing."

"What did God say?"

"He transformed me right on the spot, into one of his part-time unpaid avenging angels against queers. Isn't that divine?"

"How did he do that?"

"A lot of fasting, not sleeping, and exhaustion over and over doing kingdom come kung fu, and that put me in direct contact with God. Easy sneezy peezy."

"What did God say to you exactly?"

"That was private."

"And these are my handcuffs you will be wearing in public if you don't tell."

"Well, you see, hm ... oh, okay ... now that I'm anointed, God sends me something about once a month. Some months it's only the archdiocese newsletter but sometimes it's a list of instructions for me to follow. It's like having a magazine subscription directly from heaven. But instructions must be shredded or burned immediately after I complete what God wants from me, his avenging angel. That's how I got in trouble with you people. Nobody mentioned needing a permit to burn divine papers."

"What sort of things does God want you to do for him?"

"He wouldn't want me to say. That's why I must burn the instructions."

"Does God only communicate with you inside your head and the U.S. Postal Service?"

"No, not always, at the retreat, God also spoke to me directly through different priests.

At that point Marin and Sims both looked at their watches at the same time and Donna said, "It's time for you to see the judge in court room five."

Jimmy Jordon stood up straight, bowed, and said, "I'd let you kiss my ring, but it hasn't come in the mail yet. Do you want my blessing before I go?"

"We don't want you to be late, maybe next time."

With that said Jimmy left the room, Donna and William looked at each other inanely for a longer than expected interval. Finally, William clicked off the pocket size voice recorder laying on the table and the cops got up and left. Going out the door William said, "I'll have a transcript of whatever that gibberish was over the computer to you later today."

"Do you want to talk with him again?"

"Don't know, Donna, did we get anything useful? Can you imagine this guy planning and doing our John Doe?"

"No way. But he's like Myron Acker in that. The problem is my bosses are calling this case a waste of time."

"Yeah, the city's cop bosses say hands off without concrete proof like a smoking gun in the shooter's hand."

"But William, we have an actual eyewitness to this murder."

"Like all the other eyewitnesses in this case, not reputable. If we can even find him."

"Don't be so negative."

"Come on, he's an underage homeless prostitute, any rookie defense lawyer could eat him for a lunch snack."

"Okay, fine, we'll prove a conspiracy. Otherwise, whoever is behind these murders will keep replacing the tip of the spear."

"I don't know, Donna, isn't this out of our league? I'm a trainer at the academy now, not assigned to any cases."

"William, you know me, I've caught bigger fish. On the other hand, if you think we need help, got any ideas for aid with this crazy BDSM mess of murder?"

"Huh, good question, my old partner has a bunch of eggheads she's been hanging with lately. They just might fill your bill. You already met Oliver Kulgul about those Albany and Buffalo murders."

"What, that triple gang hit in Albany we're calling the forty-caliber hitman? Oh, wait, no, you mean the duct tape mummy and hot spring. All right then, how 'bout you take the lead with the brainiacs?"

****

Carmen shot down my suggestion of having our new Sunday Brunch Recital catered. Our consensus ended with us having a musical afternoon between brunch time and high teatime, and she served snacks and drinks at intermission. The plan from our original Sunday musicals was for each invited guest to play music, preferably on our seven-foot grand piano. There was no reason to change the plan, it worked before.

Then I checked with our resident BDSM experts and TJ said Asa did not play the piano. Also, the piano was not TJ's main musical outlet, though he played well. We settled on a compromise Asa would sing, and TJ would accompany him on the guitar. But I said absolutely no grunge rock.

In the end it turned out to have the same cast of characters as our last brunch. Noteworthy were Randy banged out a bombastic Liszt etude, Len skillfully brought a Chopin Nocturn alive, Coy and I each played adequate interpretations of matching Scarlatti sonatas, TJ and Asa did a Simon and Garfinkel medley for contrast, and Carmen's Beethoven sonata was memorable.

Ariana and Jennifer couldn't come due to a last-minute unavoidable family matter. Jennifer's mom fell and was rushed to the hospital. They were going to sing an acapella duet from Vivaldi's "Stabat Mater." Chucho had a last-minute emergency at the gay senior housing complex and could not come. Deacon Diaz decided to accompany Chucho, for clerical support instead of playing Handel for us. Coy and I like to play Handel arranged for four hands. We feel his gambling addiction caused him to be eclipsed by Bach and Scarlatti. All three men from the 1750s had equally distinctive Baroque Music styles.

At intermission during the long music recital, Carmen and Randy served drinks and healthy snacks. Seeing Randy serving our guests after being the youngest performer, having played the most difficult piano piece, gave me hope for his complete and total recovery from trauma.

However, the casual chatting during the music break was all about a new serial killer replacing Myron Acker. There were as many opinions about what to do with the situation as people were present. One thing all could agree on, if something wasn't done soon the bodies would start to pile up again.

I knew from telephone visits with Ariana we were hopefully about to have a mole with potential in the basement record room at the archdiocese. However, that was not the kind of information that should be freely disseminated, so I played dumb. It is a role many PhDs come by naturally, and I had two PhDs to support my perceived dumbass ranking.

Chapter 18.

Rodrigo Amporo convinced his Chilean recruiter his calling was super strong and so he was admitted to the seminary his junior year of high school. At the Jesuit seminary it was discovered he had a math aptitude bordering on genius level. After his ordination, he was sent to university and earned an undergraduate and then graduate degrees in business economics.

Father Rodrigo's first assignment, while wrapping up graduate work at university, was to scandal burdened Saint Ignatius' parish in Montevideo, Uruguay. The Pastor Monsignor and two of his priests had been arrested along with members of Montevideo's hoi polloi.

The arrests were for having a gambling party with underage prostitutes of both genders without paying bribes. Naturally, the Monsignor and his two priests were reassigned to other countries on other continents as soon as they made bail. The locally well-established parishioners were brought to trial, scolded severely, fined excessively, and the party's caterer was sent to prison for their miss deeds.

Father Amporo with another priest were ordered by their bishop to Saint Ignatius for salvage and rebuilding of the congregation. Once in place Father Amporo found lots of lost money in unexpectedly large quantities. The Church hierarchy acknowledged his good lucrative work with high praise and called him to Rome, Italy.

Rodrigo Amporo, a young, naïve, South American twenty-five-years of age, recent student, was acknowledged by the Vatican for his exceptional, speedy, money finding work in Montevideo. To his surprise, in Rome, Italy, he received specialized training in intelligence gathering to enhance his innate accounting abilities. After brief but intense training in covert detections, self-defense as physical exercise, and church bureaucratic lore, Rodrigo was sent to the New York Archdiocese headquarters on a covert mission.

Amporo was to officially update their computer system and supervise turning old paper records into accurate electronic 1s & 0s. The New York Archdiocese archive still relied on hunched over monk scribes' record keeping in large leather-bound ledgers. Nevertheless, the monk's work *was* superior to the archdiocese primitive, error prone early electronic recordkeeping system. It was often claimed to be the source of their many strange unaccountable accounting errors.

Just before leaving for his new assignment, Father Amporo was taken aside and told in strictest confidence there might be a little hanky-panky going on there. It was also mentioned there were other secret Vatican investigations going on in New York, but all were to keep out of each other's way, if discovered. Intended or not, the final instructions came across as ominous for such a mundane paperwork to computer assignment. Father Amporo imagined monk scribe hostility was implied.

The new priest sensed from tone and cloak and dagger formality, yet without anything definite to go on the Vatican spooks suspected more wrong doings at the New York Diocese than just *a little hanky-panky*. He was not told anything definitive to lead him to that conclusion, but the unspoken message seemed as clear as an email. On his own Rodrigo came to the self-reassuring conclusion that whatever nefarious deeds were afoot in New York, they would not be found in old dusty handwritten documents.

It was no secret to lay and clergy alike Cardinal Tommy Diddlysquat was a radical conservative homophobe cheapskate an astonishing departure from his much beloved generous predecessors. The innocent, inexperienced young priest Amporo's imagination wondered if his assignment was just about organizing old records. Was not money what the devil used to buy human souls.

Detective Ariana Bruschetti met Deacon Diaz at our brunch. The Deacon thought since Father Amporo was new to the country, he might be approachable for getting inside information on the archdiocese. Diaz gave Bruschetti the schedule Amporo heard confessions and suggested going to confession was a legitimate way to meet and size him up without anyone's notice.

She waited until Amporo was almost finished for the day, and no one was waiting. After Ariana entered the confessional, she noticed his strong Spanish accent and switched her English to speaking in Spanish. At first Rodrigo Amporo objected to her use of confession for a purpose other than was intended, then he calmed down and decided to hear her out.

Detective Bruschetti assured him, his role as confessor forbade him telling anyone what she told him, unless he was a nefarious agent of the suspect Cardinal. Joking she said, "And if you are one of his henchmen, it would be better for you to be a double agent than I have to kill you."

Just when he'd gotten comfortable conversing in his native language with her, he was gut punched by a death threat if he didn't cooperate. Not sure he'd heard her right, the priest switched back to is textbook English. It was a halting stall tactic to catch his breath as he realized he was already a double agent, secretly working for the Vatican while overtly on loan to the New York Archdiocese. And now there was this new complexity in his assignment of more than it appeared to be.

Clumsily speaking English with strong Spanish accent, irregular-regular verb conjugation, and without thinking it through first, the priest said, "What you suggest is I become a triple agent not a double to stay alive. That sounds confusing, don't you agree, and not a matter to confess?" Then he realized he'd said too much, but awkwardly clammed up too late.

Picking up on a communications problem, Ariana spoke in the slightly Americanized Italian she heard at home growing up. "I suspected the Vatican sent you here for the same reason the New York City Police Department is interested, somethings not right. Let us keep this simple and not confusing for you. You help me and I offer you unimaginable resources. What do you say padre?"

Rodrigo had not lived in Rome long, but it was total Italian language immersion. That was all they spoke, and it was close enough to Spanish for him to quickly grasp the differences. He was well educated and so were the people he worked with in Italy. Now this strange woman in three minutes had piqued his curiosity in three languages. Speaking in Roman accented Italian, he sternly said, "This is not the proper place to meet about this."

"It's perfect. You can't reveal anything I say to you under the seal of confession, and anything you say to me wouldn't stand up in court. It would be considered hearsay with no witnesses."

"What you suggest goes against the purpose of confession."

"It would keep you safe if we were to be discovered. Here's my card, if you need me for any reason, call. On my own I'll only come to confession when you are not busy and it's important."

"I'll have to pray on this first. In the meantime, you find a more suitable place to meet. Are you working with any of the other ongoing Vatican investigations?"

"No. But I suspected there would be additional inquiries going on. I was raised Catholic and there's something rotten around here."

"What exactly is your interest in the archdiocese?"

"Murder, serial murder, what's yours?"

"What else? Bureaucratic paperwork is the official version, and I'm not supposed to talk about my work to anyone outside the Vatican."

"Really, but why do you think you were sent here?"

"Like I said, I'm not at liberty to say."

"I am a police officer. It's possible I can help with your investigation."

"They told me in Rome not to trust anyone in New York."

"It's not healthy to keep things bottled up inside without an objective sounding board."

"You're probably right. I wish there *were* someone I could talk to here, in this strange country. But there is not and I'm under strict orders."

"Talk to me. I'm a clean cop. We want the same thing and together can get it faster."

"If you were raised Catholic, you'd know lying to a priest will take you straight to hell."

"I know that."

"So far, the books don't add up between this Cardinal and the last ones in ways that can be explained logically. So, now you have it, what I've found this far. Happy?"

"Not logical, like how for instance?"

"Diddlysquat is living lavishly but spending a fraction for it compared to his predecessor's grand regal lifestyles. Yet Diddlysquat's reign has produced only a tiny pittance compared to Cardinal Spillseed and O'Connor's large revenues for the Vatican."

"Huh, I wonder why that is."

"Me too, and his explanations don't come close to making sense."

"Father Amporo, since you are new to our city would you consider having dinner with my wife and me? You might be missing a home cooked meal. Disclaimer, be advised we are vegans and have a cat."

Rodrigo thought to himself, *In this strange place full of strange people even the wives have wives. Indeed, New York is as crazy as I heard.* "My day off is Wednesday."

"Is Wednesday at eight too late for you to eat?"

"No. That's fine."

"I'll have to check with Jennifer, but eight should be okay. Do you have a phone number I can reach you at if not?"

"Here, take my card and go say twelve Hail Mary's and twenty Our Fathers."

"Why? I didn't make a confession."

"It's penance for misusing the sacrament."

****

Father Amporo came to dinner at Ariana and Jennifer's home not wearing his collar. His civilian clothes were sockless leather sandals, new Italian designer denim jeans, and made to measure open neck short sleeve gray sports shirt with abundant chest hair peeking out over the top button.

He stood about six feet tall and weighed around 165 pounds. Abundant thick, straight, black hair was cut attractively to medium length above his bushy eyebrows, long eye lashes, overhanging big bright dark-brown eyes. His hairless facial features were slightly more European than indigenous, and overall look more twenty-five-year-old average-jock male than math-whiz nerd.

Murmur, the family house cat, adopted Father Amporo on sight and stayed next to him or laid on him during the whole visit. The priest brought house guest gifts, two bottles of Chilean wine one red one white. Petting Murmur the priest joked maybe a mistake had been made and his calling should have been to the Franciscans not Jesuits.

An immediate sympatico occurred for the three humans and cat. On the one hand the young South American priest felt outclassed by the two sophisticated New York women and on the other he held his own and better when the casual conversation turned to deep intellectual discourse.

Jennifer and Ariana served a lentil soup centered with a dollop of nondairy sour cream sprinkled with fresh chives, a mixed green, tomato salad topped with homemade salt pickled eggplant and drizzled with homemade dressing. The main course was a mixed vegetable casserole, served on polenta, and covered in a meatless marinara sauce. On one side were oven roasted glazed baby mixed root vegetables on the other side was nondairy buttered fresh string beans with slivered almonds. Dessert was strawberry short cake topped with nondairy whipped cream.

"I had a lovely evening, the meal was delicious, thank you so much for your warm hospitality."

"We were afraid you might be a little homesick."

"I have been, but you countered it so nicely tonight. Unfortunately, my workday starts very early and usually runs into the night."

"Do you have room for a little more dessert?"

"Really, I need to get going. Can you recommend a local cab company for me to call for a ride back to Manhattan?" Also standing Ariana said, "Let me drive you."

"No. no, I don't want to put you out."

"No problem, I'm going your way. I must check in with a confidential informant only available after midnight."

"It must be hard on a relationship not having regular hours."

Jennifer spoke right up and said, "I'm a nurse supervisor on call when the clinic is closed. Our helter-skelter schedules make the time we do have together special."

In the car driving Rodrigo to his home at a church rectory he said, "It was such a nice evening it's sad to see it end. I'm impressed you didn't bring up the matter you came to confession about. I expected you and your wife to pressure me for an answer."

"You're new to this country we wanted to welcome you. I take you at your word you are praying on helping us."

"What exactly do you expect to find?"

"A crime syndicate behind serial murder and money laundering fronted by the archdiocese."

"For this assignment I'm merely an accountant."

"Then how can that work for finding anything new? I mean it's all written down already, right?"

"It's language, and all languages have rules. Even if a person is deaf sign language has rules, and Brail for the blind has rules. But in music, the universal language, first you learn the rules to play the notes then you learn how to break those rules to make music. In forensic accounting it's learning how the rules were broken to uncover misdeeds."

"That's an easy-to-understand explanation. When do you think my prayer will be answered and you will help my investigation?"

"You should have an answer in a few days. I'm almost there. Can I ask you a personal question without offending or crossing a line?"

"You can ask. I can't promise an answer until I hear the question."

"The pastoral counseling classes at the seminary were only about heterosexual couples. Since the Church doesn't approve of same sex couples, they taught us absolutely nothing about them. As far as I know there is no same sex marriage for either gender in Chile or anywhere in South America, and the Church is working to get it appealed in Mexico."

"What's the question?"

"You have such a lovely caring home how do you and your wife maintain the loving relationship I saw with the Church against you?"

"When I was a kid, the Pope was infallible. The current Pope says, "Who am I to judge gay people. The answer to your question is *times change,*"

"I'll be honest, I don't have a clue what two women or two men could do to have sex. I mean there will be no baby at the end of it. I hope this talk isn't making you uncomfortable."

"It's not."

"I feel grossly naïve with you and your wife on one hand and at the same time you are asking me to cross ethical professional boundaries for the sake of your investigation."

"Is this tit for tat?"

"Heavens no. Like you said, times change. I have a suspicion time changes faster up here than where I'm from. Don't say anything if you are uncomfortable talking about this. It won't affect my decision. Only you have opened a box in my mind I've worked hard to keep closed. As is popular to say in English; now the genie is out of the bottle."

"In your pre-priest days didn't your hormones introduce you to sex for one?"

"My vocation started young. I went to the seminary when I was just sixteen. If you are referring to masturbation the Church considers that a mortal sin best avoided at all costs. In that department I'm probably called a late bloomer. Only since I came up here, have I started to talk to other priests about it. Back home it is never talked about by anyone ever."

"Why do you suppose secrecy is the norm?"

"Probably the difference between a homogeneous society and a heterogeneous one?"

"No offense intended I think the Church has some responsibility in fostering body shaming. Look how priests and nuns usually dress and preach about our bodies and bodily functions."

"No offense taken. You have a right to your opinion."

"If you can accept masturbation as sex for one then that opens up all sorts of possibilities for humans to have meaningful sex without the birth of a baby interfering."

"Oh, dear, I see. I don't think the Pope would approve *of that* without judgment."

"Are you aware I'm transsexual?"

"What's that?"

"Biologically I started out as a male and now I'm mostly female."

"WHAT? How is that possible you're a police officer."

"Without intending to add to your confusion, Jennifer was my wife before I transitioned."

"You know I never wanted to leave South America. It's big enough for me without all these modern living misunderstandings."

"Aren't you curious, even a little, what leads someone to being transexual?"

"Ugh! Yes, I guess."

"Imagine going through life with your right shoe on your left foot and left on right, and none of your clothes fit properly either. Add to that people expect you to be somebody else and get upset with you when you are not. Being born in the wrong body doesn't fit in any way."

"But God doesn't make mistakes."

"You'd be surprised how Brazil, Argentina, and Columbia are keeping up with North America's social progress."

"Why do you call it progress? I don't think it is progress to go against nature."

"What appears painful for some, is to expose a view of humankind's nature that has been with us since earliest times."

"Really? I'm not so sure I agree."

"Father, as I see it, both our problem is holding on to laws that have ceased to keep up or serve their intended purpose."

"Now I understand what you are driving at. Your job and mine is a lot about enforcing laws. But what did you mean just now about progress?"

"When the Jewish religion started, they had a lot of trouble with Roman soldiers. During the time of the Roman empire their legions would be away from wife and home on military campaigns for ten years at a time. The main way the men derived sexual relief was with the other men they trusted to cover their backs in battle. They were bisexual by necessity."

"I think I see were this is going."

'Because Ancient Rome ruled the known world for 1,200 years give or take a few, when the Christian religion started, they had the same problem as the Jews with Roman soldiers oppressing them."

"And the Muslims?"

"Late to the party they started after Rome fell. But they based many of their prejudices from the Jews and Christians before them."

"How come you didn't mention the Ancient Greeks? Too pagan for you?" Feeling out of his comfort zone the priest attempted a diversion.

"No ancient Rome and Greece had many of the same gods, just with different names. Before Athens was founded Greek males suffered under cruel matriarchies. When the Greek city states were founded, they preferred same sex as superior except for the obligatory breeding."

"Clearly, I knew nothing of any of this before today, but will explore it now. Did you have sex with both women and men before you changed your gender?"

"Yes."

"Would I be imposing my ignorance to ask for more in-depth details? I'm showing myself to be a total Duffus."

"To further upset your sense of propriety, I didn't transition until after I separated from the military. I'd served several combat tours in the middle east and Africa. Jennifer and I were married husband and wife five years before my change."

"I'm sitting here completely amazed. My world is so much smaller than yours, and yet so arrogant."

"Heard enough for one night?"

"No. Even though I'm feeling completely out of my depth everything you've said so far seems distant. If I'm not asking too much, I'd like to hear of a personal experience that's similar to the night of discovery I'm having."

"You want me to tell you about a sexual discovery I made?"

"If you don't mind."

Ariana explained what the letters ROTC stood for and their reduced student fee and tuition benefits for participating. As an undergraduate male, senior with a steady girlfriend, one of Ariana's duties was to drill freshmen ROTC cadets. For unknown reasons one cadet, Gilbert, showed Ariana too much admiring interest.

Up to that point Ariana as male, had only occasionally experienced gay sex as trade by accepting anonymous blow jobs in the park after a girlfriend got him over stimulated and then wouldn't put out. It was popular at that time for college students to call themself bisexual, so he did without thinking much about it one way or another.

Late one afternoon after drill practice Ariana in male form went to pee, and Gilbert walked up and took the next urinal. When Ariana glanced over and down, Gilbert took a step back showing off his unremarkable average size cock and said, "I wouldn't mind getting head from you. Just respect that I am straight." Saying that Gilbert indicated he was the opposite of straight in that day's common jargon.

The difference in their senior to freshmen ages, social scholastic class, and ROTC rank made bored Ariana decide to take the uppity freshmen's overconfidence down a peg or two. He said, "Fine, my roommate is away on a family emergency. My dorm room is this way."

They didn't speak until they were in the dorm room with the door closed and Ariana could see what had started out as a self-dare for Gilbert had turned into something he was having second thoughts about. His face showed his growing serious uncertainties over what he'd started without thinking it through.

At the same time Ariana was thinking, *how far do I want to take this prank? Or has it gone too far already I've never sucked a dick or particularly want to?*

Seeing Gilbert shit faced alarm, Ariana said, "How did you imagine this happens?"

"I didn't really. What do you suggest we do?"

"I suppose there should be rules, right?"

"Right."

Wondering if he'd really go through with anything he was about say the earlier male version of Ariana said, "OKAY! You could go trade only and lean against the door pull out your cock and think I will fall on my knees and blow you. While you are hoping against hope I don't just point my finger laughing hysterically. Which I might be inclined to do."

"That would be cruel of you."

"Okay, more friendly, you take off all your clothes wash your dick in the sink over there, lay on my bed and I lick your balls and suck you off. Then kick your sorry ass out of my dorm room, naked and throw your clothes out the window."

"I could do the first part, I guess, *except the last part would be mean of you.* I really like you Bruschetti."

"Or your best choice for me, you get in touch with your bisexual self. We go all kissy face touchy feely, I strip you, swirl my tongue around your nipples, lick your balls, blow you while I finger fuck you hard until you cum. Then I bend you over and fuck the living shit out of you with my big steel hard cock and you cum again. Pick a number." Ariana as male said this not knowing if he would or could actually do any of what he said but was aware his dick was harder than ever, and the freshman had asked for it.

Gilbert looking both turned on and off at the same time had without realizing it allowed Ariana's erotic and threatening words to take him into a spontaneous orgasm. He came vigorously from fear mixed with lust, due to unrequited love. Shuddering as a huge load embarrassingly creamed his underwear. His cum-shame face showed him realizing he'd taken a dare way too far and would now have to somehow pay up for not thinking ahead and suffer more consequences. One ROTC rule intruded pushing other thoughts away, *Take your punishment like a man so you can get the hell out of here!*

Without saying a word Gilbert turned his back to Ariana pulled down his pants and underwear and bent over spreading his ass cheeks to show his bottom hole. Fully clothed Bruschetti pulled out a rock-hard cock and took the invitation to have anal sex for the first-time mounting Gilbert saying, "If you like we can make out after I cum up your ass." While saying that Ariana was sure making out with a freshman was not something of interest for the senior, but the tight rear channel was.

Father Rodrigo's face showed conflicting emotional expressions after Ariana's tale and said, "What is a spontaneous orgasm?"

"One that happens without any physical stimulation or touching of any kind."

"Huh, one more thing I didn't know and asked about. This has been an illuminating evening."

"Let me ask you one father. Did Gilbert sin when he unintentionally orgasmed with no physical contact?"

"No. But I suspect you knew that."

"Did I sin by fucking him without a condom?"

"You know the Church disapproves same sex anything but sports, and use of condoms is always a mortal sin for all parties involved if it is to prevent conception. Yet those sins can be absolved by confession. We could even have taken care of it the other day."

"I know, but the Church also has issues with my changing genders."

"I'd absolve you."

"Thank you, but Jennifer and I stopped attending mass when I transitioned. Our parish priest at that time excommunicated me for transitioning."

"If you want, I can correct that too."

"That's okay, it's the damage of living with secrets that needs to be fixed. And the Church perpetuates it, and I doubt you're powerful enough to fix it."

"One way or another everyone's life is a struggle birth to death, and changing times or gender doesn't change that."

"Touche. In the future if you don't want to contact me directly, for any reason, there is a Deacon Diaz at Saints Peter and Paul. I don't have direct contact with him, but he can get a message to me through third parties he and I both know."

"Why shouldn't I contact you directly? I'm not put off by anything said tonight and you and your spouse lay out tasty meals."

"If you decide to help, I don't want you put in any danger from my murder investigation."

Chapter 19.

Father Rodrigo Amporo's righteous sense of superiority from following all the Church's rules was suddenly more troubled than he wanted to admit. His conversation with Ariana Bruschetti about sexuality, gender, and being human, produced doubts. He never doubted before it must be the New York ethos' fault.

Consistent with his training he threw himself into working harder, what time and energy was left after that was devoted to prayer for guidance, physically working out to exhaustion, and then exploring television like he'd never imagined. Nevertheless, the part of his being human he'd walled off up to then, cracked opened with troubling persistent erections that cold showers did not fully relieve.

After a week of hard labor, he had sorted, organized, systematized, and computerized records going back to old Cardinal Spillseed. He had only found innocent mistakes mostly from too many monk hands handling the documents and account entries. Based on his findings so far, he telephoned Ariana and said he would not participate in her investigation because he had nothing to contribute.

When he started working on record keeping since Cardinal Diddlysquat was assigned to run the archdiocese the mistakes were not from incompetence and were tricky to untangle. It was clear from the start there were traps set to confuse auditors. Rodrigo reported to his Vatican handler the books were cooked and the way it was done would take some doing to unscramble the recipe.

Just as he began to try untangling the source of large sums of money that occasionally just appeared, were mixed in with regular church funds, and then disappeared all without explanation. Someone high up in the archdiocese assigned him the additional task to cover several uncovered parishes as temporary pastor in the wilds of Staten Island, without a car.

When father Amporo showed his Vatican contact the banishment to Staten Island order, it was immediately rescinded. Then while he was back working franticly un-cooking the cooked books, he was issued an emergency order to cover a dangerous Bronx parish with an infirmed pastor. Once again, the Vatican intervened and the emergency was handled by another priest, and Rodrigo was assured his name had been taken out of rotation for vacation parish priest coverage. Just when Father Amporo thought he could concentrate on his recordkeeping assignment, a new emergency assignment was issued for him to cover a large problematic parish at the ass end of Brooklyn.

Again, the Vatican made serious threats to take complete control of the archdiocese if Amporo was not left to do his work. The archdiocese assured Vatican bullies the good father would not be assigned anywhere other than his current job. But once again expressed a serious shortage of personnel and how they saw what Father Amporo was doing as totally *unnecessary* when he could be so much more useful elsewhere.

After that Vatican directive, a series of events made the priest decide his guardian angel was vigilant protecting him from near fatal accidents. For no explainable reason accidents started to befall Rodrigo, who had always been a careful person avoiding careless mishaps. Not wanting to be seen as a troublemaker, he did not mention the almost accidents to his Vatican contact, or anyone for that matter.

Then leaving work for the day, someone pushed him out of the way when a large steel safe fell out of a high window landing mere feet in front of where Father Amporo was walking. Once again, the priest found no logical explanation how the almost accident could have happened with no witnesses top or bottom. It was a New York-style mystery to him.

The next morning a speeding driverless car came careening up onto the sidewalk right where he would have been if a kind stranger had not grabbed and shoved him out of the way. Once again, no explanation for the event was offered other than maybe he was having a run of bad luck.

Then that evening a mugger tried to stab Rodrigo with an ice pick as he walked home from his workplace. A good Samaritan seemingly came out of nowhere and dispatched the mugger instantly on the spot, breaking his neck. Then the guardian angel disappeared into the shadows as quickly as he had appeared before a heartfelt thank you could be tendered.

Next morning walking to work saying the rosary as he went, a stranger approached Father Amporo and said, "Hi, I'm Father Hector Guterres. I've been sent to bodyguard you."

The young man, slightly older than Rodrigo's age, put his hand out for a shake. Guterres was of average height, weight, appearance, and could easily blend into a crowd identified as nondescript in appearance. Except on closer look, his fine tailored priest-street-drag, expensive haircut, and athletic way of moving show he was more than an average guy.

Rodrigo was startled out of his rosery concentration, mechanically shook the offered hand, and coming to full consciousness said, "Why would I need a bodyguard?"

"It seems you're accident prone."

"I'm not!"

"Didn't a safe fall out of a window right where you were walking the other day?"

Speaking without thinking first Rodrigo said, "That was an innocent accident." His mind catching up with his mouth, he suddenly looked wary putting two and two together and said, "Did the archdiocese send you? They have been told and retold to stop interfering with my work."

"No, the Vatican feels you need a minder. It seems you stirred up a hornet's nest around here."

"If you're a priest, what qualifies you to be a bodyguard I don't need."

"One thing might be the Colt forty-five in my shoulder holster. Another, my years fighting with and then against rebels as a child soldier in Columbian jungles."

"Wait a minute, are you a Columbia University graduate? My condolences, God bless you. I heard that place is ruthlessly brutal, even savagely barbaric beyond South American coup standards."

"Based on what information?"

"Cable and streaming local television channels say the Columbia University administration is unable or unwilling to communicate with their students."

"How so?"

"They just asked the police to beat and arrest their pupils and destroy the acolytes' property just for being nonviolent. I thought these North Americans had some kind of obviously phony-baloney constitution that allowed for free speech."

"Oh, that ... it's complicated."

"It's not complicated, Columbia University has a history of cowering before students with issues. Television says this university did the same thing in 1978, invited the police to attack, beat, and arrest their students. Back home in Chile universities nurture and value students. They don't have them assaulted, jailed, and their property destroyed for expressing an idea."

"You wouldn't understand."

"I understand Columbia University must be a hellish, uncouth and savage place. Who would want to work there? It sounds more like a prison than a privileged private school. I just don't get these North Americans."

"Actually, most of the better colleges and universities, with the brightest students, also had large student protests. The violence was really, really bad at the lessor quality schools."

"What could be worse?"

"At the University of Arizona, first the police teargassed the protesting students, then stunned with gas, shot them with rubber bullets, when the bullets ran out, they clubbed students senseless with truncheons, and finally arrested them, all on university administration orders. That's even worse than Columbia University which was the harshest of the other New York schools."

"You're right, I read during the war against Vietnam the U.S. military shot down dead, with steel bullets, peaceful protesting college students on their university campuses. Apparently, in the land of mass school shootings students are not safe at any scholastic attainment. What could they be protesting to be treated so harshly?"

"It's complex. Students across this whole country protested, although not all were savaged by their school's administrators telling the police to assault them."

"I understand complex with graduate degrees in economics from honorable institutions of higher learning, that don't attack students."

"Really?"

"Well, at least not while I attended. What was so sacred it needed to disrupt student nonviolence with police violence?"

"Like the Vietnam War, making money meant more than human life."

"Explain please."

"It was none of our business. Alright, if you are going to get all pouty face I'll tell you the digest version."

Then Father Guterrez explained the country of Israel ended up with a rightwing government that didn't represent the peoples' values. The common fair-minded Israelis protested their government by the hundreds of thousands and the jails got full. So, the right wingers announced they were annexing all the indigenous people's lands they occupied for seventy years of apartheid and then left the guarded gates between them unguarded.

What the indigenous Semites heard was the last of their land was about to be stolen. Savage attackers came through unguarded gates, and it was later reported that intelligence about the impending attack was ignored. The occupied people took hostages to barter for their land after showing the occupiers they also could be savage.

The Israeli Defense Force aka IDF had asked the Israeli people to make sacrifices for them in return for a promise to protect them. The IDF didn't protect and was nowhere to be found for hours while the indigenous Semites raped, kidnapped, and slaughtered undefended Israelis.

With public protests quelled by being attacked, Israeli European leaders sent the IDF to systematically eliminate all the people on the land they occupied, by cutting off all food, water, fuel, and bombing them. The intended result was to finally give the last real estate to other European settlers and put an end to the idea of a two-state solution. Just like in the genocide in the U.S. against its first people.

This modern David and Goliath story involves donkey-carts, rock throwing children, and tunnels at war with F-16 fighter bombers, ultra-modern armor tanks, precision guided missiles, and a modern well-trained equipped infantry. After the facilitators of violence using up to date weapons of war have shed enough innocent blood, history suggests the donkey-carts are projected to win a country of their own at a ridiculously high cost for all involved.

"So, you're saying all that to hide the fact you are a Columbia University graduate, or student. Yeah, I'd be ashamed to admit it too. God bless you and your classmates."

"No. I'm from Bogota, Columbia, South America, the land of poets and philosophers. Then most recently from the Vatican, Italy."

Impromptu checking the man's authenticity Rodrigo switched to speaking Italian and said, "If what you said was true, you'd carry a Baretta not a Colt. I find all this cloak and dagger business in New York very irregular, disturbing, on top of mass student protests, it's very tiring. Now, since you disturbed me, I must start saying my rosary from the beginning again."

"What do you know about Barettas versus Colts?"

"My father is a policeman in Antofagasta, Chile. He says Barettas are the best automatic in the world."

"My Colt is for remembrance of my jungle fighting days in the Amazon. I've had a gunsmith customize it. Your father was right about Barettas. Incidentally, did a speeding car almost kill you last night?"

Speaking Italian fast to see if the stranger was authentic and could keep up Father Amporo said, "I was told that was only an out-of-control car having an accident near me. I hear they are as normal as school shootings here in North America."

"Who said that?"

"A stranger like you. He said it was not a Tesla driverless vehicle. Thirty-five of the last forty driverless car crashes were Tesla, it's expected now."

"You can't trust what you're told in the United States. Even they're government lies."

"All governments lie! … Back on topic, I've never heard of priest bodyguards and if I had I wouldn't need one. I'm only a boring non-offensive to anyone paper shuffling accountant."

Using refined, measured, Italian to reply Hector said, "Surely, you've heard of the Swiss Guards. My agency isn't Swiss, but we do their overseas work and go anywhere the Pope wants to show muscle and enforcement outside the Vatican."

"A priest packing a gun, no, that sounds incompatible. We priests are for peace."

"Perhaps you've heard of liberation theology in Central America? We used big, long guns there. Many people noticed, few objected."

Switching back to South American Spanish Rodrigo said, "Fine, but I don't have any need for your services. You may tell who sent you that. Nice meeting you Hector, goodbye."

"It's not your place to decide. You need to know your place."

"Look, Guterres, take a hint, get lost! I should have my job here wrapped up in a week or two. With luck I'll be sent back to South America or Europe at least."

"I guess New York is not your cup of tea. Personally, I love the big apple. It's fun, but then again, I'm not a Jesuit."

"You won't believe how secular sensual these North Americans are. They just up and change their gender when they want, it's unbelievably upside down here. Tell your boss I don't need a babysitter, I'm fine learning strange new things on my own."

"So, last night when that assassin tried to stab you to death, and I broke his neck that was not necessary? You trying to get dead or what?"

"Oh, that was you! Well, why didn't you do your duty! Even assassins are entitled to last rites."

"He wasn't Catholic. He looked Muslim to me."

"Arrogant! How could you tell without having pulled his pants down to check?"

"In my business Extreme Unction isn't always done timely, other factors become primary in the heat of the moment."

"I sincerely hope you will remember that in confession."

"Onwards and upwards, padre, like it or not, your belongings have been moved to a safe, secret location. I'll take you there after work. From now on, we will do everything together as long as you are in New York with people trying to kill you."

"Who says?"

"Our Vatican handlers. Also, from now on I will taste your food before you do, so don't order too spicy."

"I like spicy and don't approve of any of this."

"Do you want to get out of this alive?"

"I'm starting to dislike you."

"Hey, none of this was my idea. But believe me it's easier to just follow orders than take the consequences, Rome can be more than a bit vindictive. You know how those Italians can be."

****

The safe house was in fact a two-bedroom apartment in a small squat building with twelve apartments, four per floor in Long Island City, Queens. It was on the East River with views of Manhattan on one side and the Newtown Creek facing Greenpoint, Brooklyn on the other side.

Other tenants Rodrigo observed coming or going were pairs of males, like his arrangement. A nerdy or average looking guy with a butch looking buffed guy. It did seem odd such a small building would have two oversize twenty-four-hour doormen that nobody in their right mind would want to tangle with. Father Amporo found his belongings unpacked and laid out neatly in drawers exactly as he had them in the rectory he'd just been moved from.

Suddenly Rodrigo's daily routines included his armed shadow alongside. Monday, Wednesday, and Friday he did calisthenics for a half hour before a shower, breakfast, and going to work. On Tuesday, Thursday, and Saturday they got in a one mile run before laboring. The only time Rodrigo didn't see Hector close by was doing his work, and even there his presence was felt. After his shift crunching numbers, if Rodrigo experienced mental fatigue from his efforts, he'd go on a five-mile run to get his body to the same state of exhaustion as his mind was already.

One evening after a particularly taxing day at work, out on a five-mile run to meld mental fatigue with physical alertness, the two young priests were attacked by three older, larger, thuggish looking men. Two of them tried to waylay Hector. The one with a baseball bat was dispatched quickly and Rodrigo saw Hector trading kicks and punches with the other man.

Then suddenly he saw the third man coming at him with brass knuckles on each hand glinting from the streetlight. Rodrigo didn't have time to think, the brief but intense Vatican training in Akido took charge. As the assailant lunged forward fists flailing Rodrigo smoothly sidestepped, tripped, and pushed the man over, using his own force against him.

The assailant angrily scrambled to his feet to lunge again. He apparently thought Rodrigo would use the same defensive moves a second time, which Amporo did not. Instead, the priest got the same results defending from the opposite side. Once again, the attacker landed hard on his ass, with a thud, then pain, and a seriously damaged pride. That motivated the thug to literally fly off the ground targeting Rodrigo with murderous velocity.

Combat was ended by the sound of two gun shots, one rapidly followed the other. Hector had shot the perpetrator in the middle of his chest, then between the eyes, and said, "Problem solved. Let's get out of here."

"We going to give these three last rites? It's what we are supposed to do along with not killing them."

"Our bosses don't think they can protect you in jail if you get arrested, and I know I can't. We suspect whoever is behind the attempts on your life could have you finished off in jail. Come on we must complete this run and catch a shower before the police show up."

He stared dumbly at the three dead men prone on the ground too stunned by their recent demise to think or speak. Hector ran back, circled then grabbed Rodrigo's arm and they finished their run. All the while Father Amporo thought, *I've got to remember to take fresh oil and my last rites kit when I'm out with Father Guterres.*

Back in their safe house apartment as the two men stripped to shower Hector said, "After a kill I like to have an orgasm. It helps me sleep. Since you fought with one of the assailants do you want to fool around together?"

"Heavens no, that idea is over the top for me, I took a vow of celibacy."

"We all did. It's not realistic to expect to keep it when absolution is so handy afterward."

"Am I the only one who honors my vows?"

"I honor mine when I'm not having sex. After a night like you just had with people hired to kill you it's only natural to need a sexual release."

"Ah ha, then what exactly are you offering?"

"How about a nice hand job in the shower."

"Is that the best you can do?"

"Well, I don't know you all that well and you're going back to Rome soon if I can keep you from getting murdered."

"Why would I break my vow with you for something I can do myself?"

"Oh, all right! I'll give you a blow job but that is as far as I go with someone I hardly know."

"And you're serious. I can't believe this."

"Look at your dick. If it got any harder, it would break off."

The two young men entered the steamy hot shower and what transpired changed some of Father Amporo's beliefs from theological theoretical to toe curling concrete human. The next morning several old monks toiling away with huge ledger books in the basement archives of the archdiocese comment that father Amporo looked completely relaxed for the first time since joining them. They wondered what his secret was and could they get some too.

Released from years of stress and strain, keeping his hormones in check, Rodrigo solved the unsolvable archdiocese record keeping problems. Father Amporo broke questionable entries into two different problems rather than only the one he originally supposed needed unscrambling. Similar but different, two problems, two distinct actions, same resolution.

Problem one, when church real estate was sold, a large deposit immediately appeared added to the ledger's right column. Then a week or so later, tiny regimented, always proscribed same subtractions appeared on the left for small disbursements in service to the real estate sales recorded in that column. That was followed weeks later by a large disbursement equal to the difference in full real estate sale value minus the recently smaller amounts paid to the Church's accounts. Usually, the mysterious disbursement happened around a holiday for the remains of the sales amount when mysteriously disappeared.

The disappeared amount was always in the millions of dollars. By hook and by crook using forensic accounting tricks. Amporo discovered the disappeared money went into a nonchurch, nameless private account, in the Caymen Islands. To confuse the issue sometimes large amounts of missing money entries in the ledger were made out to *miscellaneous expenses, or other bogus entities.* This pattern repeated itself mostly when real estate was sold. It had been going on since Cardinal O'Connor retired and was replaced by Diddlysquat.

Problem part two, on a much smaller scale but confusing when included with problem number one, five hundred dollars would appear added in the right column for no reason. It was also sometimes identified as *miscellaneous income or in income.* Then often, but not always, it was followed weeks or months later by a fifty-thousand-dollar deposit added on the right, from *miscellaneous income to miscellaneous income, or in income.* Then after small disbursements subtractions on the left for: three-day high priced limousine service, three nights at eccentric hotels, escort services, videographers, and miscellaneous petty cash subtractions for meals and drinks. Then the bulk of $50,500 would eventually disappear like the real estate sales money. It would mysteriously vanish into the Caymen Islands account

What didn't jive, and glaringly finally caught Father Aporo's attention, was the archdiocese had their own fleet of luxury limousines with uniformed armed drivers. From that irregularity, a quick check of the hotels paid for with disappearing money revealed they were not of the quality or location the archdiocese would use, if they ever did use hotels for out-of-town guests. VIP Guests were always housed at the Cardinal's palace, lower classes at church rectories, no need for motorcycle hotels.

Also, every archdiocese department had a big or small petty cash account in that name. Even down in the dusty basement archives' record room was a small petty cash account box. But Father Amporo, looking among the many archdioceses' accounts, could not find a location for a *miscellaneous petty cash* account regularly handled in a special out of the ordinary way.

What was brought to notice was the difference between problems one and two being disbursement issues. In problem one, millions went into the right column from real estate sales. A few thousand were paid out to Church accounts, and then the bulk left the left column via the mysterious *miscellaneous petty cash,* easy peasy. It was always handled in the same exact way.

But with problem two, when $50,500 came in the right column, pitiful *small* expenditures were paid out on the left to *miscellaneous petty cash or in cash.* Always done sporadically and *before* a final total of the balance was paid out on the left back to *miscellaneous petty cash.* It was sloppy, and nothing was paid to Church accounts, it was the Church accounts ledgers. Unlike all the other easy to track regular petty cash, miscellaneous or in cash were well healed phantoms.

As it happened, just as Father Amporo was having his *EUREKA* moment untangling the accounting knot that had been stifling him, a geriatric monk named Martin Ambrose waddled by. Observing the sudden change in Rodrigo's body language, Brother Ambrose leaned in peering intently through his thick round eye glass lenses and whispered, "Are you all right father?"

Father Amporo nodded to the affirmative.

Still whispering, barely audibly under his breath, the monk rasped, "What happened?"

In a half whisper reply, for no reason other than imitation, Father Amporo said, "I've just solved the mystery that's been bugging me since I got here! Oh, wait, oh, dear, I still don't know where the stolen money goes. SHIT! Forget what I just said."

Brother Martin leaned in even closer, his garlic breath intense and whispered, "May I use that bit of scrap paper next to your computer?"

Feeling foolish he'd jump the gun celebrating a success not earned yet, Father Amporo turned his face away from the strong smell of garlic breath and mechanically handed the monk the reused paper he'd been scribbling numbers on.

Brother Martin scrawled something on the paper handed it back and softly murmured, "Now *that* should solve your mystery, keep it to yourself. Godspeed." And then the very, very old monk hobbled down the long hallway on his arthritic knees.

Looking carefully at what Bother Ambrose wrote, Father Amporo memorized *First National Bank of the Caymen Islands #86679,* folded the paper and put it in his pocket. Glancing at his watch, it had gotten late. tomorrow he would find the local names of signatories on that account. Then it was up to the Vatican for matching suspicious deposits from the New York Archdiocese with stolen money gone who knew where for who knew what reason.

Finished working for the day Father Hector Gutierrez met Rodrigo just before he went through the exit door, and as usual their car pulled up to the curb. The attendant got out and Hector slid in behind the wheel and they were driving in midtown rush hour traffic. After a few out of the ordinary twists and turns, Hector took out his cell phone, put it in the dashboard holder, and hit a speed dial number. A deep male voice came on the speakerphone and said, "Control."

Switching lanes and making un-signaled turns off their usual way home Gutierrez said, "Control. this is HG8. We have a tail."

"Where are you?"

"Fifty-seventh Street going toward Third Avenue and heading for the Fifty-ninth Street bridge."

"*Don't take the bridge.* Head down Second Avenue and take the Queens Midtown Tunnel."

Father Amporo turned in his seat and saw a new, dark-gray BMW trailing them. The way it was driving it had to be the car Hector mentioned. Through the windshield he saw four men inside the chase car. As they approached Second Avenue, Hector quickly switched them back to the right lane without signaling. At that point both lanes of heavy traffic on Fifty-ninth Street could drive onto the bridge. But only the right lane could also continue straight avoiding the bridge or make a right turn onto Second Avenue, which they did.

Due to traffic the chase car was stuck in the left lane. They had anticipated following their target on to the bridge. Hector made a hard right down Second Avenue. Suddenly, the tailing car was trapped in heavy traffic in the left lane trying to make a right turn onto Second. Then it was T-boned hard by a tow truck and simultaneously struck on the other side by a private sanitation truck. Amporo lost sight of what appeared to be a fatal traffic accident screwing up rush hour traffic at the lower-level Manhattan side of the Ed Koch Queensboro Bridge.

They went through the Queens Tunnel without incident and were at the safe house faster than usual. Just as their Volvo XC90 SUV drove up to the automatic steel door to open to let them into the underground garage below the safe house another big foreign made car pulled in behind them. Hector shouted, "Get down!"

With his head down, Father Amporo pushed the lever that electronically turned his right-side mirror to watch. Four men exited the vehicle behind them and started shooting automatic weapons at the automobile he was sitting in. Then the two doormen from the safehouse came out the front door firing larger caliber automatics at the intruders. The bad guys seemed to be expiring as the garage door opened and Hector drove them inside and the door automatically closed behind the dead and dying intruders.

Sitting up and turning to Hector, Rodrigo said, "I heard their bullets hit us, but none penetrated, why is that? There were a lot of bullets pinging and zinging."

"This chariot has armor plate and bullet proof glass. The question is can we get a cell signal underground?"

Hector drove them around inside the garage until he found a signal and said, "Control, we were just ambushed at the safe house. What do you advise?"

"Do you have cellphone battery life?"

"It's car charging as we speak."

"Put your passenger on."

With a head nod toward the dash-mounted cell phone, Hector indicated Rodrigo should talk.

"This is Father Amporo speaking."

"Did something unusual happen at work today?"

"Yes, I solved the mystery the Vatican sent me here to unravel."

"Why didn't you tell us?"

"I haven't wrapped it up with a bow yet."

"Can you do that remotely?"

"Why?"

"Do you know a Brother Ambrose?"

"Yes. He helped me solve the Vatican's mystery."

"He's been killed. The archdiocese says it was age related to natural causes and his body had already been shipped to Indiana where he's from. We grabbed the van carrying him on the way to the Saint Michaels Crematorium in Astoria Queens. Our autopsy indicates murder by suffocation.

"God rest his soul. He didn't deserve to be killed he was a sweet old monk dedicated to his work."

"Can you work remote?"

"I can do it with a computer if they haven't wiped all my work files."

"Let me talk to HG8."

"HG8 here."

"Do you need to change cars?"

"No. This one has bullet pockmarks but runs fine with an almost full tank of gas. I don't see any other armored vehicles here."

"Take Queens Boulevard turn left onto Roosevelt go to Woodside and Saint Sebastians on your right. I'll have agents posted along that route. Park off the street behind the rectory. A computer will be fired up with a direct link to Rome for your passenger in St. Seb's office. Expect Command to contact you en route. Control out."

As Control clicked off, Hector squealed rubber as he fishtailed them out of the underground garage from a hidden exit at breakneck speed. He soon had them driving on Queens Boulevard. Just as he made a left turn onto Roosevelt Avenue the cellphone beeped and Hector said, "This is HG8."

Then an authoritarian voice in German had a stern conversation with Hector, and the driver immediately slowed down their car speed. Rodrigo didn't understand German but if he had, he would have noticed German with a strong Swiss accent. When that conversation ended, Hector turned to Rodrigo and said, "You'll have four hours at Saint Sebastian to do your computer work and then I'm handing you off at Kennedy International Airport for a midnight flight to Rome. If I don't get a chance, it's been good working with you. Good luck in the future. God bless."

"All my travel documents are back at the safe house along with my clothes."

"You'll be met at the airport's International Departure Terminal with documents, including baggage claim tickets, your packed belongings will be on the flight."

"I guess that means I don't get to reciprocate that blow job you gave me in the shower. I really enjoyed it and was looking forward to returning the favor. With that and everything else, including your reckless driving, I've felt safe with you. Thank you, Hector."

"Don't worry about it, I was just doing my job. But I wouldn't have minded teaching you how to give head. If you hang around the Vatican long, you'll catch up on your own. Then if we meet up again, you can repay the favor as an expert."

****

Father Amporo needed most of the allotted four hours to refine and polish his exposé of fraud capped with a Caymen Island bank account number that cost a monk his life. Allowing himself a small modicum of egotism for his hard work, he sat back with satisfaction, then prayed for forgiveness for his sin of pride.

Within the last few minutes left, he sent an email to Ariana Bruschetti that said, "It is hoped my attachment of a financial file to this email will help in your investigation. Be careful, many people have died in my getting what I'm sending you. Don't wait too long, the bad guys know I'm on to them and being murderously aggressive about it. Thank you for your generous hospitality, it was the highlight of my trip here. I leave for Rome at midnight. All the best happiness to you, Jennifer, and Murmur."

The hand off at Kennedy Airport went without a glitch. As Rodrigo approached the boarding gate, he was waylaid by Ariana and Jennifer. After brief hugs the women gave him homemade food in plastic containers saying, "Airline food is not healthy. We've made enough vegan treats to see you home to Rome and back, share with other passengers. Godspeed," and they all waved goodbye.

Chapter 20.

Ariana telephoned, filled me in on the attachment she received from Father Amporo, and his sudden departure at midnight. We agreed what she had now should break open the archdiocese's crime syndicate behind the BDSM serial murders and their connection to a once-a-year magazine ad leading to homicide. And enthusiastically shared the thought we would soon see an end of murder in black leather unofficially blessed by the Church.

Then I did not hear from her for a week. When she did get back to me, it was not with a progress report, she sounded discouraged. Anxiously wanting to hear progress, I thought she was just venting her frustrations with big bureaucracies as an introduction. I tried to be a good friend and only listened until she requested an unofficial meeting outside any regular law enforcement facility. So much for yielding my interest to her needs. Knowing Ariana well, it was most likely the purpose of the call in the first place, and if I had not been listening so intently in friendship would have picked it up, before she had to spell it out to me.

Ariana wanted Coy, me, William Marin, Donna Sims and Donna's partner Jerry Parker to have a sit-down meeting. I did not probe her request although it seemed a big group for such short notice. But I did add Len to the attendees since he had been chronicling the BDSM murders since meeting Jack Warren. Having a knowledgeable scribe handy like Len could be helpful. I reserved a small conference room at the public university I also teach at for an evening, date, and time.

At the appointed time and place, all invited were present. I insisted Ariana sit at the head of the conference table since the meeting was her idea. After a brief back and forth, she took the seat reluctantly. Then she and William handed me, Coy, Donna, and Jerry photocopies of Father Amporo's attachment to an email. Recognizing there was no copy for Len, not knowing he was coming, Ariana asked for his browser address and forwarded him a copy on the spot from her laptop. Then she gave me a cross glance for neglecting to mention I had invited Len and began the meeting.

To the assembled Ariana said, "To be sure we all know each other, let's start by going around the table left to right and introduce ourselves." After all persons present spoke their name she said, "Well my friends our investigation into BDSM serial murder has an overabundance of evidence we are unable to use. Need I summarize?"

"Yes."

Yielding to the request Ariana explained blockage went local to national. "The New York City Police Department and District Attorney's Office refused to reopen the serial murder case going back many years because Myron Acker is dead, God rest his soul. They are treating the murder since his death as unrelated to all the earlier ones and refuse to link them. The New York State Police don't have the resources or jurisdiction to tackle an international murder case involving large domestic and foreign banks and multinational magazines involved in major money laundering. According to reliable sources the New York State Attorney General's office does not want to be perceived prosecuting the Roman Catholic Church without a smoking gun and blood on the floor. According to the FBI since no local or state cases have been proven against Myron Acker, and he is dead, they have no cause to open a case."

Speaking directly to Ariana Bruschetti, while closely eying the rest of us at the table, Jerry Parker asked. "Doesn't the New York City Police Department have an international crime unit floating around overseas?"

"Yes, Jerry, the city police's most elite unit is international but is only used for antiterrorism." She went on to illuminate taking that team off antiterror is forbidden by the mayor and police commissioner. Furthermore, New York's Attorney General won't open an investigation involving the Catholic Church without the governor's say so, and since the governor is running for reelection this year, she won't say go for fear of losing the Catholic vote now and in the future.

"Why am I not surprised politics interferes with good policing, as usual?" My man Coy said this with a look of disgust on his handsome face.

Donna Sim's chimed in to tell us to be aware the Federal Bureau of Investigation has investigated the interstate aspect of our many Myron Acker serial murders, unofficially off the record. "And since his death they have quietly backed off and stopped looking. That is where we are right now, nowhere, with no prospects of going somewhere."

Heads around the table nodded at the word *nowhere*.

Donna finished her thoughts to a sea of head nods. If only the archdioceses' local bank records could be gotten, they might prove a racketeering conspiracy running rotten through the New York City Archdiocese. But sadly no one is interested in issuing subpoenas in an election year.

Coy looked at each pissed off face before finally saying, "Has anyone communicated this problem to the Federal Attorney General?"

Looking down at the conference room table Ariana told us what we knew, under previous presidents the Justice Department was an independent agency in the executive branch of our federal government. Then President Frump turned it into his personal office for enforcing retaliations against free speech. At present the president is Roman Catholic with no appetite to alienate his fellow followers. Consequently, politics trumps the guilty facing justice, different party same result, around here it is called democracy.

Just then there was a knock on the conference room door and Ariana said, "Come in."

Three Catholic priests entered, two were wearing bulky overcoats. One leaned back against the door they'd just closed, and another went and stood at the opposite back corner of the room. The third walked up to the head of the conference room table.

Seeing a scheduling conflict I said, "Sorry, father, there must be a mistake, we have this room reserved for another hour."

Pulling out a chair on the left side of the conference table and sitting down, the newcomer said, "No mistake, Dr. Oliver Kulgul. I'm Father Hector Guterez and you people have something that doesn't belong to you, and we want it back."

Since he had spoken my name I said, "And what might that be, padre?"

"An attachment to an email from Father Rodrigo Amporo."

Ariana spoke right up and said, "Where is Father Amporo? If he gave it to me, he should ask for it back. That's how up and up things work."

"He's unavailable while being punished for giving out important information he shouldn't have. Please hand over copies of the attachment and delete it from your computers. He'd ask you but can't."

Coy sounding lawyerly said, "And if we refuse?"

"As you can now see my colleagues at the back of the room are pointing their latest model German manufactured submachine guns in this direction. If they start spraying bullets no one at this end of the room will survive. Don't let my good manners confuse you. We are serious and mean business."

Willaim looking for a fight said, "How do we know you aren't from the New York Archdiocese and will kill us anyway after we give you what you want?"

"Detective Marin, you'll have to take my word. I'm a priest I don't tell lies. Give us what we came for and you won't be harmed."

Feeling the mood in the room heating up I said, "To give you what you want, we require proof that is Father Amporo's wish."

"No negotiations, Dr. Kulgul."

Meeting his hard stare with my own stare I said, "I'd call that a lopsided stalemate. Wouldn't you, seven against three?"

"Huh, you have a novel approach to being intimidated. But my patience is wearing thin and we're all on the clock."

Ariana looking like a cat with a mouse said, "That's no comfort for you."

"To be a good sport, tell you what, I'll listen to each person at this table give me one wish. But that doesn't mean you won't be gunned down if you don't cooperate and give up Father Amporo's attachment."

Donna Sims using her no-nonsense state trooper voice said, "I'll bite. Ladies first, my wish is the criminal conspiracy at the New York Archdiocese face justice and is punished to the full extent of the law."

"Done, and then some. That wish is granted. Ariana Bruschetti what'll it takes for you to delete the email and give me all copies of the attachment?"

Ariana didn't pause to think and said, "That Father Amporo is not harmed for trying to do a good thing helping with my investigation."

"When I said he is being punished, I should have elaborated, his wages have been docked. He is allowed no television watching for two months and has to say six rosaries a day for sixty days. We wouldn't tolerate anyone hurting father Amporo. The Pope considers him a money finding treasure. Twice now he has found and returned stolen Church money. What do you want, William Marin?"

"What Donna said, the wrongdoers face justice."

"And you, Jerry Parker of the New York State Police, what's your wish?"

"Same as Donna and William."

"Who are you?"

"I'm Lenord Lym and wasn't given a physical copy of what you want. I'm not Catholic, may I be excused please?"

"Why didn't you get a copy?"

"Dr. Kulgul invited me without letting Detective Bruschetti know. I'm here to take notes because I cowrote a book on serial killers."

Turning to the priests in the back of the room, Father Hector Guterres said, "Lenord Lym is not to be hurt if it comes to violence."

Not sure what to think, Len said, "I'm very familiar with this case and all its twists and turns. I might even know more than anyone at this table, I'm a journalist and we see things differently than law enforcement. You're a man of God, you shouldn't go around hurting anybody."

"Coy Goff, Esquire, for what would you wish?"

My husband had a look on his face I knew too well, it was one short click shy of his pulling his gun and shooting someone. With sarcasm he said, "The next Pope continue to modernize the Church to include women and gay people."

"That's the first wish I can't grant or hasn't been so far. Nobody can tell who the next Pope will be. In any case the old Pope seems to have some milage left. Dr. Kulgul what is your wish?"

I was ready to pull my gun as soon as Coy pulled his. To distract the cleric pontificating I said, "Rumor has it from trustworthy sources that Cardinal Diddlysquat has been paying African countries to pass *kill gay laws*. I want that stopped and reversed. If they want to eat their own, it should be done on their own dime."

Out of the corner of my eye I noticed Ariana and Donna were exchanging some kind of almost hidden silent communication. Then Ariana said, "When can we expect proof you've met all our demands to receive the attachment?"

"Huh, it might just be easier to shoot the lot of you, except Lenord. We are not restricted in the exercise of our license to kill today."

With what Hector said Ariana and Donna each flopped a left hand on the tabletop. Then watching each other closely, simultaneously tapped one finger then two, and finally three fingers. Smooth as satin, both women sat back, quickly drew their service weapons, aimed, and fired.

Donna shot dead the submachine gun priest blocking the door. Her bullet hit him in the mouth and severed his spinal cord at the brain stem exiting. He slid down the door, his submachine gun discharging bullets into the ceiling acoustic tiles. The tiles' fibers caused quite a snowstorm covering him and the surrounding area in particles from above.

Simultaneously Ariana took out the clergyman gunner standing in the opposite corner of the room. Her bullet penetrated his skull just below his bulbus nose veered up and exited the back of his expensive haircut. He fell forward firing a number of rounds into the floor. His bullets tore up the wooden flooring as he slumped forward into the blood-soaked wood dust mud he had created.

The sound of gunfire ceased as quickly as it had erupted but the smell of gun smoke permeated the room's air. Fortunately, the conference room 's floor was empty at that hour, so no body responded to the loud gun reports.

"No, no, you shouldn't have done that. Now there will be consequences. Control and command will have my head for this." HG8 said this looking defeated.

As both women turned and trained their weapons on Father Hector Gutierrez, he was already holding a 1911 customized Colt 45 caliber in his hand. Catching up with what had just happened, both William and Jerry quickly drew their sidearms and pointed them at Father Hector Gutierrez.

Speaking in an even breathy soft voice Ariana said, "Now as we Italian Americans like to say, 'You can do this easy or hard.' Your choice, Father."

"That's no choice, Detective Bruschetti."

"It is. Tell us why we should give you the evidence Father Amporo gave me, or we all just shoot you dead like you intended for us."

"The Vatican will not be happy you killed two, or counting me, maybe three of their agents. You know native Italians can be more vindictive than Italian Americans."

"That's a matter of geographic opinion. Tell me, is what we Italian Americans put on cooked pasta called sauce or gravy?"

Involuntarily, Gutierrez soundlessly mouthed the answer. As soon as he did, realized Bruschetti had just bested him. If they had been fighting in the Amazon, he'd be dead.

Her face showing she'd just trumped him, Bruschetti said, "Hector, from my seat it was a good shoot we were threatened at gunpoint. Around here law enforcement calls that self-defense. Right, Dr. Kulgul?"

English not being his first language, Ariana had tricked Hector into naming what goes on spaghetti. Off balance on guard Hector Gutierrez said, "Everyone may not see it that way. If the Vatican wants, all of you and your family's can have unfortunate lethal accidents at their leisure."

Ariana got a strange no nonsense look on her face and said, "You didn't just threaten my family, did you, chump?" She clicked off her gun's safety lock again and curled her expertly manicured finger around the trigger.

Showing it across his face, Hector projected he knew he'd gone too far again, unintentionally this time threatening those present's families. To cover what might be his fatal error, he said, "Clearly you don't know who you are dealing with."

Still cop in charge, Ariana said, "You are getting closer to joining your colleagues in the great hereafter. Or could tell us what the hell is going on with Father Amporo's email attachment. Whether you are dead or alive what just happened here will get us the attention we need to prosecute this BDSM serial case. Now, I won't repeat myself again, your life hangs on a thread."

"Mmm, I'm torn. Duty dictates I shoot it out with your four guns to my one. Up until just now you seemed like reasonable people to me. You must know at this close range I could take out three of you, maybe all four before you finished me off."

At that point Coy and I drew our weapons and trained them on Gutirrez to emphasize his flawed calculation and dispel any fantasy he might have of surviving a shootout with six of us. The man had moxie in an untenable position, I would give him that. But threatening another man's family, few could survive, at least in our contemporary world.

"I'm beginning to see why Rodrigo liked you, Bruschetti, and broke rules for you. It wasn't just you stimulated him to have his first orgasm with me. He said you and your wife are great cooks. That has significant value where we come from."

Her frustration showing on her face, Ariana said, "My wife and I found Rodrigo sweet and priestly. I can't say the same for you, Hector. With all due respect are you going to get to the point, or give yourself last rites?"

"Ugh, oh, what the hell. If you give me all the attachments maybe the Vatican won't have me killed and I can talk them out of taking revenge on you. That's all I'll say about it."

The look on her face showed she meant business and then Ariana said, "That's not enough to keep your blood off our hands, talk or die."

"Turn off your recorders." In unison that task was completed by all, and then the priest told us yesterday afternoon Cardinal Diddlysquat, Bishop Boisterous, Monsignor Scattershot, Priests Badayre, and Wankervitz were summoned to Rome, Italy for a meeting. They left by private twin engine jet from Kennedy airport at noon.

Those passengers erroneously thought they were going to be honored in Italy and not aware there was no human crew flying the plane. It was flown by a new Vatican automated aerial AI system. The aircraft was preprogramed to crash into the Atlantic Ocean halfway between the U.S. and Europe. To ensure a smooth flight the cabin was filled with nitrous oxide just prior to take off.

Quickly glancing at the faces around the table, the priest said, "You didn't hear any of that from me."

Speaking to no one, Jerry Parker said, "Oh, my, that is taking vindictive to a new AI level. We've been warned something like this was coming."

Father Guterrez continued the story against his will. "Since their flight plan was erased after takeoff, nobody knows they are missing or will notice they are gone once their replacements arrive here in New York. The Vatican has transferred the money in #86679 account in the First National Bank of the Caymen Islands to its own accounts and closed #86679. Recouperation actions are being taken to claw back money promised to African countries eager to execute their gay children and parents for profit. That should cover what is known, so far"

"What is happening at the New York Archdiocese right now?"

"A search for a new more appropriate bishop to make cardinal for New York is underway. He'll do heavy house cleaning when chosen, then it's business as usual using Father Amporo's new computerized record keeping system."

Donna Sims remembered some of her unfinished business and said, "What about Jimmy Jordon who was brainwashed to believing he's a part-time avenging angel 'killing fags for Christ'?"

"Mr. Jordon had an unfortunate fatal heart attack; with his obesity and diet it was overdue. He died after someone injected a large amount of air into his carotid artery while he was sleeping. He had a peaceful death which is more than his victim could say. Are you going to give me what I came for or are we going to have a shootout?"

Since I was sure he couldn't survive a six to one gun fight, I said, "I think I understand how you must have felt getting a calling from God to live a religious life. What I don't get is why you stayed when it didn't work out. You must know a vicar running around with a gun threatening people isn't a good look for a priest."

"Dr. Kulgul, you make erroneous assumptions, inappropriate for you and your credentials. It would be so easy to just say that's none of your business and we concluded this meeting. I've already told you much more than I should have."

"But."

"But like Jesus, I'm also a teacher and must teach. I was kidnapped as a small child and raised to be a child soldier in the Amazon jungle. Like Alexander the Great, I killed my first adult male human before I reached puberty. I'd already stopped counting my too numerous dead when my calling to be a priest came. No one was more surprised than me receiving a religious vocation to dedicate my life to God. You protestants like to forget Jesus had a temper and resorted to violence when he badly beat up and physically threw the money changers out of the temple. The gang of twelve he hung out with carried weapons and knew how to use them in the New Testament."

Caught off guard, my mouth's response was not brain connected as I said, "True confession time?"

"My God knows who I am, where I come from, and my particular skill set taking life. Oh, maybe of interest to you, Oliver, he knows I'm gay because he made me that way."

I was in a quandary, let it go, or push onward for the sake of winning points and said, "We Protestants were taught Jesus was a man of peace. That's not how I'd describe you, Father Guterres."

"When he came to walk the earth, Christ was both man and God. As Christians we are expected to be both Christ like and human like him. When Jesus was not angry at how we screwed things up, he preferred peace over conflict and said so. But he and his twelve boys knew how to use swords and the knives they carried."

Abruptly I didn't trust myself to be having a theological discussion pointing my Sig Sauer 40 caliber with the safety off and my finger on the trigger. I wanted to shoot him, but instead said, "We've drifted off topic and need to wrap this up."

"Dr. Kulgul, you need to stop worrying so much about carrying a pistol because, like most of us in this room, you know how to make common everyday objects into lethal weapons at will, like Jesus. Your problem is not the number of your dead. My research shows they were all in self-defense, but rather you dig them up after burying them. How can you find peace, until you stop doing that."

Ariana had heard enough, she surveyed the conference table and said, "All those in favor of letting Father Gutierrez live, pass him your copy of the attachment I gave you."

Clearly everyone had something more to say, but we all just silently handed over our photocopies. As a group we were not of a mood to gun down another man of God that day. Hector stood, went over to stand next to Ariana's laptop computer and she brought up the email with attachment and he deleted it. Everyone with a handgun holstered it. Rolling the paper photocopies into a tight cylinder Gutierrez said, "Turn off the lights when you go, just leave the dead bodies. I'll have them disposed of."

As we bustled out of the conference room, turning off the lights, relief we'd avoided unnecessary bloodshed was reflected on every face. Coy and I exchanged an old married couple's satisfied look. It was another Queer Queries mystery solved. This time with only a small amount of gun play and inadvertently I'd been absolved by a practicing Roman Catholic priest for my killings.

****

Father Hector Gutierrez's coworkers not only cleaned up the mess their people made in the university's conference room, but they also plugged and painted over bullet holes before anyone was the wiser. With his assurances this chapter in our lives was over, there were now multiple tremendous reasons to have a big Sunday party. Everyone at our house agreed we should invite all on our cellphone's contact lists to come let down their hair and howl at the moon, and we would serve them food and drink.

All our dear friends and associates came along with people we invited but never expected to show up. For instance, Professor Jacoby and Len's whole graduate committee from the university thinking it was a celebration for his graduation.

Most of Carmen's poster responders came with plus ones. Roger, a reclusive underage teenage drag queen seamstress came alone. He had kept in contact with Carmen as a mother substitute and came in high formal drag as Marie Antionette. Randy went out, searched, and found Junior, who he felt deserved to celebrate the death of a serial killer who paid him for lethal sex without forewarning.

Even Father Hector Guiterrez and six of his associates came to our home to symbolically bury the righteous and not so righteous dead and pray for them. Also, in Roman Catholic tradition prayers were said by us all, for those who died leaving nobody to pray for them. And after that a well lubricated time was had by all.

****

The next morning, Len and I arrived at my private practice earlier than usual. I needed to get away from the refuse piles of party food disposables, cases of empty wine, liquor, soft drinks, and a half full keg of beer. The party achieved what we all needed and was a major success in blowing off steam. And the next day I refused to sully the sweet party memory with the drudgery of its cleanup. I hired a team of party cleanup professionals to put my house back together. I left them preparty photos of how it looked before the earthquake, tsunami, and heavy bombing.

On his way to his office Coy took Carmen to the airport for a much-deserved Caribbean resort vacation we insisted she take at our expense. Randy was spending quality rest and recuperation time with his father and father's new girlfriend at their weekend cabin.

Randy had convinced his father to invite Junior to tag along for his commiserating companionship that would allow father and girlfriend more private time. Normally Coy and I would discourage Randy from getting too tight with Junior. But Randy told us using the Serenity Prayer from his teen twelve step meetings, the two boys were working in tandem to forgive the thugs who raped them. He said together they were able to do what neither could do alone, and they were a good match playing video games.

Len, also looking hung over, accompanied me to the office. We had nothing to say to each other. As soon as we arrived, he scurried into his workspace reportedly to edit a magazine article with droopy blurry looking eyes.

Just after I got my shirtsleeves rolled up, lights, air conditioning, and coffee going, I dropped into my desk chair, head in hands. "Ugh. Last night," I groaned to myself. First it had been a flurry of last-minute preparations and snafus that morphed into happily greeting arriving guests, and finally socializing the night into daylight. At some point exhaustion threatened to set in, and now … here I was unmotivated sitting in my office, *Not fit for man nor beast.* BUT THE PARTY long overdue WAS WORTH IT, I just didn't want to have a postmortem.

After a long silent pause, with eyes closed, I heard the front door, and someone walk into the waiting area. I was not ready to see patients, the coffee did not have time to be ready and my next scheduled patient wasn't for an hour and a half. Craning my neck for a peek through the open office door showed TJ was the walk in. He plopped down in the same chair I had first seen him months ago and took out his cellphone.

He had been at the party until late. Maybe he had forgotten to go home and followed me to the office by mistake. No that could not be, his constant companion doggy boy wasn't present. Stirring myself into consciousness, I walked over and said, "Hey, TJ, what is up? The coffee isn't ready yet. So, why are you here?"

Looking how I felt, hungover and sleep deprived, TJ looked up from his cellphone and said, "Good morning, Oliver. You throw an enjoyable party even if they are not my kind of people."

"A thank you note would have sufficed. If you intend to continue talking, follow me."

Looking wrung out, we walked in step to my office then TJ said, "Something has been bothering me since before your party. I couldn't sleep thinking about it."

Taking my usual seat behind the desk, before TJ could, I said, "Shoot."

Sitting in one of the armchairs facing my desk he said, "What happened to all those missing videos of the murders taken by the murderer? Everyone mentioned them at the time of the murders, but not since. Why?"

"They were never found and now the case is closed, and we celebrated that last night with a party you attended."

"The murderer's video shows my husband in his birthday suit. Call me paranoid, those videos could materialize at any time and cause us embarrassment. I want them destroyed before they can hurt us."

Suddenly, I was at a crossroad: grab TJ by his belt loops and toss him out of my office, or for Willis Washington's sake, humor his grandnephew. "Me thinks the lady protests too much. Police in Maine have images of Asa in the altogether from high school streaking. New York cops took Asa's photos au-natural at the murder scene, and the court has the black and white images from the security camera I located."

"My lawyer has sued them all. Maine and New York cops have destroyed what pictures they had, and the court will soon. That leaves what the murderer recorded in the van and at the murder. Not knowing what future dangers we may face is killing me."

"Uh huh, okay I hear your concern as long as you understand what you want is about your power and control over Asa."

"What do you mean?"

"Asa likes to show off his body since high school. He even offered to dance nude for me before I hypnotized him."

"Fine then, it's all about me being paranoid for my future. I still want lose ends tied up.

"Let's see if my associates have any ideas." I'd just heard Chucho enter the outer office at his usual work time and yelled, "Hey, Len and Chucho, my office."

Still unbuttoning his outer coat Chucho entered my office and said, "What's up, boss?"

Just then Len stuck a hazy eyed head around the corner and said, "Present!"

"Do you guys remember TJ from the party a few hours ago."

Chucho yawning said, "Sure, he had that cute leather boy-dog on a leash. I never got a chance to pet your pet."

Leering, Len said, "You mean throw him a boner."

"Boys, boys play nice. TJ and I were wondering if you know what happened to the murderer's missing videos?"

Chucho shook his head no, and Len said, "They were never found, the cases were closed without them. So, they are officially nonexistent."

"We want to make it a project to find them."

"Absolutely."

"Okay, I guess an article about them would sell magazines."

TJ giving me an inquisitive stare asked, "Are you asking *me* to join in?"

"Sure, why not. It was your idea."

"All right. Where do we start?"

"Ariana Bruschetti has made this case personal for her. Let's invite her to help."

"Okay."

"I was also thinking we might want a clergy contact since the archdiocese is so involved."

"Are you thinking one of the Pope's goon squads?"

"Chucho, you still dating the Deacon?"

"Yes. But I don't want to put him at risk. Use the Pope's guys, I hear they carry big guns."

Like a flash bulb fired, droopy Len flashed brightly and said, "Wait up! We should also go after the missing left earlobes. The videos and victims' ears will make a much more marketable story, maybe a follow up book."

"Are you three available later today?"

The group nodded yes, and I answered their obvious unspoken question, "No priests with automatic weapons and licensed to kill will be invited. They make me nervous." I phoned Ariana and Nesto, and we all agreed to meet at three PM in Saints Peter and Paul's Church office.

****

When we arrived, Deacon Ernesto Diaz assured us the Monsignor was away at detox and the parish secretary left early for the day to nurse her sick parakeet. He assured us we were alone and led us to the church hall where the right number of folding chairs were arranged in a circle.

With a hand gesture Nesto indicated we should sit down and said, "Welcome. Oliver, why don't you tell us what this meeting is about?"

I brought everyone up to speed as to why we were together, then said, "Many years ago I provided security for a big reception at the Cardinal's residence. It's grand, like a palace with several fulltime domestic staff. It would be next to impossible to hide videos and earlobes there with so many paid staffers present every day. The previous Cardinals had several hidey-holes around town for their intimate endeavors. Spillseed was known to regularly party hearty out of the limelight. Any questions or comments so far?"

Having visually sized up the group, Ariana said, "Enough background, you sold me, what's the plan, Oliver?"

"You said Father Amporo's first clue of wrongdoing was finding expenses for rental limousines when the archdiocese owns a fleet of them. So, you and Deacon Diaz go to the Church's garage on the pretext of ruling out their vehicles being criminally involved transporting contraband, or some such bogus story. While looking over logbooks take note of any addresses the Cardinal or one of his recently deceased henchmen frequently visited. Then we'll scope them out."

Out of habit she said, "What you suggest is illegal."

As was his habit at work Chucho ran interference for me and said, "Hypothetically a shaky witness might have suggested church vehicles were involved in crime. Protecting the archdiocese reputation is a good thing, probably legal too."

Ariana back on procedure asked, "Fine. Let's say we do find an address of interest. How do you plan to gain entrance for a look?"

"I know a fire marshal who owes me a big favor. If he went in on an anonymous complaint, wearing a body camera, we might see probable cause for a search warrant."

"Or you could utilize unique talents of an old client from when you were a parole officer. One who no doubt also owes you a big favor."

"Ariana, with a search on for a new Cardinal for New York, time may be at a premium. Once the new man is in place, I'd imagine the Vatican will tell him to clean house. Who knows what he might turn up and throw out?"

"Okay."

TJ sniped, "Like photos of Asa in his birthday suit for sale to the highest bidder."

For some reason Nesto seemed to be looking for a fight with TJ and said, "Be realistic, my man, the case is closed, bad guys all dead, there's no point."

"My husband's pride, self-respect, and both our reputations are more than the point."

Seeing the pot going to full boil, Len said, "Remember, everyone, we don't know the actual number of serial murder victims, who they were, or where they came from. As it stands what we know is exactly like the Vatican, lots of mysteries, secrets, and nothing definite. The videos, earlobes, correspondence and or written out instructions might allow us to close this case to our satisfaction once and for all. That would give us an excuse to have another party."

Jumping out of his own skin, TJ said, "Enough talking, let's get started."

Deacon Diaz reacting to TJ's agitation said, "What, without inside help? Or outside intelligence to go on, I don't think so."

Social worker Chucho calmed the others down saying, "Wait, Oliver, tell us the plan?"

"Ariana and Nesto go to the archdiocese's limousine garage, get a look at their logbook, and record addresses frequented by the Cardinal and his gang. Don't let them say no."

Speaking right up Ariana said, "You want us to strong arm them." The looks from around the circle did not require words to explain. She yielded to the unspoken question by saying, "Oh, yeah, I do know how to do that, no problem."

I continued explaining the plan saying, "Chucho and Len, go to the Buildings Department's public information section on the fourth floor. Wait for calls with addresses from Ariana and Nesto then cellphone copy those building's plans."

"Oliver, where are you in this?"

"TJ and I will be at fire department headquarters waiting for building blueprints from Chucho and Len. Any questions?"

TJ mustering his default attitude said, "How do we know this isn't a big waste of time?"

Too hung over for his bullshit I said, "Let's get started and find out."

****

Ariana and Nesto produced three addresses, but right away ruled out two as implausible. But 404 West Forty-eighth Street was a doublewide four-story brownstone in Manhattan's Hell's Kitchen, zip code 10036. It had been the secret scene of countless now forgotten New York Cardinals' debaucheries, long before Cardinal Diddlysquat's time in charge.

Tommy Diddlysquat hadn't figured out how to sell the property to profit his beloved African "Kill Gays" laws because the ownership was not free and clear. Cardinal Spillseed's estate and the Gay Community Center had pending claims. The Buildings Department records showed the structure was still owned by the late Cardenal Spillseed Fun Consortium, and yet property tax, and current extra tax assessments were paid by the New York Archdiocese. It was hard to explain by all parties since religious organizations are tax exempt in New York.

Chucho and Len emailed the buildings plans to us, and we showed them to my fire marshal friend Gene Gilhooley. Studying the plans Gene immediately discovered a secret large party room on the first floor hidden behind a false foyer wall and oversize living room space. Entrance to the secret room was through a living room sliding bookcase concealed opening.

We set out right away in a fire marshal car's lights and siren screaming, two fire trucks and crews were at the address as we arrived. Then Ariana and Nesto showed up in an unmarked police car, followed by Chucho and Len who arrived last at 404 West Forty-Eight Street by taxicab.

Flashing his gold fire marshal badge, Gene told the assistant fire chief on the scene to get him inside. Rather than jimmy the door, which the firefighters were ready and equipped to do, the chief had the cherry picker on one truck lift a firewoman to an open third floor window and she ran down and opened the front door from the inside.

Once inside, the firefighters searched for the bogus reported gas leak and found other serious fire safety concerns. They issued multiple fire safety violations requiring immediate direct response or building condemnation. Also found was a serious crack in the building's foundation and depending on how it was managed could result in structural collapse.

Meanwhile Gene took me and my little impromptu band of investigators into the hidden room discovered because of the building's floorplan blueprint. Immediately we found a collection of fifteen missing earlobes, they were not hidden, but rather proudly displayed in a wall-mounted glass case. Gilhooley said he could envision the fire department museum proudly putting the earlobes on display after the courts were through with them.

Then out in the open, on an end table next to the Cardinal's identified armchair, we found a portable fireproof metal records box. It contained fifteen dated, alphabetized, SIM cards attached to paper records. There were receipts and photocopies of money orders and notes for planning the killings. Also, attached were completed applications from the victim with their demographic details and their fantasy wishes for a fabulous BDSM vacation committing murder.

For most present, the biggest find of the day covered the rooms' walls. There were thousands upon thousands of shelved DVD videos. Unbelievable, the cardinals had collected every episode, including *the long-lost celebrity naked cooking, and secret royal nude pantry endeavors on the Gargantuan European Braising, Broiling, and Boiling,* the worldwide longest (decades) everlasting Cookoff Show.

The others present were wowed when someone snooping around accidentally turned on the television. Then before we knew it, *Gargantuan Cookoff* videos were being shown on the secret room's giant flat screen television with surround sound. Meanwhile, I stealthily searched for, found, then purloined the only SIM card of Asa Mulroy in all his natural glory.

When everyone was still being wowed by the Cookoff Show, I slipped the SIM card into TJ's back leather pants pocket followed by a reassuring slap on his butt. Engrossed watching the show TJ reached around and into his pocket, felt the card and gave me a big smiling thumbs up. I think it was the first time I saw his face open and smiling. He was a good-looking guy when not wearing his usual ugly, angry face.

Joining the others, Gene Gilhooley was just telling Ariana the fire department had a much more adult relationship with the District Attorney than the police. He said fear of fire was universal even in high places, so, the evidence found today would be treated with much more respect than the police usually got in their sibling rivalry with the DA's office.

Having achieved our goals for the day I wished the fire department well with their earlobe archives, and reminded Gene it was rumored some of those lost, now found by us, episodes of the *Steamy Celebrity Cookoff Show* were quite valuable on the open market for fire department fund raising especially the royals baking bread in the buffs.

We shook hands all around and went our separate ways, another Queer Queries caper solved. Except, my last task would have to be fly up to Albany and explain how three men I never saw before got dead in front of my forty calibers while threatening my life with knives.

About the Author

Peter Melillo was born in New Haven, Connecticut, moved to Tucson, Arizona, at age seven, then moved to New York City at age twenty-five. In 2013, JM Snyder Books published a collection of twelve of his gay war short stories: *For Man and Country*. In total, JM Snyder Books published sixteen short stories by Peter Melillo online as e-books. In 2018 Querelle Independent published *Fairy Swatter*, six short stories with murder as a side issue, *Improbable: Gay Male Love Stories*, *Accidental Parents*, and *Queer Queries*. Peter can be reached at mabide8790@yahoo.com.